Moonflow

"A bizarre and fiercely original splatterpunk phantasmagoria of queerness, *Moonflow* is like a gay Jodorowsky film from hell. Deranged and gleefully weird, this is an impressive debut from a singular literary talent."

—Eric LaRocca, Bram Stoker Award–nominated author of *Things Have Gotten Worse Since We Last Spoke*

"Is it legal to have this much fun reading a book? I'm in awe of Karella's incredible gift for creating biting satire. This is the queer splatterpunk salvation/dissolution comic relief narrative we need in these dark times. I had a f*cking blast."

—Joe Koch, Shirley Jackson Award–nominated author of *The Wingspan of Severed Hands*

"Expert worldbuilding, genuinely creepy situations, and characters who are easy to root for. Unique, funny, and frighteningly real. This is what horror is all about."

—Sam Rebelein, Bram Stoker Award–nominated author of *Edenville*

"*Moonflow* is a deranged, horny Day-Glo escapade that is so utterly queer to its core. I adored this weirdo book."

—Jane Flett, author of *Freakslaw*

"Weird, wild, and oh-so-wretched, *Moonflow* is the trans botanical horror we need in the world right now. It will sink its tendrils into you and infect you with its spores... and you'll enjoy it."

—Drew Huff, author of *The Divine Flesh*

"Has the energy of a John Waters movie: crass, profane, packed with social commentary and bittersweet pathos—the type of art that is necessary for the current moment."

—Briar Ripley Page, author of *Corrupted Vessels*

"A triumph of queer, horny, hippie horror that'll make you cackle, gasp, and scream! With its cast of iconic characters, imaginative enchanted setting, gripping story, and mind-bending horrific imagery, Bitter Karella's *Moonflow* is a trip to die for."

—Eve Harms, author of *Transmuted*

"Karella has crafted the queer shroom trip from hell you didn't know you wanted. *Moonflow*'s dose of terror is potent and unlike anything you've ever seen."

—Emmett Nahil, author of *From the Belly*

"Transgressive, menacing fun. Karella unfolds fungal revelations in newly discovered colors, coining a language's worth of fresh and horrifying imagery."

—Naben Ruthnum, author of *Helpmeet*

"Bitter Karella is a powerhouse of horror. *Moonflow* is equal parts ridiculous, revolting, and charming. It rockets into your psyche with drug-fueled mommy-milker cults at 200 mph, and I loved every second of it."

—Lor Gislason, editor of *Bound in Flesh*

"The book that will have everyone asking, 'Who let this woman cook?' Horrific, horny, and hilarious; a cast at turns both freakish and endearing; destined to inspire cult adoration."

—Aubrey Wood, author of *Bang Bang Bodhisattva*

MOONFLOW

BITTER KARELLA

Cover design by Lisa Marie Pompilio
Cover images by Shutterstock

Author photograph by Bitter Karella

Run For It
Hachette Book Group
1290 Avenue of the Americas
New York, NY 10104
hachettebookgroup.com

First Edition: September 2025
Simultaneously published in Great Britain by Orbit

Run For It is an imprint of Orbit, a division of Hachette Book Group.
The Run For It name and logo are registered trademarks of Hachette Book Group, Inc.

Library of Congress Cataloging-in-Publication Data
Names: Karella, Bitter author
Title: Moonflow / Bitter Karella.
Description: First edition. | New York, NY : Run For It, 2025.
Identifiers: LCCN 2025000213 | ISBN 9780316581936 trade paperback |
ISBN 9780316581929 ebook
Subjects: LCGFT: Horror fiction | Queer fiction | Novels
Classification: LCC PS3611.A78466 M66 2025 | DDC 813/.6—dc23/eng/20250324
LC record available at https://lccn.loc.gov/2025000213

ISBNs: 9780316581936 (trade paperback), 9780316581929 (ebook)

Printed in the United States of America

LSC-C

Printing 1, 2025

For Marley

Content Warning

Please be aware that this book contains graphic violence, sexual assault, gore, vomit, murder, infanticide, violence against animals, and drug use.

0.

Under the trees and the earth, under the roots of the towering spruce and the mighty fir, under strata of rich black loam and rocky clay, under the carcasses of ancient sequoias and redwoods, and finally under the worms and the slugs and the crawling things that ate them all, the Lord of the Forest sleeps. His veins pulse and throb in the dark earth.

He does not like the men and the way they trample through his forest. He does not like when they pull his mushrooms from the earth and stupidly mash them between their useless flat teeth. When they come into his forest, he twists their necks and turns their feet so that they can never find their way again.

So he sleeps, but even deep in slumber, he fumes with hate.

ACT 1: INITIATION,

or The Way of What Is to Come

1.

Greetings, fellow mushroom enthusiast! If you're reading these words, it's because you too have decided to join the exciting and rewarding world of mushroom hunting. The Pamogo Forest is well known as home to a stunning variety of unusual species, some found nowhere else on Earth. Of course, harvesting Pamogo mushrooms is strictly prohibited by state and federal law, so this book should in no way be construed as an endorsement of illegal mushroom harvesting. On the following pages, you'll find a wealth of information about some of the species that you might encounter in the Pamogo. Learn and enjoy!

—Field Guide to Common Mushrooms of the Pamogo Forest, *T. F. Greengarb (1978)*

Sarah never met Madeleine in the same location twice. Before they were scheduled to make an exchange, Madeleine would text Sarah—always from a different number—to tell her where they were going to meet. Sarah wasn't entirely convinced that all the cloak-and-dagger theatrics were necessary. Her friend Damon insisted that the cops had once caught him with five grams of shrooms in his pockets, and they'd just laughed and sent him on his way. But Damon was a dude and cis and he worked a low-level office job in the financial district that required he always dress in a nice clean-cut suit and tie, so Sarah expected that the cops might not be as lenient if they caught her. She didn't relish the idea of finding out, so she went along with Madeleine's secret squirrel shenanigans.

This time, the address was an old Victorian in Alameda, spires already rattling with the bassy electronic beats of club music, revelers sprawling on the front steps and across the parched dirt of the desiccated yard. Sarah assumed that the house didn't belong to Madeleine; she wasn't sure how Madeleine always managed to find a new place for every party. She also assumed that the house definitely didn't belong to the shirtless burnout who answered her knock. He grasped the stick of a half-chewed corn dog in his free hand, mustard smeared across his bare chest, and stared at her with unfocused eyes.

She had to yell to hear herself over the THUMP THUMP THUMP of the music. "Is Madeleine in? It's Sarah. She knows me."

The burnout furrowed his brow in concentration as he struggled to understand. "Sarah? Sarah's not here, man."

"Yeah, that's funny. No, *I'm* Sarah. I'm here to see Madeleine. You know what, never mind—I'll find her."

He offered no resistance as she squeezed past him, her fingers brushing through his chest hair and coming away with a film of mustard. The burnout nodded stupidly and glared in confusion at the cat pack slung over her shoulder, but Herman, ever the little gentleman, didn't even hiss.

The foyer, the dining room, the hallway—all were filled with writhing bodies, with the heat and funk of dancers in motion, a sweaty bubbling petri dish of COVID, plague, and who knew what worse diseases. The gushing sound of strenuous vomiting echoed from the upstairs bathroom and reverberated down the stairwell, where the more lethargic revelers sat, their arms entwined with balusters. A film projector in the den was showing an old silent stag reel against a shower curtain draped over a bookcase, and a half dozen viewers sat crouched in the darkness, sucking on joints, as they watched black-and-white footage of a chubby 1920s ingenue frolicking around a fountain. Sarah squeezed between the bodies, always a few steps ahead of the mustard bouncer trailing in her wake, who was still insisting, in a voice now lost among the noise, that "Sarah isn't here, man."

Madeleine was in the palatial kitchen, holding court in a rattan peacock-backed chair with a whole battalion of new friends crowded onto folding chairs and ratty couches, around a table loaded up with pills and poppers and nugs and baggies and grinders and spoons. These new friends were probably all eggs, since Madeleine, with her easy laugh and her ageless beauty and her propensity to say things like *Sweetie, you might look nice if you grew your hair out—have you ever considered that*, attracted a certain sort of guy who was "just feeling some stuff out." Prior to transition, Madeleine had abused her body in ways that hormones and makeup had completely erased: She had beautiful sleek alabaster skin and smooth hands, her mascara always flawless and her lips always a bright cherry red that contrasted with her pale skin but matched the bright cherry red of her double-breasted business jacket with the ridiculous shoulder pads. She smoked cigarettes through an old-fashioned cigarette holder, something that Sarah had only seen in cartoons. She looked like a vampire, and Sarah was never sure if she was deliberately cultivating the look or if she'd simply never realized that the '80s were over.

"Madeleine, your man out front's dribbling mustard all over."

"Arnold, let Sarah through. And for God's sake, put a shirt on!" gushed Madeleine, clutching at the arm of one of the new eggs. "The rest of you, shoo! Mama's got business to discuss!" The crowd and the mustard guy dissipated, melting back into the party and leaving Madeleine with just her new favorite and Sarah. "Sarah, sweetie! So glad you could make it!" She leaned over to whisper loudly into the egg's ear, "You have to see this. Sarah here is the best—she's just got the most incredible green thumb."

Sarah dumped her fat ass onto a now unoccupied couch and placed her cat pack in her lap. The party was in full swing out in the living room, louder than ever, and the throbbing strobe light threw the long shadows of dancers across the kitchen ceiling. Through the crack of an open door behind Madeleine, Sarah could see a bed set up in the laundry room and two anonymous shapes writhing under a sheet. Madeleine's parties were always so sordid. Sarah didn't know how Madeleine could get high in this kind of situation. Sarah preferred the safety of her own home, an ambient chillwave mix playing, her hand stroking Herman's back. That was the way to do it. A much more spiritual high and all the better to avoid the paranoia and the bad thoughts. Sarah remembered the mustard on her hands and wiped them against her knees.

"Nice to meet you," said the egg, who was tall and buff and sporting a bushy dysphoria beard. This egg might have fooled Sarah except that hanging around Madeleine was the biggest tell of all. Just like Madeleine seemed to have a new house every time that they met, she also seemed to always find a new egg to dote on her. Sarah knew from personal experience that eggs didn't take long to crack around Madeleine.

"Sorry about Herman," said Sarah, pointing to the cat. Herman howled pitifully. He hated being cooped up. He was convinced he would never be free again, as is the way of cats. "You mind if I let him out? He won't be a problem. He loves people." Sarah didn't wait for an answer as she unlatched the pack and Herman waddled out. He was a beautiful fat black cat with big yellow eyes. He surveyed the party with interest, but he stayed close to Sarah, butting his head against her shin until she was forced to reach down and scratch his head. Herman always conducted himself like a little gentleman.

"You brought your cat?" said Madeleine.

"He doesn't like to be alone." That was all Madeleine needed to know. Sarah didn't dare leave him at home, in case the landlord changed the lock while she was out. Herman wouldn't survive that separation; he was a consummate bogmoggy—whenever Sarah closed the bathroom door, he would plant himself outside and cry until he could see her again. He loved his scritchies. "I can't stay long, sorry. Let's just do this, and I'll get him out of your hair."

Madeleine frowned but she didn't object, so Sarah started pulling plastic bags from the side pouch of the cat bag. "You really called at the right time, Madeleine. I just had a great harvest of Fire Imps—take a look at these."

She placed a plastic bag full of dried mushrooms onto the table. Madeleine pinched it between a thumb and a forefinger and held it up to the light, examining the contents with a critical eye, before passing it to the egg for approval. As if the egg would know anything about quality. Sarah was very proud of her Fire Imps (*Agaricus infernus*). Nobody grew them better than her. The deep blue color of the stems indicated a high psilocybin concentration. These were good. You could probably trip out on just one. Sarah watched, chewing her lip nervously. She really needed this sale to go well. She really needed the money.

Finally, Madeleine said, "Oh, sweetie, Fire Imps? You can't be serious. No one is taking Fire Imps anymore." She shoved the bag back toward Sarah. "They're passé."

Sarah felt her face drain. "Come on, Madeleine! You love Fire Imps." She tapped a finger desperately against the fully packed plastic bag, pointing to the product. "Look at the color—you know these are high yield. No one else grows them this blue."

Madeleine sucked on her cigarette thoughtfully and released a puff of smoke from her mouth. "I can't serve Fire Imps to my guests. They will think I'm dreadfully gauche. Very last season. That just won't do."

Madeleine could afford to be picky. But Sarah had needs that Madeleine, with her endless supply of party houses, couldn't fathom—like the need to pay the rent and the need to refill the fridge. She hadn't worked in months, not since she lost that job at the coffee shop. The last harvest was wrecked by mold. Then there was Herman's vet bill. And then Jade moved out, and suddenly rent got real expensive real fast. Damon kept saying that she should start an OnlyFans, hinting that there were lots of people who would pay good money for pictures of a naked fat girl, but Sarah knew from experience that porn wasn't the instant money solution that Damon thought it was. Besides, she had enough experience fielding annoying chasers online just from posts of dinner selfies, so she didn't relish the idea of opening those floodgates again. God, everything had been so much harder since Jade left. Sarah had sold everything that she could sell, everything except for Herman (she would *never* sell Herman) and the terrarium under the sink, and she kept that only in hopes that Madeleine would pay enough for the harvest to save her. But now what was she supposed to do?

Her empty stomach ached; she'd been living on instant ramen and ketchup packets for too long. And poor Herman got only the dry food now.

Sarah wasn't too proud to beg. "Madeleine, please. I'm in a bad spot."

Madeleine pushed the bag back across the table toward Sarah. "I'm sorry, Sarah, but of course I'll help you. You know I wouldn't leave my favorite girl in the lurch. You know I'll always help you out. When haven't I come through?"

"Thank you, Madeleine. I really mean it."

"But I need you to do something for me. Have you heard of the King's Breakfast?"

The egg shifted uncomfortably. In the other room, the figures under the sheet were reaching the crescendo of their thrusting.

"No."

Madeleine reached under the table and produced, seemingly from nowhere, a ziplock bag full of dried mushrooms. They were not Fire Imps.

"I got this sample from a friend. You *really* need to try this. As a connoisseur, I want your opinion."

Sarah did not like the idea that Madeleine had found another supplier. That did not bode well at all. Madeleine's mushrooms were white tinged with yellow, the caps tight and rounded and oily, and the fruiting bodies so tightly packed in that they all looked like one single big lumpy shroom until Madeleine started to break them apart and hand them out—one to Sarah, one to the new egg, and one for herself. Sarah turned it around in her hand to inspect the delicate fluting of the gills and search the thick knobbly stem for evidence of blue stains.

"There's no blue at all. Looks pretty weak."

"Try it before you say anything."

Sarah squirmed. "You know I don't like to get high in crowds. I don't do well."

"Just try it. Trust me. I promise you can't have a bad time on the King's Breakfast."

Madeleine and the egg popped their shrooms whole into their mouths, so Sarah sighed and, against her better judgment, followed suit. It was only one shroom, after all. The dried body was rubbery between her teeth, tasting of musk and dirt. Sarah knew it could take up to an hour to feel anything, but she was tripping minutes later.

The room was suddenly awash in colors, beautiful shades of purple and blue, like living at the bottom of an aquarium. Her whole body tingled with unexpected arousal. *Oh my God*, thought Sarah. BOOM BOOM BOOM, the beat of the music thundered louder and louder until it felt like the whole house must surely collapse. She leaned back into the chair, the exquisite softness of the cushions enveloping her, and stared at the ceiling.

Herman, grown to the size of a panther, regarded her with big yellow eyes.

"Heeeey, Herman," said Sarah. "Who's a good baby? Come sit next to Mama."

Sarah patted the cushion next to her. The giant cat jumped up onto the couch, climbed nimbly onto her lap, and started to rumble softly. Sarah scratched him between his ears and ran her hand down his back, marveling at the incredible fractal patterns improbably forming in his black fur. He seemed way fuzzier than usual, as if he'd been run through a dryer and all his hair was standing on end from static cling. The idea struck her as hilarious, and she wanted to laugh.

I think I'm going insane, said Sarah telepathically.

Herman telepathically assured her that, no, she was not going insane and that, in fact, everything was great.

"Right on," said Sarah. The couch cushions had never been so soft, so comfortable. She thought of the King's Breakfast and the marvelous mellow high she was having, despite the chaos of the party swirling around her, and that pleasant thought caused rainbow-shimmering mushrooms to blossom from the floor, spreading their gills and unfolding up toward a beautiful yellow sky (oh, apparently they were all outside now—whatever, just go with it), bigger and bigger, until they were the size of trees and Sarah was lost in a beautiful fungal forest. She saw a flickering image of someone else crouched on the couch next to her, and she was too stoned to be anything but pleased when she realized it was another her. This other Sarah was curled into a little ball, naked, her knees pulled up to her chest, her arms wrapped around her shins. A carpet of green moss blanketed her shoulders, and a constant billow of brilliant, glittering spores rose off her and floated into the ether. The doppelgänger's feet burrowed into the pillows of the couch, which were suddenly dirt, her toes turned to long stringy roots. A tangle of toadstools grew from each of her eye sockets, and a serene smile stretched across her placid face.

"Wow," said Sarah. "That is crazy."

She watched as her doppelgänger suddenly curled open like a chrysalis, something large and bright emerging, too beautiful to behold, although Sarah got the impression of a perfectly symmetrical pair of cantaloupe-sized breasts and two kindly outstretched hands. The goddess was reaching out to her and Sarah wished desperately, with the sudden onslaught of emotions that always accompanied a shroom trip, that she could reach back. In the corners of the room, friendly fuzzy things bounced and tumbled like raccoons at play, always darting away when she turned to look at them directly.

"Pretty intense, isn't it?" said Madeleine, breaking the spell. "Are you getting visuals?"

"I am," said Sarah, still staring at the blinding beauty of the emerging goddess and the full, ripe breasts upon her chest. They were huge and very distracting. "But never like this before."

Madeleine and her friend, who were both staring into nothingness, eyes wide, smiles wider, swayed to music that only they could hear.

"Where did you get this?" asked Sarah, stroking Herman's back until the cat purred so loud he rattled. The good feelings continued to swirl in her head.

Madeleine ignored the question, returning the bag to its place under the table. "Now that you've tried it, I think you'll agree that the King's Breakfast is definitely poised to be the next big thing. Someone who could grow this would really make a killing. In fact, if you were to turn your expertise to the King's Breakfast, we could *both* make a killing."

Back home, under the sink in the bathroom where Herman was forbidden to go, Sarah had a shotgun terrarium made out of an old plastic tub, filled with rice flour and vermiculite and little discs of white fuzzy mycelium carefully perched on squares of tinfoil, shoved next to a humidifier. She grew Fire Imps and Jupiter Scrotums (*Lactarius jovus*) and Pink Venom (*Amanita rosacea*), all fine cultivars and, when Sarah grew them, all very, very, *very* blue. Like Madeleine said, she just had a green thumb.

"Of course I could grow this. I'd just need to get some spores." Sarah glanced back to the empty space next to her on the couch; there wasn't even a depression in the cushions to reveal that the goddess had ever existed. But of course she never had. She was just a mushroom hallucination. Sarah could feel her sudden absence so acutely it hurt. She wished the goddess would come back.

"Oh, sweetie, that's what I like to hear!" Madeleine coughed and wrung her hands, suddenly nervous, which was weird, because Madeleine was never caught without words. *It must be the King's Breakfast affecting my judgment*, thought Sarah. That was the only possible explanation for that.

"It grows up north, in the Pamogo woods. I'd go myself, of course, but..." Again the hand-wringing, the sudden nervousness. "I don't thrive in nature. You know how it is."

Sarah narrowed her eyes. "What's wrong with the Pamogo?"

"What? Nothing's wrong." Madeleine smiled. "It's a perfectly ordinary forest."

"Is it haunted or something?" Sarah had heard that name before, but she was still too dazed on the King's Breakfast to recall any specifics. Herman trilled as she ran her hand down his back.

Madeleine laughed. "I've never known you to be scared of ghosts! Maybe it is true that sometimes hikers go missing in the Pamogo, maybe even a statistically significant number of hikers, but that's just what happens when you go traipsing around in the woods without knowing what you're doing. You, sweetie, will not have to worry about that, of course. I have a friend up in Las Brujas, a very old and dear and trusted friend, and he knows the Pamogo like the back of his hand. He's already said he's willing to be your guide. It would just be a couple days in the woods. You'd enjoy it. Think of it as camping. You'll do this for me, won't you, sweetie? Say you will."

If Madeleine was willing to pay real money for the King's Breakfast, Sarah was willing to do whatever she needed to do to grow it.

Sarah hefted Herman over her shoulder like a baby. The cat blinked in baffled confusion for a moment but quickly adapted to this new reality. "I'd need someone to watch Herman for me."

Madeleine frowned at Herman, who had closed his eyes, his tongue blepping in idiot pleasure, as Sarah kneaded the top of his head. Madeleine was a known dog person. Sarah could see her doing the mental calculations about whether it would be worth it to put up with a cat for a few days to get access to a completely new drug.

"Fine," she said finally. "I'll watch your cat."

"I'll give you instructions."

Madeleine threw up her hands. "I'll even follow your instructions."

Sarah was feeling way more hopeful when she took her leave. She even patted the egg tenderly on the shoulder as she passed. He looked like he was having major revelations under the King's Breakfast, so Sarah just said "Good luck there, friend" as she took her leave. Madeleine could deal with the fallout.

2.

Sloane Mill State Historic Park is the crown jewel in Northern California's crown of jewels! Visitors to this unique and unusual park will find adventures well worth exploring, from the innovative lumber operations of Lazarus Sloane to the unique flora and fauna of the Pamogo Forest.

—*Sloane Mill State Historic Park informational brochure (circa 1995)*

The blond girl emerged from the car, and after exchanging a few muffled words with the driver and watching him pull away and disappear up the road, she stood awkwardly on the boardwalk outside the Dank Hole. It was the only bar in Las Brujas, and a buzzing neon sign in the window indicated that it served not just beer, but ice-cold beer. Skillet and the Hell Slut stood in the shadows, sharing a joint and watching to see what the girl would do next.

"She ain't gonna go into the Dank Hole," said Skillet as she passed the joint up to her companion. "No way, no how! She's too pure for that. Lookit her. An honest-to-Gord little angel. I bet she's never even seen a dick in her life. Completely unsullied. My Gord. Just look at her."

The Hell Slut took the roach and sucked on it. "Skillet, I love you, but you don't know shit about the world. I can tell you her whole life story right now: Daddy issues, bad ones. Ran away from home at, say, fourteen. Shacked up with some smooth-talking baby face in LA or maybe San Francisco. He had her turning tricks in a week. This morning, she finally had enough. She woke up early, took all the cash from Benny's wallet—after all, it's *her* money; she earned it—and hitched her way up the PCH—"

"Benny, huh? Her pimp's got a name already?"

"Shut up. She's a frugal gal, gotta make that cash last, so she's been trading blow jobs for rides whenever she can. Except this last ride—that was just a nice retired couple coming back from their Yosemite vacation. She offered cash, but they wouldn't dream of charging such a nice young girl. The husband wanted to fuck her, though. And he would have, if he wasn't riding with his wife. He's gonna resent that wife all the way back to Oregon or wherever the fuck they're from."

"Shit. How do you come up with this shit?"

"I'm not done. Any second now, she's gonna go inside. She'll play it cool, sidle up to the bar all casual and order a beer. The bartender's not even gonna check her ID; he's gonna say *We don't get a lot of pretty ladies here in Las Brujas*. She's gonna look at him and wonder *Does he want to fuck me or father me? Or both?*

"I'm just passing through, she'll say. *I won't be here long.*

"Passing through to where? asks the bartender.

"The girl shrugs and drains her beer. Still trying to play it cool. *Dunno. North.*

"There's nothing north of Las Brujas. Just the Pamogo.

"Then I guess I'm going to the Pamogo."

"Ha ha, fuck you," said Skillet. "You're full of shit."

The girl went into the bar.

"Ha ha, holy shit..." Skillet giggled. "Fuuuuck. I dunno how you do it."

The Hell Slut passed the joint back down to Skillet. The Hell Slut was a big woman, tall enough that she had to duck to fit under the balcony and wide enough that she filled the whole boardwalk with her bulk. She was high in the temple hierarchy, second only to Mother Moonflow, and, as such, her rank came with certain privileges. She liked to take her bike down to Las Brujas on Saturday nights and throw back a few beers. Skillet came sometimes, clutching at the Hell Slut's broad backside the whole ride and shrieking in giddy glee whenever the Hell Slut revved her engine.

Skillet loved when the Hell Slut brought her along. The Hell Slut always drank until her gut sloshed and then she'd get amorous, and then later Skillet would place her ear against the Hell Slut's bloated belly and fall asleep listening to it gurgle softly. Fuck. Skillet was getting wet in her shorts just thinking about it, and she scratched at her crotch to adjust herself.

"Should we go in?" she asked impatiently.

"No. Give her a minute. She's checking out the opportunities. She thinks she can play that dumb bartender; now she's just waiting for him to offer something—advice or a place to crash or even a few bucks. He's not getting involved, though. He's not as dumb as he looks. Now she's scoping out the other lowlifes in there—the drunk bikers, the punks around the pool table, the old geezers from the fucking Elks. She thinks she could work any of them if she had to. One of them would give her a lift or a crash pad or something, if she cared to put in the work for it. But she's been working for it all day. She needs a moment. She needs to breathe. She's gonna come out again."

The girl came out of the bar again and sat down on the bench next to the door on the front porch and put her face in her hands. Skillet nearly lost her mind.

"Holy shit! How did you—"

"I been at this game a long fuckin' time, Skillet."

"I'm gonna ask her," said Skillet.

"No. Not yet."

"I'm gonna! I'm gonna do it!"

The girl was breathing deep and slow, her face buried in her hands. Now she seemed to notice that there were two other women out here with her, standing in the shadows. She could surely see the glowing red cherry of their smoke and could surely smell that they weren't smoking tobacco. Skillet extinguished the light and emerged from the shadows to approach her.

"Hey, sister," said Skillet. Skillet was a wispy girl with wide wet eyes, a shaved head, a skimpy crop top across her flat chest, and a pair of scandalously short denim shorts riding up her narrow ass. There was a splash of freckles across her cherubic face, and when she smiled, she revealed a massive gap between her front teeth. "You need a friend tonight? We're from the Sisters of the Green Lady temple and we're—"

"I'm not interested," said the girl.

"All right, all right," said Skillet, nodding. "Good vibes." She returned to the shadows without another word.

The Hell Slut chuckled. "Bad opening, Skillet."

"I had to try."

"Just wait."

Eventually, a young man—clean-cut, sandy blond hair, definitely fraternity material—came out of the bar.

"Hey, there!" He grinned at the girl.

The girl ignored him. Unlike Skillet, the young man didn't take the hint.

He pouted and shrugged helplessly. "What, not even a smile? That's cold."

Now the girl looked at him, but she still refused to smile.

"Good," whispered the Hell Slut. "Not tonight. Men always come stomping all over everything, always demanding all your fucking attention. Fuck them. Fuck this guy. Not tonight."

"C'mon," the man goaded. He stepped closer and now the girl was tensing up. "Just one smile. I gotta walk all the way back home, ya know—I need a little something to keep me warm all that way. You don't want me to freeze to death, do ya?"

The girl remained stoic.

"Hey, sister, this guy bothering you?" Skillet and the Hell Slut stepped forward together, and the girl gasped now that she could see that the Hell Slut was big, built like a bear, wearing a fringed buckskin jacket, a ring of studs through each ear.

"We're just having a conversation here," said the young man. The fact that he was still talking indicated that he wasn't a local; he didn't know whom he was talking to. He didn't know to shut up.

"We weren't asking you," said the Hell Slut.

The girl's face twisted with indecision. Skillet could tell she was fighting the urge to say *No, he's not bothering me—everything is fine.* That was what she was supposed to say, anyway. But the young man was too close, too cloying, and the girl was tired. It took so much to get away from Benny... Was she going to stop now?

So instead she said, "Yeah. Yeah, he's bothering me."

The Hell Slut grinned.

The young man's demeanor immediately changed. "Fucking bitch," he said. "You fucking whore, I just wanted to talk!"

"That's enough," said the Hell Slut. She crossed the distance to him in an instant and her arm shot out like a snake, her open hand against his face with the soft part of her palm shoved into his mouth. His eyes bulged in shock, but the Hell Slut squeezed and pushed his teeth up through his nose with a crunch. He shrieked as a cascade of blood emptied from his nostrils.

"Fucking men," said the Hell Slut.

"Get his ass!" cried Skillet, hopping up and down like a Jack Russell terrier. "Fuck him up!"

"You okay?" asked the Hell Slut, ignoring Skillet and turning away from the shrieking, crumpled mess she'd made of the man's face to look at the girl.

"Yes," said the girl, too shocked to say anything else. The young man writhed and screamed, blood gushing down his front and staining his sweater.

"You might wanna get outta here," said the Hell Slut. "There's gonna be a commotion. You got somewhere to go?"

"No," said the girl, and immediately burst into tears. The Hell Slut shifted from foot to foot awkwardly, but Skillet knew what to do. She dropped onto the bench next to the girl and threw her arms around her. The girl was too flustered to notice or object as Skillet wormed eager fingers into the soft flesh at her sides. She was a little thin for Skillet's taste, but Skillet never missed an opportunity.

"It's okay, let it out," said Skillet. "You can come with us." She looked up pleadingly at the Hell Slut and asked a question to which she already knew the answer. "She can come with us, right?"

"Of course she can. If she wants to."

"Where are you going?" asked the girl. She sniffled, liquid snot dribbling from her nose.

"North," said the Hell Slut.

"There's nothing north but the Pamogo," said the girl.

"Yeah," said the Hell Slut, grinning. "We know."

3.

*The Cat's Tongue (*Pseudohydnum gelatinosum*) is a jelly fungus, known for its gelatinous mouthfeel and barbed undersurface. It grows abundantly within the Pamogo Forest and can vary in color from white to light gray or tan. It is said to have a bland flavor.*

—Field Guide to Common Mushrooms of the Pamogo Forest, *T. F. Greengarb (1978)*

This is so stupid, thought Sarah. *I'm going to die up here.*

Here's what Sarah knew: Madeleine knew a guy. The guy's name was Andy. Andy was, according to Madeleine, "cool." Andy lived in the far north of the state, where the endless dry chaparral of California's Central Valley gave way to the eternally moist rainforests of the Pacific Northwest, in a town called Las Brujas. Andy "liked to hike" in the Pamogo Forest, the great green expanse of alders and hemlocks and cedars that blanketed the foothills of the Cascades down to the coast. "Liked to hike," Sarah assumed, meant that he had a secret little plot deep in the woods where he grew marijuana, because there was no reason for anyone to live in Las Brujas or to hike in the

Pamogo Forest unless they were secretly growing marijuana there. But that wasn't important. What was important was that Andy knew all the best mushroom spots in the Pamogo, where the constant rain made them flourish all year round in huge fungal blooms. Andy didn't know anything about spores, but Madeleine assured Sarah that he would be happy to play guide if Sarah wanted to collect some herself. Andy wanted to meet in the parking lot of Sloane Mill State Historic Park in the far north of Las Brujas. Sarah was fine with that. It sounded like a good neutral place and was probably easy to find on the map.

But it was still a six-hour drive. The car had been running on fumes; she'd had to break down and ask Madeleine for gas money. But if this worked, she wouldn't have to worry about that anymore. In the back seat, she had her backpack with granola bars, lots of plastic bags, and a dog-eared copy of T. F. Greengarb's 1978 *Field Guide to Common Mushrooms of the Pamogo Forest*, which she'd found at a Berkeley bookshop for fifty cents. She had her sleeping bag too; Andy said it would be an overnight trip.

Now Sarah was driving the I-5 from Shasta Lake—already the very edge of civilization to her thinking—to the winding unnumbered road through the mountains to a Podunk shithole in the middle of yokel country to go on an illegal camping trip to poach mushrooms in the heart of an unmapped forest with a complete rando—all on Madeleine's assurances that he was "cool."

"Yeah, I'm pretty much gonna die, ha ha," she said out loud. But she said it with a smile so that she didn't feel so bad.

Sarah didn't like the woods. It was cold and wet and there were bugs. Sarah had gone camping once as a child with her parents, and mostly she just remembered lying on the hard, lumpy ground and failing to sleep for eight hours. Oh well. At least slogging through the woods couldn't be worse than when Jade made her hike the East Bay Hills, right?

Herman will be okay without me for a couple days, she told herself. If Sarah did get killed up here, Madeleine would adopt him. Probably. Sarah really didn't want to think about Herman ever going back to the shelter.

Her '87 Tercel didn't have GPS, and phone reception had died two counties back. Her only hope of ever finding the mysterious Andy was the road map open on the shotgun seat next to her. She stole glances at it whenever the road cleared enough to risk it.

And it was raining. It rained incessantly up in the far North State, where the roads began to tilt up into the mountains. It was hard to believe that California was in the middle of a decade-long drought. Her wipers scraped across the windshield glass futilely, but the rain kept coming. The headlights of oncoming traffic blurred and smeared in the downpour, and Sarah kept adjusting her glasses in hopes that would help. It didn't.

A roadside sign loomed out of the drizzle: NOW ENTERING LAS BRUJAS. GATEWAY TO THE PAMOGO FOREST. GAS. FOOD. SLOANE MILL STATE HISTORIC PARK. The sign also had three holes in it that looked suspiciously like bullet holes. Sarah's hands clenched the wheel. This was redneck country. She hadn't dared to stop the car since Shasta Lake, and she'd stopped there only because her overfull bladder had forced her to pull into a gas station where an elderly Sikh man sat behind the cash register. His presence was reassuring; at that point, she hadn't yet crossed the border into the dark country of neo-Nazi militias and Jefferson freaks. Whatever else you could say about Shasta Lake, the weed shops and hippie gem stores brought in enough tourist traffic that it didn't feel too far off the beaten path. Not like up here. The first yokel up here to clock her was probably going to blast her in the head with a shotgun.

"Ha ha," she said again. "Gonna die up here."

Las Brujas was one of the innumerable ramshackle boomtowns that popped up all over Northern California during the gold rush, attracted prospectors from China and then prospectors from the eastern states who murdered the Chinese and burned down the Chinatown and whose descendants, a century later, added Chinese characters to the street signs in commemoration of the town's rich history. The houses were old and made of worm-riddled lumber, connected by a common wooden boardwalk like a series of Old West saloons from the movies. She passed by a bar with a sign that she could barely read through the downpour: THE DANK HOLE. The boardwalk in front was stained with big splotches of red that Sarah hoped was spilled paint. A bald man in overalls sauntered out of the bar with a metal trash can in his arms and emptied it into the gutter. He looked up as Sarah's car glided past, and for a moment, the two of them locked eyes. Sarah shivered.

A battered street sign indicated in both English and Chinese that Sloane Mill State Historic Park was ahead to the right. Sarah spun the wheel hard, hand over hand—the Tercel was old and cheap enough to predate power steering—and the car lurched down a narrow, sloping side street. The trees were thicker and the houses here set farther back from the road, so that all she could see were corrugated iron fences decorated with Gadsden flags. It was almost a relief when she finally passed into the woods and she didn't see anything except trees and rain.

Another sign loomed out of the gloom: SLOANE MILL STATE HISTORIC PARK VISITOR CENTER. She pulled into the empty parking lot labeled SLOANE MILL SHP DAY USE VISITORS ONLY, next to a low squat building. The lot was abandoned other than a State Parks maintenance truck.

Sarah killed the engine and leaned into the back seat to grab her backpack.

Tap, tap, tap. A sudden knock at her window drew her attention.

She looked up to see a paunchy man with a respectable salt-and-pepper mustache in a beige uniform and a ranger hat, standing at the side of the car. He wore sunglasses despite the complete lack of sun. Shit. Sarah realized too late that the truck was no maintenance vehicle; it was a ranger truck. Shit! Now she regretted plastering her bumper with obnoxious stickers, but most of them, other than "Bernie 2020" and the cartoon opossum declaring "Trans rights or I bites," were probably too esoteric to attract the wrong kind of attention. *Oh well. Too late now.* She rolled down the window.

"This is Sloane Mill State Park parking only, ma'am," said the ranger.

"Yes, I'm going to the park," said Sarah. And then she added, because she remembered that rangers loved to have their asses kissed, "Sir?"

The ranger shook his head, but the "sir" seemed to please him, because he was smiling now. "I wouldn't recommend going into the woods, ma'am. It's not safe for a young woman alone."

Sarah peered over her dashboard at the perimeter of the forest, blurred through the drizzle, only about a hundred yards away, beyond the edge of the parking lot. "Not safe?"

The ranger smiled and tipped his hat. "Nature is what it is. But I'd worry more about people. There's a real problem with squatters out there. Vagrants, you know. We keep sweeping them out, but more just keep coming."

"Uh-huh," said Sarah. "Way out here?"

"It's because of the bureaucrats down in Sacramento," continued the ranger, crossing his arms and relaxing his bulk against the side of her car to indicate he was about to talk for a very long time. "They give them free bus tickets to come up here, just to get them out of the city. They give priority to illegals too—can you believe it? Illegal bums get the first free tickets, before our own homegrown American bums!" He chuckled as if he'd made a very good joke. "Some real dangerous sorts, if you'll excuse me for saying so, ma'am, judging by the garbage they leave behind."

Now Sarah was getting interested. "What do they leave behind?"

"Weird graffiti. Real Satanic stuff. A lot of these hippie sorts, you know, from Berkeley. They get into drugs and Satanism, and they end up out here in the woods, shooting up and worshipping the devil. Not safe for a young woman alone."

This guy was so full of shit. Sarah had to work hard not to roll her eyes. It would not do to roll your eyes at a ranger.

"Yeah, gotta watch out for those Satanists," she said. That sounded way more sarcastic than she had intended.

"Where they ought to be is in jail; that's what's good for them." A slight note of irritation crept into the ranger's voice, as if he thought Sarah was doubting him. He had apparently picked up on her sarcasm, and he did not like that response at all.

The ranger leaned in closer, his brows suddenly knitting above his sunglasses. He craned his neck, like he was trying to see past her into the car, like he was trying to find an excuse. "I'm gonna need to see your license and registration, ma'am."

Sarah's heart fell into her stomach. She had miscalculated

with her sudden show of sympathy for squatting forest Satanists. *Shit, shit, shit.* She should have known better. She should have known you don't just have a pleasant conversation with a cop. Now she was fucked. She carried shrooms in her car often enough that she'd memorized the legal advice from late-night TV lawyer ads just for this contingency, but now that she was faced with reality, all that knowledge suddenly evaporated from her head in a panic. Did you actually have to turn over your ID to a cop when he asked for it? *Shit, shit, shit.* Could he search the car? Was there anything incriminating in the car? Other than Greengarb's book, she was in the clear, and you couldn't be arrested for just carrying a book about mushrooms, right? The country hadn't yet slid *that* deep into fascism, right?

Sarah laughed a desperately nonchalant laugh. "You don't really, do you? You're joking."

The cold reflective gaze of the ranger's sunglasses did not falter. "License and registration, ma'am."

Even as her thoughts raced in circles, she watched her dumb, dumb fingers automatically pull her license from her wallet and hand it over. *No, don't do that. That's bad. Or is it? Oh, fuck.*

The cop looked at the license and then looked back at Sarah and then back at the license. His lips moved as he silently wrapped them around the syllables of Sarah's dead name, and then a nasty smirk broke out across his rubbery ranger face. Sarah could imagine the evil glint of recognition switching on in those piggy ranger eyes behind his sunglasses.

"I'm going to need you to get out of the car," said the ranger.

Oh no.

"Why?" said Sarah, her hands tensed on the wheel. Her heart thumped in her chest. The key was still in the ignition. If she flipped it right now and gunned the engine, she might just blast out of here before he could react. What a ludicrous idea. This was the twenty-first century. You didn't start a high-speed chase with a cop unless you wanted to end up dead.

"I'm going to need you to get out of the car," repeated the ranger.

Sarah opened the door and emerged from the car. Time passed with agonizing slowness.

"You got anything in that car I should know about?"

"No? There's nothing."

The ranger pretended to study her driver's license as though it was going to tell him what to say next. "Like I said, we've had some trouble around here. Not local kids, of course. Good salt-of-the-earth kids, that's what we got here in Las Brujas. But these vagrants, they're outside agitators, you know. You know how it is."

"Right, right, of course. Sir."

"You're not involved in that sort of thing, are you?"

"No, sir."

"Good," said the ranger. "Then you won't mind if I search the car."

"I do mind, sir." Sarah's mind returned to the Greengarb book in the back seat. *Shit. Shit, shit, shit!* "I don't want you searching my car. I don't consent."

The ranger looked at her for a very long second. He flipped her driver's license between his fingers, as if there was going to be some illuminating information on the back. Finally he said, "You a lawyer?"

"No, sir. I'm not a lawyer."

"That sort of lawyer talk might work down in the city. But this is Las Brujas. This is a nice quiet community. We don't like outside agitators here. Up here, people respect the badge. Do you follow me?"

"Yes, sir, I follow you perfectly. I don't consent."

The ranger's smirk widened and he stepped closer to Sarah, close enough that she could smell sweat and aftershave. He was a finger joint taller than she was, but that finger joint made all the difference in the world right now.

"I can call up dispatch, get them to send a canine unit. Those dogs will tear up your car until they find what you're hiding. Make no mistake—they will find it. You understand that?"

"Yes, sir," said Sarah. She had no idea what to say next, but she'd already dug herself this deep into a hole—the only way out was through. "I still don't consent."

Ha ha, thought Sarah, *I am going to die. I'm not even going to get to the forest before I die. What a world.*

He moved closer to her. His mustache filled the entire world. "You look awful smug. Think you're gonna take this to some bleeding-heart judge with a sob story about your rights getting violated? You're not from around here. Las Brujas is our town. We got three of us for every civvy—"

"Heeeey, what's up here?" A second figure popped out of the building, tall and spindly and hidden under a yellow rain slicker. Sarah could just make out a face in the gloom of the hood—a sharp nose, a scruffy little beard, and droopy eyes. "Sarah? Is that Sarah?" And then, directed to the ranger, he said, "Don't worry about her, man—she's with me!"

The ranger raised an eyebrow and turned to face this new arrival.

"Oh yeah, she made special reservations for a guided interpretive walk around the premises," continued the new figure. He patted his pockets. "One sec, I got a parking permit here for her."

There was a long pause as the ranger appeared to do the mental math, trying to figure out what he could get away with now that there was a witness. Sarah held her breath. For a very long moment, time stopped.

"You know this person?"

"Oh yeah," said the new figure. "It's a special interpretive hike. It's all been prearranged. You know what we say in State Parks: all visitors welcome!"

"Fine," said the ranger brusquely. He handed Sarah's license back, shaking his head. His expression remained inscrutable for a flicker of an instant and then broke into a shit-eating grin.

No one will believe you, the shit-eating grin said.

"After all, all visitors welcome." He touched the brim of his hat.

The words dripped with sarcasm, but the new figure didn't seem to pick up on that.

"Yeah, yeah, totally, man!"

Sarah watched in stunned relief as the ranger ambled slowly back to his truck, climbed behind the wheel, and gunned the engine. He shot her a parting leer as he pulled out.

The new figure walked over to her, but Sarah kept watch on the receding red taillights of the ranger truck until they disappeared into the fog. *Good fucking riddance!* Only then did Sarah start breathing again. *Goddamn.*

"Jesus fucking Christ," Sarah muttered under her breath. Her heart was still thumping in her chest, so hard she thought she was going to die.

"Hey, sorry about that," said the new arrival, obliviously. "You are Sarah, right?"

"Yeah. You must be Andy?"

He nodded, smiling. "That's me. Welcome to sunny Las Brujas!"

He handed her a slip of paper that said "SLOANE MILL

DAY PASS" on it. "Just stick that on your dashboard and come on inside. Some of the rangers are real hard-asses about parking."

"That wasn't about parking," said Sarah.

"Naw, they're just really up in arms about parking cuz we keep getting people using the lot after-hours. It's a real problem."

It wasn't worth pursuing, so Sarah just slapped the paper onto her dashboard, shrugged herself into her coat, and followed Andy over to the visitor center, where he pulled a ring of keys out of his pocket and fumbled with the lock on the door. Sarah had assumed that the park was just a convenient meeting place, but it seemed like Andy actually worked here. Which meant that she was about to trespass on state park property with an actual state park guide. Maybe that made it legal? Or maybe that just made it worse...

"Do you actually work here? Wait, are *you* a ranger too?"

Andy pulled the door open and gestured for her to enter. "More like a caretaker. Actually, if you want to get technical, I'm what they call an interpretive specialist. Fancy way of saying that I teach tourists about the history of Lazarus Sloane and his lumber operations between 1860 and 1900. We get school groups too; every third-grade class in Las Brujas and San Bernardo comes through here for their spring field trip. There's a whole hands-on program for kids—they get to play with authentic 1860s logging equipment! Steel wedges, misery whips..."

"Hmm." Sarah wasn't very good with kids, nor did she care about the history of Lazarus Sloane. Besides that, she was still thinking about that ranger.

"It really makes history come alive for them!" continued Andy, oblivious to Sarah's polite disinterest. "The head interpreter retired about five years ago and they never replaced him, so I pretty much run the place. I have a little room in the back, kitchenette and everything."

Andy slapped the light switch and the overhead lights flickered on, illuminating the front atrium of the visitor center and a few glass display cases. He gestured vaguely at the restrooms as he pushed back his rain hood to reveal shaggy, unkempt hair.

"Make yourself at home. As we say here at State Parks, all visitors welcome! There's bathrooms over there and a kitchen in the back office. I'll be back there when you're ready."

Sarah realized suddenly that she had to piss pretty badly. It had been a long drive since Shasta Lake.

After emerging from the bathroom, she took a brief glance at the glass display cases. One was full of Native baskets, woven from willow and redbud. Another held an oil painting of a stern-eyed man with a chinstrap beard and a peacoat; the plaque identified him as "Lazarus Sloane, circa 1849." Yet another display held several yellowed animal skulls and a plaque that described common wildlife of the Pamogo woods: Mule Deer. Feral Pig. Raccoon. If State Parks knew about any psychedelic mushroom bounty it held in its own backyard, it was keeping characteristically mum about it.

There was a poster behind the front counter of a cartoon raccoon wearing a ranger hat and saying, "ALL VISITORS WELCOME!" Sarah wandered down a hallway behind the front counter where the cash register sat, past an office containing a desk and an ancient Wang VS desktop computer, to emerge in a kitchenette. Andy looked much more official now that she could see him without his rain slicker and in an official State Parks uniform; he was wearing khaki cargo pants and a beige work shirt with patches displaying the State Parks logo, a humpbacked bear against a yellow background, on the shoulders. He was microwaving a bowl of soup.

"There's instant soup mixes in the cabinets," he said. "Feel free to grab a bite—it's gonna be a while before you get hot food again."

"Thanks. I really appreciate you taking the trouble to do this."

"Happy to help. How do you know Madeleine, anyway?"

"We were in a support group together. What about you?"

"College roommates. That was back when she was a boy, of course. Oh, can I say that? That's not transphobic, is it?"

He looked at her with such an earnestly pained expression that she had to conclude he was being serious. "No, that's fine."

"Okay, good, good. Sorry, I like to think of myself as a queer ally, you know."

Wow, thought Sarah, *this guy is a doofus.*

He shook his head. "I worry about her. I think she does way too many drugs. What's she up to right now?"

"Hopefully not doing any drugs, because she's supposed to be watching my cat."

"Ooh, a cat! What's his name?"

"Herman. He's a black cat." She pulled up a photo on her phone, because she could never pass up an opportunity, and passed it over to Andy.

"Ooh, a Halloween cat," he said, nodding appreciatively. "I had cats growing up. They don't let me keep pets in State Parks housing, but otherwise . . . man! I'd have a dozen."

The microwave dinged, and Andy opened the oven to retrieve his bowl. He sipped his soup carefully. "So Madeleine says you're some kind of mushroom expert?"

"I've studied mycology." Now was not the time to mention that she'd only completed two years toward a mycology degree before depression and dysphoria derailed her life. But she still knew a little something about mushrooms. Sludge Caps

(*Agaricus ichorus*) are plentiful in the springtime, less so later in the year. If you find Blue Longstocking (*Psilocybe caeruleus*) on the south side of a log, there will almost always be Red Garters (*Psilocybe tenebrous*) on the north side. The Father of Lies (*Russula diabolus*) prefers to grow in deciduous leaf litter. The Harlot's Progress (*Bovista meritrix*) prefers to grow in fallen pine needles.

She knew enough.

"That's cool. So you grow them or something? To study?"

Sarah was beginning to get a very strange vibe off this guy. He couldn't actually be this ignorant about the true purpose of this trip, right?

"Madeleine told you what this is all about, right? Madeleine says that if we can get them to grow, there might be some money in this."

Andy's smile faded. "So you're just gonna sell them? That's the whole plan? Making money off of a free natural resource? Wow, capitalism much?"

Oh. So apparently *that* was his big objection. He wasn't against drugs; he just didn't think you should make money off them.

"Don't say it like that. It's not like I'm some evil capitalist. I really do need the money!"

"That's what jobs are for. With your expertise, couldn't you just work in a lab or something?"

"No, I couldn't." *Of course not*, thought Sarah. *Fucking look at me. I'm a fat trans college dropout. There's no work for me. What would Andy know about how things are for me? He's got a cushy job where he gets to sit on his ass all day and tell stories to tourists and no one bothers him. What does he know about real work?*

Besides, it isn't entirely about money. Sarah remembered the feeling when she was in the presence of the goddess. It would be good to see her again. Sarah really needed to see her again.

"So I guess that justifies you taking the forest's gifts and monetizing them like that. Sounds about white."

"You're white too," said Sarah, with increasing and barely contained annoyance.

Andy sighed an obnoxiously world-weary sigh and leaned back in his chair. "I promised Madeleine I'd take you to find the King's Breakfast, so I guess I'm taking you to find the King's Breakfast. But, you know, Madeleine said that one trip on the King's Breakfast could be life-changing for a person. I just don't think that's an experience that you should sell to people. It should be free for everyone."

If everyone wants it for free, then everyone can haul their ass up to the Pamogo for a camping trip with this sanctimonious prick. But everyone isn't doing that. I'm doing it and I need money.

Andy continued. "You know, the forest isn't just for our use. That's the problem with too many people—they look at a beautiful natural resource like that, and all they can think about is *How do I make money off of this?* It's just like Sloane. He thought that all this forest was just his to do as he pleased. Not even a thought to living in harmony with the land."

Andy was getting a little snotty, so Sarah thought she'd try to change the subject. She remembered the portrait in the display case out front. "So what's the deal with your man Sloane out there? I thought this was called 'Sloane Mill,' but I didn't see any mill around here. Just woods."

"That would refer to Sloane's timber mill. We don't actually know the original location, unfortunately. It probably collapsed a hundred years ago, after Sloane gave up on it." Andy brightened up, a sly grin spreading back across his face. He leaned forward as if he was about to share some delicious secret gossip. "But you asked the right guy: I am, after all, technically the world's foremost expert on Lazarus Sloane. You know Sloane used to own all the land around here? He came to California during the gold rush but didn't really have any luck."

"Did he murder the Chinese?" Sarah thought back on the bilingual street signs.

Andy squirmed awkwardly. "We know from local newspaper reports that during that period, it is true that he was involved in, ahem, altercations with Chinese mining camps."

"He sounds like an asshole."

"Yes. Well. Yeah. Sloane's life was, as we say in Parks, 'complicated.' Anyway, somehow, this guy gets his hands on a twenty-two-hundred-acre land grant; the Mexican government—remember, California is all part of Mexico back then—is just giving these things away. Sloane thought he'd finally hit it big. All he knows about this land when he gets it is that it's forest and, hey, trees are useful, right?

"He thinks he can use it for timber. No dice, though. The damp literally just rots his timber mill from the inside out, and all his equipment rusts."

"So how'd that all turn out for him?"

Andy shrugged. "Not too good. He started losing it, probably because of undiagnosed syphilis, and his diaries really get a little...weird toward the end. By the way, one more thing—I don't know what Madeleine told you, but when we're in the Pamogo, you need to do everything I say. I don't care if you've been camping before; the Pamogo isn't like any other woods. It's dangerous. People die out there."

Sarah grimaced. She could feel Andy's eyes sliding over her, judging her already. She was short and fat with stubby little legs and a wide ass that overflowed the edges of her seat. Her thick glasses kept sliding down her squashed nose. Her weedy blond hair was pulled back into a ponytail that she hoped looked "sporty," but honestly probably only made her face look rounder and more moonlike. Andy clearly did not think she was up to roughing it. He was right, of course, but Sarah still didn't like it.

"And on top of that, we are technically trespassing. This whole forest is State Parks property. Actually, it's under the joint stewardship of State Parks and the Federal Accumulation Agency. And if you wander far enough north, then the Bureau of Land Management gets involved. But the point is, *if* we run into any rangers out there, let me do the talking. If they figure out that you've got a backpack full of magic mushrooms, they're gonna bring the hammer down."

Sarah remembered how the ranger earlier had wilted away once Andy showed up. "Okay. Understood."

Andy stood up and carried his empty bowl to the sink. "We can head out into the park once it gets dark," he said. "Then no one will notice us till we're in the thick of it."

"When it gets dark? You don't want to start while we still have a little sunlight?"

Andy turned to face her, folding his arms across his chest and leaning back against the counter. "Trust me. In the Pamogo, it won't make any difference."

4.

I do not anticipate I shall have to remain long at the mill. Once actual operations commence, I shall entrust the oversight to my foreman, and I shall simply earn money from a distance like an east coast robber baron. To think I ever imagined that the wealth of this new country was in gold! What folly! Timber is the future, of this I am certain.

—Diary of Lazarus Sloane
(California State Parks Archives)

Deep, deep down in the earth, Skillet and the Hell Slut, covered head to toe in rust-red muck, paused in their work to share a joint, as was their way. It was dark in the compost pit, darker now that evening was upon them, and their work was illuminated by only a few guttering candle lanterns strategically placed around the perimeter and the rising moon far above them. The flickering candlelight cast long shadows across the walls of the pit and made the slick mud glimmer.

Skillet didn't like mucking after nightfall. The pit was always unnerving, the way that the steam rose from the muck so that you could almost see inhuman shapes in the mist if you looked hard enough, or the way that the wind playing above sounded suspiciously like ghostly moaning, but it was worse after dusk. Some of the sisters refused to go near the pit, as if it was haunted. The pit was a good twenty-minute hike from the temple, through treacherous woods where the power of the Lord of the Forest was strongest, but the sisters were able to safely traverse his domain because they had faith in the Green Lady, who kept him at bay.

Still, they were always aware of his presence, out there in the forest, watching, waiting.

Skillet wasn't scared of the Lord of the Forest or any other ghosts. Skillet was not religious. She just didn't like not being able to see what she was doing, that was all.

"We shoulda been done hours ago," grumbled Skillet, kicking her shovel in a huff. "This shit is thick as clay. It's way too dry. We need some fresh fertilizer and soon."

"What's the hurry? You on some schedule? Got some pressin' appointment or something?" The Hell Slut lifted her shovel with a grunt and planted it deep in the muck. It stood upright when she released it. "We'll get fertilizer when the Green Lady wills it."

"Then she better fuckin' will it soon, or we'll have to listen to Pickles whine." Skillet held the joint between two fingers and blew a plume of smoke. Her bloodshot eyes practically blazed in the darkness. "Fucking Pickles! The fuck does he care? It produces enough!"

They were both naked other than a thick coating of mud. The work was dirty and the smell was awful, but Skillet loved watching the Hell Slut sweaty and glistening and gradually gathering a thick coating of rancid slop all over her thick thighs and hanging belly. Skillet clenched her toes, squishing mud between her digits.

"Fucking Pickles!" she said again.

"I don't like him either. But Mother Moonflow trusts him and that's the way it is."

Skillet rolled her eyes. "Mother Moonflow says a lot of stuff."

"You need to shut your gob, you little shit. Mother Moonflow is the chosen prophet of the Green Lady. I wish you wouldn't disrespect her like that."

"She's not even here! What does it matter? She ain't psychic! Heaven forbid there be *one* superpower she doesn't have!"

"That fuckin' attitude is gonna get you in trouble. Especially with Pickles looking for a reason to get you in trouble. I can't protect you forever."

Skillet grinned. "Yes, you can! Nobody's gonna give you shit. C'mon, you wouldn't leave ol' Skillet out to dry, would you?" Skillet slithered up to the Hell Slut and humped her leg, mud squelching.

"I'm not in the mood, Skillet. You're really testing me."

"C'mon! Think about it. Maybe when we're done, we could sneak into the cellar, have some fun?"

"You know I don't like the cellar, Skillet."

Skillet did not stop, and eventually the Hell Slut rested a massive hand on the crown of Skillet's head and scritched, reveling in the texture of her bristly scalp. Skillet fluttered her eyelids.

"You would make my life easier if you just played along," said the Hell Slut morosely.

"I don't fuckin' play along," said Skillet, still humping. "Skillet plays by her own rules. That's why you love me, you fuckin' dumbass. If it was up to you, you'd still be back home with the Jesus Freaks, *playing along* in their dumb barn church."

"Fuck you, Skillet."

"Are you down there? Do you need help?" said a voice from

above, drawing their attention away from their revelry. A dark figure stood at the lip of the pit above, peering down at them. Backlit by the rising moon, her face was lost in shadow. But as she attempted to scale down the sheer walls of the pit, they recognized the Dank Hole girl.

Skillet snorted as the Dank Hole girl's feet slipped in the wet soil and she slid the last several feet, smearing mud down her front and landing on her bottom. She was wearing unwieldy rubber waders, hitched up to her armpits, which made Skillet laugh. Most of the sisters preferred to wear waders when they were on pit duty. It was only Skillet and the Hell Slut who dared to muck in the nude.

"Don't laugh," said the Hell Slut.

"But—"

"Cut her some fucking slack—she's new," said the Hell Slut, extending a hand. The Dank Hole girl took it and gasped as the Hell Slut lifted her back to her feet.

"What are you doing here?" Skillet sniffed. She didn't understand why the Dank Hole girl kept hanging around them. They had rescued her from the frat guy at the bar and delivered her unto Mother Moonflow. In theory, their association should be complete. The Dank Hole girl should leave them alone now. Under some other circumstances, certainly, Skillet would be happy to take this chick to bed, but right now Skillet was really busy trying to get the Hell Slut in the mood. This Dank Hole girl was totally cramping her style!

"Thanks for taking care of that guy," said the girl. She wrinkled her adorable little nose at the smell. She stepped gingerly among the piles of muck and slime, unsure of herself, her feet sinking deep into the burbling and farting ooze.

"Sure. No problem." There was a pause long enough to be

awkward. The Hell Slut changed the subject. "What did you think of Mother Moonflow?"

"She's incredible. I never thought about it like that before. But everything she said...It just makes sense, you know?"

"Yes!" said the Hell Slut, casting a meaningful glare at Skillet. "It *does* make sense, doesn't it?"

"Whatever," said Skillet.

"I've always thought that it must be like that. That there must be a goddess behind this all, right? I mean, feminine creation, right? They keep trying to deny it, telling us we come from *God* or something, but I've always felt like that can't be right. Mother Moonflow just explained it so well. I've never seen it so clearly. Praise the Green Lady!"

"Yes! Exactly! See, Skillet? She gets it!"

"That's great. That's really great. I'm glad you're both having so much fun with your religion. But we're kinda busy, ya know? So if you would just head back up, I'm sure Mother Moonflow could put you to work in the nursery or something..."

"I asked if I could help you down here."

"That was fuckin' stupid," said Skillet, and the Hell Slut cuffed her on the back of her skull. "Ow! That fuckin' hurt!"

"Yeah, and you're being fuckin' rude. She wants to help. I think that's real fuckin' nice of her." The Hell Slut held out her shovel for the Dank Hole girl to accept. "Take it and get to mucking. We won't get a good harvest unless we get to work."

"What will you use?"

"Pfft." The Hell Slut held up her hands, each as big as a catcher's mitt. "I got these, don't I?"

"Yes!" The Dank Hole girl beamed. "Praise the Green Lady, you do!"

"Yeah, praise the Green Lady, I do."

The Dank Hole girl and the Hell Slut resumed mucking, the Hell Slut plunging her naked arms into the raw earth. The Dank Hole girl handled the shovel awkwardly. It wasn't even just that her slender arms were too weak to swing it properly. There was the very obvious fact that she clearly had no intuitive knowledge of dirty work. *She's such a city girl*, thought Skillet.

Skillet watched them work for several seconds, watched the light play off the flexing, tensing muscles in their arms and backs, before she returned to work. The back of her head was still hurting, but not from the blow, and she was just *fuming* about this little cockblocker. She had a bad feeling in her stomach that this girl was going to be trouble.

Later, Skillet was still fuming. The Dank Hole girl kept fluttering around the Hell Slut, like one of those little birds that rides in a crocodile's mouth, and that prevented Skillet from getting any pussy.

The Sisters of the Green Lady gathered in the big room for the evening meal, all twenty of them seated on pillows around a kotatsu made from a single slice of an ancient bristlecone pine. All except for Mother Moonflow, who was in seclusion and took her meals alone. In her absence, Pickles ladled out vegetable soup into bowls, sliced chunks of dark marbled meat from a roast, and passed portions down the line. They all waited for him to deliver the benediction before they began to eat. The big room was clean, the only room in the temple that the sisters bothered to scrub with any regularity, so you could still see the veins in the warped oak wood floors and the spray-painted portraits of the goddess on the walls. A ragged rainbow of Tibetan prayer flags had been slung across the room, dangling limply from the high ceiling. If they were going to eat here, it should be clean—for better appetites. On certain days, though, when the wind blew from the north or when one of their number had completed a tour of duty in the compost pit, the rank odor of death was inescapable and all but the heartiest of the sisters would lose their will to eat.

"Bless this meal, Green Lady. Your pain sustains us, your sacrifice holds us, we dwell in the shadow of your sorrow forever, and we will not forget. Bless your prophet Mother Moonflow and all your daughters, and bless the little sisters of the forest..."

The Hell Slut sat opposite Pickles at the foot of the table, staring at her bowl of broth. There were chunks of anemic carrot and black potato floating in it. The vegetable garden behind the temple was finally bearing fruit, but they needed to do so much more before they could finally be self-sufficient. Then they would no longer need to go begging in the world of men.

The Hell Slut reeked. The Hell Slut always reeked after pit duty, even when the pit was dry, and no amount of bathing or perfumes or essential oils could cut through that rancid stink. The only cure for the smell of the pit was time. The Dank Hole girl didn't care about the smell. She clung tightly to the Hell Slut's sequoia-sized arm as Pickles droned on, then slipped a little hand under the fabric of the Hell Slut's tank top and gently stroked her chest.

The Dank Hole girl had lived with her pimp in San Francisco until she couldn't take it anymore, stole his money, and hitchhiked up the PCH until fate brought her into contact with the temple. Her pimp's name was Mel, but otherwise the Hell Slut had been right about everything.

"We give thanks for all of these and more. For the green blades of grass. And the blue of the sea. For the binding of the Lord of the Forest. For all of these and more, we give you thanks, our Lady. Bless."

"Bless," murmured the sisters.

"Bless! And bless Mother Moonflow!" cried out the Dank Hole girl with all the embarrassing zeal of a new convert. She giggled nervously at the awkward silence that followed her outburst, but the Hell Slut patted her reassuringly on the shoulder and pulled her closer.

"Yes, that's right." Pickles nodded. "And bless Mother Moonflow! Thank you for reminding us, new sister."

They all took their spoons and began to eat. The soup was bland and unspiced, and the chunks of potato were mushy in a way that suggested rot rather than overboiling. The meat was soft and greasy with the flatulent taste of overcooked turkey.

"So," said Pickles, casually dragging his moistened finger around the rim of his glass so that it squealed. He acted as if the noise didn't bother him. He tossed his long snarly hair—rampant split ends made it frizz out like a halo because he refused to cut them. "The pit is still dry. The pit should be at least wet by now. Can anyone tell me, why isn't the pit wet?"

All eyes at the table turned to the Hell Slut.

Skillet jumped to her feet. "Shut your fucking mouth, Pickles! Don't you talk to the Hell Slut like that!"

A smug little smile crossed Pickles's face. "I don't understand the hostility, Skillet. I was just asking a question—"

"Sit down, Skillet," said the Hell Slut.

"Did you fucking hear what he—"

"I heard it. Sit your ass down, Skillet."

Skillet huffed and dropped back into her seat.

The Hell Slut turned her attention to Pickles. "Okay, boy, what exactly are you saying here? You saying we don't keep the pit filled? The pit is filled when the pit is supposed to be filled. You got that, *boy*?"

Pickles maintained his composure, but a vein in his forehead throbbed visibly.

"You know it moves according to its own cycles." The Hell Slut guffawed. "Oh no, I guess you wouldn't know anything about that, would you?"

The sisters all laughed except for Pickles, which is to say that *all* the sisters laughed, because Pickles was not, technically, a sister. Sometimes they forgot that he wasn't a sister; sometimes he forgot, but they always remembered in the end. Pickles's eye twitched and he pressed his lips together, but he didn't say anything.

The Dank Hole girl crouched close to the Hell Slut and snuggled into her lap just like a kitten. The Hell Slut gently lowered her hand down upon the crown of the Dank Hole girl's head and stroked her flaxen hair.

Skillet was mad. She didn't like that the Hell Slut had told her to sit her ass down; she never would have said that before the Dank Hole girl joined the temple. And she really didn't like how the Dank Hole girl was always hanging off the Hell Slut, so that everyone was just thinking about the Dank Hole girl and the Hell Slut now.

And soon no one would be thinking about Skillet and the Hell Slut.

The fact that the Dank Hole girl was already welcome at the table showed that Mother Moonflow definitely considered her to be a high-value addition to the temple. And, thought Skillet miserably, why *shouldn't* she be a high-value addition? She was *super* hot—in a conventional way—with those blue eyes and those blond locks. Skillet expected that the Dank Hole girl was probably very much to Mother Moonflow's tastes, which Skillet assumed to be pedestrian.

Skillet suddenly imagined the Hell Slut riding into Las Brujas on her hog alone and wanted to cry at the thought. And then she imagined something far worse—the Hell Slut riding into Las Brujas with the Dank Hole girl on the back of the hog, clutching the imaginary Hell Slut's backside and shrieking in giddy glee.

Skillet could tell from the rhythm of her breathing that Aphrodite wasn't asleep.

Aphrodite, the outline of her swollen belly faintly visible in the starlight through the window, rustled suddenly under her sheets and sat up in bed. "Who's there?"

"It's me, Sister Aphrodite."

Aphrodite relaxed. "Sister Skillet? What are you doing here?"

Skillet usually slipped into the Hell Slut's room after dinner, but there were other sisters that she sometimes visited too. Skillet could not stop replaying the events of the evening meal in her head. *Sit your ass down, Skillet.* And then when Skillet went to the trapdoor beneath the Hell Slut's room, she was certain she heard voices in there—two voices, giggling and breathy, and the Hell Slut speaking with a tenderness that she had never used with Skillet, not even when she was drunk. Skillet did not enter.

"I was thinking," said Skillet, "of how it pleases Mother Moonflow for us sisters to know each other."

"Yes, Sister Skillet, but... I'm just kind of tired tonight. And little Athena takes so much energy." Aphrodite rubbed her pregnant belly to punctuate the point.

"I understand," said Skillet, "but I was just thinking of Mother Moonflow's wishes..."

There was a pause and then Aphrodite said, "Of course, I was being foolish. Please. Join me."

Skillet slid into bed and curled around the pregnant woman like a snake. She put her little hands on Aphrodite's belly and felt the life within. She was due any day now. Skillet found Aphrodite's expanding belly fascinating, though it was too firm and round for her taste. She preferred the Hell Slut's spongy middle—flesh you could sink your fingers into.

"I can feel the baby," said Skillet.

"Yes. Athena's going to be a mighty warrior, the Green Lady reborn in flesh. I can't wait to meet her."

Aphrodite seemed to want to say more, but Skillet burrowed between her legs and the conversation ended.

They stopped giggling when they heard a knock at the trapdoor. It was Pickles, his face thrown into stark relief by the flame of the beeswax candle clutched in his hand.

The Hell Slut grunted. "What do you want, boy?"

"Mother Moonflow just had a vision. From the Green Lady herself." He held a slip of paper up to the Hell Slut. "This needs to happen quickly, before the birthing ceremony."

"That's cutting it a little close."

"It's important. She's not taking any chances. We don't want anything to go wrong this time."

The Hell Slut crouched into a squat with a grunt and plucked the paper from his fingers, giving the words a quick glance before crumpling the paper in the palm of her hand. There was a name and an address on the paper, nothing more. That would make this job a little harder; they were going in nearly blind. The Hell Slut was naked, and Pickles stared defiantly into the middle distance to avoid seeing her hanging breasts or the tangle of pubic hair under the roll of her gut.

"This guy's in San Bernardo. That's a fucking jaunt."

Pickles didn't like swearing, and he especially didn't like the heavy scent of rut that hung in the air of the Hell Slut's room. He staunchly endeavored to ignore the nude young woman lounging on the mattress behind her.

"Then take one of the cars. Do this right, Hell Slut, and we'll see the Green Lady reborn in flesh."

The Hell Slut sighed, her gaze flicking back to the mattress and to the Dank Hole girl. It was after dinner. That was usually fucking time. But it must be important if Mother Moonflow was interrupting fucking time.

"Fine. Tell Mother Moonflow I'm on it. What is he? Geologist? Surveyor? I hope it's a surveyor. They're the fucking worst."

Surveyors were the pinnacle of toxic masculinity, with their incessant need to dissect and catalog the unknowable contours of Mother Earth. All the Sisters of the Green Lady hated surveyors.

"All that I know is on the paper. And Mother Moonflow tells me everything that we need to know." Pickles couldn't keep the edge out of his voice, and that made the Hell Slut chuckle. She loved when she got to him. "There's one more thing. Before you kill him, Mother Moonflow wants you to give him a message. Tell him it's for Aphrodite and the Green Lady."

The Hell Slut snorted. "If he even remembers her. But fine, whatever. I can tell him that."

"I suppose you'll want to take Skillet."

The Hell Slut paused. That conversation at the compost pit had bothered her, and Skillet's behavior at dinner was unhinged—the hot-tempered violence that women should be above. Mother

Moonflow always said that anger was a man's emotion. It was unbecoming. Skillet would know this if she just took Mother Moonflow's lessons a little more seriously! She was getting complacent in her faith, forgetting the way of the Green Lady. The Hell Slut's gaze flickered momentarily to the Dank Hole girl in the corner. Her passion to know the Green Lady, her thirst for knowledge, her need for meaning... They were like a breath of fresh air after Skillet's casual blasphemy.

"Maybe not this time."

"Good. Glad to hear it. Praise the Green Lady!"

"Praise the Green Lady."

Pickles bowed his head and scuttled down the ladder. The Hell Slut shut the trapdoor.

"Fucking little toady," muttered the Hell Slut. "Burns me up how that little weasel thinks he's got Mother Moonflow's ear."

The Dank Hole girl lounged in bed, watching the Hell Slut as the bigger woman wriggled into her pants. "Is it gonna be like when you smashed that guy's face in Las Brujas?"

"Kinda." That wasn't the entirety of it, but it was close enough and it was all that the Dank Hole girl really needed to know. It was too soon to scare her with all the gory details of the Hell Slut's work.

The Dank Hole girl stretched in bed. "Can I come? I want to come."

"You won't enjoy it."

"You don't know that. I know there's bad people in the world. You think I'm so naive just cuz I'm pretty."

The Hell Slut laughed as she pulled on a tank top. "Oh, you're pretty, huh? Just gonna blurt it out like that? You're awful sure of yourself."

The Dank Hole girl smirked and rolled her shoulders. "If I

wasn't pretty, would I be here with you? You could have any girl, couldn't you?"

The Dank Hole girl was the worst kind of girl. She was petite and blond with perfectly formed, perfectly symmetrical breasts and a perfectly plump little pussy. She knew how hot she was, and she didn't see any reason to pretend otherwise. The Hell Slut couldn't understand how this girl had ended up under Mel's thumb for so long. How many weeks, months, years had she lived under his control, turning tricks and taking beatings? The Hell Slut couldn't fathom letting a man do that to you.

As a kid, she had calmly accepted her parents' teachings that women were the inferior sex, designed by God to suffer under the yoke of marriage. She didn't believe that anymore. Mother Moonflow had set her free. Back at the farm, there were so many sermons about the sinfulness of women, how they craved sex like wild beasts yet denied it to men out of spite. The Hell Slut was already bigger than both of her parents by the time she was fourteen—taller and also broader—but that was an advantage on the farm, where the women were expected to work chores while the men sat in a circle in the barn, discussing the finer aspects of doctrine. Father would preach to the family on Sunday mornings, telling them all about the love of Jesus and the evils of women. Women were temptresses, venal and plush with sin, and the Hell Slut nodded along with all her cousins, but everything her father said only made her more and more curious, his vivid descriptions of women's wiles making her tingle strangely. It was only after she recognized the truth in the face of Jesus in the icon above the family's mantel that she started to understand: Those big sorrowful eyes, those slender hands, those red kissable lips. She was beautiful, the woman of sorrows, but only the Hell Slut could see it. She instinctively knew she should not speak of the Lady Jesus to her parents; they would not understand. They thought all women were sinful, but the women who lay with women were the most sinful of all. The worst kinds of sluts.

And sluts go to hell, Father always said.

Well. So be it.

But even after she resigned herself to a life of sin, the Hell Slut had never thought that she could have any girl. She was too big, too ungainly, a thundering ox built all wrong, so that even Father couldn't find the energy to wholeheartedly condemn her as a woman—though he seemed to find her mannishness even more offensive. For years, the Hell Slut was certain no woman other than the Lady Jesus could love her, no woman could be so selfless. Sure, Skillet would gush over the Hell Slut's gut and swoon over her love handles, but that was all pillow talk. Skillet wasn't good for it. Skillet just wanted sex and she'd say anything to get it.

But the Dank Hole girl's words gave her a silly fluttery feeling in her stomach, made her feel like a dumb schoolgirl. It was a new sensation for the Hell Slut.

"I've seen stuff," continued the Dank Hole girl. "I watched Mel stab a john once and just spill his guts out on the floor. Is it weird that sometimes I fantasize about Mel finding me? I like to think of what you'd do to him."

More than anything, the Hell Slut wanted to kill Mel. She wanted to squeeze his cheeks slowly until his face imploded.

"I gotta level with you. It's not gonna be like in Las Brujas. I was just fooling around with that guy. This time, we're playing for keeps." She held up Pickles's paper scrap between two fingers. "There's no guarantee this'll go well."

The Dank Hole girl sat up. Her face was serious. "Stop acting like I'm a child. I understand this. But I don't want to sit here and worry. I wanna be with you at the end. Ooh, we could die together? It would be like Bonnie and Clyde."

The Hell Slut rumbled deep in her chest, a laugh. The idea of the Dank Hole girl sitting here, fretting and waiting for the Hell Slut's return like a good little 1950s housewife, was beyond funny to her.

"You're fucked up. You're more fucked up than I gave you credit for."

The Dank Hole girl pouted. "I thought I was being romantic."

"Oh, you were. Very romantic. Fuck. Okay, let's do it."

The Dank Hole girl clapped her hands in delight, a radiant smile spreading across her face. The whole room seemed to light up when she was happy. "You mean it? Praise the Green Lady! I can come?"

"You can come. But I'm taking a big risk on you, here. You gotta be cool and you gotta do what I say."

The Dank Hole girl jumped from the bed and threw her arms around the Hell Slut, pressing her breasts into the Hell Slut's chest and squealing with excitement. Her arms didn't reach all the way around, but that was okay. The Hell Slut understood what she meant.

"Can I have a code name?"

"A what?"

"A code name! Like, you all have such cool names! The Hell Slut isn't the name you were born with, right?"

"What do you want to be called?"

The Dank Hole girl ran her fingers down the Hell Slut's chest. "You tell me."

The Hell Slut ran a massive hand through the Dank Hole girl's flaxen hair, marveling at the color. It was beautiful, just like her. Like golden waves of grain. Like Sunny Delight.

"I'm gonna call you . . . Sunny Delight."

Sunny Delight made a face. "Like the orange juice?"

"Yeah. Exactly. Like the orange juice. You like it?"

Sunny Delight laughed. "That's silly. But I like that you gave it to me. So praise the Green Lady for my new name!"

This girl really *was* romantic. She snuggled deep into the Hell Slut's chest, and the Hell Slut wound her arms around the newly christened Sunny Delight. *She's so tiny*, thought the Hell Slut. *She's so tiny and pure.*

5.

*Quinine Conk (*Laricifomes officinalis*) is a wood-decay fungus that causes brown heart rot in conifer trees. Known as "the bread of ghosts" among some Indigenous peoples of the Pacific Northwest, the large fruiting bodies served a ritual purpose and were sometimes carved into elaborate masks to guard the graves of shamans. It is said to have a bitter taste.*

—Field Guide to Common Mushrooms of the Pamogo Forest, *T. F. Greengarb (1978)*

The Pamogo summers are wet and the winters cold; the rain never stops, not entirely, and the fog sits heavy across the canopy. From the foothills of the Cascades to the crest of the Pacific Ocean, the forest stretches across five counties of the far northern tip of California and bleeds, where it's not aggressively held back, across the border into Oregon. In theory, the wilderness overlaps the territories of the Wintu, the Shasta, and the Achomawi peoples, but they all found reason to avoid the woods, and the white settlers who came later, usually so eager to gobble up the acres, mostly found reason to follow suit. It stands today, endless miles of bigleaf maples and Douglas firs and ash and spruce, their roots and branches incestuously intertwined, all silent and still but for the rain and the insects that swarm in big buzzing clouds in the underbrush. No deer graze in the forest undergrowth, and no bears forage in the foothills; maybe you'll hear the occasional flutter of a crow or starling in the treetops, but even the birds sense that they're intruders here. *We don't want you here*, the forest seems to say as it closes up around the unwary traveler. *You would do well to leave.*

It was just around dusk, when the sun was dipping behind the hills and the sky was turning purple behind the eternal gray of the clouds, that they crossed the threshold that separated FEDERAL ACCUMULATION AGENCY, KEEP OUT from PAMOGO STATE PRESERVE, KEEP OUT.

"Don't worry about the signs," said Andy as he swung one leg and then the other over the low barbed wire fence and waved his flashlight to indicate that Sarah should follow. "They say they patrol, but they don't."

"If they catch us, we can just say, 'Hey, you said *all visitors welcome*,'" said Sarah. "We just took you at your word."

Andy's face was hidden in the darkness of his yellow rain hood, but his eyes twinkled and his breath billowed into the cool night air in big gouts of steam. Then he laughed, loud and raucous.

"Yeah. Yeah! Ha ha! All visitors welcome, indeed!" He paused. "One last thing... It's no big deal, really. But while we're in there, you need to be alert for symptoms of PCS."

Sarah stared at him. "PCS?"

"Pamogo catatonia syndrome. Something about the Pamogo messes with your head, and some people just can't take it. That's probably why there's never been any Native settlements in the Pamogo. Technically, we are right now within the ancestral territory of the Wintu people—"

"Uh-huh," said Sarah. "Are you going to give it back?"

"But the Pamogo doesn't appear within Wintu lore." Andy barreled ahead with his lecture, pointedly ignoring the interruption. "In fact, there's no mention of it before Sloane's arrival."

"That's convenient for State Parks."

"Officially, that's all because of PCS. But some of the townies around here have a different take. They say the forest is alive, it's got a spirit, and it doesn't like tourists. If it catches you, you go insane and wander these woods until you die of exposure. Or worse... Anyway, if you start to feel weird, you better down one of these."

He held out his hand; there were three yellow capsules in his palm.

"It's Leviathan's Favored Son. In pill form."

Sarah didn't even bother growing Leviathan's Favored Son (*Sarcoscypha cenobytis*). In her esteemed opinion, it was a garbage mushroom. No visuals. No good feelings. All it did was numb you. You ate one and an hour later you woke up missing an hour.

"What's this do?"

"Scrubs your memory. The Parks Department used to issue them to rangers, back when rangers would patrol the woods. There's a whole barrel of 'em back at the visitor center. The point is, if you start to feel scared for no reason, don't hesitate. Just pop one down the hatch. That fear is the first symptom of PCS. Who knows, maybe ol' Sloane wouldn't have lost it if he had some of these."

"How does scrubbing your memory help?"

Andy shrugged. "Dunno. Of course, afterward there's no way

of knowing *why* you took one, since you just won't remember. But, hey, there must have been a good reason, right?"

"Yeah, sure." Sarah started to put the pills into her backpack, but Andy said, "No. Put them in your pocket. Keep them handy."

Sarah nodded. These theatrics gave the whole enterprise a delightfully wicked sense of adventure; despite herself, she felt a rush of excitement.

"Then again, maybe it's not PCS at all. Maybe they just made that all up to hide the real truth." Andy held up his hands and waggled his fingers in mock drama. "Maybe there really is something in these woods that's terrible to behold, that you'll go mad when you see it. Maybe wiping your brain is the only way to protect yourself when it catches you. Think about it." Andy stepped into the bushes and vanished.

She stood for a moment, letting those last words sink in, before she followed.

They trudged in silence for a while, the only noise the trickle of raindrops and the steady hum of insects singing their secret love songs in the gathering dusk. The gnarled treetops hid any hint of the evening sky, so once they were under the canopy, all Sarah could see was the light thrown by her flashlight and, bobbing along ahead of her, the light thrown by Andy's. It was tough going. Andy made good time, striding through the thick underbrush on his long legs, while Sarah waddled along, puffing, behind him. She felt a stab of panic every time Andy's spindly figure dodged out of her flashlight beam and into the darkness.

Every so often, Andy would abruptly change direction, and Sarah could only do her best to keep up. How did he know where to go? He wasn't reading a map or looking at a compass or even following a trail, as far as Sarah could see. He must have come this way before, but the ground cover was so thick it was as if they were the first humans to ever venture this way. It felt like they were walking off the edge of the world. The ferns were waist-deep, and Sarah could feel her sneakers sliding in mud with every step.

She wasn't used to physical exertion like this—even back when she lived as a boy, she hated exercise, and that was when she actually had some muscle tone. These days, it was all hidden under girlish pudge. Her thick legs rubbed together when she walked, so that the inner thighs of her jeans always wore out first. HRT had only made her fatter, except for her tits—which remained, in Sarah's estimation, disappointingly petite.

"Could we take a break?" puffed Sarah finally, gasping as she doubled over to lean her hands against her knees. Her coat and jeans were drenched, and she was sweating despite the chill in the air.

"The faster we move, the faster we get there," said Andy without breaking stride.

"Please," muttered Sarah. She inhaled deeply through her nose and exhaled through her mouth, willing herself to catch her breath. The constant drizzle was really getting to her; she was absolutely soaked, and her glasses kept fogging up from the choking humidity. "I'm not built for this sort of thing."

Andy paused, frowning. "We really should keep moving."

Sarah groaned. Honestly, he was really starting to annoy her with this attitude. She bit her tongue. *Don't piss off your only guide when you're in the middle of nowhere*, she thought. *Just think of the King's Breakfast. That'll make everything worth it. All I have to do is get a few spores, enough to start growing my own batch... Madeleine will pay through the nose once she gets a taste of your new crop. Think of Herman. I can finally give him wet food again.*

"How are you even finding your way?" she said out loud. "You're zigzagging all over the place!"

"That's how you have to move in the Pamogo. You know that movie *Stalker*?"

"No."

Now Andy finally paused. "You don't know *Stalker*? By Andrei Tarkovsky? It's a classic of Soviet cinema."

"I'm not really a big movie buff."

"Oh my God. How can you *not* know *Stalker*? I thought all trans women knew *Stalker*."

Sarah glared at him over the frames of her glasses. *Oh, here it comes.* It seemed like every day she learned a new thing that everyone knew about trans women.

"Why would trans women all know *Stalker*?" she said, struggling to keep the annoyance out of her voice. She was already crabby about being wet and winded; she didn't need the world's weirdest microaggression to be mad about.

"You need to see it. When we get back to civilization, I'm going to make you watch it."

Sarah couldn't think of anything she wanted to do less than watch a movie with Andy.

"You didn't answer my— Christ, okay, whatever, I get it, you really like this movie. What's it about?"

"I can't explain it. You really just have to see it."

Sarah rolled her eyes, knowing that wouldn't be the end of it. Sure enough, a minute later Andy continued: "It's about this place called the Zone, where everything's weird. The normal laws of physics don't apply here. And the only people who know how to safely go into the Zone are called stalkers."

"So are you're saying the Pamogo is like the Zone?"

"No, that's not what I'm saying. I'm saying that anything you think you know about forests? You can just forget it here. The Pamogo isn't like any other forest on Earth. Things get weird here. Like, here, check this out." Andy paused in the path and rummaged through his backpack, eventually pulling out a small compass. He held it out so that Sarah could see the needle spinning wildly.

"See that? Compasses are completely useless in the Pamogo. It's cuz of the electrical storms on the Cascades slopes; it just plays haywire with magnetism. And forget about maps. They've tried to draw maps of this place, but the woods are never the same way twice. It's the rain, you see. It makes the undergrowth grow super aggressively, so it doesn't matter how many times you try to hack your way through here... The path's always gone by the time you get back. Some people say it's even worse than that. Some people say that the woods seem to move and twist between visits, almost as if it doesn't *want* to be mapped."

Sarah thought about what Andy had said: *They say the forest is alive, it's got a spirit, and it doesn't like tourists.*

Andy shoved the compass back into his backpack and zipped it up, slinging it over his shoulders again. "You don't survive a day in these woods if you don't know what you're up against."

"And so you're basically a stalker, is that it? You're saying you understand these woods?"

Andy looked at her with a sad, pitying expression. "You really just have to see that movie," he said, and turned back to the non-existent trail.

"Oh, get off it." Sarah grunted, hoisted her backpack, and wobbled after him. Andy was really starting to fucking annoy her. *Just think of the King's Breakfast*, she told herself. *Just think of the King's Breakfast.*

Sarah didn't know how much time passed, how many hours she'd wasted trudging through ferns and shrubbery, before she suddenly realized that she was crunch-crunch-crunching tiny bones underfoot. She pushed through the hemlocks into a clearing where a tidy pile of mossy, blackened bones—skulls and ribs and femurs and especially tiny little delicate fingers—towered as high as her head over the forest floor.

"What the hell."

"Yeah, don't freak out," said Andy. "It's just a raccoon graveyard. You find these in the Pamogo. Don't act so surprised—of course there's raccoons in the Pamogo."

"I'm not surprised that there's raccoons here! I'm surprised that..." She motioned at the tower of bones as if the reason for her confusion should be self-evident.

"It stands to reason, of course, that there are raccoons in the Pamogo," continued Andy. "This is part of their range. It makes perfect sense that raccoons should live here."

"So?"

"No one ever sees them, though. You only ever see their bones."

Sarah was quiet.

"The reason, of course, is that raccoon bones are quite fine." Andy was back in tour guide mode, evidently quite happy that he had this opportunity to show off. "The unique wind currents, generated by the alternating pressure systems of the mountain storms, pick up bones as they pass through the woods before converging in specific spots, known scientifically as terminal gyres. It's all perfectly normal."

"What the hell."

"See, the old-growth trees act as natural wind tunnels."

"What the *hell*."

The sight filled Sarah with a sick, nauseous feeling in the pit of her stomach. She looked up. Even in this clearing, the treetops reached across to blot out the sky and block the stars.

"You coming?" asked Andy.

"What? Oh. Yeah."

They passed through quickly. Sarah kept her eyes to the ground so she wouldn't have to look at the tower of bones, but there were more bones littering the path, delicate and fine, like the bones of babies.

Later, they skirted the edge of a gully, where it was so dark that Sarah had to keep her flashlight trained on her sneakers to make sure she didn't slip and tumble down the slope. She could hear Andy ahead of her, slop-slop-slopping through the mud, and then he stopped abruptly and said, "Okay, gonna turn left in about four steps, ready?"

"C'mon, how are you doing that?" said Sarah. "Tell me your big 'stalker' secret. Cuz it really feels like you're just randomly zigzagging around."

Andy was quiet in the darkness for a moment, then he said, "Don't freak out."

Sarah rolled her eyes. "Why would I freak out? Is there another pile of raccoon bones here?"

"Look down in the gully."

"Fine."

She aimed her flashlight into the ditch, illuminating bracken and ferns and swarming clouds of gnats and then, just when she was ready to give up and say *There's nothing there*, something green. Everything in the Pamogo was green, but this wasn't the rich, soothing mossy green of plants. It was a violent electric green. It took Sarah a moment to understand that she was looking at a raincoat and that the raincoat was worn by a man lying at the bottom of the gorge. Sarah gasped out loud and almost dropped her light.

"There's a guy down there!"

"Yeah, that's Greensleeves. Don't worry about it, he's dead."

Sarah made the same face of absolute confused disgust that she'd made earlier when she saw the raccoon graveyard. Andy didn't notice it in the dark, so he kept talking.

"He's been down there, oh, at least ten, twenty years? As long as I've been coming here. You can track your position by the bodies."

Greensleeves lay at the bottom of the gorge, his back to them, his head tucked under his arm, his legs curled up against his belly, contorted by rigor mortis into a fetal position. His tattered raincoat was dusted with black blooms of creeping mold.

"You track your position by the *bodies*?! Is that how you've been finding the path? By bodies?! Jesus Christ, the whole time? How many?"

Sarah had seen a documentary once about mountain climbers on Mount Everest, about how people died on the slopes of that mountain every year. About how, with the extreme altitude and the extreme geography, no one could bring down the bodies that perished on those great heights. About how the bodies just lay there, stiff and frozen, as successive teams of mountaineers passed by, unable to do anything. About how climbers relied on the bodies as grisly milestones to track their progress and mark their path.

"I told you not to freak out. These woods are dangerous. People die here."

"How many bodies have we already passed tonight?"

Andy paused, mumbling under his breath as he counted. "Three so far. Counting Greensleeves."

"Three?!"

"Yeah, and that's why I told you to listen to me. Unless you want to add us to that number."

Sarah was quiet. Greensleeves died here, on this slope, many, many years ago, long before Sarah decided to come on this venture, long before Andy ever started stalking here. Who knows how long he'd lain here before even that? How many lonely years at the bottom of this ditch before he was discovered?

The gorge was so choked with brambles and moss that Greensleeves nearly disappeared among the green. Slightly down the way, a chunk of earth had fallen into the ravine from the crest, clearing a path of upturned red dirt through the thicket. It must be recent; Sarah suspected that nothing stayed red for long in the Pamogo. Sarah could already see green runners and creepers stretching across the red path, ready to reclaim this fallow area for the forest. Something occurred to her.

"Hey, have you ever gone down there to take a closer look?"

"What? No, why would I do that?"

Sarah chewed on a thought for a moment. "I want to see something. Hold on."

She picked her way down the red path, stumbled toward the end, and lurched her way to the bottom of the gorge. She stood only a few feet away from Greensleeves. Andy stood silently at the crest, his face hidden in the dark of his rain hood, watching.

Sarah hunched over the body, put her hands against Greensleeves's side, and gently shifted the body toward her. *Gently, gently. It's old, it's just bones*, she told herself, *nothing gross here anymore, it's fine.* Her breath came quicker, billowing in front of her eyes in big misty clouds.

Years of exposure to the elements had worn away most of Greensleeves's clothing other than his eponymous plastic raincoat, but even that was mostly just ribbons of soggy fabric now. All that was left of Greensleeves himself was brittle papery skin stretched tightly over bones. His face was a grinning rictus. Two aggressive whorls of twisty black toadstools burst from his empty eye sockets. Slug Shanties. *Phallaceae strigilis.*

"Just as I thought!" crowed Sarah. "Slug Shanties!"

"Are those anything?" called Andy as he watched Sarah cut away the caps.

"Slug Shanties? Yeah, these are a good time. They're a specialized anthropophagic fungus, so they only grow on dead flesh."

"That's wrong. You shouldn't mess around with his body like that!"

Sarah carefully dug the mushrooms free from his sockets. When she was done, she let go and Greensleeves rocked back to his original position, silent and still, as if he'd never been disturbed at all. Sarah stood up. She knew all about Slug Shanties from Greengarb's book, knew that pulling shrooms from corpses wasn't anything new, so she was bristling at Andy's judgment. Not that there was anything respectful about the situation to begin with. Andy was using the poor guy as a road marker, for crying out loud!

"He won't mind," she said, and immediately felt stupid for saying it. The cadaver didn't respond; it just continued to lie there.

Something—a beetle or a cockroach or a big fat grub—suddenly wiggled in Sarah's hand and she yelped. She dropped the mushroom clump and quickly brushed her hand against her sweater in a panic. Upslope, Andy chuckled ruefully.

"That's not funny!"

"It's a little funny."

Sarah aimed her flashlight into the underbrush to search for the lost Slug Shanties. They lay across Greensleeves's side. There was no grub among the roots. Instead, the roots themselves were twisting and writhing like a nest of white worms.

"What the hell?! The roots are alive! They're moving."

"Oh yeah, that happens sometimes. It's because of the weird acidity of the soil here in the Pamogo. They'll stop in a minute. It's perfectly normal."

The roots curled and uncurled like grasping fingers. When Sarah put her hand near them, one quickly wound around her index finger. But the root had no strength in its grip, and she easily snapped it by flexing slightly. A few seconds later, true to Andy's word, the roots completed their dance and lay still. Now Sarah felt confident enough to pick the Slug Shanties up and put them in a plastic bag.

"Criminy. Dead bodies, live roots, mountains of raccoon bones...Is there anything else about the Pamogo you'd like to tell me about?"

"There's always more to talk about with the Pamogo," called Andy. "You done down there?"

"Yeah. I'm done."

She hefted herself back up the ridge where Andy was waiting.

"That's messed up," said Andy. "What are you gonna do with those? Sell them too?"

"Maybe." Madeleine would probably pay top dollar for some good Slug Shanties. They were always in demand.

Andy sighed. "The whole world's just a dollar sign to you. Let's go, I wanna get some more miles behind us before we break for the night."

6.

Attempts to use Indian labor have failed—not even tame Indians will enter the forest, out of some ignorant heathen superstition & idle laziness. Have assembled a fine crew, 30 workmen strong—mostly strong-backed californios & chinamen, also some mulattos & irishmen. Soon my lumber mill will be the envy of all Alta California!

—Diary of Lazarus Sloane
(California State Parks Archives)

Behind the temple stood a muddy patch of earth that the sisters charitably referred to as "the vegetable garden." Aphrodite usually helped Skillet in the garden, but Mother Moonflow had ordered her to be on bed rest until the baby arrived.

Not that it mattered now.

Skillet wallowed in the mud, up to her elbows in muck as slippery as liquid shit, and occasionally her hand fell upon something solid under the slime and she pulled a soft blackened lump from the earth. Skillet hissed angrily under her breath. The ground was too wet; all the carrots and potatoes that she planted turned to rot. It wasn't her fault. Not even a master gardener could work with this sloppy soil and this anemic sunlight. But Mother Moonflow had high hopes that the sisters would eventually be able to feed themselves, and Skillet could feel Mother Moonflow's disappointment like a physical weight bearing down on her.

At least the mushrooms were thriving. The perimeter of rotten logs was positively bursting with fresh mushroom blooms—greasy black Jack Mackerels (*Morchella piscis*) with their shifting rainbow sheen like a beautiful oil slick; squat little Jolly Bottles (*Calvatia vitrimus*) with their friendly coral-pink stems and their bloody crimson caps; wet gooey Jizz Bombs (*Agaricus abominatio*) with their bulging gills and their sticky, drippy sap. At least the temple's pharmacy would be well stocked.

Skillet broke off a chunk from a Jack Mackerel and shoved it into her mouth, just a nibble to top off her buzz. She needed it. Just to take the edge off.

In the distance, she saw the Hell Slut stride off into the forest; the Dank Hole girl skipped along beside her. Skillet watched them leave. Word among the sisters was that Mother Moonflow was sending the Hell Slut away on some important assignment, something to do with the birthing ceremony. Skillet knew exactly what that meant. She was going to kill a man. The Hell Slut always took Skillet along with her when she went to kill a man. They had killed plenty of men together. So why was she taking the Dank Hole girl instead?

Skillet almost didn't notice Pickles until he was standing over her. He squinted into the distance.

"I see the Hell Slut and Sunny Delight are off," he said.

"Sunny Delight?"

"Oh, you know. The new girl. With the blond hair." He pantomimed running a comb through his own tangled mane.

"She's already got a name?" said Skillet miserably. She wished that she had never spotted this girl outside the Dank Hole. She wished the Hell Slut had never stopped that frat guy.

"Hmm. Yes, she's really become part of the temple quickly, hasn't she? We all do love our Sunny Delight."

Skillet felt like her body was too small to contain her sudden boiling rage. The Jack Mackerel was going to hit soon, and Skillet was even madder knowing that Pickles was going to ruin a perfectly good high.

Pickles cleared his throat. "I spoke to Mother Moonflow about your behavior at the evening meal, sister. I didn't want to, but I had to."

"My behavior? You started it—"

"You were very aggressive," said Pickles. "If the Hell Slut wasn't there to calm you—"

"If the Hell Slut wasn't there!" repeated Skillet, incredulous.

Unbelievable. Fucking unbelievable. Pickles of all people was trying to play politics, trying to rise up through the ranks. Who did he think he was? His robe was open, and Skillet could see the scar that started at his navel and ended where his dick used to be. Pickles dribbled piss constantly from the hole between his legs, and no amount of perfume could ever completely cover the acrid tang of stale urine.

"And I know you've been sneaking into the cellar again."

"All the sisters sneak into the cellar! It's no big deal!"

"Mother Moonflow doesn't want anyone down there unsupervised. It's dangerous to go alone!"

Skillet rolled her eyes and flapped her hand in the *blah, blah, blah* gesture.

Pickles was not impressed. "Mother Moonflow has assigned you back on pit duty."

"I just fuckin' did pit duty! That's not fair!"

"That's Mother Moonflow's orders. You'd do well to remember that the Green Lady protects us because we follow a better way." He clutched his robe closed, turned on his heels, and marched back toward the temple, wet mud squelching between his bare toes.

"Fuck, fuck, fuck." Skillet swore under her breath. "Fucking little tattletale!" She felt like the ground was slippery and shifting beneath her feet. She was losing everything—the Hell Slut was enamored with fucking Sunny Delight, Mother Moonflow was pissed at her, and if this kept up, soon she'd be even more reviled than fucking Pickles among the sisters.

Skillet was in free fall.

"Fuck you!" shouted Skillet, louder now, but Pickles was already out of earshot. "And fuck Mother Moonflow! She's not the boss of me! Fuck the Green Lady!"

Several sisters sat in a circle farther down the incline and closer to the tree line, sewing a patchwork quilt. They paused in their work to look up in shock at the source of the commotion. Skillet stomped through the garden, still swearing, past the line of sewing women, and, her swears turning to angry tears, started picking up speed as she neared the tree line. She needed to get out of here. She needed to get away from these people!

Fuck Pickles! Fuck Mother Moonflow! Fuck the Green Lady! Fuck everything!

Now she was running, as fast as she could through a forest this thick, running and crying and yelling, and she threw herself into the mud and beat her fists against the ground, howling. She was losing the Hell Slut. She was losing everything. Without the Hell Slut, she was nothing, she was shit. The Hell Slut kept her together; the Hell Slut kept her sane. Without the Hell Slut, was she even human? Just a shitty little creature, a worthless goblin that should just live here in the mud—that was what she should do, just live here in the mud forever.

Skillet screamed, raking her claws through the dirt. It was a sound somewhat like a donkey's bray and also somewhat like a goose's honk. She hung her head, her forehead touching the dirt.

Then she was quiet, except for the gasping sobs, and when the words finally came, they were words that should not be spoken.

"Mother Moonflow's got the Green Lady's ear," mumbled Skillet, "but whatever. That's fine. The fuckin' Green Lady never listened to me anyway. Fuck the Green Lady in her fuckin' cunt! So I'm not talking to her. I'm talking to *you*."

Skillet was snorting and drooling, strings of thick phlegm dangling from her slack lips and sniffling nose.

"The Hell Slut thinks she can just throw me away?! Just throw away Skillet! And Pickles, fucking Pickles! Tattling on me to Mother Moonflow?! And Mother Moonflow!" Skillet was spitting in raw fury, her enemies list growing in her head. There was more than enough spite to go around. "Who the fuck does she think she is, telling me how to live? I hate them all! I want to see this whole stupid temple burn to the ground, I don't care! Destroy them! Do this for me and . . . I'm yours forever! Whatever you want, my body, my soul, my pussy, it's all yours, I swear it!"

I do not have the face of a man.

Skillet arched her back, a sudden bolt of electricity running down her spine, and she wretched, yellow bile exploding from her mouth and spraying across the clearing. She never heard the voice; the words blossomed, fully formed, inside her brain. She knew she hadn't thought them, she knew that something alien had put them in her head, and she knew they were true. She gasped, her eyes darting around the clearing. *Shit.* She shouldn't have eaten that Jack Mackerel. It was really fucking with her head. She was having a bad time. Skillet wished this were over.

"Ugh...Fuck...My head!" Skillet grabbed at her head, grunting, as if she could squeeze these alien thoughts out of her brain through sheer will.

Something rustled in the bushes and Skillet tensed. It wouldn't be Pickles. Pickles never came into the woods. He was too afraid to leave the temple grounds.

"Skillet?" said a familiar voice.

Skillet relaxed.

A scrawny young woman with wild ginger hair emerged from the bushes; it was Effervescent Bubbles. Skillet knew her well. She was young, barely legal, a spindly beanstalk so shy about her petite breasts and shallow curves that she always draped her body in that ratty poncho to hide what she should have flaunted. She carried a plastic bucket under her arm. Skillet had not noticed that she was among the women sewing the patchwork quilt, the women who had observed her meltdown. "Are you okay?"

The thing about Effervescent Bubbles was, she liked men. It was obvious from the few times that Skillet had shared her bed that she was always trying to pretend that Skillet's flat chest and shaved head were enough to satisfy her. The sisters at the temple all had different levels of antipathy for men: Mother Moonflow railed against the sins of the patriarchy in sermons delivered directly to her ear from the Green Lady, and the Hell Slut loathed men with a personal fervor that sometimes shocked even Skillet. Skillet herself didn't mind men. She found certain things about them pleasing, in fact. A half-cocked devil-may-care grin, a light dusting of stubble across a double chin, a downy fluff of penicillin fuzz sprouting between flabby pecs—these were all things that she could appreciate, even if no man could ever compare to the pleasing round plumpness of a ripe woman in full bloom. But Effervescent Bubbles downright liked men, as much as she tried to hide it. *What a hard fucking life that must be*, thought Skillet.

Skillet wheezed, her chest burning like she'd swallowed an ember. *It's just the Jack Mackerel hitting*, she thought. *Of course that's all it is. It isn't like any of this is real or anything.* It wasn't like she had actually just communicated with something from... beyond. That was ridiculous. There was nothing out there. It was all just some goofy story that Mother Moonflow told to keep everyone in line. Skillet was too smart to fall for that bullshit.

"I'm fine," snapped Skillet, wiping her nose and rubbing the puke remnants from her chin. "I just ate a bad shroom. You heard all that?"

"No," said Effervescent Bubbles. She shook her head. "I didn't hear anything. Mother Moonflow says we shouldn't go into the forest alone. I thought you came out to scavenge, so I thought you might want help?" She held up the bucket.

The forest held a rich bounty for those who knew its secrets, and the sisters had explored the deep woods thoroughly, confident that Mother Moonflow's benevolent guiding wisdom would keep them safe from the wiles of the Lord of the Forest, no matter how deeply they probed. Here and there, hidden among the roots of the tall, tall trees that blocked out the sky day and night, in the deepest of shadows, they could find little reminders of the civilization that had failed time and again to tame the Pamogo woods: abandoned ranger stations, crumbling loggers' cabins, the occasional fire watchtower collapsing by degrees under the weight of creeper vines. The forest was always taking back what belonged to it.

Skillet lurched to her feet, wiping her muddy hands across her shirt. Pickles probably expected her to report for pit duty, but Skillet had no intention of following orders now. "Good. Yes. That's absolutely what I was doing. C'mon. Let's go scavenge."

Now that the moment had passed, now that the Jack Mackerel's influence had waned and the fear had dissipated, Skillet wished it had been real. She wished that something had heard her.

But under the trees and the earth, under the roots of the towering spruce and the mighty fir, under strata of rich black loam and rocky clay, under the carcasses of ancient sequoias and redwoods, and finally under the worms and the slugs and the crawling things that ate them all, something had.

7.

*The Western Jack-O'-Lantern (*Omphalotus olivascens*) is an orange-to-brown-colored poisonous mushroom. It can be differentiated from edible chanterelles by the fact that it has gills rather than ridges. It is faintly bioluminescent.*

—Field Guide to Common Mushrooms of the Pamogo Forest, *T. F. Greengarb (1978)*

Sarah was startled when her cell phone rang. She was sure that with the thick trees looming overhead, all reception would be blocked. Indeed, when she pulled her cell phone out of her pocket to check, she saw that she had no bars. Yet the phone was still buzzing insistently. The caller ID spat out a line of nonsense gibberish, claiming the call was coming from a series of exclamation marks and ampersands.

"I should have warned you about that," said Andy. "That's the electrical storms on the Cascades again; they make electronics go haywire in here. I don't even bother bringing my phone anymore when I hike in here."

"I don't have any reception. How is anyone calling?"

"No one's actually calling. It's just a glitch. Ignore it."

Sarah watched the cell phone vibrate, urgently insisting that "!!!&&&!&!" wanted to speak with her. Finally, after long seconds, she pressed her finger against the "Ignore" button and the phone fell silent. "!!!&&&!&!" did not call back. That was when she noticed that she had also received a string of several dozen text messages, all from unknown numbers.

"I'm getting texts too," said Sarah.

"I'd just turn your phone off. It's only gonna drain the battery."

As Andy turned back to the path, morbid curiosity compelled her to scroll through the received messages. They were mostly in Cyrillic and Chinese characters, so if they meant anything, Sarah couldn't understand, but there were several in what approached English gibberish. One said:

>DRAIN&* THE BATTERY *@!!!***

And the other said:

>DONT$$@IGNORE*%^

She rolled her eyes. She hated how, even way out here in the dead zone of the Pamogo, your cell phone continued to spy on you.

At a certain point, Andy stopped and announced, "We'll camp here, okay?"

"Oh my God, yes." Sarah was dying. Her calves throbbed, her back ached, and she was so exhausted that she didn't even have the strength to be mad that *now* Andy was good with breaking. She slid her backpack off her shoulders and collapsed ass-first into the dirt. She could hear Andy scrambling around in the darkness, a backpack unzipping, and then the slosh of a thermos. They fumbled around in the dark, flashlight beams stabbing into the treetops as they struggled to extricate their sleeping bags from their knapsacks.

“How much farther is it?” asked Sarah.

“We’re almost there. We’re in the deep woods now, so no one’s gonna find us here. Get a few hours’ sleep; you’ll need it. There might even be some light when we wake up. You believe me now that the Pamogo’s not like other forests?”

Sarah thought back on the darkness, on the raccoon graveyard, on Greensleeves. “Yeah.”

“Ya know, Sloane even talked about this sort of thing in his diary.”

Sarah sensed that Andy wanted her to prod him to keep talking; the guy went into serious tour-guide mode whenever the topic of Sloane came up. That was what happened to you when they trapped you in a job long enough—you started just doing it even when you were on your own time. It was like when Sarah worked as a barista and realized with horror one day that she suddenly cared about coffee filtration systems. “Fine, I’ll bite. Tell me more about Sloane.”

“Funny story,” said Andy, although Sarah doubted that. “Remember I mentioned that timber mill? After he got this land, he convinced some San Francisco magnate to finance that whole plan. It’s a fiasco from the start. First, the local wood’s all too porous for construction, so he’s got to import everything from miles away. You’d think that would be his first clue that a sawmill’s a bad idea, but Sloane’s persistent.”

“Sucks to be him.”

“But that’s not the only thing. During construction, he’s losing so many men that he can barely even keep it going. And I don’t mean that his guys are quitting on him; I mean they’re literally getting lost in the forest. They’re building this mill, and every day guys are just going into the woods for a smoke and disappearing. The project foreman disappears for three days because he went to take a piss and couldn't find his way back. They clear footpaths through the woods, but they literally just grow over in days, so they have to start stringing ropes between trees just so that they'll have something visual to follow, but the ropes just rot through."

A chill ran down Sarah's back. She could feel the oppressive darkness of the forest all around her, and she thought about what it must have been like, almost two hundred years ago, to be an old-timey mill worker suddenly lost in all that.

Andy continued. "The men who work there had a safety protocol: Never go where you can't see the mill. As long as you have a visual on the building, you can find your way back to it. But the minute it disappears behind the trees? You're out of luck."

"You're full of shit."

"No, it's all true!"

"Sure it is. It's a nice spooky little story, really gives you the chills. Could probably use a little more of a punch at the end, though. And on that note, I'm gonna get some sleep. Thanks for the campfire tale, Andy."

Andy paused and then said, "You're not really just gonna sell the King's Breakfast, are you?"

"Oh, this again? This is really a problem for you?"

"I just don't think people should make money off something like that. I've heard it can really change your life! You can't put a price tag on that."

"It's not just about the money! I've tried the King's Breakfast; I know all about— Wait a second, what do you mean 'you've heard'?"

Andy shrugged.

"You're kidding me."

"I don't like putting foreign substances in my body."

"You do it every time you eat! You have got to be joking! Are you straight edge or something?"

Andy shifted uncomfortably. "No, I smoked marijuana once."

"Oh my *God*. I can't believe you're lecturing me about *monetizing the connection to the divine* and shit, and you haven't even tried them! Ridiculous!"

Now Andy was on the defensive. "No, I just—I just wouldn't want to have a bad trip."

"That's the risk you take!" cried Sarah, now so indignant that she sat up in her sleeping bag. "Sometimes you just have to go through hell to get closer to God! That's the whole deal!"

"I just don't see why you would want to put yourself through that."

"It can be a good thing! Sometimes it's your brain trying to show you things about yourself, things you need to know but you buried too deep."

"If they're buried too deep, they should probably stay buried."

Sarah threw up her hands. "Fine! Maybe it's not for you! It's not my business."

Andy must have been more interested than he indicated, because he didn't let the conversation drop. Instead, he asked, "So what's it like?"

Sarah rubbed her face. She remembered the vision she'd seen on the King's Breakfast at Madeleine's party, watching her doppelgänger bloom open and something transcendent emerge. It was an embarrassingly on-the-nose hallucination, probably something to do with dumb gender feels. And now she was here, in the Pamogo, because she wanted Madeleine's money... but also because she was desperately hungry to see that goddess again, to feel her close. She felt, deep in her heart, that the goddess was the antidote to the loneliness she had felt since Jade left. If she could just see the goddess again, she wouldn't feel this ache. She wanted to see the goddess reach out her hands again, and she wanted to take them.

"It's hard to explain. Your brain shows you things."

"Like what?"

"You wouldn't understand. You probably think it's something you can experience and, after you're done, you'll be the same person. It isn't until you're inside it that you understand that's not the case. But there's no going back; there's only forward. You have a secret knowledge that makes you different. It makes you crazy. But if you haven't experienced it, you won't understand."

"No, I get it! It's like your transition, right?"

"Oh, fuck you. I don't need this."

"Sorry, was that bad? Was that transphobic?"

"I— Look, you seem like an okay guy and all, Andy, but you don't know what the fuck you're talking about. I'm just saying... I think the King's Breakfast is worth trying."

"Since you're so gung ho to sell me on this experience, maybe I will try it one of these days. Here, I'll make a deal. I will try the King's Breakfast if you watch *Stalker*."

Sarah groaned and tossed in her sleeping bag. "Fine, whatever! It's a deal."

"Really? That's good, I actually have *Stalker* on DVD back home. We can watch it in the visitor center theater when we get back."

"Sure, sounds great. Just let me sleep, please."

She heard him take another pull from his thermos. She had a terrible feeling that this conversation was going to continue. True to her fears, Andy blurted out, "So why did you want to be a woman, anyway?"

"Oh Jesus. I'm definitely not having *this* conversation. Good night." Sarah rolled over, turning her back to him, and pulled her sleeping bag up to her chin.

"C'mon! I'm just asking. It's okay to just ask. Madeleine said it wasn't transphobic to ask that."

Sarah sighed. She wasn't about to get into the details, not now, not here, and certainly not with this doofus. For once, her better judgment was going to win out. But just like Andy couldn't keep his mouth shut about Sloane or the mill or *Stalker*, it just came tumbling out of her: "I wanted tits, okay?"

She heard Andy giggle into his flask. "That's understandable. I think everyone wants that."

"No, I mean... You know what, never mind, you wouldn't get it."

Sarah stared into the dark, painfully aware of the pathetic nubs on her chest. She'd started too late and genetics had fucked her over. Not like Madeleine, who grew big perfect boobs in just a few months on the titty skittles. No such luck for Sarah. But that wasn't the worst of it. Sarah didn't just want tits; she wanted absolutely huge tits, massive tits that sagged to her waist or maybe lower, ridiculous cartoonish tits that would threaten to break her spine every time that she tried to walk. She remembered her mother, whom Sarah had decidedly *not* taken after, complaining about how carrying those big heavy breasts around all day made her back ache by the evening, so, of course, Sarah absolutely *knew* the reality of what huge tits meant and she knew it was silly to want them and she knew that even if she could ever afford the surgery to get them, she wouldn't because why would she. People already thought she was a freak just for being a girl; the last thing she needed was for anyone to know about this weird secret need. She was careful never to mention it—not to her parents when she came out, certainly not to any gatekeeping doctors who would probably see it as evidence of mental psychosis and take away her pills. No, no one could ever know.

But after this trip was over, she would probably never see Andy again in her life. She definitely wasn't going to be sticking around to watch any old Soviet movies. And they were all alone in the forest right now.

"I want gigantic knockers," said Sarah. "Like, just absolutely stupid big ones."

Andy sucked on his flask. He seemed to be gradually realizing that he was wrong and he did not, in fact, understand how she felt. In the distance, something shrieked.

"What the hell was that?!" said Sarah.

"Probably just a raccoon," said Andy. "There's raccoons in the Pamogo, after all."

"That didn't sound like a raccoon."

Andy sucked at his thermos again. There was a long pause. Then he yelled out, at the top of his lungs, "Any raccoons out there, you better shut up! We're trying to sleep! So be quiet... unless you wanna go at it!"

Silence hung in the air for several seconds.

"See? Just raccoons."

"What was that about? You gonna fight raccoons?"

"Maybe I will." She could tell by the tone of his voice that he was annoyed his posturing hadn't impressed her, and he flopped over in his sleeping bag with a resounding finality that signaled the end of the conversation. *Thank God for that*, thought Sarah.

"Anyway. I hope you get your breasts someday," he said.

"Yeah. Sure. Thanks."

Within minutes, she could tell by the rhythm of his breathing that Andy was asleep. Sarah did not have any such luck. The damp air and the firm ground were hard on a city girl, and she twisted and turned for what felt like hours until finally frustration and boredom reminded her that her cell phone still had some juice and maybe that amusing glitch had texted her again. She worked it out of her pocket and pressed a button, the screen lighting up as a brilliant blinding white square in the infinite black of the Pamogo night. The glitch had, indeed, sent her more gibberish texts, but it had also sent one that said:

>WATCH SIGNS&&&@!

I hate that cell phones listen to your conversations, thought Sarah. *That's creepy as hell.*

After several more messages composed entirely of Wingdings, there was a second English message:

>DREAM&!!&

Sarah texted back:

>Hello, glitch. What are you dreaming about?

That seemed to agitate the glitch, because it responded immediately and in English:

>WAKE@@

Sarah snorted.

>are you having a nice nap, glitch?

>&$^&****&&@@@

>lol don't swear at me, i'm just being polite

>WAKE

>ok that's better, i guess. are you really just a glitch in the phone? or are you a real person talking to me?

There was a pause and then the glitch wrote back.

>I SLEEP UNDER THE ROOTS AND THE DIRT AND CRAWLING THINGS%%@@

>I DO NOT HAVE THE FACE OF A MAN&&@

"Okay, that's enough of that," mumbled Sarah, quickly shoving her cell phone back into her pocket. Although she spent the next several hours repeating in her own head that it was nothing to worry about, just the random firing of circuits confused by the Pamogo electrical storms creating the uncanny approximation of a human mind, it still didn't help her sleep. It kept creeping into her thoughts, unbidden, until she finally succumbed to exhaustion and fitful dreams.

8.

There are rumors that the forest is not healthy. The trees block all sunlight during the day & all moonlight at night. the glow of kerosine lamps reveals that already the workers grow lazy & listless from laboring in the dark. It is like living inside a tomb, thick with oily smoke trapped by the branches above. Nevertheless, I am optimistic about progress.

—Diary of Lazarus Sloane
(California State Parks Archives)

The empty field was full of cars, most of which had been stationary for so long that weeds grew between their plates and vines hugged them down into the dirt. But a few were still mobile, and the Hell Slut picked out a sleek yellow '76 Sturgeon because Sunny Delight squealed in excitement at the color. "It's like a big banana," she said. The Frog Sisters, whom the Hell Slut had also brought along as backup for this job, didn't object, so that was their ride even though it would have been smarter to pick something less conspicuous and with four doors. The Frog Sisters always wore identical black gowns and hid their faces behind identical black veils and spoke only in unison; the Hell Slut suspected from their behavior that they were identical twins, but having never seen their faces, she couldn't be sure.

"Where did all these cars come from?" asked Sunny Delight.

"Don't worry about it," said the Hell Slut. Then she dug into the dirt under the undercarriage of a ruined Studebaker until she found what she knew was there: a sealed lockbox, which she opened to reveal a stack of wrinkled bills and a motley assortment of car keys, chintzy jewelry, and disemboweled cell phones. She found the key for the Sturgeon on a grinning plastic skull key chain and peeled a few bills off the top of the stack, not a lot, just what they'd need for gas and maybe a couple of meals along the way. The Hell Slut never took more than she needed when she went out on assignment, because there wasn't any telling how long this money would need to last. The sisters didn't use money, because money was a concept invented by the men. They lived off the land, scrounging what they could. This cache, gifted by the grace of the Green Lady, was known only to Mother Moonflow's inner circle, only for emergencies when they needed to breach the world of men and go among them. Sunny Delight watched, but she didn't ask where the money came from. She knew better than to ask that question.

No one knew about this secret automobile graveyard, and no one knew about the hidden road—just one lane of gravel, constantly churned by enterprising roots and advancing underbrush—that snaked through the woods and dumped out onto the unmarked State Parks service road. Budget cuts ensured that State Parks had long since abandoned it, though you could occasionally glimpse the husks of abandoned ranger jeeps rusting on the shoulders. The mouth of the service road was barred by a locked gate, but the Hell Slut pulled another key from her ring, and soon they were barreling down the freeway toward San Bernardo.

The trip was uneventful, though Sunny Delight kept up a

steady stream of chatter the entire way and the Frog Sisters dozed. San Bernardo was a midsized town in the foothills, just skimming the western edge of the Pamogo as California gave way, spiritually at least, to Oregon. It was designed not so much to be lived in, but rather to be driven through. The highway expanded to five lanes of cracked, sunbaked asphalt here, lined with an endless series of gas stations and fast-food joints. A giant plume of smoke dominated the southern horizon, evidence of the wildfires that consumed the Central Valley every summer.

"Might as well get some chow," the Hell Slut said, and pulled off the road into the parking lot of a greasy spoon with a big flashing neon sign that said JOE'S DINER.

"Get whatever you want," said the Hell Slut. It was a rare treat that the sisters got to eat like this. They started with drinks, and the Hell Slut uncorked her flask and added a little moonflow to each soda. Moonflow would heighten their senses and strengthen their resolve; they would need it tonight. She ordered a tuna melt with seasoned waffle fries, and the Frog Sisters (as usual) got one grilled cheese sandwich each. Sunny Delight spent ten minutes studying the menu and then interrogated the waitress about what kind of dressing came on the house salad. They had Thousand Island, French, and Italian. Sunny Delight hemmed and hawed and finally asked for Italian on the side.

"I'm trying to be healthy," she said in response to the Hell Slut's amused smirk.

"You don't need to watch your figure anymore," said the Hell Slut. "You're one of the sisters now. You can eat whatever you want. No man's gonna give you shit ever again."

"It isn't about *that*." Sunny Delight huffed angrily. It was all a moot point, though, because when the salad came, it was mostly cheese and bacon bits anyway.

Sunny Delight started to recite the benediction as the waitress placed her tray before her, but she trailed off uncertainly when her companions failed to join in. The waitress was a professional and pretended not to hear anything.

"Aren't we going to say the benediction? Mother Moonflow's benediction?"

"We only give praise to the Green Lady for food that the Green Lady provides," said the Hell Slut. "This shit is man's food. Look at it! Unhealthy. Fatty. Probably chock-full of carcinogens. And bad for the planet too! We wouldn't insult the Green Lady by attributing it to her."

"Oh. But... then we shouldn't eat it, should we?"

"No, no, it's fine. You're allowed a cheat day. It's no big deal. Just one of the benefits of getting to go off campus."

"So the other sisters back at the temple... they're not allowed to eat like this? That doesn't seem fair. I feel like the Green Lady wouldn't approve..." Sunny Delight looked troubled, a shadow of doubt passing over her face. *Poor kid*, thought the Hell Slut. It was always so hard watching the new converts try to figure out the rules. It was kind of adorable. Sunny Delight was just so darn earnest about everything!

"Don't worry so much. Mother Moonflow says it's fine. She's the prophet of the Green Lady, so she would know."

"I'm sorry. Of course it makes sense. If Mother Moonflow says it's fine, then of course it makes sense."

"Yeah, that's right: If Mother Moonflow says it's fine, then of course it makes sense," said the Hell Slut, but saying it out loud suddenly made the whole idea very much not make sense. She grimaced at the sudden cognitive dissonance.

Silence hung heavy over the table for a long instant before Sunny Delight attempted conversation again. "So who's this guy we're after?" The Frog Sisters looked to the Hell Slut and then to Sunny Delight and back, as if anticipating an entertaining exchange.

"He's Aphrodite's baby daddy. He's gotta die for the birthing ceremony to work."

Sunny Delight looked upset, as the Hell Slut had expected she might. New sisters sometimes had difficulty with this concept. "That's it?"

The Hell Slut picked up her tuna melt and ripped off a bite with her teeth, an avalanche of wet fish chunks and liquid mayonnaise spilling out the far end of her sandwich. "That's enough," she said through bulging cheeks. "Look, it's not that complicated. Nine months ago, Aphrodite went out and got herself pregnant by some, I dunno, some hiker or some fucking surveyor. She really took one for the team; she's a trooper. There's a few gals at the temple who don't mind letting men touch 'em. A few bisexuals, some pans…"

"A couple political lesbians," added the Frog Sisters.

"And anyway, now we gotta bump him off. But it's fine, he's a man. They're all scum."

"Not all men," said Sunny Delight.

The Frog Sisters looked back and forth between Sunny Delight and the Hell Slut again, as if anticipating an even more entertaining exchange.

"I feel bad just killing some random guy," continued Sunny Delight. "I'd feel better if he was a bad guy, like a pimp or a cop or a rapist."

"Mother Moonflow told us to kill him," said the Hell Slut by way of ending the discussion. "And she said this kill is vital for the birthing ceremony. This guy needs to die if we're gonna see the Green Lady reborn."

Sunny Delight did not look reassured. The Hell Slut did not understand what kind of sick Stockholm syndrome had left Sunny Delight with the occasional warm feeling about men—sometimes not even men in the abstract, but some of her old clients. The ones who sat with her, who talked to her in soft voices before they raped her, complaining about their shrewish wives or their stressful jobs, about how no one else understood them. Sunny Delight naively took them at their word. The Hell Slut never would have done that. She would have ripped them out, root and stem.

Only one man had ever touched the Hell Slut. Back when she believed in the Christian god and loved the Lady Jesus with all her heart, she knew that her father and mother would never understand her feelings. But Uncle Steve, third in line of the uncles, might. He was the one elder who recognized in the Hell Slut something more than just another woman, a purpose in her other than breeding. He would show her how to fix things, letting her watch as he tinkered with that old motorcycle in the barn, sometimes even letting her work the tools as he stood over her shoulder and explained what to do. He called her "kiddo" and "champ." He was the one whom she told about the Lady Jesus.

Uncle Steve put a reassuring hand on her shoulder and looked into her eyes and had the decency to sound slightly sad when he said it, but he said, "Sluts go to hell."

Then he said, "This isn't a punishment, kiddo. It's a lesson. Don't worry. We'll correct this right now."

The Hell Slut didn't experience what happened next, but she saw it happen. She watched it from a distance outside her body, far, far away, so far that it was almost like it wasn't happening even though she knew it was. The Hell Slut was bigger than Uncle Steve, so she could have stopped him if she'd wanted, but she didn't stop him; she just stood there and let it happen, so in years to come, the Hell Slut imagined that she must have wanted it. There was no other explanation.

That was when she knew that the sermons of her father were wrong. Women were not the vessels of sin. It was men. She hated them, every one of them. Even the Lady Jesus. The Lady Jesus might look girly, but he was still one of them. That was why he did nothing to stop Uncle Steve.

The Hell Slut could tell that she wasn't doing a very good job of reassuring Sunny Delight. That was more Skillet's forte. She wished Skillet were here, even if Skillet was being fucking weird lately, all cold and cranky. The Hell Slut knew exactly why. Whatever. Let Skillet be jealous for once. The Hell Slut was rather enjoying that. It wasn't often that girls felt possessive of the Hell Slut.

"Okay, look. Do you trust me?"

Sunny Delight nodded.

"Then we're doing the right thing when we do it the way Mother Moonflow wants. The Green Lady sent her a vision."

"You're right, of course. Praise the Green Lady! Praise Mother Moonflow!"

The Hell Slut ordered a coffee, topped it off with an extra shake of moonflow, and gulped it all down, because they still had a ways to go. They paid in cash because cash was all they had, and the Hell Slut left an extra fifty dollars as a tip, because the money wasn't hers and the waitress really seemed to be working hard. They piled back into the Sturgeon and were back on the freeway in minutes. Sunny Delight fell asleep in the shotgun seat, and the Frog Sisters dozed in the back seat again. Somehow, though the Hell Slut could not figure out how they did it, the Frog Sisters also snored in unison.

The Hell Slut had not killed that many men, if you really thought about it, but that was only because as much as she enjoyed the results, the actual act was hard work. The first murder was Uncle Steve, who could have avoided the whole thing because the Hell Slut gave him ample warning. Early in childhood, the farm elders had recognized her strength and tasked her with wringing the necks of chickens. He should have guessed that the Hell Slut would put that strength to use eventually, but he underestimated her. The hard part was making the decision, but once she put her mind to it, the actual act was relatively easy—Uncle Steve didn't even wake up before his head was on backward. After that, she ran through the drainage ditch behind the barn, all the way down to the road, and she ran down the road and she kept running and she never stopped until the day Mother Moonflow took her in. Mother Moonflow, the prophet of the Green Lady, took one look at the Hell Slut and put her hand so gently on the Hell Slut's cheek and said, "You don't gotta run no more, Big Mama. You got a home here. You'll always have a home here with just us gals." And the Hell Slut knew then that she would do anything for Mother Moonflow.

Uncle Steve's culling was for herself, but the men she killed on Mother Moonflow's orders? Those were righteous kills. The Hell Slut watched road signs flick by, one by one, as the Sturgeon ate up the miles. DEER CROSSING. SPEED LIMIT 70 MPH. SAN BERNARDO 80 M. It was their job, their solemn duty, to carry out Mother Moonflow's will, to eliminate the men she told them to eliminate.

Her gaze flickered over to Sunny Delight momentarily. The girl was small and delicate, her soft lips slightly parted in her sleep, her blond hair falling over her shoulders like a golden waterfall. Sunny Delight might not understand the wisdom of Mother Moonflow's orders, but she was young. She had not been long at the temple; she would learn. Tonight, someone was going to die, and as much as Sunny Delight insisted that she was ready, the Hell Slut knew she wasn't. No one could ever truly be ready. She was taking a huge risk bringing an untested newbie along on this mission; if she'd had any sense, she would have brought Skillet. But the thought of watching Skillet bounce with excitement in the passenger seat, as she always did when they went out to kill, just made her sick to her stomach. It was so gross.

The Hell Slut still remembered her first kill in service to Mother Moonflow and to the Green Lady. It was a guy they knew only as Master Choda, from the graffiti that they found on a broken beam in the old mill when they were first repurposing it into their temple: the words "MASTER CHODA" and a crude drawing of a penis that looked like a conchiglie noodle.

Mother Moonflow told them that the Green Lady could not abide this desecration of their sacred space and that Master Choda, who the Green Lady informed her through a vision now lived in a van with an airbrushed eagle on its flank, parked on the banks of the Klamath River in unincorporated Siskiyou County, must die. The Hell Slut had experience with killing, so Mother Moonflow tapped her to complete the deed. The Hell Slut generally didn't enjoy killing, but she was good at it, and after she had done it once, she found that the act came easier.

Skillet, whom at that point the Hell Slut knew only as *that new kid*, came along, because Skillet wanted to.

The Hell Slut left that night, and she raced her hog along the darkened roads of unincorporated Siskiyou County, churning gravel in the bike's wake, Skillet clinging to her broad backside and shrieking in giddy glee, until she spied the painted van parked under a bridge next to the remains of a campfire and a pile of spent spray cans, evidence of Master Choda's perfidy.

Master Choda himself sat crouched in the open back of his van, nursing a beer. He was a thick, chunky guy with a horseshoe mustache, a bulging hairy gut, floppy man breasts like suet, torn jeans, and a leather vest, no shirt. They watched him for twenty minutes from a patch of bushes across the overpass, but Master Choda was too drunk to notice them.

"How you gonna do this?" said Skillet.

"I didn't really have a plan. I'm just gonna go down there and finish it."

"Gord, *you* don't know anything! Let me show you. Let me help you. Wait here, I'll go down. I'll tell him I heard he got the hookup, right? Then I'll lead him over under the bridge and start sucking his dick, and that's when you come down and do your thing, okay? You got it?"

The Hell Slut nodded. That did sound like a better plan.

Skillet went down, and the Hell Slut waited as she pounded on the side of the van for Master Choda's attention. Then she and Master Choda conversed briefly, quietly, in hushed voices that the Hell Slut could not discern. Eventually, as she promised she would, Skillet took Master Choda's hand and led him under the bridge, and they stood behind a piling. After that, the Hell Slut came up behind him, more silent than a woman of her size had any right to be. She grabbed him by the shoulder and by the roots of his hair and yanked his head backward so that his spine burst through his throat and a torrent of blood poured over Skillet below. He fell with a thud, already dead, so he didn't feel the bloody furrows Skillet's teeth scraped down his shaft as it popped from her mouth. She looked up at the Hell Slut with giant wet eyes.

"Holy shit," she said. "You popped his head like a fuckin' dandelion." She grinned, her teeth a blinding white in the pit of her red-streaked face. "Wow. Hi. You're real big. You're a real big gal."

"Shit, not now."

"Can't help it. Horny," whined Skillet, bouncing in place, dribbling blood. "He got me all hot an' bothered. C'mon, it's not my fault—I didn't know he was gonna be hot! Let me just touch you, just once? Let me just touch you and I promise we'll go."

"Skillet, this chump might have friends. We gotta go."

"Sure, whatever. Just let me touch your belly, 'kay? Just let me touch you and I'll be down for anything."

Her goblin hands were tiny, shaking and reverent as they explored the sagging flesh around the Hell Slut's middle, but soon the Hell Slut felt herself melting under their grasp even as she promised herself that she wouldn't, that they really needed to go *now*. The Hell Slut had never imagined what it could be like, not even when she entertained fantasies of the Lady Jesus. They made love on a pile of moldy blankets in the back of Master Choda's van, the shreds of his foreskin still caught in Skillet's teeth. Skillet tore open the Hell Slut's jeans and buried a face still covered in Master Choda's blood into the brush between her legs and ate her for hours, and later they rooted through the corpse's pockets until they found his car keys. They loaded him into the back and Skillet drove the van, the Hell Slut following on her bike. They milked his body for the all-important dead man's seed, and then they disposed of the carcass discreetly.

It was obvious from their success that she and Skillet made a good pair. But that was all in the past. Now she had Sunny Delight.

The Hell Slut gripped the wheel, and the Sturgeon roared down the freeway, drawing them ever nearer to their date with destiny.

9.

*The Candy Cap (*Lactarius camphoratus*) ranges in color from cinnamon to reddish brown and has a distinctive wavy cap. It is said to taste of maple syrup, with hints of burnt sugar, butterscotch, or caramel.*

—Field Guide to Common Mushrooms of the Pamogo Forest, *T. F. Greengarb (1978)*

Sarah awoke from fitful dreams, already fading. She tried to hold on to them, but they vanished like vapor with the dawn, and all that was left was that sick lingering unease that comes after your brain decides to dream something it shouldn't—it was the unease that came after dreams of killing your mother or fucking your brother. She couldn't help but think of Greensleeves and how she'd disturbed his body to pluck mushrooms from his eyes. It was silly to think that his ghost was punishing her with nightmares, right? Sarah didn't like the feeling.

She didn't want to get up yet; the air was chilly and her sleeping bag was so nice and warm. Besides, it couldn't be morning—it was still dark, so dark that she might as well have her eyes closed. It was only when she remembered that it was always dark in the Pamogo that she thought to check her phone. Nine thirty a.m. Shit. She sat up, pulling her quilted sleeping bag over her shoulders to bundle herself against the morning cold. She fumbled for her flashlight and flicked it on, aiming it over at Andy, who was still snoring softly.

Sucking air between her teeth, she lurched to her feet. She tiptoed over to her pack, placed a pill under her tongue, gnawed on a granola bar, and sat down on an exposed root to wait for Andy's awakening.

She aimed her flashlight upward in a futile attempt to see where the trunks of the Jeffrey pines and red cedars produced branches, but they were too tall. Her flashlight beam dissipated into the gloom long before it revealed any trace of the distant canopy. She sat and waited, pulling her coat tight around her shoulders against the cold and the damp. Rain continued to drizzle.

The trees had not looked this tall last night, this packed together. She remembered what Andy had said, how it was impossible to map this forest because the undergrowth grew too fast, too aggressively. But the trees shouldn't change *this* much between evening and dawn, should they?

Should they?

This was making her nervous. Way more nervous than she ought to be.

She shook Andy's shoulder. "Hey, Andy. Andy! Wake up!"

"Hmm?" He blinked one bleary eye open.

"Where are we?"

"What? We're in the Pamogo." He closed his eyes again.

"No, I mean— Where are we? Everything looks different."

"It's the Pamogo. Everything always looks different."

"I'm serious! It looks..." How could she articulate this? Why was she suddenly feeling so nervous about the woods? Why was she so sure they were different, when she couldn't even remember what they *should* look like?

"Fine, fine. Gimme a second." He sat up and stretched, unbothered, and then languidly got to his feet and puttered around camp for a moment before disappearing into the bushes. He was gone for a minute, then two. She heard the splash of piss against leaves and waited, impatiently, for Andy to finish his morning relief and get back to business. More minutes passed in silence before she heard the rustling of bushes that signaled his return. The Andy who emerged from the bushes wore a worried expression, his jaw set, his brow furrowed.

"What's the matter?" said Sarah, although she had a sinking feeling that she knew. Her instincts were right. This was not the same campsite where they had gone to sleep.

"Nothing's the matter." Andy wouldn't stand still and, more worrying, wouldn't look her in the eye. He marched around camp, peering into the distance and muttering to himself.

"I can tell something's the matter. Andy. What's wrong?"

He paused, scratching his head. "So, don't freak out."

Sarah immediately started to freak out. "I knew it! We're lost!"

"No, no, of course not. We're not lost; we're just a little off course from where we need to be. Just gimme a sec—I need to get my bearings."

We're lost, thought Sarah, panic rising again. *Shit. Shit, shit, shit.*

According to Andy, the only way to find your way through the Pamogo was to navigate by landmarks. As soon as you were off course, how were you supposed to find your way back? This forest was massive. She'd seen it on maps, a great green glob spreading across the ass end of the North State. But it felt even bigger, vaster, deeper when you were here in the thick of it, all alone.

Retracing their steps back to Las Brujas was a pipe dream; she couldn't remember any of Andy's zigzags in the darkness last night. If they were lucky, they might blunder their way to the coast and then follow it to civilization. But that would require them to know which direction was west. She remembered Andy's wildly spinning compass. Hell, in the perpetual darkness of the Pamogo they couldn't even use the sun or the stars to get their bearings.

"We should have reached Mr. Bojangles by now," muttered Andy, apparently referencing another corpse marker unfamiliar to Sarah. "Or if we veered off course yesterday, we should have seen the Big Hat Man or at least Longshanks..." He turned on Sarah. "Did you move Greensleeves? You must have moved Greensleeves. That's the only explanation."

Sarah had another awful thought about Greensleeves's ghost. Shit. No. She was just panicking. There was no such thing as ghosts or forest spirits or whatever. It was just her and Andy, alone, in the forest, lost.

Sarah snarled. "Get off it! You just don't want to admit that you got us lost!"

"You shouldn't have messed with Greensleeves! You should have..." He stopped short, as if a thought had suddenly occurred to him, and he started patting his pockets. "Oh no, oh no, oh no..."

"What?"

"Leviathan's Favored Son. I had three. Now I just have two."

"Calm down, I've got mine right here." Sarah wiggled her finger into her watch pocket. She found one capsule, then two. Andy could tell from her confused expression.

"I know I had three. You gave me three, right? I remember three."

"We must have taken them in the night," said Andy. "Shit."

"That doesn't make sense. I remember going to bed here. You're saying that we both woke up in the middle of the night and took those pills for no reason?"

"Not for no reason. Something must have happened!"

"Oh, fucking hell!" Sarah rolled her eyes. She could not believe this. Andy got them lost, and now he was trying to blame it on a ghost! "And then what? We saw your stupid forest ghost and then wandered around until we found another campsite and just bedded down again? How does that even make sense?"

"Do you have a better explanation?"

"How would I know?!" Sarah gestured impotently at the surrounding trees. "You're the stalker! You tell me! Where are we?"

"I don't know," wailed Andy. "We could be anywhere!"

Sarah plopped down into the dirt. What had happed last night? She knew she'd dreamed; she could just barely recall the fleeting image of *something*. It tickled the edges of her perception, and she shuddered to think of what it could mean. What revelation was so terrible for them to recall in waking light that it had compelled them to swallow their pills and take their chances wandering blind in this eternal forest?

Something had happened after she ended her conversation with that phone glitch and bedded down for the night. But what? She pulled out her phone to check her history and was surprised to see a whole new slew of texts.

"The reception doesn't work here," said Andy.

"I'm not calling anyone! I'm checking the phone glitch!" The glitch had continued to send her gibberish all night, well after she had gone to sleep, a constant deluge of Wingdings. She quickly scrolled down the list with a flick of her thumb.

>&^&&&&

>???@@@$$

>NICE NAP&&&

>DREAM&&

>DREAM SLEEP&^&&

The timestamps revealed that the messages continued over the course of hours, and it was only much, much farther down the thread that Sarah finally saw her own response:

>I know someone's out there! I can hear it!

>is that you???

>tell me if it's you

>please tell me if it's you

>who is it?

>what does your face look like

>tell me

>please tell me

>where are we

>is that you??? are you a person??? Is this real?

>please

After that, there was just more gibberish from the glitch. Sarah stared at her last message. There was nothing around them but endless green. Any trail from the night before was gone, already swallowed up by the teeming undergrowth, as if they'd never even passed through. The air was still and silent. Sarah could feel the forest waiting. In the distance—but not far *enough* in the distance—something shrieked again. Sarah was pretty confident that it was not a raccoon.

10.

*The Crown-Tipped Coral (*Artomyces pyxidatus*), distinguished by its thin branching stalks and yellow to pink color, is sometimes consumed as a remedy for gastrointestinal problems, as it has a strong laxative effect. It is said to have a peppery flavor well suited for sauces and soups.*

—Field Guide to Common Mushrooms of the Pamogo Forest, *T. F. Greengarb (1978)*

Sarah sat among the ferns, resolutely and stupidly staring at the trees. She could hear Andy going in circles—he would stomp off into the underbrush, and she'd hear him tromping around for ten to fifteen minutes and then he'd return, even more disgruntled than before. He'd been doing that all morning. He didn't dare stray too far from camp without his bearings, in case he couldn't find his way back. So he was useless, absolutely useless. Sarah was so pissed. Pissed that she'd put her faith in Andy's failed stalking skills, pissed that she was going to die out here and rot in the woods, and, above all, pissed that he'd yelled at her about Greensleeves.

Maybe some future Pamogo hikers would use her corpse

as a marker on their journey. Maybe someday some lost hiker would be saved by finding her body. *Maybe there's beauty in that*, she thought, but no, that was stupid and she couldn't convince herself.

It was all her own fault. She should have left well enough alone. But no, she had to go and mess up everything. If she'd left well enough alone, Jade would still be living with her and the rent would be covered and she never would have had to even come to the Pamogo.

But she hadn't. And here she was.

Jade was a popular East Bay artist, a sculptor who built contraptions from trash she scavenged from the Emeryville mudflats. Critics in the *East Bay Express* liked to describe her work as "bold" or "daring" or "a vivid exploration of what it means to occupy space." That meant that she had no trouble landing exhibitions in abandoned warehouses in Oakland, which, Jade told her, was the place to be. Nothing was more prestigious than a show in an abandoned Oakland warehouse. They met through Madeleine, who knew all the local artists and liked to tell them she "knew a good hookup, she'll take care of you." The first time they met, Sarah sold Jade ten grams of Blood Sapphires (*Agrocybe sanguines*). And Sarah got to go to the receptions, which she could still be going to if she had kept her mouth shut, living a pampered life as Jade's awkward fat girlfriend, always hovering at the edge of wine-and-cheese tables as Jade gave interviews to regional art magazines. It was fine. It was always fine.

Sarah knew early in their relationship that Jade's foremost concern was always going to be her own comfort and convenience. She was just lucky that so many things that Jade enjoyed happened to line up with what Sarah needed, so that was fine. The art shows were fine. The strenuous hikes in the East Bay Hills, when Jade would clamber nimbly over rocks like a sweat-glistening gazelle and Sarah would struggle along behind, were fine. It was always fine. Everything was fine. That was just the deal that Sarah accepted. After Jade walked out and Sarah was left with the hunger of her new loneliness, she knew that it had been gluttonous to want more. But the relationship had been going for so long, so many years, always just fine, and somehow, in her greed, Sarah had finally fucked it up.

The important thing was, things had been fine. They could have been fine forever. But no. She'd had it made and she blew it.

She checked her cell phone. There were more gibberish texts. Of course. She sighed and typed back.

```
>you still here, glitch?
>HERE$%
>i'm in a real jam, glitch. things ain't good
>JAM REAL?@@@
>we're lost in the pamogo woods
>no way to leave
>absolutely fucked
>nothing out here but trees, no markers
>probably gonna die out here ha ha
>what do you think I should do, glitch?
>god I miss herman:(
>what will happen to him:(:(
>I keep hoping this is just another bad dream
>maybe I'll wake up
>ha ha ha
```

The glitch didn't respond. Sarah watched her cell phone with mild disinterest. She was just waiting out the clock now, wasting juice until the inevitable. She thought maybe the electrical storms had subsided enough to fix the glitch, when it suddenly wrote:

>YOU SHOULD@@@

>LEAVE WOODS@@%

>that's not real helpful. how do you think I should do that?

>I WILL SHOW YOU&&&$%$

>I WILL&&&@#MARKERS

>that's a whole lot going on there, glitch. what's this about markers? you know about the bodies?

>GREENSLEEVES&&&&&

Sarah stared at that last message. Obviously, her phone was simply spying on her, repeating her own words back to her. Everyone knew that phones did that, right? But somehow, the fact that it knew Greensleeves...

>do you know how to get back to greensleeves???

>NO BACK&&&

>FORWARD&$$

>FOLLOW&&&

I must be insane, thought Sarah, but she wrote back.

>how do I follow you, glitch?

>who are you? what happened last night?

The glitch did not respond.

She heard Andy slogging through the ferns toward her, so she put her phone away. She didn't react to his presence until he was right behind her.

"Hey," he said.

"Hey. Do you know where we are?"

"No."

"Great. That's just great."

"Listen, the smart thing to do is stay put and wait for help. State Parks is going to notice when I don't show up for work, and they'll send someone looking for us. All we have to do is set up a camp and—"

"Oh, is that all we have to do? How long is it gonna take before they notice you're missing?"

Andy was insistent. "Someone will come looking," he said.

"No, they won't. You have a touching level of faith in the world. Everyone's gonna move heaven and earth to find you, won't they? That's not the way it works!"

Andy didn't reply.

Maybe that was the way it worked for Andy. He was so earnest, so sickeningly sweet in his naivete, that maybe the world just felt sorry for him and would bend to his will to avoid disappointing him. But it didn't work that way for Sarah. It never worked that way for her.

She buried her face in her hands. "Oh, God, and who's gonna look after Herman?!"

"Herman? You're worried about your cat now? Be reasonable—"

"He needs me! God damn it, you wouldn't understand."

Jade didn't need her. But Herman did. At least someone did. And she was absolutely failing him.

"I didn't say waiting was a good option. But it's our best option."

She glanced at her phone. The newest message read:

`>GO NOW***&&`

Andy was still talking, but Sarah didn't hear a word he said. She was fascinated by the possibility. Could it be that this phone glitch knew where they were? Maybe the connection wasn't as hopeless as they thought; maybe some sort of tracking signal was getting through...

And somehow, for some reason, the phone was translating that into gibberish texts?

It was possible. In all the infinite realities, it was at least possible.

And, to be frank, it sounded like a much more attractive option than sitting and waiting for State Parks rescue workers or death, whichever came first. Sarah was reasonably sure she could guess which would come first.

"That's a terrible option. I have a way better idea. I say we just pick a direction and walk."

"That's really not—"

She held up her phone. "The glitch says we should go."

Andy gave her a pitying look.

"I'm gonna be the stalker now, okay? You can stay here and camp, but I'm going to take my chances and follow the phone glitch."

Sarah lurched to her feet and squared her shoulders, rolling her backpack into place.

"You're being hysterical. You'd just be wandering aimlessly!"

"I'm not wandering aimlessly," said Sarah, laughing mirthlessly. "I know exactly where I'm going! Maybe I'll even meet that forest ghost again, and this time, I definitely *won't* take any of those stupid pills!"

She looked at her phone. The glitch had texted `WALK&&&`. She had only 50 percent battery power left, but she was going to entrust her life to the directions of a phone glitch. Why not? She just had to hope it led her *somewhere* before her phone died completely.

She started walking, and several seconds later Andy, apparently out of options, fell in line behind her.

`> FORWARD&&`, said the glitch.

`>LORD OF THE FOREST&&& ALL THESE WOODS`

>UNDER MY&& HANDS&&&

>I SLEEP UNDER THE ROOTS&&&&AND

>I WAKE%&&&

>FORWARD&&&

Here goes nothing, thought Sarah. *I'm coming home, Herman. I'm coming home.*

Time dragged by. Her phone was at 40 percent now. She felt a lead weight in her stomach every time that a little bar in the battery icon vanished. Andy trudged in silence behind her, and she felt a weird guilt for leading him on like this. Her cell phone would periodically buzz and deliver a new text: &&&& or !!! or, if she was lucky, something marginally coherent like NOW&. Somehow, though, Sarah knew what the messages meant. She thought she knew, at least. Somehow, though she couldn't explain it to herself, she could tell when a random string of ampersands meant she should turn left or a bunch of question marks meant turn right. Somehow, she was certain that her lizard brain was decoding these messages.

Maybe.

Or maybe she was just getting them more and more lost. That was certainly also a possibility. She tried not to think about that possibility, though it had a way of gripping the imagination.

Eventually, to break the silence, she asked, "Why do you think we took Leviathan's Favored Son?"

"Probably that forest spirit," said Andy. "That's usually what people blame it on."

"The Lord of the Forest?"

"What?"

Sarah held up her phone. "It's something the glitch said. The Lord of the Forest."

"Oh. Sure. Maybe it was the Lord of the Forest."

Sarah rolled her eyes. "No, I mean, why did we *really* take the pills? What's really going on?"

"I don't know."

Sarah didn't ask again. What could possibly have happened during the night? What awful thing had befallen them? What horror, too monstrous to remember, had compelled them each to resort to amnesia to continue living?

What was out there? Was it watching them? Following them?

She remembered the texts she'd sent to the glitch the night before, during the hours erased from her memory.

>I know someone's out there! I can hear it!

>is that you???

>tell me if it's you

>please tell me if it's you

>who is it?

>what does your face look like

Sarah tried really hard not to think about *it* following them.

Was it following them? She felt the hairs on the back of her neck rise, and she struggled to ignore the sensation. Surely, there was nothing to follow them. It was just like Andy said, an electrical glitch. There was nothing out there.

"Ration your water," Sarah reminded herself in fevered mumbles. Why was she reminding herself? She was just reciting garbage that she half remembered hearing from contestants on reality shows. It wasn't like she knew the first thing about wilderness survival; she was a city girl—she hated even tagging along on those annoying hikes that Jade loved so much. Sarah would always lag behind, huffing and puffing, her shirt drenched with sweat, begging for just a moment to rest. She didn't know how to survive an afternoon in a backyard tent, let alone days in the middle of the forest!

She thought of Herman, poor stupid Herman, sitting in the window, his paws neatly tucked under him, his big golden eyes staring, mewling pitifully for Mommy, who wasn't ever coming back. Would Madeleine take him in when Sarah didn't return? No, that was a fantasy. She would just leave him at the shelter. Sarah couldn't bear to think about Herman in one of those cold, empty cages.

She had to shine her flashlight at her watch to know that it was evening, because it was dark as a tomb day or night here. Sarah was exhausted. Her feet ached. She was out of granola. Hunger tied her stomach in knots, so much so that she even missed ramen and ketchup. And someone was following them.

"Someone's following us," said Sarah.

"What are you talking about?"

"Can't you feel it? There's someone out there." She was certain. There it was, the steady tramping of foliage, the squish, squish, squish of boots through mud. The rhythm was distinctly human—the one, two, one, two of bipedal footsteps. Quiet and stealthy, like a thief in the night, pausing when they paused, moving when they moved.

"There's no one out here," said Andy. "We're as deep in the Pamogo as you can get. There isn't another living soul for hundreds of miles."

"Someone is following us," said Sarah resolutely. "I can feel it." She hadn't survived this long not knowing when someone was stalking her. She knew she was right. She could feel her hackles rising; there were greedy eyes out there in the forest, watching, waiting.

>I WAKE&&

>I WATCH&&&

>FORWARD&&&&

An even blacker darkness was coming. Her phone was dying

faster and faster out here in the wilderness, and who knew how long the flashlight batteries would last. *I need to conserve my power*, she thought numbly, and the knowledge that they would soon be trapped in complete blackness filled her with a new dread.

In the distance, Sarah once again heard that familiar shriek that she was absolutely positive was not made by any raccoon. It sounded human. It had to be human. Someone was fucking with them.

"Someone's fucking with us," said Sarah. "There's people out here. I know it!"

Andy just shook his head in frustration, but she was dead certain.

Sarah paused, gasping, and leaned her hand against a massive sequoia, its gnarled trunk a big black column in the gathering gloom. It existed in the midst of a knot of tangled vines, also black in the eternal dusk, that looked like spider legs. Something embedded in the trunk, like a tumor, glinted in the dim light of her flashlight beam.

She looked closer. A line of crooked yellow nubs: teeth. There were teeth embedded in the bark. She could see the brown veins of plaque lacing the hills and valleys of their crowns.

"What the fuck? There's teeth in this tree!"

Just above the teeth, there was something else.

"What the hell is that?"

Andy stumbled up beside her and let out an excited gasp.

"What's that? Whoa!" He ran his fingers over the teeth without regard for hygiene, then tapped what looked like a knot in the trunk. "Look, there's more. There used to be a skull here. See? There's his nasal ridge."

A thin sliver of bone protruded vertically from the tree, just above the teeth. From the right angle, you could almost see the skull's invisible grin in the placement of the teeth and the pits of the eyes still faintly visible below the membrane of the bark. Now Sarah could see it clearly: the bumps and ridges in the tree bark where, below, the tree in its oblivious growth had enveloped the long rope of vertebrae and then the bulge of a rib cage. The dead man's pelvis and anything below was lost among the nest of the tree's roots.

"Is this…is this another corpse marker?" asked Sarah hopefully.

Andy ran his fingers over the ridge of the dead man's nose, so entranced by the discovery that he forgot any squeamishness, and Sarah felt a stab of annoyance that this was the same guy who'd given her such guff for messing with Greensleeves. "I don't recognize it. By the looks of it, he's been here a long time. It must have taken a hundred years for the tree to grow around him like this! You know, this could actually be one of Sloane's original mill workers? And that means Sloane's mill can't be too far away!" He brightened. "Can you imagine? If we're the first to rediscover Sloane's actual mill! It would be huge for California history!"

One hundred, two hundred years ago, some poor bastard hired to build a folly of a sawmill wandered into the forest to take a piss and never returned. How long was he out here, lost, wandering in the pitch black, before he finally sat down and died? The faint outlines of the skull made it look as if the tree itself wore a screaming face.

How long would they be lost out here, wandering in the pitch black, before they suffered the same fate?

She checked her phone: 35 percent battery. The glitch had sent another message.

>GO&&&

>SOON YOU WILL ARRIVE&&&

>SOON WE WILL MEET&&&

Sarah typed back.

>are you the lord of the forest?

>I AM THINGS&&& I SLEEP

>WAKE WHEN

>THE GODDESS WAKES&&&

Sarah felt suddenly lightheaded. She glanced over at Andy, but he was preoccupied with the discovery of the skull tree. She stepped away from him and turned her body, just enough for a bit of privacy. She didn't need him watching her type. This wasn't something he needed to know about. Sarah typed with sweaty, trembling fingers:

>what do you mean 'goddess'?

>what's the goddess?

>i met her

>when i took the king's breakfast at madeleine's party, i'm sure i met her

>will i see her again?

>i need to see her again

>FOLLOW&&&

>FOLLOW AND&&&

"Andy," said Sarah, her voice a low croak. "Andy, we have to keep moving."

"Which direction?"

Sarah held up her phone. "This way. C'mon. We need to follow."

ACT 2: LIMINALITY,

or The Experiences in the Desert

11.

The foreman has not been seen for 2 days, I must assume he has abandoned his post. I am losing more men every day. Searching for them is eating into the construction time, and I despair that the mill will be complete before winter.

—Diary of Lazarus Sloane
(California State Parks Archives)

It continued to drizzle.

Sarah was still certain that someone was out there. Her phone was at 25 percent, but that didn't matter now. She could hear them, scampering away when she turned to confront them. The sudden rustling was too big, too clumsy, too human to be a raccoon. She was convinced. Instead of running away, she was in pursuit. If she could just find their unseen stalker, Sarah was certain... Whoever they were, they were definitely a person, and a person meant that they must be close to civilization.

They weren't following her anymore. She was following them. Whoever it was, they seemed to sense the shift in fortunes. Instinctively, like a wild animal, they knew that they were now the hunted, and they fled before Sarah like a rabbit from a hound. But Sarah was determined. She would attain her quarry. Andy followed along, but he was too depressed to question why Sarah now zigzagged through the forest. The phone was leading them toward the stranger.

>i hear something out there, glitch

>is that you?

>are we catching up with you?

>GO&&&&

But she was still surprised when, blundering through the brush, they came across a house.

"Is that a house?" said Andy. He ran his flashlight beam over the structure, up and down, as if it would eventually reveal a deception. But no, it was definitely a house.

"I thought you said no one lived in these woods."

"No one does! It must be one of the old stations for Sloane's mill. We must be really close to it!"

The eminent discovery of this incredible historical relic filled Andy with excitement, but Sarah was more concerned with the fact that whoever was following them, or leading them, was here. She had a terrible feeling that the glitch was leading them here. She had a terrible feeling that the glitch, or whatever had been speaking to her, whatever had been leading her on, whatever she had been so naively following, was inside.

She tapped at her phone:

>glitch? we're at a house

>what is this

>is this your house?

>do you live here

>INSIDE&&&&%%%

Sarah stared at that last response.

`>are you inside?`

`>INSIDE &&&`

"Are you still wasting your battery?" Andy's voice jolted her out of her own head, and she nearly dropped the phone.

"No! Christ, don't scare me like that." Sarah inhaled deeply and exhaled. She didn't like what she was about to say. "We have to go in."

"Okay, sure." The idea did not seem to faze Andy at all. *In some ways*, thought Sarah, *he's lucky he doesn't know we've been following a phone glitch or that this phone glitch is now telling us to go inside this creepy house. Ignorance is bliss. This lucky bastard!*

The house was little more than a small wooden shack hidden in the dip of a ravine, nearly invisible under a cascade of moss, its shingled roof caved in under the weight of vines and bushes. Sarah ran her flashlight along the side until the beam revealed a missing door and a sucking wound of an exposed entrance. Ragged wisps of curtains still dangled in the smashed windows. Inside was yet more darkness. It was hard to tell in the surrounding gloom, but Sarah was certain the darkness was moving. She could sense someone or something within.

"There's someone in there."

"I told you before, Sarah, there's no one else out here."

"You're wrong."

This was it. She had come this far, trusting in the benevolence of a phone glitch. She might as well go the distance.

"C'mon."

She tried to pick her way down the embankment but lost her footing in the mud and tumbled the final leg of the trip on her ass, yelping and bellowing. She slammed into the side of the house, knocking a rain of dirt and leaves free from the overhanging eaves as the force of her impact reverberated through the structure.

"Ow! Shit!"

Her flashlight slipped from her hands and rolled away, the beam smothered by bramble.

"Shit! Shit! Shit!"

She sensed that whatever was within the house had suddenly paused in its movements. She wasn't sure how she knew—it wasn't a sudden silence or even a stop in the vibration of the wood. But something was paused, waiting. Something knew they were here now.

Andy watched, silently, from the ridge.

"Are you coming? Get down here!" she whispered, motioning him forward. She was certain that their unseen pursuer was close, obviously inside. Andy could at least be useful as backup. If they had to fight, they would be at a disadvantage, probably at every disadvantage, but at least there were two of them. Andy came skittering down the slope, stopping himself before he slammed into the side of the house.

"Stay close! There's someone in there! Be ready!"

"Be ready for what?"

Sarah rolled her eyes. Getting lost had been a disastrous blow to Andy's self-confidence, and ever since he'd been completely useless for anything. "I don't know! Just... just be ready!"

She crept along the side of the house, one hand touching the wooden wall, spongy with rot. She saw something stir within just as she was too close to avoid being seen. Or heard. She turned on the light on her cell phone. The beam was anemic compared to her flashlight, but it worked for now—23 percent battery. Whoever was inside the house must surely have been able to see her flashlight fall, even assuming that they didn't hear

Sarah's blundering approach, yet they made no move. They were waiting. They were waiting to see what Sarah did next.

Slowly, slowly, she crept forward, wet sneakers squelching in the damp underbrush.

"Stay close! Be ready!"

"Be ready for what? What are you doing? There's no one here."

And then, all at once, she lunged forward. She fumbled but regained her footing and spun around to aim the cell phone beam through the open door.

Now that she was closer, she could see through the open door that the inside of the house was a large, open room. The walls, slick with moisture, were permeated with great sleeves of brown bracket fungus and swaths of lichen, and blue mold bloomed along the wooden seams in intricate whorls that looked sickeningly familiar. The trails of mold almost made sense in their infinite loops and twists, but her eyes refused to see the pattern.

The room was empty.

She tried to talk, but nerves choked her voice and her words came out in a low whisper.

"Hello? Are you in here? Glitch? Is that you?"

She stepped through the door, throwing her cell phone beam across the room. Dry twigs and broken glass crunched under her sneakers. The air was thick with mold, so musty it almost felt poisonous. Spores and dust motes floated languidly in the beam of her light.

"Glitch? What are you talking about?" said Andy behind her. He pointed his own flashlight around the room, but his beam didn't reveal anything new. "I told you there wasn't anyone here."

"No, no, that doesn't make sense! I was sure of it!"

"Did you hear someone?"

"No, I just—I just felt..."

Sarah returned her attention to her phone, but for once, the glitch was silent.

On the one hand, their situation hadn't changed—they were still lost in the forest, destined to die of dehydration or starvation or exposure. But on the other—Sarah felt strangely relieved. Only now that the threat had passed and she felt the tension start to leave her body did Sarah realize how terrified she had been that they really would meet someone in this house, that they would suddenly confront the grim majesty of the Lord of the Forest himself, whatever that was.

And then Andy had to flash his beam into the corner.

"Hey. There's a door over there."

Sarah froze. She turned to look.

There was, indeed, a naked opening in the far wall. It was short, coming up only to waist height, possibly leading down to some kind of subterranean storehouse, and hidden beneath an aggressively overhanging shelf of bracket fungus. Nothing was visible beyond it but black.

That must be where they needed to go.

It must be down there.

Sarah approached it slowly, cautiously, as if the absolute blackness beyond might itself somehow lash out at her. Already, she could hear it. Something was indeed in there; something was dodging down the sloping corridor, skitter, skitter, skitter—she could hear the scrabbling of little feet like rats across a rooftop. Whatever it was, whoever it was, they did not want to be caught.

Either that, or they wanted Sarah to follow.

Sarah fingered the remaining pills in her watch pocket. She might need them soon.

"You still got your pills, Andy?"

"Yeah, I got them. Why?"

"Okay. Hold on to them. We might need them again soon."

"What? What are you talking about?"

She took a deep breath and aimed her cell phone flashlight down the corridor. It was a wrecked mineshaft collapsing under its own weight, the packed-earth walls white with roots. It did not look sturdy, but she had to chance it. She ducked under the bracket fungus doorjamb and edged forward, one hand along the wall, which was wet with slime, her other aiming the cell phone's light ahead of her.

"What is it?" called Andy from behind her. Sarah cringed. That idiot was too loud. It was like he was totally oblivious to the reality of their situation.

"I think...I think it's the Lord of the Forest!" she hissed.

She couldn't see Andy's reaction in the dark.

As the slope leveled out, Sarah could see that there was a room ahead. It was dimly lit, too dim to make out anything other than squirming shadows.

The light flickered, like it was cast by flame. There should not be a light down here.

The corridor emptied into another room, identical to the first except that the ceiling here sagged even worse. In the center of the room, the ceiling had burst under the pressure and dumped a column of vines and dirt and leaves onto the floor. Mushrooms and lichen coated these walls even more thickly than in the first room. An abandoned candle lantern sat on the floor, flickering ominously and casting dancing shadows across the mold-soaked walls.

The candle was still lit.

There were no other doors in this room.

It had to still be here.

"Hello? Hello! Are you here?!" She threw her light here and

there and into the corners and then across the ceiling and then right over there, right in the right place, to catch a glimpse of something standing at the far back of the room, shrouded in shadow. Sarah yelped and flashed her beam on it again and fell backward as she beheld the full horror.

It was not the Lord of the Forest.

Instead, it was a small woman with huge limpid eyes and bare feet stained black with mud. She was cutting mushrooms, Saint Sebastian's Bones (*Hygrocybe sagattis*), from the wall with a paring knife and dropping them into a plastic bucket at her feet, and she turned to stare at Sarah, blinking and grimacing in the flashlight beam. She looked like a forest goblin. A second woman, taller, thinner, with frizzy red hair and a threadbare poncho, stood beside her, holding a second bucket.

They were definitely human. Everything about their appearance screamed *INSANE HILLBILLY*, and Sarah was certain from a glance that they were the sort of hicks who would probably either rape your corpse or eat it, but they definitely would not bury it.

But they were still human.

And that meant they were help.

Sarah kept her distance, her eyes on the goblin's knife.

"Don't be frightened!" she said, raising a hand in a friendly greeting. "We're friendly! We're lost and we need help."

The goblin regarded her coolly for a moment, just long enough that Sarah started to worry it might not understand English. Or possibly language at all.

Finally, the goblin spoke.

"Hey, sister, what's happening?" she said in a shrill, whistling voice, dropping the knife into the bucket and raising her hands in a similar friendship display. "We've been expecting you!"

"You have?" snapped Sarah. "Have you been following us? Are you the glitch?"

"Oh thank God," sighed Andy, entering the room behind her. His shoulders sagged with visible relief, and this time he nearly dropped his flashlight. "Please, we need help! We're lost!"

"Hey, hey, don't worry, it's okay, calm down!" The goblin walked toward Sarah and threw her frail little arms around her without warning, hugging her tight. Sarah felt tiny claws sink into her spongy back fat and felt eager, malevolent fingers testing her bra straps through the fabric of the sweater. "You ain't lost no more! You found the Sisters of the Green Lady!"

It was too much. In a panic, Sarah stumbled and pulled away. The goblin fell back, still grinning. "Sorry, sister, I forgot you been livin' among the normies. You ain't used to the way us sisters express free love! Don't worry, you'll get used to it!"

Meanwhile, the poncho girl approached Andy and put her arms around him in an awkward embrace, her hands hovering over his shoulder blades, before she stepped back, her face going pink. "Welcome!" she mumbled. "Praise the Green Lady!"

"Um, hi, thanks," said Andy.

"Have you been following us?" repeated Sarah, who was surer of it than ever.

"Now why would we be doing that?" The goblin tilted her head quizzically. Her eyes glowed in the blue light from Sarah's cell phone. "You two are a long way from home. Just what are you doing out here in our woods, anyway?"

"Hiking," said Sarah, remembering their agreed-upon lie.

The goblin and the poncho girl exchanged bemused looks. "Nobody hikes out this deep in the Pamogo, sister!"

Sarah gestured toward Andy. "He's like... like a stalker?"

The goblin tilted her head the other way. "Like the Tarkovsky film?"

"Yes! Exactly!" Somehow the fact that this goblin was familiar with Soviet cinema was reassuring.

"Ya know, I'd really like to help you two…" The goblin tapped her chin thoughtfully. "But shit, you're both phallic alecs. Oof, I dunno. Mother Moonflow's not gonna like that, is she?"

"Mother Moonflow says phallic alecs reify the patriarchal structure," said the poncho girl.

"Exactly! What she said." The goblin jerked a thumb toward her companion.

"We just need a telephone," said Sarah desperately. "We'll be out of there so fast you won't even know we're there! You have a telephone, right?"

"Of course not, Mother Moonflow says that telephones are phallic."

Sarah didn't know how to react to that.

"See, it's a lesbian separatist commune," explained the goblin.

Sarah was quiet. Behind her, Andy also seemed to be out of words. The goblin smiled, and her smile got wider and wider until she broke into a laugh.

"Haaa! You really believed that. Ha ha, dumb lesbian separatist cult in the woods! Right? Of course we'd think everything's phallic, right? Ha ha!" She elbowed the poncho girl, who seemed reluctant to laugh, in the side. Maybe it wasn't a very good joke.

But the goblin was so amused by it that Sarah had to chuckle, her body relaxing a little. This goblin might be a weirdo living deep in the heart of an uncharted forest, but at least she seemed to have a sense of humor about it. She couldn't be *that* far gone.

"Ha, yeah. You really had me going."

"Haaa..." The goblin's laughter petered out into a wheeze. "But seriously, no, we don't. Sorry to tell you this, but there ain't nothing but Pamogo out there for miles. Try getting a signal here on a cell phone. And of course, we're totally off the grid as far as landlines. You know what landlines are, right? You know, the old kinda telephones? Plugged into the wall? Mother Moonflow talks about them sometimes?"

"Oh. Yeah, I know about those." Apparently from the sound of it, Mother Moonflow was, in fact, not an invention for the sake of a bad joke but a real person and the presumable head of the goblin's little cult. "You have to help us, please. We'll talk to your Mother Moonflow; I'm sure we can explain everything!"

The goblin seemed to think that was hilarious. "Oh, you'll talk to Mother Moonflow? Ha ha, you bet you will!"

The poncho girl looked suddenly panicked and tugged at the goblin's shoulder before whispering something urgently in her ear. The goblin pulled her aside, and the two of them conversed in terse, hushed tones for a very long, awkward minute. Sarah got the distinct impression that the poncho girl was not sold on this plan and, in fact, was not convinced that Mother Moonflow, who apparently thought that "phallic alecs" reified the patriarchal structure, would appreciate their presence.

"Phallic alec?" asked Andy.

"Oh come on, you can guess. It's probably some sort of discourse thing." Sarah did not like that phrase. It did not bode well for what was going to come next. But it was either go with these two or keep wandering lost in an uncharted forest...

Finally, the goblin appeared to win whatever disagreement was going on, because she turned back to Sarah with a big grin.

"I guess we can't just leave you here. Y'all can barely take care of yourselves! But don't worry... Mother Moonflow will make sure you're nice and comfortable!" She motioned to her companion to gather up the buckets. "Let's get these two back to the temple."

The clearing was filled with concentric rings of tree stumps, suggesting that the large wooden structure at its center was probably a derelict lumber mill. Didn't Andy say something about that? Yeah, Sloane had failed at logging back in the 1800s. But the mill still stood, a jumble of impossible jerry-rigged spires and turrets, five stories of worm-riddled timber, every window now plastered over with wooden boards, every wall painted in a hodgepodge of psychedelic images—rainbows, peace signs, big Smurf mushrooms with red caps covered in white spots. Sarah could see the sky for the first time in days, gray gloomy clouds, and she wanted to cry from relief. Oh, apparently it was day again. How many hours had she been awake? Time had felt like molasses ever since she had entered the Pamogo.

Skillet, as the goblin revealed her name to be, grinned even wider. "You're gonna love the sisters. And the sisters are gonna love you!"

There were people here too. She could sense curious eyes watching her through the slats of the boarded-up windows. A burly woman, shirtless, a peace sign made of raised welts on her bare chest, sat on a stump, watching them pass. She was sucking on a bong made out of a smashed soda can, sitting in a miasma of skunky smoke. Kids played in the dirt, pausing at their approach. One of them glared at Sarah with eyes too emerald green to be real.

Sarah raised a hand in a friendly wave. The green-eyed girl narrowed her eyes and hissed like a cat. Just like Herman when he heard the vacuum cleaner. God, poor Herman. Sarah's heart ached thinking about him.

A man with long black hair emerged from the building and ran to meet them. "Skillet! Where have you been? You can't just go running off into the—" He paused and recoiled as if shot when he saw Skillet's guests, his black-tipped fingers tugging at the puka shell necklace that dangled from his neck. "Phallic alecs!"

"That's right, Pickles!" said Skillet. "Two of them! Tell Mother Moonflow I got two phallic alecs for her!"

"Where did you find them?! You can't bring phallic alecs into the temple!"

"Fuck you, Pickles! I didn't ask your goddamn opinion!"

Pickles looked from Sarah to Andy and back again.

"We just need a telephone," said Sarah.

Pickles stiffened. "Whatever you need, you'll need to talk to Mother Moonflow about that." Without another word, he rapped his knuckle against a door painted with a giant vagina. There was no mistaking the pink clamshell ripples surrounding a dark oblong portal, the big round pearl painted right at the apex of the chasm clearly meant to indicate a clitoris. A muffled voice from within said something. Pickles nodded and motioned for them to enter.

"Mother Moonflow doesn't usually take guests in the sanctuary," said Pickles with the breezy nonchalance and easy smile that only schadenfreude could bring out. *Someone's in trouble and it's not me*, said that smile. "It's the holiest room of the temple, reserved exclusively for the prophet of the Green Lady. And you phallic alecs have to go and sully it like this. You're lucky she's even talking to you. But by all means, go on in. Mother Moonflow will see you now."

12.

The foreman returns! Says he became lost in the forest after losing sight of the mill. A likely story! I suspect that, like so many of his degenerate bog-dwelling countrymen, he possesses a debilitating weakness for spirits. The men are spreading tales that some monster lurks in the woods.

—Diary of Lazarus Sloane
(California State Parks Archives)

The sanctuary was hot and stuffy, dimly lit by candles in censers suspended from the ceiling, and filled with the overwhelming stench of patchouli. The walls were covered in graffiti art of green Horus eyes and blue Venus symbols, and the floor was buried under layers of ragged Persian carpets and embroidered boho pillows. In one corner, a boombox nestled among towers of battered CD jewel cases softly piped Enya's "Orinoco Flow." A woman sat on a futon in the center of the room, naked other than a pair of reflective round John Lennon sunglasses that flashed in the candlelight. Her white skin glowed in the low light, and her body was toned and supple, such that only the faint laugh lines around her mouth and the subtle streaks of gray in her long black hair gave away her age. She had the biggest breasts that Sarah had ever seen, hanging down into her lap. They were comically gigantic, big enough that Sarah wondered if this woman could even walk bearing their weight. She was nursing a swaddled baby at her left teat.

Most importantly, there was a tray on the futon next to her, and on the tray were the desiccated remains of the King's Breakfast. The King's Breakfast! It was right there! After all they'd been through, it was right there! Sarah wanted to signal to Andy, to let him know *LOOK*, but Andy seemed distracted by the gigantic breasts. As Sarah watched, the woman reached over, plucked a dried stem between her fingers, and popped it into her mouth.

She swallowed, looked up, and smiled. "Hey, Big Mama. Big Daddy. The Sisters of the Green Lady bid you welcome. I am Mother Moonflow, divine prophet of the Green Lady. Find a good place to park your bottoms and let's rap. Good vibes!"

"Good vibes!" said Andy, sitting down. "I'm Andy."

"Good vibes," said Sarah, a little less certainly, as she settled into a squat. "Sarah."

Mother Moonflow winced and gasped, suddenly cradling the swaddled baby. "Ow, ow, ow! No bitey, no bitey, no bitey!" She carefully pulled the baby away from her breast, her nipple popping free with a wet sucking sound. It was as big as a wine cork, still glistening with baby spit. Mother Moonflow placed the baby on the floor, where it immediately rose up on all four legs, shook itself free of its blanket, and revealed that it wasn't a baby at all: A raccoon stared up at Sarah for a split second, chattered angrily, and scampered into the nearest pile of pillows.

Sarah was suddenly aware of all the movement in the shadows; the room was filled with raccoons, prowling around the walls and staring out at her with beady reflective eyes, their chattering faintly audible over the room's new age soundtrack. She could detect a musky animal stench beneath the overwhelming patchouli reek.

"There's raccoons in here," she said, and immediately felt stupid.

"Oh, don't worry about the little sisters," said Mother Moonflow. "They come and go as they please; there's tunnels under the rugs somewhere. We believe that raccoons are sacred to the Green Lady, embodying her best qualities by living free of patriarchal hierarchy! So you don't mistreat the little sisters, not on my watch! The forest belonged to them first, and we're just here to share it."

Sarah scanned the room again. There was a second door, across the room from the one through which they'd entered. It was small, only coming up to waist height, like the door in the house in the woods, but there was a padlock on it. It was painted with an angry, leering face—a wide mouth full of pointed teeth, and, sprouting from between red eyes, two curling horns. Sarah couldn't stop looking at that door; it was the only thing in the room that wasn't painted in soothing tones of blue and green, and it made her strangely nervous. But there was no reason to be nervous. She would never need to see what was behind it, after all.

"First things first," said Mother Moonflow, pressing her hands together into a prayer pose. "Know that this temple and all who dwell within this temple are under the protection of the Green Lady. Now I don't know what's goin' through those phallic alec noggins of yours, but the Lord of the Forest, he is a bum trip and he is not allowed within this space. So don't even think about conjurin' no phallic energy here!"

"Of course," said Andy. "We wouldn't do that."

Sarah was still staring at the waist-high door. The art was mesmerizing, so vivid the colors looked dayglow. Sarah was thankful it gave her somewhere to look that wasn't Mother Moonflow's chest. Mother Moonflow noticed her staring and grinned.

"You dig that art, huh? That's mine, by the way. I'm a bit of an artist too. That's my rendition of the Lord of the Forest. Ya know, that cat I was just yappin' about?"

"You know the Lord of the Forest?" said Sarah. Of course, of course, of course. It all made sense. Somehow that phone glitch must have been secretly tapping into the network, right? And somehow it must have been picking up ambient chatter and repeating the words of this weird forest cult back to her, right? Of course. It all made perfect sense, if you thought about it.

"Yeah, Big Mama, he's a real bum trip."

Sarah dared to push a little harder. She had to know. "So if you know the Lord of the Forest, does that mean you know the goddess...?"

"Course we know the Green Lady, Big Mama!" said Mother Moonflow, folding her arms over her chest even as her smile never faltered. The flickering candlelight reflected in her opaque glasses, two flames dancing over her hidden eyes. "But how exactly do you two phallic alecs know about the Green Lady? And what're y'all doing in our woods?"

Andy cleared his throat. "Actually, as a state park, these woods really belong to all the people of California."

That was, thought Sarah, the absolute worst thing he could have said. Did this guy literally have no survival instincts at all?

"Y'all are with State Parks?" said Mother Moonflow. "Are y'all rangers?"

"We're not with State Parks!" said Sarah quickly. "We don't know anything about State Parks! And we're not rangers! We totally hate rangers! Just yesterday, this ranger was hassling me over in Las Brujas—"

"Oh, yeah, about the parking," said Andy.

"It wasn't just about the parking," said Sarah darkly. "It was not about the parking at all. Trust me, this ranger was bad news. You can imagine, right? I mean, you can imagine?"

Sarah nodded desperately, hoping that maybe there was some intuitive female connection happening. Mother Moonflow's smile went flat and serious.

"Oh, Big Mama, I know exactly what you mean! I apologize for my phallophobia—I was letting it overwhelm my sister solidarity. We accept all allies here, even phallic alecs."

"That's good!" said Andy. "I do like to consider myself an ally."

"Right on, Big Daddy."

"Orinoco Flow" ended and restarted.

Andy kept talking: "So who's this Green Lady? I haven't heard of this."

Mother Moonflow laughed. "Typical phallic alecs! That's the thing with phallic alecs: You're all so preoccupied with your own selves that you can't even conceive of something different. The Green Lady is the divine feminine, man. She's the mother of us all! The yin to the Lord of the Forest's yang! In the beginning, the Green Lady was consort to the Lord of the Forest! But that was less enlightened times, man. We stopped all that when we found a better way. Now we keep the Lord of the Forest locked down, man, at arm's length, so he can't exercise that toxic masculinity. We keep him locked up tight, using the real power of a woman!"

By way of explanation, she grabbed at her bushy crotch and

squeezed. Laughing, she plucked another mushroom from the plate and placed it neatly on her tongue, then curled her tongue back into her open mouth and swallowed.

"Without him in the picture, the true power of the divine feminine is unstoppable!"

"Interesting, many cultures have origin myths very much like that," said Andy. "But doesn't that upset the natural order? To have feminine without masculine?"

Christ, thought Sarah. *He thinks they're talking about fucking folklore. Any idiot can tell that she's talking about religion. We have been rescued by crazy people.*

Mother Moonflow laughed and shook her finger. "That's binary thinking, man! We're way beyond that. But I'm not surprised a phallic alec would think that way. No offense, but you're just not on our level."

"I could be on that level," said Sarah suddenly. She really wanted to hear more about this Green Lady. The goddess had a name. The goddess was the Green Lady.

"No, you couldn't. Sorry, Big Mama, I know you're trans and I dig that, it's very valid. Right on. But I'm talkin' about real women. Y'all phallic alecs don't got it in ya. But y'all came to us at a very auspicious time. Heck, y'all might even call it divinely inspired! Almost as if the Green Lady herself might have brought ya here..." She tapped her forehead.

Sarah thought back to the text messages. *Something* had definitely brought them here.

Mother Moonflow snapped her fingers. "Of course! The Green Lady musta sent ya here to be witnesses, to take the news back to others of your kind! To know that the world is about to change!"

"Change?"

"Here at the Sisters of the Green Lady, we believe that someday the Green Lady herself will come to us. In the flesh! Imagine it: a divine world for women, where a woman has the power of a man. We are making that day a reality. But you'll understand everything tonight, because tonight you will both join us for a very special ceremony—to welcome the Green Lady back into the world!"

Mother Moonflow clapped her hands, and Pickles poked his head in through the door. He was struggling to contain a growing tide of bodies behind him. A commotion was just audible through the crack in the door, and Sarah could see curious faces behind Pickles, straining to see inside. "Mother Moonflow?"

"What's all the rhubarb out there, Pickles? You got all the sisters gathered?"

"Yes, there's . . . a lot of curiosity about our . . . visitors." Pickles was picking his words very carefully.

"Right on. I'd better lay down how it is." Grunting, she struggled to her feet, her breasts swaying. She motioned to her guests, bangles and bracelets around her wrist jangling. "Follow me, cats—I'll introduce you to the sisters."

Outside, a crowd of several dozen women had gathered, mumbling and muttering among themselves. They were a motley assortment, in various states of undress and uncleanliness, and the large woman with the ritually scarified peace sign across her bare chest stood in the front row, her arms folded and her face sullen. The emerald-eyed child, oblivious to the tension in the air, rolled around at her feet like a puppy, yapping and growling.

"Hey, sisters and systers, y'all have probably already heard the big news," announced Mother Moonflow, one hand on Sarah's shoulder, one hand on Andy's shoulder. "Seems some of our sisters found these two cats lost in the woods and did a most groovy rescue. I want you all to give a righteous temple welcome to Andy and Sarah!"

"They're phallic alecs!" yelled a plump, ruddy-cheeked woman from the back of the crowd. She had swampy green hair and wore a Sedona patchwork dress made of squares of burlap and denim. "Why should we welcome them?"

A murmur of agreement rippled through the crowd. Sarah did not like this situation. She did not like this situation one bit. Pickles was sitting off to the side, fingering his puka shell necklace and grinning wickedly. He would be the sort to enjoy their misfortune.

"Miss Trix is right!" yelled the peace sign woman. "We don't want no man in the temple! And we don't want no he-she either!"

"Whoa, that is not cool! You know we don't use those words around here. Around here, we call them by the proper term—they're phallic alecs! Don't forget yourself, Virginia Dentata."

The peace sign woman hung her head, properly shamed.

"And the rest of you, I don't want none of this unmellow talk. I'm saying it right now for all you cats to hear: These two are cool. I got a premonition from the Green Lady that these two phallic alecs are here for a reason. They're gonna witness the birth of the Green Lady for the whole world to know!"

The crowd exploded into indignant babble, and Mother Moonflow raised her hands for silence.

Virginia Dentata was livid. "But, Mother Moonflow, we can't have them at the birthing ceremony! They'll get their phallic energy all over everything! They'll ruin it!"

"No way, man, that's yesterday's doctrine. We've taken precautions. Right now, the Hell Slut is on a supersecret mission that's gonna make sure the birthing ceremony goes according to plan—and she's taken Sunny Delight and not one, but *both* of the Frog Sisters along with her!"

The crowd liked that and people started to cheer, other than Virginia Dentata, who continued shaking her head at this news.

"So I want y'all to just keep on keepin' on! And tonight... these two phallic alecs will be the first outsiders to ever see the Green Lady!"

The crowd cheered harder.

Mother Moonflow nodded her head toward Pickles. "Pickles, why don't ya show our guests around? They probably ain't never seen anything like what we got here. And tell the gals to set up some rooms for them. You dig it, baby?"

"Yes, Mother Moonflow, I dig it."

Pickles motioned for them to follow him and they fell in line; the sisters parted to let them pass, still cheering after Mother Moonflow's speech, and one or two even attempted to clap the visitors on the back as they passed. Sarah cast one more glance back at Mother Moonflow as they left. She had returned to the sanctuary, and through the open door, Sarah saw her raise her arms triumphantly and shout along with the chorus of "Orinoco Flow" while the raccoons around the perimeter of the room chattered and cackled in response.

13.

Had the men dig a trench & clear a path to the new latrine. It was slow work in the thick, root-bound mud, but at least no longer will the men get lost in the woods when they go to relieve themselves.

—Diary of Lazarus Sloane
(California State Parks Archives)

They reached San Bernardo late. The moment they pulled off the freeway, the Hell Slut sensed that they'd made a huge mistake. It wasn't just the cruiser parked in every driveway or the cold blue light shining from every porch—the houses were too nice, darling little whitewashed bungalows, each with its own little neatly manicured lawn. No flower beds, no xeriscaped little deserts. Only lawns. The only houses this nice in any city are cop houses.

"Hell Slut," said the Frog Sisters in one voice from the back seat. Apparently they were awake now. "Hell Slut, this is a cop town."

Sunny Delight flinched at that, clearly unnerved to hear those two voices in such complete harmony, and even the Hell Slut was startled. The Hell Slut knew the secret to the Frog Sisters' act.

There wasn't any psychic link between the two, no matter how much they liked to play up the twin angle. They just rehearsed everything that they said, for hours, for days. Neither one ever said a word unless she was absolutely assured that the other was also going to say it at the exact same time. It was a hell of an act. Hopefully it would come in handy tonight.

"It's okay, kids," said the Hell Slut. "Trust me, I'll get us all home safe. I won't steer us wrong." The Hell Slut did not like this. Cops were toxically masculine, with their male swagger and their phallic guns, and they could fight back better than any surveyor. Mother Moonflow should have warned them. Instead, she had sent them unprepared into this nest of vipers. This whole thing seemed wrong, wrong in a way that made the Hell Slut's scalp itch and her palms sweat. But she was loyal to Mother Moonflow, and if Mother Moonflow tasked her with a mission, she was going to fulfill that mission no matter what.

Sunny Delight turned, her eyes suddenly wide. "Are we gonna kill a cop?"

They were. But there was more to it. Sunny Delight would find out soon enough.

"Probably. Don't freak out on me now, Sunny."

"Cops are dangerous! Some of my clients were cops and..." She trailed off. "Cops are dangerous."

"Not to me, they aren't. The only thing they know is guns. I don't have that limitation. This little piggy's ours to barbecue." She kept her eyes glued to the street. "Trust me, Sunny, I've dealt with cops before. Every oinker thinks he's fucking Dirty Harry. But look at me! I'm still running around free."

"You know what they do when they catch cop killers?" said Sunny Delight. "We'll get the chair! If we even get a trial!"

"That's why they're not gonna catch us."

The car was quiet, the weight of the Hell Slut's words hanging in the air. The Hell Slut was being flippant for Sunny Delight's sake. It wouldn't do to upset the girl, not now, not when she needed to be calm more than ever. But the Hell Slut was nervous. She gripped the Sturgeon's wheel and licked her lips. *Just play it cool and you'll be fine. It's after dark, so they'll all be out hunting. It's all cool.* In the back seat, the Frog Sisters were silent, but their white hands flopped in their laps like beached fish.

"We're getting close. Everyone, bottoms up." The Hell Slut pulled her flask from her hip and swigged a deep pull of moonflow. In the back seat, the Frog Sisters did the same without hesitation. Sunny Delight held her flask to her lips but looked to the Hell Slut for confirmation before she drank.

The Hell Slut nodded. Sunny Delight gulped her moonflow and gagged loudly. The others shared a good-natured chuckle at her discomfort, but the Hell Slut was too busy thinking to laugh for real.

She scanned the street signs—she couldn't tell if they were on the path toward a main road. Gardenia Way. Shady Grove Drive. Jasmine Lane. Any one of these could empty out into a cul-de-sac. Better to keep going straight and hope it cut all the way through.

"Sunny D, keep a watch out. Tell me if you see Wisteria Drive."

There was a commotion in front of a house ahead. About a dozen cops were out in the driveway, all hollering. One fired his gun nonchalantly into the air to a chorus of hoots. Bang bang bang! *Shit. They shouldn't be here,* thought the Hell Slut. *They should be out hunting. But looks like tonight they're waiting for the prey to come to them.*

There was no turning back now; a sudden stop and three-point reverse would only attract more attention. Their only hope was to pass unnoticed. She sailed the Sturgeon right past them, but the cops stopped hollering and all turned to stare. *Shit. Shit, shit, shit.*

No lone cop would dare stop them. They'd see the pentacle bumper sticker on the Sturgeon's ass and stay away, cuz magic scared the shit out of cops. But this was different. There were enough of them gathered together to make them feel brave, safety in numbers, and they were on their home turf, and—this was the most important part—they were all hopped up on adrenaline and ready to chase.

They all had identical cop mustaches and crew cuts, so the Hell Slut couldn't tell them apart even if she tried. One was wearing a black T-shirt with the Punisher logo stretched so tightly across his barrel chest that the decal was peeling, and the Hell Slut felt, from the intensity of his stare and the alpha male posturing of his deep chest-swelling breaths, that this one was probably the leader. She wondered briefly if he was their target, if any of this mob was. The Punisher watched them pass, his little piggy eyes gleaming under his brow. The other cops watched with interest, ruddy pink skin pulled tight over bones as thick as armor, eyes staring out from little chinks in their anvil-shaped skulls.

The Hell Slut adjusted the rearview mirror to watch the cop mob fade into the distance. When they were a block away, she let out her breath. The cops weren't interested in a chase. That was good.

Sunny Delight sagged in her seat, evidently feeling the same relief. "Oh my gosh, that was intense. Why do they all look like that? Even the cops down in San Francisco look like that!"

"Cops stopped breeding with civvies long ago, because civvies just couldn't understand the stress of being a cop," said the Hell Slut. "Now cops only breed with other cops. The new cops are bigger, their bones stronger, and their skulls thicker. You'd probably break your hand if you tried to hit one. That's why you leave the hitting to me."

Sunny Delight sat up in her seat, suddenly alert, and pointed at a street sign. "Wisteria Drive!"

"Good eye, Sunny D, good eye."

The Sturgeon turned a corner and drifted to a stop on the curb of a darkened side street, where the streetlights were fewer and farther between. It was dark other than the headlights of the idling Sturgeon and the cold blue glow of porch lights. Then the Hell Slut killed the lights, and the world plunged into darkness.

"Here's our stop," she said.

Hal Sampson. 125 Wisteria Drive, San Bernardo. Like all the other homes in the neighborhood, it was a neat little white bungalow with a well-manicured lawn. An American flag dangled limply from a flagpole under the front porch eaves. There was a cruiser in the driveway.

"What do you think?" asked the Frog Sisters in unison.

The Hell Slut narrowed her eyes in concentration and stared at the scene. "Obviously, we already know he's a cop. Second generation, grew up in a cop home, cop values. High school athlete, even got a scholarship, but lost it cuz of an incident involving, gonna say, hmm, racist graffiti. Married his high school sweetheart, who agrees with him that the incident was exaggerated and he was robbed. Attends church every Sunday, probably Lutheran. Comes home afterward and beats his wife. No kids. Hmm. Almost one, though. She miscarried when he shoved her down the stairs."

"It's a one-floor house," said the Frog Sisters in unison.

"Basement stairs."

"There's no basements in California," said the Frog Sisters in unison.

"This house has a basement."

"You can tell all that from just looking at his house?" said Sunny Delight.

"No. It's just a hunch." She shifted in her seat. "Remember the plan, Sunny D? Me and the Frog Sisters are gonna go in and take care of this guy. You stay out here. You're our getaway driver."

Sunny Delight nodded bravely, but she was trembling. Things were starting to get real for her. The Hell Slut put a hand on her shoulder and squeezed.

"You'll be okay. Nothing bad's gonna happen to you. We're gonna go in and finish the job. Once we go in the front door, you start your countdown. If we're not back out here and in the car in ten minutes, you turn tail and drive outta here, okay?"

"But..."

"Just like we agreed."

Sunny Delight nodded numbly.

"Listen. After this is all over, maybe you and me... Maybe we can take a little trip down to San Francisco sometime? Maybe pay a visit to your old pal Mel? I got some shit I wanna discuss with him."

Sunny Delight released a giggle too high-pitched to disguise her nerves and nodded. "I'd like that."

The Hell Slut smiled and squeezed her shoulder one last time. Then she kicked open her door, extricated herself from the Sturgeon, and marched up the flagstone path leading to the front door. The Frog Sisters trailed behind.

The Hell Slut pressed the doorbell. They had to do this fast, strike quick and hard, get in and get out. They were at a disadvantage. The Hell Slut never used guns; she killed only with her hands. That was her way. But this guy would have guns, lots of them. They just had to off him fast before he could reach them. It was after dark, though, so if the Hell Slut knew cop brain, he would either be fucking his wife or be passed out in his recliner in front of the TV. Either way, he would be unarmed. After a few minutes, she heard a rustling inside and the door opened a crack. The face of a middle-aged blond woman with impeccable makeup peered out.

"Yes?"

"Mental health check, ma'am," said the Hell Slut.

"What?" Confused, the woman opened the door wider so that she could poke her head out. Now the Hell Slut could see her clearly. She had the put-together look of a former model, fighting the ravages of age with the typical tradwife combo of Botox and kale smoothies. Her supple body was ensconced in a tight white tank top with a plunging V-neckline and high-waisted mom jeans. Her blond hair was coiffed for a night on the town, and her makeup was perfect, the pink flush of concealer disguising the green bruise below her left eye socket. *Hal Sampson got himself a real milf*, thought the Hell Slut, but she didn't have the time to admire Hal Sampson's taste. One hand shot out and thrust the door open while the other grabbed the woman's face and roughly pinched her mouth shut. The woman's eyes bugged out of her head and she tried to twist away, but the Hell Slut was already pushing her backward, striding into the house, and slamming the woman against the closed door of the broom closet opposite the entrance.

"Stay," said the Hell Slut. "Don't make a sound."

She let go of Mrs. Sampson and the woman slumped to the

ground, sobbing quietly under her breath. She was a woman used to following orders, so hopefully her instincts would kick in and she would obey.

The living room was a vast chamber, blanketed in thick spongy white carpet. The Hell Slut's senses were heightened by moonflow; the dimensions of the room were bigger than expected. A newscast in which a clean-cut young man in a suit used lots of red and blue graphics to explain the threat of Mexican gangs was playing on a massive flat-screen TV against the far wall, among an arrangement of commemorative Disney plates. There were *a lot* of plates and also an oil painting of Jesus Christ, beatific smile and all, holding his bloody stigmata hand out to Mickey Mouse. A leather-cushioned La-Z-Boy occupied the center of the room, and the Hell Slut could hear the steady rise and fall of loud wheezy cop snoring. She tiptoed around the recliner and discovered a middle-aged man wearing only black socks and Jockey shorts. He had the cop crew cut and matching respectable salt-and-pepper mustache, and his hairy paunch filled his lap. Several drained beer bottles littered the floor.

"Hal! Hal!" screamed Mrs. Sampson suddenly.

Hal Sampson stirred in his sleep and grunted, blinking his eyes open just before the Hell Slut's fist came down. He squirmed out of the way, and the fist that should have cracked his skull instead slammed down on his shoulder blade, prompting a bellow like a wounded buffalo's. Hal Sampson slithered out of his recliner with a speed surprising for his age, physique, and line of work. He hit the floor and lashed out with one hairy leg, knocking the Hell Slut's feet out from under her. She toppled and hit the spongy carpet, ass-first. *Shit. I underestimated Hal Sampson*, thought the Hell Slut. This was not the time for regrets. He was on top of her now, straddling her and slamming her face into the floor with one meaty hand until her nose exploded against the carpet. When he thought she was too stunned to react anymore, he grabbed at her hands. At first, she was confused by the move, but then she realized he was trying to twist her arms behind her back, like he thought he was going to cuff her. Oh my God, did he think he was going to arrest her? The very idea was laughable.

"Hands behind your back! Stop resisting! Stop resisting!" Hal Sampson shouted in her ear, and she could smell the beer on his breath. "Come into my frickin' house— Who sent you? Who sent you? I knew you would try this!" Now he was yelling at the tradwife: "Donna! Call dispatch and tell them there's been a home invasion. Tell them the suspect has been subdued—"

No, this was not going to do at all. If they got through to dispatch, it was all over. No way the Hell Slut was going to be able to take out a whole gaggle of cops. She needed to end this now.

"Fuck you, Hal Sampson," she gurgled through a mouthful of blood. "We came for you. You're going to die."

Hal Sampson wasn't used to anyone talking back once he had their face to the ground, and it showed, because he flinched. But he recovered quickly.

"Oh, you think that, do you?" he growled. "What are you? Who sent you?" He slammed her face into the carpet again, so that the Hell Slut blew bubbles into the spreading pool of blood boiling from her nose. He shouted for the tradwife again. "Don't just sit there! I told you to call..." His command trailed off as he suddenly realized that the Hell Slut wasn't the only outside presence in his house.

"Shrooms are groovy! Kill the pigs!" chanted the Frog Sisters from the atrium, hovering over the prone, sobbing form of Donna Sampson.

"What the hell?! What the hell is this? Get the hell outta my house!" bellowed Hal Sampson. Instinctively, he reached for a radio that wasn't there to call for backup that wouldn't come.

The Frog Sisters continued chanting, stepping over Donna Sampson and entering the living room. Hal Sampson stared, mesmerized.

The Hell Slut didn't know a whole lot about the background of the Frog Sisters before they joined the temple, but she did know that they had performed a stage act for years. *Magic or comedy or something, I guess. Maybe burlesque.* The important thing was that was where they perfected the talking-in-unison thing. The Hell Slut had tangled with cops a few times in her youth, back when neighbors would hear her elders conducting church in the barn and call in the cops to escalate the situation, and the Hell Slut knew one thing with absolute 100 percent deadass certainty about cops: They were all fucking dumb as shit. They all believed that Black people had special brains that made them good at crime, that the world was run by Jewish space lizards, and that ghosts were real. Hell, most cops would shit their pants rather than tell a goth to stop loitering in the 7-Eleven parking lot. If a kid with black eyeliner gave a cop a weird look, he'd spend the next decade telling all his dumbass cop friends about how he met a real-life Satanist and only just managed to escape being sacrificed to the dark lord himself, because of his elite cop skills.

So when a cop was confronted by something like the Frog Sisters? Oh shit. He couldn't take it. He was just about to lose his goddamn mind.

"Who are you? What do you want?!" shrieked Hal Sampson. "Are you BLM? Antifa?"

He's not so tough without his gun, thought the Hell Slut. He was distracted, so she rolled. She threw her weight, knocking Hal

Sampson off-balance. He toppled over, crashing into a decorative Chinese table and knocking a lamp to the floor, where it shattered. The Hell Slut was up now, coming at him again, but Hal Sampson had recovered from his initial shock at seeing the Frog Sisters. He ducked and dodged, and the Hell Slut fell into a bookcase, sweeping a collection of bric-a-brac to the floor. Hal Sampson went careening down the hallway, bouncing wildly off the walls, and, as the Hell Slut followed, ran into a room at the far end and locked the door. The Hell Slut could hear the bolt turn. *Shit. That's got to be the master bedroom, and that's got to be where he's got the gun safe.* The Hell Slut could already imagine him crouched down in front of it, desperately spinning the combination dial as he peered over his shoulder, waiting for the Hell Slut to bust down the door. There was no time.

She stepped back from the doorway, and sure enough, gunshots blasted through the flimsy balsa wood. The Hell Slut would wait until Hal Sampson tired himself out. If they were unlucky, he would barricade himself in that room like a little bitch. Classic cop move. But Hal Sampson struck her as more of a cowboy type.

"Hal Sampson," called the Hell Slut in a singsong voice. "Don't hide yourself away. We've got your wife out here."

Hal Sampson bellowed from the other side of the door, but his voice was so muffled she couldn't tell if he was making threats or demands. He was mad, that much was for sure.

She turned to the Frog Sisters. "How long have we been in here?"

"Two minutes."

"Okay, okay. Any second now."

Then something unexpected happened. The front door flew open and Sunny Delight ran into the room, tripping over Donna

Sampson's huddled form and pinwheeling into the living room with a shout.

"What the hell?!" The Hell Slut was momentarily distracted from Hal Sampson's roaring. Another gunshot blasted another hole through the bedroom door; the air was thick with smoke and sawdust. "What are you doing here? I told you to stay in the car!"

"Praise the Green Lady! Praise be!" shouted Sunny Delight, waving her arms above her head as she twirled through the living room, oblivious to the wreckage and the smoke and the crying of Donna Sampson. "I had to tell you—I just had a vision! The Green Lady spoke to me! I heard her voice! I heard her voice in my head!" Sunny Delight tapped her finger to her temple. In her excitement, her voice was getting awfully loud and awfully shrill.

"A vision from the Green Lady!" cried the Frog Sisters in unison, and they dropped to their knees in supplication.

"Tone it down, eh? We don't want the neighbors to hear us in here! What the hell's going on with you? What did the Green Lady tell you?"

"She told me to come in and see you! She told me that I love you! I love you, and if you're about to die, then I don't want to live without you! I want to be by your side always . . . my true Hell Slut!" She grabbed the Hell Slut's big hand and peppered it with sloppy kisses. "Praise the Green Lady!"

Sunny Delight laughed in pure, unfiltered joy, delirious tears streaming down her cheeks as she gazed at the Hell Slut with naked affection. "I love you *so* much! Please, I just want to be with you! I don't care about anything else! Ever since you saved me from that guy at the Dank Hole, you're all I can think about! Nobody's ever done anything like that for me before . . . Nobody's ever stood up for me like that!"

Hal Sampson fired another volley through the door in a cloud of sawdust and asbestos. The Hell Slut flinched, but Sunny Delight was too caught up in her own story to notice.

"The Green Lady made me realize I need to be here, by your side! Like Bonnie and Clyde! I can't sit in the car while you fight! If we die, we die together!" She hooked her arm around the Hell Slut's elbow and pulled her close.

"Praise the Green Lady!" cried the Frog Sisters. "Praise be!"

"Stop it! You're all gonna ruin everything—we need to focus!"

Sunny Delight's face started to crumple. "Don't you love me too? Why won't you say it? The Green Lady..."

"Oh shit," said the Hell Slut, suddenly understanding the situation. "You drank too much moonflow! Sorry about this, kid." She grabbed Sunny Delight and spun her off toward the Frog Sisters. "Get her out of the way! She's having visions! Not now, not now!"

Sunny Delight tumbled into the Frog Sisters, knocking them to the floor. At the same time, Hal Sampson fired several more blasts through the door and then, as predicted, threw it open and came roaring out, gun drawn and pointed directly at the Hell Slut's brain.

"Stop resisting!" he bellowed. "Hands in the air! Where I can see them! Hands in the air!"

"No! Don't kill her, I love her!" cried Sunny Delight, tearing at her hair in frustration and rolling across the floor. She pointed at the Hell Slut from the ground. "The Green Lady protect you!"

Hal Sampson kept his gun pointed, but Sunny Delight's outburst distracted him long enough that the Frog Sisters were back on their feet, chanting again.

"Go ahead, pull the trigger," gambled the Hell Slut.

And he might have. In any other situation, Hal Sampson

might have pulled the trigger. But behind the Hell Slut, swaying and mumbling with their long dark hair and their matching black veils and their matching black gowns, the Frog Sisters continued to chant. And the Hell Slut knew that Hal Sampson knew, deep in the pit of his stupid cop heart, that these people in his house were no ordinary people—they were avenging demons, sent by Satan himself to kill Hal Sampson and drag his soul to hell. There was no other possible explanation.

"Pull the trigger and see what happens," said the Hell Slut, taking a step forward, pressing Hal Sampson back toward the end of the hallway. "Pull the trigger and see if I die."

She knew that he knew, deep in his cop heart, that she wouldn't die. You couldn't kill a demon with a bullet. And he was scared, too scared to test it, too scared to find out the truth... Because if he fired and she didn't fall, what then? The prospect was too terrible to admit. Good. That was exactly what the Hell Slut was hoping for.

"Shrooms are groovy! Kill the pigs!"

Hal Sampson backed away from them, fear in his eyes. He couldn't decide where to point his gun, flipping from the Hell Slut to one Frog Sister and then to the other Frog Sister, back and forth, his wrists getting shakier by the second.

"No, you can't kill her! I won't let you!" cried Sunny Delight, breaking free of the Frog Sisters and lunging across the room. What the hell was she doing? The Hell Slut watched, baffled, as Sunny Delight jumped in front of her.

"The Green Lady calls on me to protect my love!" She rolled her head to glance over her shoulder and fix the Hell Slut with a dreamy smile. "Don't worry, my love! The Green Lady will deliver us!"

Oh shit, she's gonna be a human shield.

The Frog Sisters' chants were in Hal Sampson's head, and that was the only reason that his hand jittered, and that was the only reason that when the gun discharged, the bullet didn't immediately perforate Sunny Delight through the neck. Instead, it diverted upward—just as the Hell Slut regained the presence of mind to clamp her hands on Sunny Delight's shoulders and shove her to the floor. The Hell Slut felt a sudden burning pain in her shoulder, and she knew she'd been hit. That was fine. She would just put that knowledge in a little box in her head to process later. There were other issues to deal with at the moment. It was just one bullet—she would be fine.

It was fine.

The important thing was, Hal Sampson tried to shoot Sunny Delight. The Hell Slut felt her temperature rise. This was no longer just a job. This was personal. This miserable piece of shit just tried to shoot Sunny Delight!

Hal Sampson didn't understand what was happening, since he had clearly just shot the Hell Slut but the Hell Slut did not die. He was not used to people not dying when he shot them. That was why the Hell Slut didn't fear cops. They couldn't function if their guns couldn't finish their jobs for them.

"You miserable piece of shit!" snarled the Hell Slut, wheezing with pure unholy rage. Adrenaline was pumping through her system like a drug; she was so furious that her vision was going blurry, her racing heartbeat blowing rhythmic geysers of blood from the hole in her shoulder. She shoved Sunny Delight aside and took a step forward. Hal Sampson tried to retreat, but she smacked the gun from his hand with her good arm. It went off one final time, and the Hell Slut felt the heat of the escaping bullet just graze her shin as it blasted impotently into the carpet. A less meticulous killer would have grabbed for the gun and turned it back on Hal Sampson. But the Hell Slut killed only with her hands. Now Hal Sampson's head was within reach. He was staring at his lost gun, his lip quivering in panicked confusion, like a perplexed baby in the split second after it loses its bottle and before it begins to cry. The Hell Slut was tired of fooling around. She grabbed his head in both hands, ignoring the pain that flowed through her arm like electricity, and twisted hard.

"Aphrodite sends her regards!"

Hal Sampson did not betray any recognition of the name, but the Hell Slut didn't expect much. Hal Sampson's encounter with Aphrodite was probably nothing more than a random truck stop seduction or possibly a stop and frisk that went really well for him. Even if he remembered it, chances were that he and Aphrodite hadn't even exchanged names.

His spine tore with a satisfying crunch, and that was that. He dropped to the floor, and just to be sure, the Hell Slut raised her leg and put her boot through his head so hard that a chunky stew of brains and bone burst across the carpet. Sunny Delight screamed, tearing at her hair in fear and confusion.

"You killed him! By the Green Lady, you did it! Praise the Green Lady!"

"Yeah, great." The Hell Slut sighed, wiping the sweat from her brow with one giant arm. She was exhausted, her whole body aching with tension, and they weren't done yet—they still needed to get out of here without any of Hal Sampson's cop cronies catching wind of what they'd done. And Sunny Delight's head trip wasn't going to make that any easier.

And, oh yeah, the gunshot wound.

She sank to her knees. Sunny Delight ran to her. The Frog Sisters knew the drill and did not need to be told what to do.

They descended on the corpse, ripping the Jockey shorts away, and started pumping its shaft. One, two, three, one, two, three, quick staccato jerks calculated to achieve maximum turgidity fast. Time was of the essence. Hal Sampson's heart was stopping, his blood was slowing; they had only minutes—maybe even less—before entire system shutdown.

"Oh my God, he shot you! Hold still. Put pressure on it—we've got to stem the bleeding!" cried Sunny Delight, oblivious to the Frog Sisters' machinations. It was as if a switch flipped in her head, and now suddenly Sunny Delight was taking charge. She grabbed a doily from an upturned end table and pressed it into the wound. "There's got to be a first aid kit around here somewhere! There's got to be some rubbing alcohol! And get some towels!"

"And find the liquor cabinet," added the Hell Slut.

"It's okay, you're gonna be okay! The Green Lady protects you. We'll get you home, Doc Clopper will get you fixed up..." Sunny Delight's chatter trailed off as she noticed what the Frog Sisters were doing. The late Hal Sampson's dick was rigid and purple.

"Don't worry about it," said the Hell Slut. "That's the other part of our mission. I didn't want to tell you before. We just needed to get some sperm."

Sunny Delight stared. "Why do we need sperm?"

"For the birthing ceremony. It'll all make sense later, I promise you. Just remember, this is all according to the Green Lady's plan."

"Yeah, of course. The Green Lady."

Hal Sampson's body remained limp as his erect dick finally twitched and the Frog Sisters collected the offering in a glass jelly jar.

"Enough of that. You two, find that first aid kit," said the Hell Slut, still holding her wound.

The Frog Sisters nodded in unison, secreting the precious jar among their persons, and they left the Hell Slut alone with Sunny Delight in the decimated living room, sitting in a vast pool of blood, some of which belonged to the Hell Slut, some of which was still spilling from the now-cooling, now-spent body of Hal Sampson. Donna Sampson still huddled in a whimpering heap by the front door. She was babbling the Lord's Prayer under her breath, and the Hell Slut pressed her hand into the soaked doily against her shoulder wound to stanch the bleeding and let the pain distract her from memories of her parents' sermons in the barn. She did *not* like hearing the Lord's Prayer.

"Quiet," she snapped.

"Hell Slut! Stop it!" scolded Sunny Delight. She turned to Donna. "She doesn't mean it; she's just a little upset right now."

Donna Sampson fell silent. Donna did not seem to understand that something wonderful had just happened, that she'd just been freed from a prison and suddenly her whole life was spreading out before her, fresh and new. Sometimes it was hard to get people to understand that. Sometimes people preferred to stay shackled, and you had to lead them gently to liberation. The Hell Slut had a sinking feeling that breaking through this woman's defenses was going to be beyond her limited social skills. She didn't like killing women, but she couldn't leave a witness.

That was going to be a problem.

14.

The Green Lady, she of the divine yoni from whom all good things come, bestows the gift of sapphic unity to all who accept her offer of feminine community and live in harmony with her tenets. She awaits any woman who would experience the spiritual fulfillment of lesbian union.

—Shining Clitopia: The Way of the Green Lady
(mimeographed pamphlet, date and author unknown)

After Mother Moonflow dismissed them into Pickles's care, he took it upon himself to show them around. Pickles was less interested in answering Sarah's two most pressing questions—"What's this about a birthing ceremony?" and "So where, exactly, do you keep the King's Breakfast?"—than he was in explaining the architecture of the building.

Andy was fascinated. "This isn't Lazarus Sloane's actual mill, is it?"

"In fact, it is!" Pickles regarded Andy with sudden interest. "Lazarus Sloane abandoned this mill over a hundred years ago, but there's no sense in letting it go to waste. Us sisters took it over cuz possession is nine-tenths of the law."

There was little to indicate, other than the general shape of the temple, that it had once been a lumber mill. Over the years, the sisters had jerry-rigged it into something far more, a project mostly overseen by Virginia Dentata and Miss Trix, according to Pickles, since they were both carpenters before joining the temple, and now the building was a honeycomb of tiny rooms connected by so many ladders and so many trapdoors. The floor was warped, and the walls were wet with mold and mildew—the constant rain was slowly rotting the building by degrees—but "we do what we can!" said Pickles. There was the main room where the sisters took their meals, seated around a massive slab of petrified bristlecone left over from Sloane's failure, and there was the sanctuary, where Mother Moonflow spent her days in meditation, but the rest of the rooms were small and cramped, demarcated by erratic walls jumbled from scavenged wood slats, particleboard, and corrugated iron. Spaghetti clumps of wires ran along every wall, squeezing through drilled knotholes to power naked incandescent bulbs strung from the ceiling. The wires had to be connected to something, and Sarah wondered if there was a generator somewhere on the grounds or if they were illicitly tapped into some power grid. How many underground miles of forbidden forest did those wires have to traverse to siphon off power from some unwitting strip mall or office building back in Las Brujas?

Some of the rooms were playrooms; the temple included at least a dozen kids, who were always underfoot and who didn't seem to belong to anyone. ("Oh, yeah, we love the little shits," said Pickles when Sarah asked about them.) There were other rooms that had been claimed by the raccoons and were now spray-painted with big *X*'s to indicate they were off-limits. Still others were bedrooms, furnished with simple futons and pull curtains, although Sarah didn't get the impression that the sisters cared much for privacy—when Pickles took them around the grounds, there was a young woman behind the toolshed, robes over her head, fingers buried knuckle-deep in the downy fluff between her spread legs. A pair of women—older, thicker, heads graying—were entwined in the hollow beneath one of the temple's many ladders and didn't break apart at their approach. As they passed unfamiliar faces, Pickles pointed them out as Marsha Mallow and Captain Beef Curtains and Zooty Zoot Zoot and Charlotte the Harlot and other far-out names that Sarah couldn't hold in her head. Everyone seemed extremely involved in their lovemaking.

"Don't worry, you'll get used to it," said Pickles, who'd suddenly become quite gregarious after their meeting with Mother Moonflow. He wore a wide and genuine smile, so that Sarah could only surmise that they must have passed some sort of test in the sanctuary and now Pickles was quite happy to have them here. "We believe in free love here at the Temple of the Green Lady. So where are you from specifically?"

Andy was originally from Barstow. Sarah was from Chico, transplanted to Oakland.

That knowledge delighted Pickles. "Ah, the Bay Area! I'm from San Francisco myself. Of course, I haven't been back since I was a kid. What's it like now? Is King Willie still in charge?"

"Sorry, who?" said Sarah.

"King Willie! You know, Willie Brown!"

"Not since the aughts. Just how long have you been here?"

Pickles ran his fingers through his hair, pulling away large snarly gobs of tangles. "Oh, I never leave the temple. This is our sanctuary away from the world of men."

"Ah," said Andy. "But aren't you—"

"Andy," said Sarah. "Shut up."

Pickles kept talking, oblivious to the interruption. "Only Skillet and the Hell Slut have to go to town anymore, for supplies. What is it that you two do in the world of men?"

"I'm a mycologist," said Sarah. "Andy's an interpretive specialist."

"What's that?"

"I study mushrooms."

"No. I mean, what's an interpretive specialist?"

Sarah looked to Andy for an explanation.

"It's like a teacher," he said.

Pickles brightened. "Oh, excellent! You know what, you two are just what we need. Follow me, I know just what you two need to see."

He led them to a bare muddy garden, where Skillet was sitting on a tree stump and sharing moonshine out of unlabeled brown bottles with Virginia Dentata and Miss Trix. Skillet saw their approach and waved them over. To Sarah, Pickles said, "I'm gonna leave you here in the care of these ladies... and Skillet. She's supposed to be our gardener, but you can see what kind of success she's having. Maybe our little mushroom doctor here can give her some pointers."

"Fuck you, Pickles," said Skillet.

"Now remember, Sarah is cool. I know she's a phallic alec, but Mother Moonflow has declared her cool."

"Yeah, yeah, we get it," said Virginia Dentata, spitting a wad of phlegm to the ground. "We wouldn't dream of hassling this delicate little flower."

Pickles took Andy's hand and tugged at his sleeve. "I'm going to take your Andy to see our school. As a teacher, you'll really get a lot out of it. Don't worry, I'll have him back to you for supper."

Andy gave her a pleading look as he was led away, and the last thing Sarah heard was him complaining that he wasn't *technically* a teacher, he was an interpretive specialist, which was actually quite different.

Skillet laughed. "Fuuuuck, thank Gord we're rid of them, right? Just us girls now. Sit down, join us."

"Can't believe you brought these two phallic alecs into the temple," said Virginia Dentata, scratching at her bare chest. "That's fucked up, Skillet. Bad aura. Phallic shit."

"I'm standing right here," said Sarah. "And maybe you weren't paying attention, but I'm cool. Your Mother Moonflow only said it about a hundred times."

Sarah remembered quite clearly how Virginia Dentata and Miss Trix had reacted to Mother Moonflow's announcement. But she was under official protection now, and she felt extremely gratified to rub that in these fucking terf-ass bitches' faces.

"Yeah, dumbass, she's cool," said Skillet. "I thought y'all liked listening to Mother Moonflow?"

"Well," said Virginia Dentata. "Mother Moonflow knows the will of the Green Lady." She gazed at Sarah with unblinking brown eyes. "So I guess you're cool until I hear otherwise."

"If the Green Lady told her, it's cool," concluded Miss Trix.

"Glad that's settled." Skillet handed a bottle to Sarah and motioned for her to drink. Sarah took a sip of the acrid liquid and sputtered. The three other women laughed.

"Good shit, huh?" said Skillet. "We make it ourselves. Miss Trix has a still in the back. We gotta make everything ourselves since we're living off the land—our own liquor, our own weed, our own shrooms."

Sarah glanced over at the garden and noticed, for the first time, the explosion of mushrooms: Cat Claws (*Clathrus felicia*) and Thief's Luck (*Lepiota jinx*) and Old Methuselah (*Agaricus geriatrica*). But no King's Breakfast.

"I noticed Mother Moonflow was eating the King's Breakfast," said Sarah.

"That's a little gift from the devil, you might say," said Miss Trix.

Since starting this journey, Sarah had expected she would be collecting spores from some patch of wild mushrooms out in the woods. But it looked like instead she was just going to buy some. She cursed herself silently. If she had known this was how things would turn out, she would have brought cash. What were the odds that this weirdo forest cult was equipped to accept digital payment? Sarah cleared her throat and asked the all-important question that would determine everything from here on out: "Could I buy some?"

"You don't want that," said Miss Trix. "The King's Breakfast is an aspect of the Lord of the Forest. It just puts the Lord of the Forest in your system, and you don't want him poking his roots into your mind. You'd rot from the inside real fast."

"Mother Moonflow seemed to be doing okay," said Sarah pointedly.

"That's cuz she's the prophet of the Green Lady," said Virginia Dentata. She slammed down her jar. "You phallic alecs wouldn't understand. Within her body, the King's Breakfast is transmuted from a phallic vibe to a yonic tonic. It's gotta be feminized."

"Huh, that's interesting," said Sarah, getting annoyed. "So you're telling me that something masculine can be made feminine. That's really interesting. Why don't you tell me more about that?"

Skillet started laughing, but Virginia Dentata held up a finger for silence.

"Hold it. Look over there."

She nudged her bottle to indicate a section of rotting fence about twenty feet away, toward the edge of the clearing, where a fat raccoon perched on a splintering post and regarded them with black eyes.

"You see that raccoon?" Virginia Dentata whipped her bottle at the raccoon's head. The bottle spun through the air, arced up, and smashed into shards against the raccoon's pointed snout, knocking it to the ground. The women guffawed loudly as the stunned raccoon hit the ground and lay there, paws in the air. "Maybe don't test me, phallic alec."

"Jesus," said Sarah, recoiling in shock. "I thought raccoons were sacred to you guys!"

"What's this? Some phallic alec thinks she knows my religion more than me? Is that what I'm hearing?" Virginia Dentata accepted another bottle from Miss Trix and tipped it down her throat. "Can't believe you're gonna be at the birthing ceremony."

"Oh, it's gonna be lit!" giggled Miss Trix, grinning. "Mother Moonflow's gonna induce Aphrodite into labor tonight, and we're all gonna welcome a new sister into the world."

"Not just any sister," said Virginia Dentata. "But you wouldn't understand."

"You don't know that," said Sarah. "I just might."

Virginia Dentata sucked on her bottle. "This temple is dedicated to the Green Lady, the essence of womanhood. That's what we're building here. A shrine to womanhood. A birthing canal for the spirit like you've never seen, like you ain't ever gonna see."

"Lay off her," said Skillet.

"I'm just spitting facts," said Virginia Dentata. "We don't just practice free love here; we *perfect* it. We perfect the love that only a woman can have for a woman. And nine months ago, we did perfect it. We all did. We've been trying for a long, long time and it finally happened. Aphrodite's child will be the first child ever to be born entirely of woman."

"What are you talking about?" Sarah did not follow.

"We all fucked in a big pile, just us gals. And now Aphrodite is pregnant. Pregnant with a child that has twenty mothers. A daughter with no father. The Green Lady reborn in flesh."

15.

*The Chinese Lantern (*Lactarius chinoiserie*) is a species of milk cap, notable for the thick blue fluid it exudes when cut or damaged. The light blue flesh has a distinctive brittle consistency and a chewy mouthfeel. The Chinese Lantern is prized as an aphrodisiac, but unsupervised consumption may result in prolonged emissions. It is said to taste of charnel smoke.*

—Field Guide to Common Mushrooms of the Pamogo Forest, *T. F. Greengarb (1978)*

The classroom looked like the other rooms in the temple, except that it was covered floor-to-ceiling in little handprints in garish yellow, blue, and red finger paints. Finger painting must be part of the curriculum here, although Sarah didn't think there was much of a curriculum at all. The kids snapped and growled and rolled around on the floor and occasionally wrestled and generally ignored Effervescent Bubbles as she struggled to corral them.

"What do you mean, twenty mothers?" asked Andy.

"I mean they think they made a baby with a big all-woman orgy and they're gonna deliver this super-femme baby tonight," said Sarah. "And where have you been?! I've been looking all over for you!"

"I've been right here, watching how they run their school. It's really something, actually! Right now, the kids are getting in touch with nature by—"

"Goddamn, I don't need to hear about this." Sarah grimaced as a trio of children rolled past in a snarling tangle. "Has anyone said anything about the way back to Las Brujas? When can we get out of here?"

Andy was squatting down into the fray of wild children, distributing snacks from a wicker basket. The snacks appeared to be diced bits of unidentifiable root vegetables, and the kids reacted with predictable disdain, spitting them on the floor and throwing them at each other. Andy was like the world's most patient kindergarten teacher, thought Sarah. Who else would allow himself to be pressed into service as a lunch aide?

"I haven't really asked. You know, I think they're using a really interesting variant of the open classroom model here—"

"These people are bonkers, and I think we need to get out of here as soon as possible."

"And go where? We don't exactly know where we are."

Sarah hated that he was right. "Christ, are you fucking Effervescent Bubbles?"

Andy looked aghast. "Language! There's kids here!"

Sarah was pretty sure that these kids did not understand language. She was pretty sure that something had gone very wrong in their critical development. Nearby, the emerald-eyed girl was holding down a redheaded girl and chewing on her hair.

"These kids are not going to notice. Answer me, are you fucking Effervescent Bubbles? Is this what this weird teacher's pet act is all about?"

"Effervescent Bubbles and I were just talking about her school! I think they've got the right idea about a lot of stuff here—for example, just collecting the mushrooms that they need, not selling them."

Sarah groaned. "Not this again!"

Andy shook his head. "You're not even a little inspired by how they're living in harmony with the forest?"

Sarah glared at Andy. She felt like she was on the verge of making an important discovery. Madeleine hadn't been able to grow the King's Breakfast—no one had—but somehow these weirdo cultists living in a shack in the woods had managed to get these incredibly finicky mushrooms to grow in profusion. Sarah needed to learn more if she ever hoped to replicate their success. And Andy was giving her guff about it! Rescue had revived his self-confidence, but Sarah was beginning to think she preferred him when he was hopeless and depressed.

"They're not living in harmony with anything! I just saw one of them throw a beer bottle at a raccoon! This woman cult shit is super terfy and I'm pretty sure they're gonna sacrifice us to, I don't know, whatever that Green Lady thing is, and you want to hang out here and navel gaze with a goddamn teenager!"

"First of all, Effervescent Bubbles is actually twenty, and she's really mature—"

"I do *not* care," whispered Sarah, lowering her voice as the emerald-eyed girl slithered past, growling. She smiled and nodded. The green-eyed girl lunged without warning and plunged her teeth into Sarah's leg, deep enough to draw blood, and Sarah instinctively jerked away with a curse.

"Ow! What the fuck?!"

"Language!" scolded Andy again. And then to the girl he said, "No! No bitey! You know better than that!"

The green-eyed girl grinned stupidly, her mouth dribbling red. She fell back into the fray of squirming kids.

"Oof, I should have warned you about that one, she's a biter," said Andy. He bent down to examine the puncture. "You might wanna see Doc Clopper about putting something on that before it gets infected."

"Whose kids are these, anyway?" said Sarah, massaging her wound. Blood welled up through the denim fabric. She rolled up the leg of her jeans to inspect the damage and found streaks of red oozing down her shin. She thought about the sisters trying to orgy into existence a thing that could never be, a girl with no father, and wondered if all these screaming children were failed experiments, dumped into this joke of a school to be forgotten. She scanned the room, suddenly suspicious.

"Everyone's," said Andy solemnly. "It takes a village, as they say."

"They're all girls too."

Andy was not following. "So?"

"So? Don't you think that's kind of weird?"

This whole cult felt increasingly fucked up, but all this free love and woman-on-woman orgy stuff was hardly any more sordid than anything that went down at one of Madeleine's parties. Probably far less sordid, actually, considering that these women made a religion of it.

"This whole situation is super weird. I do not want to stay here. I want to go home. I want to go home now. Andy, are you . . . are you joining this cult? Are you for real?"

"No, of course not! You're being ridiculous!"

"You've done nothing but talk about how great they are! God, only you would fall for this shit!"

Andy pressed his lips together. "As an ally, I think—"

"Oh, shut the fuck up! You sound like a doofus. This whole situation is insane. You saw their Mother Moonflow! She just walks around naked all day and you think this is all normal?"

"I didn't say it was normal. I just think, you know, it's a valid way of living."

"What is wrong with you? Did you see the size of her tits? I feel like I'm going crazy that no one else seems to even notice this!"

Andy coughed in embarrassment, rolled his shoulders, and looked off into the distance, pretending that he didn't hear her. "Honestly, I just figured you'd be in with Skillet by now. She's really into you."

"Why would you think that?" huffed Sarah.

"The way she was looking at you earlier."

Sarah remembered. At their first meeting, Skillet practically groped her. If she didn't know better, she would have thought Skillet was trying to pull her bra off. But it didn't make sense that Skillet would be into her. That was just silly.

"Honestly, I think Skillet is just handsy with everyone."

"All these women seem pretty handsy," said Andy, stroking his beard thoughtfully.

"Oh, go play with your child bride!" snapped Sarah. "I'm done talking with you!"

Andy laughed. A sudden yelp from Effervescent Bubbles drew his attention. She appeared to be trying to start some kind of lesson, but the kids were not interested in sitting still or being quiet.

Andy raised his voice: "You know, if you really want to engage kids at this age, you have to get on their level and really connect with them. See, in State Parks, we try to apply the interpretive principles of Freeman Tilden, and Tilden talks about how interpreting for kids is way different than interpreting for adults."

Sarah watched in disbelief as Andy began explaining the basic principles of interpretation to Effervescent Bubbles.

"He can't even see *ritual Satanic cult human sacrifice* two inches in front of his face," she mumbled, shaking her head. "Jesus *fucking* Christ. I cannot believe him. I cannot believe any of this."

Doc Clopper was a sour-faced old crone with long ribbons of white hair and Coke-bottle glasses, wearing an oversized tie-dyed T-shirt with a cracked decal of a cartoon horse and the words "PEGASISTERS DO IT IN THE STABLE."

"That's a nasty bite. One of the little shits did that, huh?" Doc Clopper examined the green bruise on Sarah's shin left by the emerald-eyed girl's teeth. She shook her head and dipped her hand into a tub of greasy ointment, which she smeared over the wound. "I keep telling Effervescent Bubbles she needs to keep those hellions on a leash. You think she ever listens to me? I'm only the one who's gotta keep bandaging people up."

"This happens a lot? Whose kids are they?"

"Various." Doc Clopper slapped a length of gauze around Sarah's leg and stepped back to admire her handiwork. "That should hold you. Keep an eye on it and come back if it turns black. If you value keeping your leg, that is."

What passed for an infirmary was little more than a closet lined with shelves filled with glass jars full of leaves and seeds and esoteric oozes, and stacks of gleaming vacuums and pumps and tubes that Sarah could only assume were scavenged from hospital dumpsters. Posters lined the walls; Sarah initially assumed they were medical PSAs, but they turned out to be zodiac charts.

There was a cot, where Sarah sat and stared up at the painting on the ceiling above her, done in a flat Grandma Moses style, of a green woman with large breasts and a big pregnant belly, tangled vines of hair streaming out from under a spotted mushroom cap perched upon her head. *That must be the Green Lady.* Sarah could almost just believe it depicted the same goddess that she had seen at Madeleine's party. That made sense. People tended to think in archetypes when they experienced psychedelic trips, and it wasn't uncommon for different people to report remarkably similar images. It made perfect sense.

But it only reminded her how much she needed to see the goddess—the Green Lady—again.

And how much she needed to find the King's Breakfast.

There were also trays of mushrooms laid out, and Sarah recognized Forbidden Idols (*Fomes occultus*), Harod's Delight (*Boletus tyrannicus*), and, most exciting of all, the familiar white and yellow-tinged caps of the King's Breakfast. Doc Clopper, satisfied that she had dispensed her medical duties, had turned away from Sarah and was attacking the shrooms with an electric blow-dryer. Sarah needed to keep her talking if she was going to find out where they grew them.

"That's an interesting choice," said Sarah, who would never use a blow-dryer. Heat could damage the psilocybin. "I use a fan at home."

Doc Clopper paused the blow-dryer and adjusted her Coke-bottle glasses to regard Sarah with a withering glance. "Thanks for the advice, but I think I know what I'm doing. I am a doctor, after all. Not like anyone around here ever listens to me. Why would they? Not like I have any medical knowledge or anything..."

Sarah was not eager to listen to Doc Clopper's gripes. She needed information.

"Where do you grow them? Do you have a special place or...?"

"What do you care? They're not for you. These are for Mother Moonflow. She's gotta have a constant supply so she doesn't lose contact with the Green Lady. Then we'd never get things done around here!" Doc Clopper upended the tray and dumped this most recent batch of shrooms into a large mason jar. Grunting, she screwed on the lid and shoved it up on a shelf. "Of course, it's easy for Mother Moonflow; all she's gotta do is have visions. I'm the one who has to do all the actual work!"

"Could I give you a hand? I'd really like to know more about these mushrooms."

"Yeah, well, that ain't happening. I've got enough problems without playing nursemaid. If you ain't dying, then I don't know why you're still hanging around."

This was useless. Maybe she would have more luck talking to the other sisters. Mother Moonflow had designated her as "cool," so she hoped that meant someone would be willing to show her this mysterious mushroom garden. "I'll get out of your hair."

"See that you do."

Something occurred to Sarah right as she crossed the threshold of the infirmary. "You said Mother Moonflow never comes down from her shroom high?"

Doc Clopper shot Sarah another withering glance, her eyes magnified into squirming blobs by her thick glasses. "Did I stutter? She's always in contact with the Green Lady."

At that moment, a stringy-haired woman appeared at the threshold of the doorway, pushing Sarah aside. "Yo, doc, you got a minute? We got an emergency. Aphrodite's got contractions."

"How close are the contractions?"

"Uh...I don't know?"

"Fine, fine, I'll check it out." Grumbling, Doc Clopper slammed her blow-dryer to the counter and followed the stringy-haired woman. She shot a parting glance at Sarah. "Don't touch anything while I'm gone. Especially don't touch any shrooms!"

"I wouldn't dream of it."

Actually, though, she would dream of it—if the King's Breakfast meant that she could see the goddess again, and maybe the Green Lady was just their name for the goddess and maybe if Sarah just took one, she could see her again and—

"See that you don't. I'll know!"

Now Sarah was alone in the office. She wouldn't get another chance. Now was the time to snoop.

The jars of mushrooms were useless for her needs; the drying process would have killed any lingering spores. She needed a living sample.

There was a mini-fridge in the corner, humming, tangled spaghetti cords running through a hole in the wall, with a handwritten Post-it note on the door that said "MOONFLOW." Inside, it contained glass jars of various sizes, mostly filled with thick white liquid. There were also jars of other liquids that Sarah did not immediately recognize.

More interesting was the file cabinet in the corner marked "PRIVATE!" Sarah was way past caring about that. She pulled open a drawer of hanging manila folders; each was marked with a wacky name that Sarah assumed must belong to someone in this cult. Apparently Doc Clopper was actually keeping medical records. It was time to commit some HIPAA violations.

She hoped that maybe, just maybe, there might be a file labeled "King's Breakfast," something that would helpfully explain where they were growing these mushrooms, but there was not. There was, however, a file labeled "The Green Lady (Experiment 13)."

Sarah flipped it open. It contained a few loose-leaf pages with basic medical information.

Earthly Name: Athena
Vessel: Aphrodite, Goddess of Love
Mother: The 20 Mothers

Father: Unidentified Highway Rest Stop Man (POST-NOTE: Green Lady has identified the father as Hal Sampson. 125 Wisteria Drive, San Bernardo. Hell Slut dispatched to retrieve dad sperm.)

The ritual was completed without incident, Mother Moonflow presiding. 20/20 participants report orgasms, indicating high probability of successful fertilization of the yonic egg. Physical incubation successfully started in reproductive womb, but success of spiritual incubation in yonic womb remains uncertain. Successful birth will reintroduce physical manifestation of Green Lady into gender ecosystem, long-term results unknown without corresponding reintroduction of physical manifestation of Lord of the Forest. Prediction as per Mother Moonflow's prophecy is new world of feminine power and dominance (Good).

"This is useless," muttered Sarah, shoving the folder back into the file cabinet. This was more gobbledygook about making a baby with twenty mothers, but it only served to confirm what Sarah already knew: This cult was absolutely wackadoodle bananas. Even the doctor believed this crazy shit!

Another folder caught her eye: "Moonflow, Mother." That was more promising! After all, Mother Moonflow was the only person in this cult who was allowed to eat the King's Breakfast. Maybe her file had some extra information...

But at that moment the door to the office suddenly swung open and Doc Clopper returned, grumbling under her breath. Sarah crumpled Mother Moonflow's pages down the front of her sweater and slammed the drawer shut with her hip. She turned and grinned stupidly at Doc Clopper.

Doc Clopper scowled. "Didn't I tell you to get lost?"

"Yeah... I was just..."

"Then get lost! And stay outta my things! That's private medical info. If you want to know something, just ask."

"Just ask?"

Doc Clopper flicked her blow-dryer back on and attacked the drying mushrooms again. "Look, who are you shtupping?"

"What?"

"It's a simple question. Who are you shtupping? I know what you're after. Everyone comes in and goes through my files when they want to know if their new fuck buddy has the clap or something, cuz they're just too damn embarrassed to ask. So tell me: Who're you hooking up with?"

"You got me," said Sarah, who thought it better to pretend she was doing anything other than trying to find the King's Breakfast. She said the first name that came into her head: "It's Skillet."

"Yeah, that's no surprise. I could tell by looking at you it was gonna be Skillet. That's your own funeral. Skillet's a frickin' virus factory—herpes, chlamydia, *and* the intangible squirms. Not to mention phallic vapor. You stick your dick in her, it's gonna fall off. But maybe that's what you want."

"That's good to know," said Sarah, who had never heard of the intangible squirms or phallic vapor and was beginning to have even graver doubts about Doc Clopper's medical expertise. "I'm gonna get out of your hair for real now."

"The big thing, though, is Skillet's got a weird fricking vagina," continued Doc Clopper, unbidden. "Real messed up. Looks like she sat on a hot plate or something."

"Cool. That's good to know. I'm gonna get out of your hair for really real now."

"Horse piss."

"I'm sorry?"

"Before you go, horse piss. You got some, right? I only need a little."

"I don't know what you're talking about."

"C'mon, don't hold out on me. Just a little, a taste." Doc Clopper ran her gray tongue over cracked, dry lips.

"I really need to get out of your hair for real now," said Sarah, and she left the room, still clutching Mother Moonflow's file inside her sweater.

16.

The trees of the Pamogo are damp, their wood soft & bad for timber. Even the mill itself, constructed from Pamogo trees, seems destined to rot. I am driven to despair by these failures.

—*Diary of Lazarus Sloane*
(California State Parks Archives)

Mother Moonflow's pronouncement that the visitors were cool had permeated throughout the sisters, and it seemed that nearly every door of the temple was open to Sarah. After leaving Doc Clopper's office, she wandered, unsupervised, down the hallways. The whole building was decorated with graffiti of the Green Lady in various manifestations, usually with huge breasts and a round pregnant belly. She always had her mushroom cap, and different artists had chosen to draw her vagina with varying levels of detail depending on how easily embarrassed they were. There were other pictures, less flattering, of a towering figure with a massive dong and branching coral fungus antlers. Sometimes the two were drawn in congress.

Something about the figure with the massive dong and the branching coral fungus antlers was uncomfortably familiar. She was certain this must depict the Lord of the Forest that they kept talking about, but it was more than that. The image tickled her brain, like a bad dream best forgotten.

Her mind wandered back to Mother Moonflow. The woman was on a constant drip of psychedelic mushrooms, and that seemed positively bonkers. What did it do to your mind to live constantly in a hallucinogenic haze? No wonder she was coming up with insane ideas about making a super-femme baby! And how high were these other women that they were all going along with it?

Behind the garden, Miss Trix strummed a guitar, while a girl with a tattered sundress and long frizzy hair that fell over her eyes gyrated to the tune and slapped a tambourine against her hip. A small group of women sat cross-legged on the ground, surrounding a heavily pregnant woman with a lopsided pixie haircut. Sarah stood in the back to eavesdrop on the song.

"Gather round, sisters and systers!" sang Miss Trix, attacking the guitar strings with a vengeance. "Come hear my empowering song! I sing of the power of the Green Lady! Correcting unempowering wrongs!"

There were several verses, during which Miss Trix attempted to rhyme "vulvonic flower" with "uterine power" and then asked multiple times, "Why can't we live like the raccoons? Who climb in the trees up above? Empowered to live in harmonic peace? Sleeping in burrows and showing free love?"

The song didn't make any sense to Sarah, even less when she considered the anti-raccoon violence she had already witnessed earlier, but she still dutifully clapped along with the rest of the crowd when the song concluded. The other women crowded the pregnant one, clapping her on the shoulder and rubbing her belly, apparently their way of congratulating her. The girl in the sundress continued to gyrate and smack her tambourine as if she didn't notice that the song had ended. Her eyes drifted independent of each other.

"That was great," said Sarah. "I really like your song."

Miss Trix propped the guitar against her leg and nodded toward the pregnant woman. "I've been working on it for Aphrodite's birthing ceremony. Just the right harmony to welcome our new little sister. I wanted to write a song that would really empower her!"

"I think you really communicated that. I definitely got that out of it. Hey, I wanted to ask you, we were talking about the King's Breakfast earlier. Any chance I could see where you grow it?"

Miss Trix was quiet for a long moment. "Did Mother Moonflow say you could?"

"She said I was cool."

"I don't know that you're *that* cool. Sounds like you're being greedy for instant gratification. We don't show it to outsiders. Sisters only. Outsiders wouldn't understand."

"I'm a mycologist. I think I'd understand."

Miss Trix sneered. "You think it's like an ordinary mushroom. You don't understand. The King's Breakfast comes from the Lord of the Forest. It's dangerous if it touches a mind that's not ready. It takes years of study and meditation and theory before a sister is ready to know the secret of the King's Breakfast. You probably haven't even read *Shining Clitopia*."

"The source must stay pure," piped up Aphrodite suddenly from the audience. "Sisters only. It's the law."

Virginia Dentata was doing laundry in a washtub full of soapy water, beating a pile of wet clothes with a washing paddle and grunting dramatically with every swing, working up such a sheen of sweat that the peace sign on her chest practically glowed red. Sarah did not want to talk to this bitch, but she might know. Instead, she laughed in Sarah's face when she asked about the King's Breakfast.

"You gotta be kidding. That's not for outsiders. You don't even believe in the twenty mothers."

"You're not serious, right?" said Sarah. "You don't actually believe the baby has twenty mothers?"

Virginia Dentata paused, dropping her paddle. It hit the ground with a wet slap. "We didn't *literally* plant the seed, if that's what you mean. Of course we didn't *literally* do that. But what's a man put into his seed, anyway? His soul? No, he just cums and then he forgets about it. No man ever put as much of himself into his seed as we put of ourselves into the psychic vibrations that night. See, by attuning all our yonic energy to the rhythm of the Green Lady, we overrode whatever that man put into his seed. It doesn't matter who he was; his seed no longer contains his lineage. It contains our"—she motioned with her finger to indicate the collective around the temple—"chromosomes. That's where the sex is."

Sarah couldn't keep her mouth shut. Why couldn't she just keep her mouth shut?

"And you think you did that?" she said. "You really believe you willed your chromosomes into that baby?"

"Mother Moonflow herself led the ceremony," said Virginia Dentata, temper starting to flare. "It was a beautiful ceremony. I came, like, three times. Miss Trix came *four* times. What aren't *you* getting here? You don't think women are good enough to do that, huh?"

"I never said that," said Sarah.

What was she doing? Was she really going to come this far, survive this long, only to throw it all away by goading a backwoods freak into killing her? And for what...because she couldn't keep her mouth shut and let her believe her clearly delusional theory about mind-projecting DNA into a fetus by the sheer power of her feminine orgasm?

Virginia Dentata was in her face now, spittle foaming at the corners of her mouth. Sarah flashed back to the ranger at Las Brujas. Eerily familiar.

"You saying we can't change sex, but you think *you* can do it? Typical phallic alec."

"Those things," said Sarah, "are not the same at all."

Virginia Dentata snorted and picked up her paddle. Sarah tensed, but Virginia Dentata simply resumed her work hitting the clothes. SMACK. SMACK. SMACK. She brought down the paddle with unnecessary, ostentatious force, maintaining eye contact the entire time. SMACK.

"So the answer to your question, phallic alec, is NO. I'm not gonna show you where we grow the King's Breakfast. Keep your money. It ain't good around here."

Sarah thought it was churlish to complain about her accommodations, but when Pickles led her to the rusted skeleton of an old Volkswagen Microbus at the bottom of a gorge, teetering at the very lip of the forest, she had to say something.

"Really?"

"Sorry, no one warned us you were coming; this is the only free room that doesn't smell like raccoon piss. It's not so bad. Think of it like camping."

"I've already had my fill of camping."

"Look, sweetie," said Pickles. "It's this or literally camping. Take your pick."

The microbus was draped in moss, ferns sprouting from empty wheel sockets, and what little wasn't covered in vegetation was covered in graffiti—so much graffiti, layer upon layer, that it was just a rainbow mélange, although Sarah could still pick out the odd "FUCK THE PIGS" or "SATAN 666." The rear door was missing from its hinges, and the only furnishing inside was a lumpy mattress that dipped in the middle around a human-sized sweat stain. Sarah was just happy for some privacy so she could finally read through Doc Clopper's papers. "Fine, I'll take it."

"Good girl! When you hear a bell, that means that dinner's served in the big room. You're welcome to join us. Afterward is the birthing ceremony. Attendance is mandatory for that. Mother Moonflow's orders."

After he left, Sarah rifled through the map pockets on the backs of the seats and then through the glove box, where she found a mimeographed pamphlet stashed away like a hotel Bible. She scanned it briefly, but *Shining Clitopia: The Way of the Green Lady* mostly just contained impenetrable discourse:

> *Only the lesbian experiences total freedom of spirit, unbeholden to the demands of the earthbound phallus. The only pleasures derived from non-lesbian sex are those of the flesh, they do not nourish the soul. It is only through the sexual aspects that can only be known by women with women—the gentle touch, the loving word—that one can achieve elevation to a higher plane, a plane free of power disparity and miscommunication.*

The illustrations, obviously drawn by Mother Moonflow, were more interesting. They depicted the Green Lady, with her mushroom hat, and the Lord of the Forest, with his coral fungus antlers. The Green Lady did look somewhat like the goddess that Sarah had seen. The breasts were the right size, at least.

The Green Lady makes herself known to us through the sacrament of moonflow, dispensed by the great holy tit.

Sarah read that sentence several times, but her brain refused to accept it as anything other than figurative. She flipped the pamphlet this way and that, looking for anything else useful, but she ultimately tossed it aside and concentrated on the stolen medical file.

Name: Moonflow, Mother. Blood type: O+. Allergies: none. Living relatives— This last part had been blacked out with a Sharpie.

One page bore crude outlines of Mother Moonflow's body from front and side views, recognizable by the ridiculously gigantic breasts, with transparent plastic overlays of her circulatory, reproductive, and "yonic" systems. The yonic system was completely devoid of organs or glands, being mostly arrows showing the flow of "yonic energy" throughout Mother Moonflow's body, detailing how her magical boobs turned the masculine King's Breakfast into feminine moonflow.

Okay. So apparently that whole thing about the holy tits of moonflow wasn't a metaphor. This was a real thing that they believed.

"No, of course it's not real," muttered Sarah. "This is ridiculous. Criminy, these women know nothing about biology."

A fraying plastic card slipped from the stack of papers and clattered to the metal floor. When Sarah bent to retrieve it, she was surprised to see that it was an old state ID card with a photo. The photo showed the face of a woman who was instantly recognizable by her long black hair and crooked nose. The name on the ID card was not, however, "Mother Moonflow." That was not surprising. The name was "Diane Tibbitts."

"Tibbitts? No wonder she changed it."

Sarah pulled out her cell phone and attempted a quick Internet search for the name. Surely, there must be something—some digital trail to explain who this woman was or how she'd ended up here, in the woods, leading a cult—but she still couldn't get any reception.

The only thing that seemed to work at all was that glitch. She had only 20 percent power left; the phone's screen was already dimming as it put itself into power saver mode.

What the hell, thought Sarah, *it's worth a try.*

`>glitch do you know anything about mother moonflow? Or diane tibbitts?`

`>PROPHET OF THE GREEN LADY&&&&@@@`

"Yeah, I know that. She told me that herself! Do you have any information that you don't just get by spying on my conversations?"

`>WAKE&&&`

"Hey, whatcha doing in my van?" Skillet leered at her from the open door, chomping a peach and dribbling juice down her chin.

Sarah fumbled her phone and it dropped on the floor, but she was quick enough on the draw to think of an excuse. "Nothing! Just reading about Shining Clitopia."

Skillet tore a chunk of peach with her teeth, and a glop of combined saliva and peach flesh fell from her lips to the ground with a plop. "Oh, *that*. Good luck understanding any of that bullshit. Mother Moonflow likes pretty words. So Doc Clopper says you were askin' about me."

Sarah casually shoved the medical papers into the nearest map pocket. "Oh no, not like that—"

"It's okay. I don't mind. Maybe ol' Skillet's been thinking about you too. And I hear you've been going around, asking about the King's Breakfast. I don't think Mother Moonflow would approve of that, seeing as you ain't a sister. She's real protective of that. Then again... you're thinkin' about me, I'm thinkin' about you... Maybe we could work something out?"

"Like what?"

Skillet dropped the remnants of her peach, wiped her sticky hands across her denim-clad bottom, and climbed into the van. She flopped onto the mattress next to Sarah, so that their noses were almost touching. Sarah remembered Andy's words. Skillet couldn't be interested in her. It had to be a joke.

"You don't pick up on hints, do ya?" said Skillet.

Sarah had gone on three dates with Jade before she had the courage to ask if they were on a date. She wasn't used to anyone being this direct.

Skillet took Sarah's hand and ran a finger over the lines in her palm. "Look, there's gonna be a big party tonight, right after Aphrodite pops out her baby. Drugs, sex, food. All that good stuff. So tell you what... we'll trade. You do something for me, I'll do something for you. I show you where we grow the King's Breakfast, you come with me to the birthing ceremony. Like, together."

"Like a date?"

Skillet grinned and closed Sarah's palm with her other hand. Skillet's fingers were still sticky with peach residue. "Ha ha! That sounds so formal. I mean, it doesn't have to be a date. Maybe we're just two gals enjoying each other's company, huh? If you prefer that. What do you say?"

Sarah had not been asked on a date before. Neither had ever

asked the other out when it came to Jade. They just started hanging out, and eventually it seemed like they were in a rut without ever having formally passed through the "dating" phase.

She remembered Doc Clopper's warnings. But it felt so good to be desired.

"I think a date would be lovely. I would be happy to attend the birthing ceremony with you, Skillet."

"Cool, it's a deal!" Skillet seemed in no hurry; instead she pulled a withered joint from the watch pocket of her fraying denim shorts and held it up between her thumb and forefinger, as if to tempt Sarah. "We gotta kill a little time first. Wanna pregame?"

These women sure smoked *a lot* of weed. But a little one-on-one smoke sounded just fine.

"I wouldn't refuse."

Skillet pulled a butane lighter from her other pocket. She sparked it with a single flip, held it to the joint in her mouth until the cherry glowed, and then flung it away into the shadows. She sucked on the roach with a squealing gulp before passing it to Sarah. They lay on the mattress and looked out at the temple through a corroded hole in the roof. It looked so peaceful in the evening, silhouetted against the setting sun. Candles glowed behind the boarded-up windows, flickers faintly visible between cracks in the slats.

"Ya know, this is technically my van. Maybe someday I'll get it running again."

This van would definitely never run again.

"I come out here sometimes, when I need to be alone," continued Skillet. "Just to get away from all that religion an' stuff."

"Do you really believe all that religion? About the baby having twenty moms?"

Skillet shrugged. "Dunno. Everyone else does."

"What about the Green Lady? And the Lord of the Forest?"

"I don't like to think about that," said Skillet, visibly tensing. "I guess it makes sense, whatever. Ya know, male and female mushroom gods. I guess that makes sense."

"Not really. Most mushrooms are actually hermaphroditic."

Skillet laughed. "Ha ha! You son of a bitch, that's hilarious."

"What's the deal with Effervescent Bubbles?" asked Sarah suddenly. She hadn't seen Andy in hours. There was no way that he and Effervescent Bubbles were still talking about historical interpretation.

"You wouldn't want to be with her. She's damaged goods. Mormon. Grew up on a compound outside Salt Lake City. Child bride to an alderman."

"Shit, poor kid," said Sarah. "That's a hard life. Whatever, it's none of my business what she does. I guess she could do worse than Andy. He's an idiot. He means well, but he's got no common sense. I don't know how a guy like that survives."

"It's easy for guys to survive. They don't need smarts."

"Yeah, that's for damn sure." Sarah sighed, wiping her brow.

"Effervescent Bubbles ain't even that interesting," continued Skillet. "You should hear some of the other sisters' stories! Virginia Dentata used to belong to an autonomous womyn's collective llama farm up in the Dakotas. Miss Trix was a roadie for the Vegetable Lasagna Experience, back when they played Woodstock '99. Doc Clopper was a street medic during Occupy, you remember that? And the George Floyd protests. And she was part of the schism between the Universalists and the Exclusionists at BronyCon 4."

"What about Mother Moonflow?"

Skillet shrugged. "Who fucking cares. Thinks she can tell me what to do."

"You don't know anything about Mother Moonflow's background?"

"I know she started this temple. I know she's the prophet of the Green Lady. What else is there to know? Nothing I care about."

Sarah took a chance. "Have you ever heard the name Diane Tibbitts?"

"Nope. Never heard of her."

The loud ringing of a bell signaled dinnertime, calling the sisters back to the temple.

"That's our cue." Skillet sat up, stubbing the joint against the wall. "C'mon, let's go see the King's Breakfast. Trust me, you're gonna love this. There ain't nothing like it!"

"Shouldn't we go to dinner?"

"Do you want to see the King's Breakfast or not?"

"Yeah, of course!"

"Cool. Follow me, then."

Skillet hopped out of the van, and Sarah followed, all thoughts of Diane Tibbitts forgotten.

17.

Lesbian sex remains the truest form of connection between humans, beautiful in its deep intimacy and mutual trust. The orgasm is an added benefit but far from the objective—pure love is the real goal. This alone is incomprehensible to non-lesbians, who practice lesser forms of love which can only manifest on a physical level without the deeper spiritual possibilities of lesbian love. This is also why the mainstream media never correctly portrays lesbian sex, because it can only imagine the violence and coercion of penetration.

—Shining Clitopia: The Way of the Green Lady
(mimeographed pamphlet, date and author unknown)

Diane, the younger daughter of the Tibbitts family, used to draw her as far back as she could remember. Throughout her childhood, that scribbled green figure appeared in all her art, sometimes hiding in the background, sometimes taking center stage. Her parents, who had little interest in art, didn't care, but Diane's older sister, Emma, recognized in Diane a talent and encouraged her as a big sister should. Diane didn't know a name for the green figure, but she could sense her, feel her lurking on the other side of some thin veil that separated the two of them. Sometimes, as she aged, she thought of the green figure as a guardian angel, sometimes as the spirit of womanhood itself. And sometimes she liked to fantasize that she was the green figure, full of all the green figure's power and rage.

When she was seventeen, Diane had long straight black hair and big tits that made men ogle her. She also had a crooked nose, and she knew she had a crooked nose because her father, every one of her ex-boyfriends, and several of the artists she ended up rooming with after high school had all independently commented on that aspect, and she knew there was no way they could have coordinated that. That might have made some girls cry, Diane told herself, but not her. Diane never cried. Her father didn't care when she dropped out of high school senior year. He agreed with Diane that school wasn't helping her. But Diane thought it was pointless because she was going to be an artist; her father thought it was pointless because the main purpose of a girl's education was the chance to snag a husband. He liked to brag about how Emma had given up on that whole silly nursing career idea after Chet proposed. Diane couldn't stand her father's blowhard pontificating, so she left. Berkeley was where the artists were. She worked in a record store and supplemented her income by selling her paintings to tourists on the corner of Telegraph Avenue and Channing Way, and that was usually enough to pay her share of the rent for a studio apartment above a crystal store. She burned sage in honor of the goddess in all her forms: Hecate, Demeter, Bast. She shared the apartment with other artists, all men, but she felt among her own there. The other artists often brought girls home, mostly models who would pose nude for portraits that inevitably looked awful but that the artists claimed were avant-garde, and those girls would usually end up crying at some point—usually over some triviality, like when the artists revealed that they didn't believe in traditional monogamy. The models, who always claimed to be very hip and mod when they first arrived at the threshold of the Telegraph Avenue apartment that served as the collective's studio, would always suddenly become very conservative. Afterward, when the models had left cursing them in between sobs, the artists would turn to Diane and say, with honest confusion in their voices, "I just don't get these birds" and "They're not like you, of course—you're groovy. You're not like other women. You get it."

Diane did get it, and she silently decided those models were stupid to not get it. The men were not complicated, and it was embarrassing that women should fall for their wiles. Women, who were more levelheaded and intelligent, should rightfully run this world if only they didn't allow themselves to be ruled by the men. It was infuriating.

Those other women thought they could rely on their beauty and their tears to get what they wanted, but they were inevitably disappointed. Diane congratulated herself on being smarter than the other women, so smart that she was almost the equal of a man. In another life, if she'd been born different, she surely would have been the leader of them all. But the honest truth was that she could easily resist the artists because none of them appealed to her. They were all dirty Bohemians, constantly stoned and rarely bathed, and their art was mediocre at best. The walls of the studio were cluttered with dozens of interchangeable pastel images of sad-eyed waifs and the occasional caricature of Richard Nixon in the "Keep on Truckin'" pose.

Diane's paintings were much deeper—they were personal

cries of rage. They were empowering. She channeled the feminine mystique into her work—paintings of Hecate, Demeter, and Bast. By all rights, her work should be on the walls, but the other artists always found excuses why she should give up the space that was rightfully hers. They had lots of excuses, but Diane knew that it was because she was a woman. It was just not fair.

There was one artist, though, who respected her, not just as a "woman who was not like other women" but as an artist. His name was Wilder, and Diane thought that was a beautiful name, so natural and exotic, recalling the lush woods and grassy meadows and the antlered god of the male aspect, although after the incident, she always referred to him in her mind as simply the Pig. He had brown hair the color of the wet seashore, and he wore his peasant blouse open to the navel to show off the delicious curls of dark hair across his chest. He loved his mother and spoke of her often, how she inspired him to love women and treat all women like mothers, and Diane believed him because his voice was soft yet rough, gentle yet manly, and it gave every word he said the exquisite ring of truth. He had that easy male confidence that made people want to listen to him, so that no one would ever think to object when he pulled out his guitar for an impromptu sing-along, and everyone agreed when he suggested they spend the communal food budget on lentils and granola. Diane was jealous; that kind of power would have been her birthright, if only she hadn't been born a soft, useless woman. Wilder wore flowers in his hair, and sometimes, after he'd finished strumming a cover of "Blowin' in the Wind" or "Time of the Season," he would braid flowers into her hair too. He bragged about his sexual prowess, but not in a crude way. That made some of the models giggle when they were all collected together for a Be-In, but Diane reacted dismissively—which was probably why he found her so intriguing. He was an artist as well, although Diane felt that his ornate still lifes were derivative of the Arts and Crafts movement, but he appreciated her own paintings as no one else in the collective did.

"These are good," said Wilder when he looked at her work. "You're really good. It really captures the true essence of femininity." He pointed at the green woman with her long leafy hair and her parted green lips. "Who's this figure represent? Gaia?"

Diane shrugged. "No, she's... she's hard to explain. She's womanhood. She's the goddess."

"Far out. I dig it."

Diane truly believed that he did.

He pointed to a sigil in the corner. "What's this mean?"

"That's nothing. That's just my signature."

Wilder was smarter than the other artists, and he could immediately suss out that it was more than a signature. "It's more than that. I can tell this means something profound." He looked at her with sad eyes, like he was asking her permission to know. No man had asked her permission for anything before. The sense of accomplishment was intoxicating. "Can you tell me what it means?"

"It represents my connection to the divine feminine, through the phases of the moon. It means Moonflow."

"Moonflow." Wilder said it as if testing out how the word felt on his tongue. "That's real groovy. A beautiful name for a beautiful woman."

Diane was too smart to fall for that line. "I'm not beautiful."

"All women are beautiful," he said. "It's cuz you're expressing the true essence of woman just by being. It's a power—and no man can touch it. That's why men are so jealous; that's why they keep you down, they try to stamp it out. But I can sense that strength in you because you are a true woman, Moonflow."

Before that moment, no one had used the name she had secretly given herself. When Wilder said it, she might have almost believed it was true—that a man could be jealous of a woman.

It was on a retreat to a distant forest, when the artists did plein air painting among the trees and took drugs to open their minds to the artistic possibilities of nature, that Diane found herself alone with him in the cellar of the old sawmill that now served as a rustic artists' sanctuary. He produced a quorum of exotic mushrooms and fed them to her, lovingly, his fingers so gentle, and she ate them willingly. She believed that he understood her art, understood her, and that was the only reason that she let her guard down and allowed him to take her, to have her, to pleasure her, and they made love. It was the most wonderful experience in her life so far. She could tell he had very powerful seed, as powerful as he was. She touched something sacred, something that she could never possess, and when he came in her, she saw visions.

She saw the Lord of the Forest in all his fullness, the mushroom god properly attired with his branching coral fungus antlers and his always erect, always dribbling phallus. Great mats of fuzzy green moss grew down his spine, fat toadstools sprouted from his shoulders, saucers of brown-and-yellow bracket fungus blossomed from his thighs, and whorls of blue lichen crisscrossed the fish belly–white skin of his chest. When he walked, his dick flopped heavily between long, long legs. His face was not like the face of a man.

Wilder held her face between his hands even as his countenance flickered between man and god. He ran his fingers through her long, long hair and said, "I can feel that strength in you, Moonflow." It was cheesy, and even at the time she knew it was just a line, but it made her cry. Those tears were the first and last that she ever shed.

Her period was late that month. She woke up feeling nauseous. She could tell the signs, and she was furious because she was smarter than that. When she confronted Wilder, he just seemed annoyed that she had interrupted his painting with such a triviality. "How do you know it's mine?"

Diane didn't cry then. She wouldn't. "What am I supposed to do?"

The Pig shrugged, barely turning from his canvas. "You're a groovy chick. I'm sure you'll figure it out."

"I'll tell your mother."

The Pig started to cry. "How could you," he sobbed. "How could you. That would break her heart!"

That was the first time she understood all those dumb models, understood what they were going through, felt their shame. *They were my sisters this whole time*, she thought. *They were my sisters and I never even realized it.* She left the studio after that and she did not return. She had some dignity, after all.

She prayed for deliverance to all the goddesses—Hecate, Demeter, Bast—but they were powerless in the face of a man's negligence. The men were too strong. *We need a place away from them*, she decided. Only then would she be free.

But even now, she remembered the vision she had received in the Pamogo woods, remembered the electricity that had coursed through her as she felt the Lord of the Forest enter her. More than anything, she longed to feel that again, and she was determined that she would.

She needed the mushrooms, so later, she returned to the old

mill in the woods, to the cellar where it all happened, and there, in the deep-down dirt, she planted the first spores and waited for the new world to be born. This was where she would live, away from the men, away from their draining demands and their grasping needs. She would live in the dream world of the King's Breakfast, and she would never come down again.

18.

*Hell's Courtesan (*Russula jezebelus*) is a white mushroom covered in large black spots, often forming a death's head pattern upon its broad, sloped cap. It is said to taste of grave dirt.*

—Field Guide to Common Mushrooms of the Pamogo Forest, *T. F. Greengarb (1978)*

The temple was trimmed in flower garlands and wired-up speakers, and torches were lined around the perimeter of the clearing, all in preparation for the birthing ceremony. But the sisters had all answered the summons to dinner, so no one remained to impede Skillet and Sarah as they crossed the clearing.

Sarah could feel eyes watching her from behind the sealed-over windows in the temple. Two figures stood on the temple roof, silhouetted against the last rays of the dying sun. They were probably just keeping watch; that was probably a normal thing that you had to do when you lived in an abandoned sawmill in the middle of a forest. But were they meant to keep guard against external threats, or were they there to keep everyone in line? What would happen right now if Sarah made a run for it?

If she just bolted for the tree line? Did they have guns up there? Could they just blast her through the head at any moment?

Skillet approached the vagina door and tapped lightly. No response.

"Almost there! I'm really not supposed to do this," said Skillet. A feral grin spread across her face and she opened the vagina door, revealing an infinite black void. A patchouli miasma billowed out, so thick and cloying that Sarah nearly choked on it.

"Where are you taking me?" asked Sarah. But Skillet didn't answer; she was already inside.

This can't be right, Sarah thought, panic rising in her gut. She wanted to turn and run, but she couldn't run and it didn't matter, because suddenly there was no place to run to. The world was gone; there was nothing but darkness, nothing but darkness and that door. She moved through the door.

For a second, she thought there was someone in the room. No, of course not, none of that was happening. It was just a trick of the light, the undulating shadows thrown by the last few candle stubs still burning. The sanctuary was exactly the same as earlier: the same piles of boho pillows and Persian carpets, the same patchouli-burning censers, the same vague raccoon reek, and right there, in the epicenter of the room, Mother Moonflow, same as before.

Mother Moonflow turned to look at them with pure white eyes. Sarah flinched back.

"Don't bother her," whispered Skillet. "She's deep in trance."

Now that Sarah looked closer, she could see that Mother Moonflow's head lolled drunkenly on her neck. Her mouth hung open, long ropes of drool dangling from her lips, and her eyes were rolled so far back into her head that red veins laced the white sclera. She was leaking from her nipples, and a raccoon sat at her feet, lapping at the resulting puddle. Other raccoons moved under the piles of blankets like sharks under a sea.

"She's always peaking during dinner. We'll be out of here before she comes down." Skillet made a beeline for the waist-high door and grappled with the lock on the rusty dead bolt.

Sarah stepped carefully around the periphery of the room, staying out of Moonflow's reach, in case the woman suddenly revived and grabbed at her ankles.

"You sure about this? Are we supposed to be here?"

"Nope!" said Skillet cheerfully. "No one's supposed to mess with the King's Breakfast, not before it's feminized. Beyond this door, the Lord of the Forest holds sway. You're gonna love it! All the sisters love it. Except the Hell Slut, she's really not too keen."

Sarah kept her eyes on Mother Moonflow. "Can she see us?"

"Naw, reality doesn't exist for her right now. Besides, if she remembers us, she'll just think we're hallucinations. She's so stupid she doesn't think anyone could figure out her whole routine." Skillet giggled.

Then she said, oh so casually, "So you got anyone back home? Boyfriend?" Then, more hopefully: "Girlfriend?"

"No." Sarah kept her eyes on Mother Moonflow. The comatose woman twitched sporadically in her trance, sending ripples through her giant breasts like waves through a quiet ocean. "The closest thing I have to a relationship is talking to a phone glitch. Don't ask. Jade and I broke up..." She struggled to do the math in her head. "Six months ago, I think?"

"Six months, huh? Sucks. So what happened? Problems in the bedroom, ha ha?" Skillet jammed a hairpin into the lock and twisted, then rattled the door. It did not budge.

Christ, this goblin had no decorum at all. "That's kind of a personal question, don't you think?"

"Is it?" Skillet giggled and shrugged. She slapped futilely at the dead bolt.

Sarah paused. After this was all over, she would probably never see Skillet again in her life. "No. No, it wasn't that. Not really. It was stupid. So Herman—he's my cat—he was sneezing for days, he just couldn't stop, so I made a vet appointment and it turned out I had to meet with Madeleine that day. So I asked Jade if she could take him and she said, 'I can't do that, I have a reception later on. Couldn't you ask someone else?'"

Skillet nodded, waiting for more. Sarah didn't say more.

"What, that's it?" said Skillet. She looked up from her lock-pick work.

"Yeah."

"And did she have a reception?"

"Yeah."

"Then why didn't you just ask someone else?" Skillet was still smiling, but the subtle furrow of her eyebrows gave away her confusion.

"I don't know," said Sarah. She kept watch on Mother Moonflow, who was obliviously blowing bubbles with her spittle. The raccoon rolled onto its back, chattering and waving its stubby legs drunkenly.

Why hadn't she just asked someone else? It was perfectly reasonable for Jade to do her reception; there was no reason that Sarah should expect her to skip it to take Herman to the vet. Herman was her cat, after all, right? Jade was always reasonable. How could she explain it? How could she explain how much she hated having to always go to Madeleine or to Damon or to whomever, hat in hand, to ask for favors that they would always grant but always with that sad pitying expression that clearly asked, *Why isn't your girlfriend doing this instead? Doesn't she love you?*

And apparently that stupid vet appointment was the final straw, the thing that finally pushed her to tank her whole relationship and her whole life.

Skillet giggled madly, struggling to contain her laughter. Mother Moonflow slumped forward without warning, plopping her forehead against the pillow of her breasts.

"Ha ha! You're stupid, Sarah. You're so stupid! What are you, a dumbass?"

"Yeah. I guess." Sarah felt like an idiot. Words were coming out of her that probably shouldn't. *Yes, problems in the bedroom. That sounds like a less stupid reason to break up. Let's go with that.* "Also, yeah, bedroom problems. She liked sex, but for her, it's just a thing you do. She could do it with anyone. It didn't have to be me."

Skillet's laughter abruptly stopped. "Shit, I'm sorry, I shouldn't laugh. Now that ain't funny." Skillet left her work to pat Sarah on the shoulder, a pat that turned into a rub. Skillet kept massaging, but she didn't say anything. She stroked Sarah's hair. Sarah did not object.

"I get that. You wanna be wanted, don't you?"

Sarah thought about the goddess at Madeleine's party, about those kindly hands reaching out for her and about how she wished she could reach back.

"Yeah," said Sarah. Her voice creaked a little. "Yeah. See? You understand!"

"You musta been awfully lonely." Now Skillet nibbled at Sarah's shoulder. She moved her other hand under Sarah's double chin and tilted her head back, turning Sarah around to face her.

Sarah shook her head and hissed, "Mother Moonflow is sitting right there!"

"I don't care."

"We'll be caught!"

"I don't care."

This was so unfair. Finally—finally!—someone wanted her, and it turned out to be a freak in a cult out in the middle of the woods. Figures it would be the biggest freak on Earth who would actually want her. But this wasn't safe, Sarah knew. These Green Lady sisters were too much into the whole *womyn* thing. Seemed dangerously terfy, to be honest, even if Skillet knew what she was, what she had between her legs. And, yeah, sure, they hadn't killed her *yet*. But there was always a *yet*.

A gentle knock at the door.

"Oh shit," hissed Skillet. She dropped like a sack of potatoes, pulling Sarah to the floor. "Lie still, don't move."

The door creaked open and Pickles slunk inside, carrying a shallow bowl of liquid. He swore under his breath and kicked the drunk raccoon; it chattered and rolled over, snapping at his toes before it lurched uncertainly back into the surrounding piles of blankets. Pickles placed the bowl on the futon next to Mother Moonflow and bowed low before her.

"Your dinner, Mother Moonflow. It's soup tonight."

Mother Moonflow did not respond. She was still leaning forward, her long hair pouring over her face and breasts, obscuring her features.

Sarah hardly dared breathe. In the dim light, she could barely make out Pickles's shape; his black house robe billowed when he bowed, like the wings of a big black bat. But even more distracting, she could feel Skillet lying on top of her, feel the warmth of her little froggy body, feel the thumping of her little heart.

Pickles continued: "We had absences tonight. Skillet and her phallic alec were missing; so were Effervescent Bubbles and her phallic alec. I hate to think what they were all getting up to."

Mother Moonflow gurgled and petted the top of Pickles's head, playing with his split ends. His words must have penetrated her trance, because she momentarily returned to Earth and said, in slurred words, "Baby, you could be a rock star with this hair."

Pickles gasped and bowed even lower. "Thank you, Mother Moonflow! Oh thank you! I will never forget that you said this! I will never forget! I promise!"

Mother Moonflow burbled in idiot bliss, her mind returning again to the ether, while Pickles kissed her toes and babbled words of gratitude. It was extremely embarrassing to witness. It reminded Sarah uncomfortably of her relationship with Madeleine before she came out.

At length, Pickles rose from the ground, wiped his eyes, adjusted his robe, and then frowned, his eyes falling upon the small door in the corner. Something attracted his attention. He padded toward it, gingerly picking his way through the pillows, and Sarah, beneath Skillet, couldn't hold in a terrified little gasp as he passed close to them and the trail of his robe slithered over their outstretched feet. But if Pickles heard anything, he must have believed it was coming from the raccoons prowling the edges of the room, because he did not pause. He moved to the door and briefly inspected the lock, touching the place where Skillet's machinations had caused some of the rust to flake off. Perhaps he expected the lock to bear some revelation. But it didn't, so eventually he backed out of the room, closing the door behind him.

19.

Two more men missing. The Irishmen are quick to abandon their work from fear of goblins & bogeymen. The Chinamen are likewise under the thrall of unchristian superstitions, but their native industriousness binds them to their work regardless. Eastern wall collapses, wood is rotten.

—*Diary of Lazarus Sloane*
(California State Parks Archives)

The Frog Sisters returned with supplies—two bottles of alcohol—and the Hell Slut swigged vodka as they dumped isopropyl alcohol over the wound. It stung like hell, so much so the Hell Slut had to grind her teeth to dust to avoid howling out loud. Sunny Delight tied a bath towel into a makeshift tourniquet, but it was already soaked with blood. Doc Clopper would probably read them the riot act for doing it wrong, but what other choice did they have?

Afterward, Sunny Delight and the Hell Slut sat in the wreckage of the kitchen, huddled together in the doorway of the open refrigerator, which hummed as it cooled the entire room. Sunny Delight was finally starting to come down from her moonflow high, and the Hell Slut was just starting to be drunk enough to function again. The Frog Sisters were making out, which they did occasionally when they were bored.

"How'd you learn to treat bullet wounds, anyway?" The Hell Slut tilted the vodka bottle back again, sucking the dregs. She was more than tipsy, but the liquor was keeping the pain at bay.

"My friend Jackie got stabbed by a john once."

"Sorry to hear that. She okay?"

"No, not really." Sunny Delight frowned and changed the subject. "I'm sorry I didn't listen to you. I thought the Green Lady was talking to me, I really did. And I…I was afraid you might need help." Her eyes strayed over to the fresh corpse splayed across the living room floor and arranged so she could just see the smashed head from her vantage point.

"Listen, Sunny D, don't go around saying that you saw the Green Lady. That won't go over well."

"But—"

"The Green Lady only reveals herself to Mother Moonflow. Mother Moonflow is her chosen prophet."

"You've never seen her?"

The Hell Slut shook her head. Of course the Hell Slut had never seen her. The Green Lady was the truest embodiment of the divine feminine; why would she ever choose to show herself to a creature like the Hell Slut? But the Hell Slut felt a little prickle of jealousy that Sunny Delight had seen her. That wasn't fair.

"What was she like?"

"She was beautiful. A beautiful glowing presence. Soft and warm, like a mother." She looked over at the body of Hal Sampson, the bloody reality intruding on her fantasy.

"You're lucky you saw her—that's a real honor." The Hell Slut was woozy from alcohol and blood loss, but she staggered to her feet with some assistance from Sunny Delight. "We gotta leave."

"You're in no condition for that!"

"Too bad. We can't stay here." She motioned for the Frog Sisters to follow, and she stumbled back to the living room, her boots squelching in the blood-soaked carpet.

Donna Sampson was still sitting on the floor where they had left her. She was shrieking and wailing and praying and would not shut up.

"What are we gonna do about her?" asked the Frog Sisters.

"Shit. I guess I better talk to her." The Hell Slut looked down at Donna and cleared her throat. "Okay, listen, Donna, we don't got a beef with you. This isn't personal. Now I want you to turn your head, okay? You're not gonna move, do you understand?"

Donna Sampson was used to obedience, so she turned her head and exposed her neck, so delicate and slight, so easy to snap. She squeezed her eyes shut and a whimper escaped her throat, like she knew what was coming. The Hell Slut inhaled a deep lungful of air, bracing herself for what she needed to do. She was the Hell Slut and she did what needed doing. She had to do it. There couldn't be any witnesses. There wasn't any other choice.

"You're not actually gonna do anything, are you?" Sunny Delight's voice, high and shrill, broke through the cloud of her thoughts.

"Sunny D, I wish you'd stayed in the car like I told you to—"

"You can't do this! She should come with us! She's a woman—she deserves the choice! She could be a sister!"

The Hell Slut snorted. "She's too far gone. She's too used to living under the sway of men. She wouldn't want to come with us."

"She deserves the choice!" said Sunny Delight hotly. "Is that what you thought about me? Was I too far gone?"

"No, that was different..."

"Let me talk to her!"

Sunny Delight shoved the Hell Slut aside and squatted down next to the blubbering woman, so that they were eye to eye. "Donna?"

Donna again looked up with watery brown eyes.

"Hi, let me introduce myself. I'm Sunny Delight! And this is the Hell Slut and these are the Frog Sisters."

Donna nodded dumbly.

"I am so excited for you today! You're about to receive a wonderful gift—the gift of sisterhood! I know it might be confusing at first, but you have to understand. The Green Lady called us to visit you and free you from the shackles of patriarchy! Now she's calling you to come with us. Haven't you ever wanted to escape from the men? It was hard to accept when the Green Lady first called to me. I used to be a whore down in San Francisco, letting the men take me for their pleasure. But when I came to know the Green Lady and accept the plan that she has for us, for all women... then I knew that I wasn't just created for the men to use. I'm so much more! And so are you! Won't you come with us? You can start a new life, the life you were meant to live." She looked to the Hell Slut. "She can come with us, right? If she wants to?"

Damn, this girl picks things up fast, thought the Hell Slut. *That was even better than Skillet.*

"Yeah, if she wants to."

Sunny Delight offered a hand. Incredibly, Donna Sampson nodded and accepted it. Sunny Delight squealed in excitement as she helped Donna to her feet. Donna was too stunned to react when Sunny Delight threw her arms around her in a bear hug.

"We've got a new sister!" crowed Sunny Delight. Donna didn't hug back, her hands hovering, stunned, in the air and her eyes staring blankly at nothing.

"That's great," said the Hell Slut. "Let's get the hell out of here. Check the coast."

The Frog Sisters peeked out the front door and nodded back at her. The Hell Slut grabbed Hal Sampson's body by the scruff of his thick cop neck and dragged him across the living room, paused to nod at the whimpering Donna, and then lugged the corpse out the door after the Frog Sisters. Sunny Delight followed, leading the placid Donna. As they loped down the flagstones, the Hell Slut looked at the cruiser in the driveway and noticed, for the first time, that the logo on the side wasn't that of any city police force. It was a humpbacked bear on a yellow field enclosed within a blue circle: California State Parks. Hal Sampson was a ranger.

Whatever. No time to worry about that now—they needed to get out of here before anyone saw them. The Hell Slut could only imagine the orgy of carnage that would ensue if that cop mob up the block got a whiff of this bloodshed. The Hell Slut popped the trunk and used all her strength to make Hal Sampson's folded body fit. He would make a fine fertilizer. She slammed the trunk shut and scanned the horizon. All the houses in the cul-de-sac were dark.

Sunny Delight sat behind the Sturgeon's wheel, sobbing in big hiccuping gulps as the enormity of their crimes hit her. The Hell Slut slid in next to her and touched her shoulder. "Sunny D. Not now. Please."

Sunny Delight nodded, snorting loudly as she bit back more embarrassing tears, threw the Sturgeon into drive, and pumped the gas. The car lurched away from the curb, awkwardly circled the cul-de-sac, farted its way back down Wisteria Drive to the corner, hung a left, and sailed right past the still-hopping cop mob up the block.

"Maintain speed," said the Hell Slut. "Don't slow down. Don't speed up."

Sunny Delight's foot jittered on the gas pedal, and the Sturgeon drifted in fits and starts past the most dangerous thing in the world. It was dark inside the car, but the Hell Slut could see the tears on Sunny Delight's face glistening in the anemic light thrown by the streetlamps.

"It's okay. It's okay. You're doing great. You're doing so good."

Sunny Delight nodded curtly. She was terrified, trembling like a leaf. The silhouette of her little froggy body reminded the Hell Slut of Skillet. My God. How could this girl be so like and so unlike Skillet? Sunny Delight had come with her on this trip because she... because she wanted to be with the Hell Slut, wanted to experience this with the Hell Slut, because this was what the Hell Slut experienced. Despite everything that had happened tonight, Sunny Delight did not appear to be horny at all. That was another big difference from Skillet.

"Keep going. Just keep driving. We're good. We're good."

The car kept going. Then, all at once, Donna Sampson kicked the door open and threw herself from the car, screaming as she hit the asphalt. The cops perked up at the sound. The Punisher pointed, and several cops loped toward Donna's tumbling body.

"Shit, shit! Hit the gas! Fast!" yelled the Hell Slut. Sunny Delight slammed her shaking foot down, and the car lurched up to speed as they rounded the curb and the cop party disappeared behind another row of identical white bungalows.

The Hell Slut glanced at the rearview mirror just as the scene vanished around the bend. There was a beat. Then she saw the cops turning the corner behind them, a whole phalanx of them.

Sunny Delight spun her face toward the Hell Slut, abject fear pouring over her features. "What is it?! What is it?!"

"Fucking Donna Sampson! She ratted us out!"

"We told you," said the Frog Sisters. "We told you."

"What's going to happen?!" cried Sunny Delight.

"Nothing, nothing, just keep going."

In the rearview mirror, the Hell Slut watched the lead cop, the one in the Punisher shirt, throw back his head and call. The bellow reverberated through the Sturgeon's Detroit steel frame, and the Frog Sisters bounced up and down on the rattling bench seat. The wheel vibrated under Sunny Delight's hands like chattering teeth. Blue lights flashed on in houses on both sides of the street.

"Shit. Buckle up, kids," said the Hell Slut, reaching across the console and grabbing hold of the wheel with her left hand. Her head was woozy with alcohol and moonflow, but she needed to concentrate. "I'll take the wheel, you hit the gas. Floor it, I'll do the rest!"

Sunny Delight released the wheel like it was on fire, and stomped obediently on the pedal. The Sturgeon kicked into gear. They had to move fast, but this was a residential neighborhood and the cops had speed bumps every ten feet to keep their prey slow. The car hit a bump, and the Frog Sisters nearly hit the ceiling. Behind them, cops were loping down the center of the street, baying for blood, all paws and claws. More and more of them were pouring out of houses on either side.

Thank the fuckin' Green Lady the cops ain't driving, thought the Hell Slut, spinning the wheel as the Sturgeon careened over the curb and around the corner on two wheels. *Then we'd really be toast.* But no, in all the excitement, the cops didn't think to jump into their cars; they were hunting on foot. The Sturgeon lumbered out in front of the pack, like a wounded elk, but cops were closing in from all sides now. *Shit shit shit.* The Hell Slut saw the end ahead, where the through road reconnected with the main drag. But the cops had it all planned out—there was a whole row of them blocking the exit like dragon's teeth. Now, one cop? The Sturgeon could knock him down like nothing. But a whole line of cops, standing arm in arm across the road? Shit, might as well just plow right into a brick wall.

The Frog Sisters were whispering among themselves.

The Hell Slut spun the wheel, and the car slid around a corner, as smooth as butter. *Any god listening, let this not be a dead end.* Any god listening had a real sick sense of humor, though, cuz right there in the middle of the street, a gaggle of cop kids was trying to pull the legs off a stray cat. They looked up and started squealing.

"Gas! Gas!" shouted the Hell Slut as she pulled the wheel and hunched in her seat. "Everyone, duck down!" The Sturgeon bucked as it plowed through the crowd. The cat went flying over the hood, spitting and yowling, and reappeared moments later in the Sturgeon's rearview mirror. It landed gracefully on its feet and bolted into the dark as a barrage of bullets descended on the car.

The Frog Sisters sat up. A bullet pierced the rear window, which spiderwebbed into cracks immediately, and passed through the head of a Frog Sister before exiting through the windshield and away into the night. The Frog Sister with the broken head slumped forward, spraying a crimson arc of gore in her wake; the remaining Frog Sister said nothing, since—without her sister—she no longer had anyone to say things in unison with, but she immediately threw up her grilled cheese. The Hell Slut cursed, Sunny Delight screamed through tears but kept her foot down, and the Sturgeon plowed over the curb, tires bucking and more cop kids scattering like bowling pins. The car glanced off a Little Free Library designed to look like a birdhouse; it exploded into a maelstrom of Bibles and self-help books. A hailstorm of bullets descended on the car, but the Sturgeon's armored Detroit steel chassis repelled the bulk of them; one bullet hit at just the right angle to crack the valance window and skim the back seat, perforating the head of the remaining Frog Sister. She slumped over her departed twin, brains spilling to the floor.

The steering wheel spun out of the Hell Slut's hand, and the car flew across a cop lawn in three bounces. And this cop, get this, this cop was the one cop in the whole world who didn't have a neat little manicured lawn—he had a tree, a goddamn Japanese maple, right there in the middle of the green and right there in the middle of the Sturgeon's path.

The Sturgeon hit the tree with a crunch that threw the Hell Slut against the dash so hard her nose exploded again. The Hell Slut howled and tasted coppery blood in her mouth. The rear-view mirror was cracked and askew, but when she looked, she could see the cop horde rushing in on them.

The Punisher leaped onto the Sturgeon with a victory screech, his weight denting the roof. Another cop tore at the door, too frenzied to pause long enough to understand how to work the handle. More cops were closing in, guns drawn, barking orders. The cop kids circled, waiting for the adults to eat their fill so they could move in for scraps.

"They're all around us!" cried Sunny Delight. The Hell Slut looked at her through a haze of blood. A dark red drop dangled from her eyebrow, and she watched it fall. "What do we do? We're out of options!"

"Sorry, kid," said the Hell Slut. She put her fingers to her nose and felt the blood, warm and sticky. "This is it. End of the line."

"N-no," said Sunny Delight, shuddering. If she had known better, she would have realized the utter hopelessness of the situation. But Sunny Delight didn't know better. She slammed the Sturgeon into reverse and hit the gas. The Hell Slut had forgotten one very important detail: The Sturgeon was an all-American classic, two and a half tons of chrome and steel, designed by proud American engineers to take a beating and built by proud American teamsters before car manufacturing became the exclusive domain of foreign homosexuals, and as such, the Sturgeon could not be killed by any tree grown of seed. Tires spun, flinging grass and mud into the air, and the Sturgeon disengaged from the maple. The Punisher went flying as the Sturgeon rocketed backward, and the Hell Slut watched as several other approaching cops stopped and turned tail just a split second too late to avoid going under the Sturgeon's tires. The car bucked and the cops crunched underfoot, while the corpses in the back seat slithered back and forth on a tide of blood and vomit.

"Holy shit! It's working! Keep going! Don't stop!"

The cops screeched in bewildered rage. The Sturgeon rolled backward down the block at full speed, did a doughnut at the junction, and pinballed across Gardenia Way and back toward the freeway entrance.

"Don't go up the ramp!" yelled the Hell Slut. "It's gonna be crawling with cops by now."

"Then what do I do?!"

"Hold on," cried the Hell Slut. "Keep going! Don't stop!" She pumped the reclining lever and the seat dropped back; the Hell Slut wriggled into the back seat and kicked the door open. "Spin the wheel, spin it!"

Sunny Delight rolled the wheel and the car turned sideways.

"Sorry, gals." The Hell Slut shoved the first Frog Sister out.

The body tumbled wildly, spraying blood and brains, and bowled into the line of advancing cops. The Hell Slut kicked out the second Frog Sister corpse and watched it spin into the fray before she slammed the door shut. Sunny Delight twirled the car into reverse, and the Sturgeon blasted toward the human barricade that signaled the boundaries of cop town.

The line of cops, momentarily relaxed when the Sturgeon vanished from view, reconsolidated; the cops hunkered together, shoulder to shoulder, like a single massive mile-long crustacean shrugging into its armor. Sunny Delight did not hesitate and the Sturgeon smashed into them at full tilt, crumpling the rear like an aluminum can and forcing the trunk to pop open and smash against the shattered rear window. The car lurched as a tire blew and the line broke. Cops churned underneath, and the Sturgeon spun into the open street.

"Brakes! Brakes! Under the ramp, under the ramp!" shouted the Hell Slut, grabbing the wheel and jerking hard. There was a parking lot under the freeway. The Sturgeon slid over the curb and twirled in circles, remaining tires screeching, rubber burning, until it skidded to a stop in the shadows behind the on-ramp. The Hell Slut slapped the headlights off and twisted the key to kill the engine. The Sturgeon died with a long, drawn-out groan.

Sunny Delight was hysterical, her pupils pinpricks of insanity in her bulging eyes, her face streaked with sweat. "They're gonna find us! They're cops!"

"Shh. That's exactly right. They're cops. Shh."

They sat in the darkness and waited, the only sound their haggard breathing. Long moments passed, and then a parade of cop cars poured out of cop town, lights flashing, sirens blaring, and, one by one, flew up the ramp and onto the freeway. The Hell Slut released a breath she hadn't realized she was holding and felt the tension instantly drain from her body. It worked. Holy hell, it actually worked.

"Heh. I knew it. Fuckin' dumbass cops."

The Hell Slut turned to Sunny Delight with a grin, but Sunny Delight was trembling, her eyes wide and her mind far away. "Oh my God. Oh my God," she mumbled, new tears spilling down her face. "I'm sorry, I'm sorry, I'm sorry... I killed the Frog Sisters, oh God..."

The Hell Slut was silent. This was all messed up. She'd never lost anyone on assignment before. The poor Frog Sisters. RIP. There wasn't time to mourn now, so the Hell Slut put the knowledge of their deaths into a little box in her head to process later. There would be time enough, back at the temple. Shit, she shouldn't have taken Donna Sampson. This was all her fault. This never would have happened with Skillet. Skillet would have been able to talk Donna Sampson into staying put. Skillet's foot wouldn't have jittered on the gas. But the Hell Slut wasn't going to say any of that now. It wasn't the time.

If Mother Moonflow had just warned them what they would be up against...

"No," said the Hell Slut. "You didn't shoot them, you didn't kill them."

I killed them, thought the Hell Slut. *It's all my fault.*

But out loud she said, "We all know the risks. We all know the dangers. But it's the right thing to do, just as Mother Moonflow says."

Sunny Delight laughed hysterically.

"You really came through. Shit, Mel's not gonna know what hit him when we see him. There'll be time to worry about them later, but we need to think about us. Gimme a sec. I need to think."

Sunny Delight nodded and blew her breath out through her mouth.

The Hell Slut opened the door, swung her feet to the asphalt, and put her forehead into her hands. Her thoughts were racing. This was all wrong. Her arm was turning white and losing feeling below the tourniquet, and this whole fiasco might have completely tanked the birthing ceremony. And she had lost the Frog Sisters. She'd never lost anyone before. She had really fucked this up. This was not good. This was not good at all.

Sunny Delight continued to blubber until the Hell Slut stood up and wandered away from the car. In the chaos, the Sturgeon's trunk had come unlatched, revealing a shallow pool of body fluids and Hal Sampson's corpse marinating in its own juices.

She needed to focus. She needed to get Sunny Delight out of here.

We don't have a lot of time. Every cop in the state's going to be looking for a banana-yellow '76 Sturgeon with a dead ranger in the trunk.

They would definitely need a new car.

20.

*The Murder of God (*Lactarius deo*) is a dark purple toadstool that grows in bifurcated clumps resembling a pair of hands with interlaced fingers. It is carnivorous, catching insects and small mammals in the sweet-smelling but sticky ichor that pools in its "palms." These creatures are dissolved and digested over the course of months. The Murder of God is warm to the touch and appears to throb gently when observed. Its stalk is laced with veins. It does not speak in human voices.*

—Field Guide to Common Mushrooms of the Pamogo Forest, *T. F. Greengarb (1978)*

Candles glowed behind the boarded-up windows, flickers faintly visible between cracks in the slats. The two women snuggling together under the ladder were still there, asleep in each other's arms. The sisters seemed to pretty much bed down anywhere; Sarah wondered if they even had assigned rooms or if they just played musical beds constantly.

They ran back to the van, giggling hysterically the entire way, so that the sisters now returning to their work after dinner glared at them in annoyance. But Sarah didn't care; she was so relieved, so exhilarated after that near miss. She couldn't believe that they had escaped without notice! She couldn't believe that Pickles hadn't seen them, lying right there on the floor in a pile among the rugs and the pillows! She couldn't believe that Mother Moonflow had slept through the whole thing! She couldn't stop laughing from the sheer beautiful absurdity of it all!

"He didn't see us! The dumbass looked right at us and didn't see a thing!" howled Skillet, rolling around on the mattress and clutching her belly with laughter.

"How did he not see us?! Was it really that dark?"

"The raccoons! That room's always full of raccoons, just rutting away. He musta just seen this big ol' blob lying among the blankets and just thought we were a couple more raccoons just doin' it!"

Sarah couldn't stop laughing. The very idea! Pickles had looked right through them and just thought, *Oh yeah, there's something squirming around on the floor there in the dark, must be raccoons fucking*, and he'd just rolled with it.

"Ha ha! Yeah! Just a couple of raccoons fucking in the blankets!"

"Just raccoons messin' around! That was it! Sorry I didn't get you your King's Breakfast, though."

"It's fine. It was almost worth it for the adventure."

"Yeah. We had fun, didn't we? Good fun." She giggled.

Sarah lay on her back, and Skillet lay curled up into a croissant next to her. Maybe it was the lingering marijuana high or maybe it was the thrill of their shared escape, but... Sarah was feeling better than she had since coming to the Pamogo. Better than she had felt in weeks. Better than she had felt since Jade left.

"I can't believe Mother Moonflow slept through that entire thing!"

"She's so stupid!" laughed Skillet. "I hate that stupid bitch and her stupid fuckin' hippie bullshit act. Thinks she's so much better than me! Ya know she put me on extra compost pit duty? She's always doing shit like that."

"Why?"

"Cuz she sucks! She thinks I'm just some little freak, like I'm not worth nothin' except to keep the Hell Slut happy. And now the Hell Slut doesn't want me anymore."

"You don't seem like a freak," said Sarah, which wasn't true. She was pretty sure that Skillet was an absolute freak. She touched Skillet's hand.

"But if that's the case, why don't you just leave?" Sarah felt stupid asking the question, because there were always a million things keeping you tethered to every awful thing in life and she knew it. But she still asked.

Skillet looked at her like she was crazy. "Ha ha! And go where? I'm just a little fuckup. You know she let the Hell Slut go off without me? I'm not nothin' without the Hell Slut."

"Well," said Sarah, "you have me now." She rolled onto her side and looked at Skillet, *really* looked at her. Skillet was kind of cute, in a psychotic sort of way. Sarah was going to choose to ignore her misgivings. Outside, the peak of the temple loomed over the trees in silhouette against the rising moon. Sarah remembered Andy's story about Sloane's workmen. *As long as you keep the mill within your sight, you won't get lost.*

"What's your story, Skillet? I told you my story. Tell me yours."

Skillet flipped over and smiled wide, revealing pink gums. "Oh, you're gonna laugh! It's real funny. I was a champion high school dick sucker, so dear ol' dad got them to put me in the nuthouse, ha ha! Can you imagine? Committed for liking dick too much?"

"Jesus," said Sarah. "Skillet, honey. That's not funny."

"It's not? Maybe you had to be there."

"I don't think I had to be there to know. That's terrible that he did that to you, honey." She moved her hand to Skillet's knee. The marijuana was still hitting her. She only ever called anyone *honey* when she was high. "I'm so sorry."

Skillet paused, as if she had never considered the possibility that what had happened to her wasn't funny, as if there was no possible other way to react to her story than with gales of hysterical laughter. She stared at the hand cupping her knee.

"Yeah. Yeah, I guess it's not that funny. It's actually kind of fucked up."

"Honey, it's really fucked up. I'm sorry."

"It's fine, they let me use the computer sometimes, for socialization. That's where I found Mother Moonflow's posts first. After I got out, I kinda just wandered. Goin' to bars and stuff, pickin' up dudes. And girls too. And then when Mother Moonflow started the temple, I came here. Figured, well, I sucked too much dick, now I can eat too much pussy, ya know?"

Sarah didn't know, but she nodded anyway. It felt like she was expected to nod.

"But damn, you shoulda seen me back then. I sucked 'em all—big ol' dongs, itty-bitty chodes, boy dicks, girl dicks. I'll suck yours, if you're cool? You're cool about that, right? You ain't a prude?"

Sarah's face felt hot and flushed; she hoped it wasn't obvious in the gathering dusk. She could feel the marijuana lighting up her veins and her dick stirring at Skillet's horny talk. *No*, thought some rational part of her brain that seemed to be calling from a million miles away, *that's a terrible idea. There's no way that fucking around with Skillet is going to end well.*

Skillet shook her head, laughing. "You ain't scared, are ya? Playing coy? Afraid I'll bite it off? Ha ha! C'mon, let me have a go. You ain't ever had it like me." She wiggled her tongue through the gap between her teeth. "Gord, you're so fuckin' hot, I can't stand it. C'mon. Roll over. Let me massage some of that tension away. You been working hard."

Sarah did as she was told, even though she knew where it was leading. Skillet's hands fluttered across her shoulders, squeezing the tight, knotted muscles through the soft padding of Sarah's fat.

"That good?"

"Yeah. Did you mean what you said before, Skillet? When you said you didn't care if Mother Moonflow caught us?"

"I didn't get to finish."

"Oh? What else were you going to say?"

"That you're hot. Just looking at you drives me crazy, and you've been driving me crazy since I first saw you in the woods. I think you're real sexy. I want to fuck you, Sarah."

That was direct. There was no misinterpreting that signal.

"Shhh," said Skillet, still stroking her back and drawing close. Skillet nibbled at Sarah's shoulder. "You're so soft and plush, so ripe. I love how big you are. How much do you weigh?"

"I... I don't know."

Skillet grunted in frustration but she kept nibbling, little tiny kisses all along Sarah's shoulder and neck. "Ugh! C'mon! Work with me, sister! I need a number or I can't get wet. Gimme a number."

Sarah said a number.

"Oh my Gord," murmured Skillet, her lips brushing Sarah's sternum. She reached below the sag of Sarah's potbelly and squeezed a handful of soft blubber. "I wish we had something to feed you besides fucking potato soup and raccoon meat. Mmm, what do you like to eat, Sarah? Say what you like. What's your favorite food? What's the naughtiest treat you eat?"

What am I doing? "Tiramisu."

"Ooh, decadent. If I had tiramisu, I'd feed you *so* much. Oh my Gord, I'd make you *so* fat."

"Tell me my breasts are huge," whined Sarah.

"Oh, you want big tits, do you? That's adorable." Skillet gurgled into Sarah's ear. "Your tits are *so* big. I'd make them even bigger. I'd feed you tiramisu till you're so fat that they sag all the way down. Huge. Bigger than Mother Moonflow."

Sarah hummed quietly in bliss, and the tingling pleasure coursing through her body made it hard to resist, and the weed was making her dumb. Her dick was stirring despite her best efforts to stave it off. *Oh God, no. Not that.* "Not there. Please. Not yet."

Skillet would not be deterred. Sarah rolled over and now they were together, Sarah staring into that grinning goblin mug, Skillet's hands all over her, squeezing, probing.

"Mmm." Skillet purred, her breath so warm on Sarah's earlobe that the hair stood up on her neck. Skillet's hands continued to knead the soft flesh of Sarah's flanks, drawing closer to her crotch on every rotation.

"What do you have under here?" said Skillet, slipping her hand into the crevasse under Sarah's belly and smoothly popping open the fly of her jeans. Sarah wanted to say something, but Skillet was too fast and her hands were down Sarah's pants and abruptly around her cock. "Does it still work or do I gotta muff ya, hmm? Yeah, I thought so."

Sarah was simultaneously relieved and extremely annoyed.

"I ain't sucked a girl dick in so long, not since before I came to the temple." Skillet lowered her voice, as if there was anyone else who might hear. She crawled over Sarah like a centipede, all tickly little arms and legs. "I sucked off my entire junior class, ya know, all the boys, all the girls. My dad found out and he busted my face for it, gave me this." She grinned widely and pointed at her gapped teeth. "Joke's on him—it made me even better at it." She wiggled the tip of her tongue between her teeth lasciviously.

Sarah's breath quickened, and her nipples stiffened under her sweater. *Oh God, no. God, I can't do this. I'm gonna get myself killed.*

Skillet slithered into Sarah's lap and pushed her backward until Sarah was lying flat on the floor. Sarah raised her butt off the mattress so that Skillet could strip down her jeans. Skillet nipped at the elastic waistband of Sarah's underwear with her teeth. "What size are these?" she mumbled through clenched teeth. "Extra large? Extra extra large?"

"Please...stop talking," sighed Sarah. Skillet's questions reminded her too much of all the chasers online: *How much do you eat? Could you sit on me? I just think it would be interesting if you ate a whole cake. Have you ever intentionally gotten yourself stuck in a doorway?* But no girl had ever wanted her before. Not like this. It wasn't like Jade, who'd tolerated her. Skillet was vibrating with desire.

"I can't help it, Sarah. I just want you so much. My Gord. This body, it's so perfect. So big and round." Skillet was grinding her crotch against Sarah's soft thigh now, soaking through her shorts and smearing her juices. "You want big titties, huh?"

"Don't say it like that, please. It sounds so sleazy."

Skillet peeled Sarah's underwear away with her teeth and buried her face between Sarah's legs. Sarah's girl dick was painfully erect now.

"You should stay with us," breathed Skillet.

"I can't," huffed Sarah, her plump cheeks so shiny and flushed, her bosom rising and falling. "My cat."

"You gonna give all this up for a cat? We could have so much here."

Sarah's body was trembling so hard her flesh jiggled. Skillet poked her tongue through her gap and lapped at Sarah's girl dick like a dainty little cat. Sarah arched her back and sighed.

21.

An odd occurrence. A stranger appeared at the periphery of the camp this morning. At first I mistook him for one of the lost men, no doubt returning after some tomfoolery. I shouted and approached, but he vanished before I was able to see his face. Have enquired among the men but no one else saw him.

—Diary of Lazarus Sloane
(California State Parks Archives)

The Hell Slut rolled her new Toyota Corolla into the space between a rusted-over station wagon and a busted compact where, until very recently, a much more stylish '76 Sturgeon had lived. The Sturgeon was, as far as she knew, still languishing under a San Bernardo freeway entrance with the Frog Sisters' brains across the bench seat. Luckily, the Hell Slut had had little trouble securing alternative transportation; this Corolla had, until very recently, belonged to an acne-studded teen working a late shift at a San Bernardo Jack in the Box. The Hell Slut would have been happy to end that teen to secure the ride, but luckily for him Sunny Delight had an easier plan. She distracted him at the counter, twirling long strands of golden hair casually around her index finger as she bit her lip and furrowed her brow and pretended to have sooo much trouble deciding which burger to order that she just needed the help of a big strong man to suggest an answer. Sunny Delight had perfected her technique working Bay Area johns from the back room of Mel's apartment, and she was good at it, good enough that the cashier failed to notice when the Hell Slut, outside in the parking lot, smashed his window and hot-wired his engine. That meant he was extraordinarily fortunate, although he probably didn't feel that way upon discovering his loss, because it meant that Sunny Delight and the Hell Slut were long gone, but he was still alive and his face would remain intact. Some people are just born lucky.

The Hell Slut barreled past Joe's Diner without registering it and blasted down the freeway like a bat out of hell, not stopping once, foot slammed so hard on the gas that her leg threatened to smash through the undercarriage, weaving wildly between semis, but she didn't care. She was powered by a cold hard determination she had never felt before, not even in the midst of a kill, every muscle in her body tensed, like a coiled spring ready to blow, her mind racing, the sucking bullet hole in her shoulder throbbing, the purple creep of infection already faintly visible on her bicep under the sheen of blood. She was the Hell Slut, who always did what needed doing, and she didn't regret doing what needed doing, and Sunny Delight was on the seat next to her. They made excellent time. Now they were home, safe and sound. The California freeways had been crawling with cops, rangers, and highway patrolmen, but once they crossed the threshold onto the abandoned service road and disappeared into the Pamogo, they were home free.

The Hell Slut shifted into park and stared into the darkness of the surrounding Pamogo. A fat raindrop hit the windshield. That was the first signal that it would be raining hard soon. She pulled the key from the ignition. In the passenger seat, Sunny Delight stirred and stretched, yawning. The Hell Slut reached over and brushed a finger against her cheek.

"Hey, Sunny D. Wake up."

"Are we back?"

"Yeah, we're home."

The Hell Slut knew this forest as well as anyone could; the Pamogo was strange and hostile—it twisted its paths beneath your feet and tried to confuse you to your death. But the Hell Slut could read the trees as well as she could read people, and she knew when a pictogram carved into a trunk was signaling her to turn left and when a rotted fencepost jammed into a thicket was signaling her to turn right.

Something was off.

The rain drizzled down, and the wind whipped through the branches above. Twigs snapped and cracked, but it wasn't the wind. The Hell Slut looked up. Shining in the darkness, dozens and dozens of reflective eyes stared down on them. The trees were full of raccoons.

"Holy hell," said the Hell Slut.

"I've never seen raccoons outside before," said Sunny Delight. "Why aren't they in the temple?"

The Hell Slut did not want to think about what could have driven the raccoons from the temple. She could feel it in the air. Something big was coming.

Sarah snorted awake. God, these dreams. This last one was worse; she could sense it, even though she couldn't remember it. She felt itchy, like her skin was on fire, a weird sensation that made her wish she could tear herself out of her body and fly away free from it. It made her wonder, again, about Andy's weird claims about Pamogo catatonia syndrome and the Lord of the Forest and what had really happened while they were blacked out on Leviathan's Favored Son. She rocked herself into a sitting position, grunting as she felt her belly shift over her lap. Skillet was asleep on the filthy mattress next to her, curled up into a little ball like a dozing cat. Sarah dangled her legs over the edge of the mattress and out the missing bus door. It was late, but the trees here were sparse enough that she could see the peak of the temple silhouetted against the sky. Here in the depths of the Pamogo, where the only light came from the few candles and bare light bulbs still burning in the temple windows, you could see the full richness of the night. The velvet heavens were filled with tiny pinpricks of light from distant galaxies, so many more than you could see in the city.

Her cell phone was buzzing in her jeans pocket. When she inspected it, she found more glitches.

`>&&&&`

`>hey glitch`

`>i only have 5% battery left. this might be the last time we talk`

`>HEY GLITCH ^$##&*`

`>thanks for everything. i don't know what you are, i don't know how you did it...but you got us out of the woods! we got rescued by this cult and`

`>haha`

`>i'm really stepping in it now`

`>i don't know if even your words of wisdom can help me now`

>i just fucked around with this chick who likes fat girls

>i'm fat btw

>she was so horny, i've never been with a girl who got so horny for me b4

>pretty crazy huh?

>I WILL WAKE HORNY*&%$#@@

>haha i like you glitch, you always know what to say

>FUCKED AROUND WORDS OF WISDOM@$

>idk it was nice

>lol do you think I'm falling for her or something? lolo

>imagine if we gay married lol

>and id just live in this weird woods cult with my cottagecore goblin wife forever lol

>i wonder if she likes cats

>CATS WIFE%%$%$ NICE

Sarah's clothes lay scattered over the floor of the van. She quietly gathered them up, careful not to wake Skillet, and put them on. She could escape now, she realized, without Skillet following her, maybe find Andy, but Sarah didn't want to go anywhere. *This was stupid. I'm making stupid decisions again*, thought Sarah. *And I guess I just will until I die.*

>good talk, glitch

>GOOD TALK

The battery finally emptied; the phone went black. *I guess that's the end of that relationship*, thought Sarah.

Sarah looked up as a shadow passed over her, big and bulky. The biggest woman that Sarah had ever seen was standing about twenty feet away, watching her. Her face and shirt were crusted with blood. Another woman, smaller, daintier, blonder, stood behind her, also staring. Sarah had not seen these temple freaks before.

"Hello?" said Sarah.

"You're in Skillet's van," said the woman. "Who the fuck are you?"

"It's okay," said Sarah quickly. "Skillet's right here." She reached out and shook Skillet's shoulder until the small woman snorted awake.

"Someone's here." Sarah lowered her voice. "She's covered in blood."

"What?" Skillet looked out at the bloody woman and immediately perked up. "If it isn't the Hell Slut! You get your guy?"

"Who the fuck is that?" said the Hell Slut, ignoring the question.

"This," said Skillet proudly, "is Sarah. She's new. She's my Sunny Delight."

Sarah had never seen a woman as big as this. She was huge, possibly seven feet tall. And fat, huge fat. It dawned on Sarah that the Hell Slut had a history with Skillet. Of course. Of course she did. Of course Skillet was just going around fucking fat girls. It would be too much to hope that they had some actual connection, that Skillet wasn't just like every other chaser. The Hell Slut locked eyes with Sarah, and she almost felt like they had a brief moment of understanding. As if the Hell Slut was thinking the exact same thing.

Skillet threw her arms around Sarah. "See, I don't even need you anymore! I don't even care that you're fucking around with that little whore! It doesn't bother me at all! We're in love!"

"Skillet, is this your ex?" said Sarah. God, she was tired. She was so very tired of all this.

"Ex? I'm an ex? What is this normie bullshit? Skillet doesn't have exes, cuz that would imply she has relationships!"

"I have plenty of relationships!"

"We all know what you are, Skillet. Don't pull this shit."

"Don't you fucking say it!"

"You're a chaser."

"You take that back! I am not! We have a connection! I just happen to think that fat is beautiful! It's a legitimate belief! You wouldn't know about that kind of thing!"

Skillet leaped from the truck and launched herself at the Hell Slut, who instantly swatted her to the ground. Sunny Delight gasped in surprise and stepped back. The marijuana dulled Sarah's response time but she still shouted.

"Ow! Fuck!" Skillet rolled around on the ground, clutching her nose. Sarah jumped from the van and ran to Skillet's side.

"Skillet! Shit! Are you okay?"

"I'm dying," wailed Skillet, although she clearly wasn't. "I can't believe she called me a chaser! That's so fuckin' dehumanizing!"

Sarah cradled Skillet's head close and looked into her eyes. Sarah was stupid to ever think there was something here, but she'd been so lonely since Jade left. She just wanted someone to tell her she was pretty, and God damn it, Skillet was the first to do it. Skillet was bawling again.

"You hit her," said Sarah, glaring accusingly at the Hell Slut. "How could you do that? I thought you loved her!"

"You don't know anything, you stupid bitch. Who do you think you are? Just some new bitch dragged in off the street, and now you think that you're the fucking Green Lady's special little gal."

"I don't care about the Green Lady! I'm not part of your cult! I— What happened to your arm?!"

Sarah saw that the Hell Slut's arm was locked into a crab claw, her shoulder wrapped with bloody bandages.

"I got shot."

"You got shot?!" Skillet sat up, eyes wide, tears ceased, the fight forgotten.

"That's not all. The whole thing…it was fucked. We lost the Frog Sisters."

"You lost the Frog Sisters?!"

"Who are the Frog Sisters?" asked Sarah.

"We lost the Frog Sisters," said the Hell Slut. She rubbed the bridge of her nose and sighed miserably. "No, that's not right. *I* lost the Frog Sisters. I need to have a fun little talk with Mother Moonflow."

Skillet started to laugh a loud, braying laugh.

"It ain't funny, Skillet."

"It's hilarious!" shrieked Skillet, laughing even harder. "It's happening! The Lord of the Forest, that ol' son of a bitch, he's coming through!"

"Fuck you, Skillet," said the Hell Slut. She stomped away, Sunny Delight following her, leaving Skillet to laugh and laugh and laugh. Sarah watched Skillet roll around on the ground, flailing and shrieking.

Eventually, she regained enough composure to speak again.

"I did it all!" wheezed Skillet. "It's all me! And they're all too stupid to know it! You know, if it weren't for me, you would be raccoon bait."

"Yeah, yeah, I know."

"No, you don't get it. I didn't just find you. That wasn't just coincidence. I asked the Lord of the Forest to bring you here and he did!"

Sarah paused. The Lord of the Forest. She kept hearing that

name. The phone glitch. No. There was no way. There was no way that could actually be connected with this.

Sarah could feel the oppressive dread of a revelation approaching; she knew that awful feeling all too well. But she couldn't avoid it now. Things were moving forward, whether she wanted them to or not.

"What did you do, Skillet?"

"The Green Lady ain't ever done nothing for me! Mother Moonflow and all her women's lib bullshit. It ain't for a creature like me; she don't count me. She don't count us. You know it. So I prayed to the Lord of the Forest, and fuuuuck me, it looks like he answered. And damn if he didn't know what I like!"

"You asked the Lord of the Forest to send me?" That was absurd. There was no way. But the phone glitches, the unseen pursuer in the woods, even the lost hours of memory from Leviathan's Favored Son...Was it all part of some sinister plot against her, some weird conspiracy to use her for...for what exactly?

"I wanted to see this whole stupid temple burn! I wanted to get even with Mother Moonflow. And all of them. For taking the Hell Slut away."

"You're using me to get back at Mother Moonflow?" Sarah struggled to follow the chain of logic. "So...you killed the Frog Sisters?"

"No, no, it's not like that! It's kinda obvious, isn't it? A pair of phallic alecs, here in the temple."

"No, it's not obvious! Mother Moonflow seems extremely unbothered by the whole situation, to be honest, so I'm not seeing what the angle is."

"Oh, she's unbothered now. But things ain't done yet. The Lord of the Forest, he's fuckin' wily. That's what they tell me. And something tells me he ain't done pullin' the strings. By the time this is over, there ain't gonna be no Mother Moonflow and no Pickles and no Sunny Delight and nobody to tell me how to do nothin'! Then it'll just be you an' me..."

"What the fuck?! This is all so messed up."

"What? We could have a thing going! You still gonna give this all up for your cat?"

Sarah dropped to the ground and buried her face in her hands. This was all so incredibly tiring. All this time, she had been looking for the King's Breakfast because she needed the money, yes, but there was more, and she hardly dared admit it to herself: The vision at Madeleine's party, the goddess who'd looked at her with benevolence and love, had reached out her hands for Sarah, and Sarah wanted to take those hands and she wanted to be one with that goddess; what a vision, what a beautiful thing, to be with someone who wanted you, and now here she was, letting some chaser have her way, and *God* she missed Jade, why did she ever let Jade slip away, why did she ever let it all come to this? But through it all, through the fog of misery and confusion, one thing still broke through like a crystal clear clarion call from heaven: She needed to get home to Herman. Herman was a good boy, a good boy who sat outside the bathroom door and cried if he couldn't see Mama, a good boy who curled up by her pillow at night and rumbled if you rubbed his ear, a good boy she couldn't ever abandon.

"Yeah," said Sarah. "I guess I am."

The clearing was decorated with strings of flowers stretched between poles, trellises with creeping vines, flaming torches, and, hidden among the foliage, speakers with wires trailing back into the temple. Mother Moonflow would be presiding, after spending time in seclusion with Aphrodite, where she calmed Aphrodite's jangled nerves with stories of the Green Lady. The sisters were already gathering in the clearing in anticipation of the blessed event to come.

A candle burned near the vagina door that led to the sanctuary, Pickles standing guard in front as he usually did. He looked up at the Hell Slut's approach. Women gasped and pointed, stepping aside as the Hell Slut, still painted with blood, purposefully strode through their midst.

"Outta my way. I'm gonna see Mother Moonflow."

Pickles frowned. "Not like that, you're not. You're covered in blood!"

"Outta my way."

"She's in seclusion, getting ready for the birthing ceremony. She's not to be disturbed."

"I've had enough of you!" She grabbed Pickles by the neck and slammed him into the wall.

"Hell Slut! Stop, please!" Sunny Delight was tugging at her arm, frightened by this display, but she didn't have the strength to halt the attack. The Hell Slut's fingers tightened, digging into Pickles's throat until he gasped and sputtered, his face going red and his eyes bulging. He clawed uselessly at her hand, but the Hell Slut held him pinned fast against the wall and watched him writhe. The Hell Slut found it deeply satisfying to witness.

"Hell Slut! Stop it!" Sunny Delight was beating her fists against the Hell Slut's back, but it was barely a tickle. It was cute how much the sight of violence upset her, but the Hell Slut realized Sunny Delight might be in a raw state after having watched her kill that ranger. She was not enjoying this show like she had enjoyed seeing the frat guy at the Dank Hole eat shit. This was actually upsetting her.

Other sisters were gathered around too, all shouting different things since everyone was confused and no one knew exactly what was going on. They were mostly yelling at her to let go of Pickles, because they didn't understand the situation. Aphrodite was crying.

Aphrodite clutched at her belly and grimaced. "Please, stop! You're stressing out Athena!" She howled and dropped to her knees. No one noticed; they were all trying to get a good look at the fight. Aphrodite toppled backward, landing on her butt, and moaned, lifting her belly in the air and spreading her legs.

The sisters' attention was still on the Hell Slut. At some point during the exchange, the vagina door had opened, because now Mother Moonflow was standing beside the Hell Slut, watching this whole little spectacle play out. Pickles glanced desperately at Mother Moonflow, his jaw flapping, unable to get enough air to beg for her help.

"Hell Slut, you got something to say, come inside and say it," said Mother Moonflow. "But let him go. I ain't gonna say it again."

"Let him go!" cried Sunny Delight.

The Hell Slut hesitated but she loosened her grip. Pickles slid down the wall into a choking, wheezing heap.

Mother Moonflow turned to the assembled crowd. "I don't want none of you touching Pickles, ya dig? That would be most unmellow. Are you sponging what I'm spilling? Wait here till I'm done." Mother Moonflow disappeared back into the sanctuary, leaving the door ajar for the Hell Slut to follow.

Inside the sanctuary, Mother Moonflow was spray-painting a picture on the wall as Enya's "Orinoco Flow" continued to play.

In the dark, it was hard for the Hell Slut to parse the image, but as she approached, she realized it was yet another picture of the Green Lady as she manifested in Mother Moonflow's visions—a green woman with a mushroom cap and a large pregnant belly like a moon.

And how she apparently appeared in Sunny Delight's visions, thought the Hell Slut. That was just not fair. The Hell Slut had been with the Sisters of the Green Lady since the beginning; she had obeyed Mother Moonflow's every tenet and command, killed more men than anyone, drunk more moonflow than anyone, and yet she did not receive visions of the Green Lady. It was just not fair.

Mother Moonflow turned and looked at the Hell Slut, her glasses two blank discs reflecting the candlelight.

"What's the deal, sis? What's got you so mad you gotta be hasslin' Pickles?"

The Hell Slut crouched down on one knee and hung her head. Even squatting, she was still as tall as Mother Moonflow. "I failed you, Mother Moonflow. I lost the Frog Sisters."

Mother Moonflow clucked her tongue. She sprayed paint into her hand and lathered it between her legs. Then she pressed her naked ass against the wall, and it wasn't until she pulled away, the bare flesh parting from the sticky wood with a wet slurping sound, that the Hell Slut could see the perfect red outline of Mother Moonflow's vulva on the wall.

"You bring the body back?"

"Hal Sampson? Yeah."

"Right on, Big Mama! You got the baby batter, too?"

The Hell Slut proffered the jar, which Mother Moonflow received with reverence. She held it up to the light, tilting the jar this way and that to test the viscosity of the ooze, as if she were a connoisseur inspecting the legs on a glass of wine. The seed glowed with unholy luminosity.

Just in case Mother Moonflow hadn't heard, the Hell Slut repeated, "I lost the Frog Sisters."

Mother Moonflow did not seem interested in the loss; she continued to stare at the jizz jar. In a quiet voice, she said, "Dead dad seed is real powerful stuff, Big Mama, and this is the most powerful I've seen in a hot minute. This shit, it can be dangerous if you don't know how to use it. When the Pig fucked me and shot his high-potency man sperm up my uterus, it was a failure. But that was my fault. I came when he put his dick in me. I shouldn't have done that. That orgasm weakened my safeguards, and his man sperm overpowered my yonic essence. We won't make that mistake again. Females giving females orgasms, that's the only way to force the man sperm to our will."

The Hell Slut was really confused. None of this made any sense. Somehow, all of this sounded very stupid. It had never sounded stupid to her before. She must be mistaken. Of course she was mistaken. Mother Moonflow would never say something stupid. Her head was pounding.

"Now that Hal Sampson's dead, his sperm won't contain his DNA anymore. That's just medical science. And Athena will be born only of the twenty mothers!"

"But he already fucked Aphrodite while he was alive! The Frog Sisters died for this! For nothing!"

"Cripes, Big Mama, you sound like a stuck record. That's yesterday's doctrine! The Green Lady just told me in a vision that the DNA erasure is retroactive, so they ain't died for nothing. Or they wouldn't have, if they'd actually died."

"They did die! I saw them!" The Hell Slut didn't know what to say. She was slowly progressing from despair to anger, anger that

Mother Moonflow wasn't listening, anger that Mother Moonflow was more interested in a jar of spunk than in the loss of two of their sisters. She was heady with rage, but there was no one here whom she could punch.

"No, they didn't, Big Mama. You're confused. They're fine, they're right outside."

"I got shot for this!"

"No, you didn't, Big Mama. You been hittin' the moonflow too hard. You're fine."

The Hell Slut touched her shoulder where she was certain that the bullet had hit her, but felt only smooth flesh.

"But the ranger shot me—"

"He manifested as a ranger, huh?" Mother Moonflow unscrewed the top of the jar and jabbed a finger within; she dabbed a fingerprint's worth of the substance behind each ear and onto the backs of her wrists. "I need you, Big Mama. I need you to do exactly what I say. Everything depends on tonight. Everything depends on you doing exactly what I say."

"What did I... ? I don't understand—"

"The moonflow helped you do what you had to do, Big Mama. That's all you gotta know. Hal Sampson appeared however he had to appear so that you could finish the job."

"But then... who did we really kill?"

Mother Moonflow shrugged. "Hal Sampson. The details, Big Mama, are all academic. But hey, would it feel better if you thought he was a surveyor? I could tell you that."

"It wouldn't make me... I don't know."

Doc Clopper rapped on the door, not waiting for a response before she threw it open and poked her head in.

"Hey, I hate to interrupt this little kaffeeklatsch you two've got going. But thanks to Big Mac over there, Aphrodite's going into labor. We can't wait any longer. This baby is coming, like it or not."

Mother Moonflow stood and stretched, raising her arms over her head so that her breasts lifted. She looked at the Hell Slut. "I need you with me here, Big Mama. We started this journey together. I can't finish it without you."

"Right, right..."

"Remember what I told you when you first came to me? 'You'll always have a home with us gals.' And I meant it. You've been a loyal sister, Hell Slut; you've always come through for me. You come through tonight and I'll see that you always do have a home with us gals. I need you to say it, Big Mama. Are you with me?"

"I'm with you."

"No matter where it goes?"

"No matter where it goes."

"There will come a time, very soon, when your loyalty to me will be tested."

"Of course I'm loyal! Anything for you, Mother Moonflow, always!"

"Say it again. What did I tell you?"

"'You'll always have a home here with us gals.'" The Hell Slut would remember that to her dying day.

"That's right. As long as you're a loyal sister, you'll have a home here with us. But if not...? Dang, sis, I'd hate to think about that." Mother Moonflow turned toward the door. "Anyway, enough bummer talk! Let's welcome Athena of the Twenty Mothers. The Green Lady reborn. It's time."

She swept out of the sanctuary, handing off the jizz jar to Doc Clopper as she passed, the Hell Slut following in her wake. The Hell Slut had no idea what had just happened, but Mother

Moonflow needed her and she had promised to be with Mother Moonflow the whole way. That was all she needed to know.

Pickles crouched down in supplication, and Mother Moonflow scratched the top of his head as she passed, running her fingers tenderly through his scraggly hair. If only he would cut his split ends, he might have hair as beautiful as Mother Moonflow's. If only. He cowered back as the Hell Slut emerged behind Mother Moonflow, and that, at least, gave the Hell Slut a small twinge of satisfaction.

"Gather the sisters around," said Mother Moonflow. "Where are those phallic alecs? We don't want them to miss a second of this. Come on, it's time to begin. It's gonna be a real groove!"

Pickles nodded and hurried away, eager to play whatever part he was to play in the drama to come. The sisters rushed about the clearing, completing any last-minute setup—stringing up more flower chains and setting up folding chairs—while the Hell Slut watched the chaos with numb detachment. Two women in identical black gowns and identical black veils brushed past her.

"I thought you two died."

The Frog Sisters bowed their heads slightly, a gesture that the Hell Slut could not parse.

"You did come with me to San Bernardo, right? You were there?"

The Frog Sisters shrugged and continued on their business without another word. The Hell Slut rubbed her face. She was certain that she had watched the Frog Sisters die. There was not a shred of doubt in her mind. It seemed so real. Fucking hell, she must have gotten hold of an especially potent batch of moonflow. She touched her shoulder again, just to remind herself that she was in reality now. She had to be in reality now. This was definitely reality.

Mother Moonflow looked over her shoulder. "You coming?"

"Yes, Mother Moonflow."

She brushed past Sunny Delight, nearly knocking her to the ground. Sunny Delight chased after her and touched the Hell Slut on the shoulder. "Hey! What did Mother Moonflow say? What happened in there?"

"Nothing. It's time. The birthing ceremony is happening."

"Praise the Green—"

"Not now," said the Hell Slut gruffly, and she was too preoccupied with her own thoughts to see how Sunny Delight's smile vanished.

22.

*The Fox Candle (*Russula vulpes*) grows in large clusters of black toadstools. The stem is long and slender, while the cap is tall and peaked with a slick, oily appearance. It is said to taste like children's fear.*

—Field Guide to Common Mushrooms of the Pamogo Forest, *T. F. Greengarb (1978)*

The sisters linked hands to form a large circle in the clearing outside the temple. Someone started humming and swaying, and soon they were all humming and swaying. The humming and swaying was hypnotic, and Sarah felt herself humming and swaying along. A heap emerged from the dark and humped its way toward her. Only when it spoke did she recognize the voice.

"Take my hand, honey," said Pickles. His robe was striped with mud and clods of dirt and covered in leaves. He wore a raccoon mask, painted with stripes, over his face. "We gotta get you to the best seats in the house."

Sarah was too surprised by his appearance to say anything. She obeyed without question and let him escort her over to a raised stage, where Andy was already sitting on a metal folding chair, his hands awkwardly folded in his lap. Sarah climbed onto the stage and took a seat.

"That's perfect," said Pickles. "Now you just have to put on your masks!"

From under the stage, Pickles pulled out an unwieldy papier-mâché abomination with a massive leering grin, two curling horns, and a beard made of dyed chicken feathers.

"I'm not putting that on," said Sarah.

"Actually, each of you need to put one of these on." Pickles was already diving under the stage for a second mask. "We're trying to keep all the phallic energy locked in this little area here, so it would really help out if you could just put on the masks."

"Sarah, don't make a fuss. I'll put it on." Andy picked up the mask and hoisted it over his shoulders. He turned and the mask glared at Sarah with giant red eyes. A muffled voice from within: "How do I look?"

"You look fantastic, really great. Just great."

Pickles was arranging the second mask on the floor of the stage. Sarah felt the need to repeat her earlier refusal. "I'm not wearing that. How about your mask? I'd wear something like that. Do you have anything like that?"

Pickles vibrated with visible frustration. "Fine. Here. Just take it, why don't you?"

He yanked the mask from his face and threw it at her and then stomped off, his mud-splattered robe trailing behind him.

Christ. She really didn't expect this to be such a big deal.

Still, everyone else was wearing masks. She suddenly felt stupid that she wasn't. She grabbed Pickles's discarded mask and snapped the string around the back of her head.

"You should have just put it on," said Andy's muffled voice. It echoed inside the massive cavern of his ridiculous mask.

"I am not wearing that thing. Jesus! Can you even see anything in that? And where have you been all day?!"

"Effervescent Bubbles and I were talking about historical interpretation."

"Sure you were. Listen. Skillet brought us here."

"I know, I was there."

"No, I mean she made some kind of fucked-up deal with the Lord of the Forest, and it brought us here. It manipulated us to come here, Andy! I don't know what the fuck that thing is, but I swear to God it made us take Leviathan's Favored Son! It made us get lost in the woods! It was the phone glitch! It's all part of a plan!"

"The Lord of the Forest?"

"Yeah, that…that thing you were talking about! The forest thing! The reason people get lost in the Pamogo! I swear it must be that! Shit, Andy, we are so fucked. We are going to die."

The leering mask did not answer. "Are you high now?"

"What? No! I smoked a little weed earlier, but I'm fine now! I'm serious, Andy!"

"Did you already get some of that moonflow?"

"I haven't had any moonflow! Andy, we need to leave—"

The CHUNK of a CD drive snapping shut cut off Sarah's words. Someone, somewhere, turned on a boombox and the speakers rattled to life, blasting the opening chord of "Orinoco Flow."

"Sisters, we're gathered here tonight to mark a totally groovy occasion," said Mother Moonflow, raising her voice above the music, her face and bosom illuminated by torchlight. "We got some phallic alecs in attendance tonight—let's give them a real chill temple welcome!"

A chorus of animal hoots and hollers rolled out of the

darkness. Sarah felt all eyes on her. Well. There was no escaping now.

Mother Moonflow continued. "Tonight is the birth of a new kind of woman, born only of woman, free of man's taint. Born from the love of twenty totally mod lesbians and the sperm of a dead man, she will be the Green Lady reborn in flesh!"

The sisters, shrouded in deepening shadow, continued to hum and sway. Only when the flickering torchlight fell upon a face or an arm or a breast for just the barest slice of a moment before it was consumed back into the dark did Sarah recognize a new truth: The sisters were all naked, except for masks. They all wore masks. Some wore simple domino masks, black or gray or purple, and Sarah could confirm that when a laughing white face would suddenly lurch into the light. But others wore more elaborate Venetian masks, peppered with glitter and festooned with feathers and ferns. Still others wore the heads of animals—wolves and cats and birds. Mother Moonflow was the only one not wearing a mask. Sarah goggled once again at the size of those breasts; could they even make a robe big enough to accommodate those knockers? *Shit. Stop thinking about that.* The last thing that she needed was anyone noticing her excitement.

The circle parted, and a trio of women entered to join Mother Moonflow: Two masked women whom Sarah did not recognize (although she assumed the smaller one wearing a horse mask must be Doc Clopper) were escorting another masked woman, recognizable by her round pregnant belly, into the ring. The pregnant woman wore the head of a bird of some kind; she had plump full breasts with big puffy nipples. The horse had smaller, subtler breasts, ripe in maturity. The final member of the trio, who was gigantically tall and gigantically wide, wore a wolf mask. She had fat heavy titties that sloped majestically against her gut. A thick animal tongue that did not belong to any human flopped limply from the mouth of the mask like a slab of roast beef.

The horse handed off a jar of some precious unguent, and the sisters passed it from one to another, anointing their pulse points. It smelled like fresh pear blossoms.

"Praise the Green Lady!" yelled Mother Moonflow.

"Praise the Green Lady!" called out the sisters in response. They raised their linked arms.

"When the Green Lady walks among us in mortal flesh," cried Mother Moonflow, lifting her hands to the night sky, "know that the world will be different! No longer will we suffer under the thumb of the phallic alecs! No longer will we be forced to live in exile! It will be a world where a woman is just as good as a man!"

Her white skin positively glowed in the rising moonlight; the manicured patch of black hair at her crotch was like a tiny window into darkness. She swayed on her feet, humming, and the sisters hummed back. Sarah got the impression that something very profound was about to happen. She couldn't keep from staring at Mother Moonflow's pendulous chest, those thick swollen nipples. *Christ.* The ceremony had begun.

"Now let all sisters who wish to partake of the sacrament c'mon down!"

Sarah watched as, one by one, the sisters dropped hands, stepped forward from the circle, and approached Mother Moonflow. The first to reach the center was a woman in a cat mask, who kneeled, placed her hands beneath one of Mother Moonflow's sagging breasts, and lifted it to her mouth. She began to suckle. Another woman, wearing a cow mask, kneeled before her other breast and did the same.

What the fuck, thought Sarah. After several seconds, the cat and the cow each stood up, bowed, and returned to their places in the circle.

"C'mon, everyone, step forward and get yourself some sacrament," repeated Mother Moonflow. "This moonflow ain't gonna drink itself!"

Holy shit. Holy shit. No way. This is absolutely ludicrous—there is no way that this can really be happening. Mother Moonflow's breasts billowed in the pale light, wobbling ever so slightly as she gestured. Sarah remembered all the nights she'd prayed before she fell asleep as a kid: *Let me wake up a girl. Let me wake up with breasts. Let them be huge.*

Sarah needed to get down there. She needed to get in on this.

"What are you doing?" said Andy from within his mask. "I don't think we're supposed to leave this section."

"Who the hell cares?" Sarah stumbled in her haste, her feet tangled in the legs of the folding chair. Everything had led to this moment. She had seen the goddess at Madeleine's party one time, and she ached to see her again. Just one more time. This might be her last chance. This might be her only chance.

I'm just gonna keep making bad decisions till I die.

Even if she had to die, though, she was going to see the goddess again. She was going to feel that warm presence, bask in her unearthly glow. She needed to. She had never needed something so badly in her life before. She knew without an iota of doubt in her brain that she needed to go down and take that sacrament, experience moonflow, see the goddess again—please let her see the goddess again—or she was going to regret it forever and ever and ever.

No, thought Sarah, *you can't do this. You can't get yourself killed. You have to stay alive for Herman.*

Think about Herman.

There was no way that she could pull this off. They would recognize her immediately, if not by her body then by her girl dick. But the image of the goddess was too bright and too big and too holy to allow any other thoughts in her brain. So she was behind the stage, stripping out of her jeans and her sweater and her underwear and adjusting her raccoon mask, and she was jogging toward the circle. She could hear Andy's voice, now muffled by distance as well as his mask; he was probably pointing out how insane it was that mere minutes ago, she was ranting about how they ought to be getting out of here and now she was running *toward* the birthing ceremony, or maybe he was just scandalized by her nudity. Whatever. Who cared about that? Who cared about anything other than seeing the goddess again?

A woman with a weasel mask was there, standing between two women in frog masks, all humming and swaying. The weasel had a flat chest and a fucked-up vagina, like she had sat on a hot plate.

"Skillet!" said Sarah.

"Aw, look who's come to join us!" said the weasel, releasing the hand of one frog and holding her own out toward Sarah. "C'mon. Hold my hand."

Sarah didn't care that Skillet had tricked her, had planned some weird fucked-up shit with the phone glitch or whatever; she didn't care that this weasel was an obvious chaser. Nothing mattered but getting that moonflow.

The ring of sisters opened to accept her easily. The weasel took her left hand, a frog took her right, and now they were humming and swaying as if she had been part of their circle since the beginning.

"You ready for moonflow?" giggled the weasel.

"Can I be ready?"

"No." The weasel squeezed her hand. "We'll go up together."

The weasel let go and took a step toward Mother Moonflow. Sarah stepped forward too.

What am I doing? she thought.

Together they walked forward, hand in hand. Sarah's heart jackhammered against the back of her ribs. Every step felt like an eternity as she walked up to Mother Moonflow, who smiled her serene smile and nodded.

"Hey, Big Mama. C'mon down!"

The weasel kneeled at Mother Moonflow's left tit. Sarah kneeled at the right. Mother Moonflow reached out with her slender alabaster fingers and took Sarah's palsied hands in her own and guided them to touch her breast. It was soft and warm. Sarah could see the older woman's cork-sized nipples stiffen with arousal before her eyes.

"Far out," said Mother Moonflow. "This is a real trip."

Sarah took that as an invitation; she had to move now or she would lose her nerve. She put her mouth to the nipple and sucked. Mother Moonflow's milk was warm in her mouth. Sarah's eyes rolled back in her head, and she sucked and sucked and sucked. *Holy shit. Make this real. Green Lady, moon goddess, whatever, just make this real.* It was stupid, but Sarah wanted to believe, she needed to believe, that this was doing something, that she was taking something of Mother Moonflow's essence into her, and that maybe, when all was said and done, she would awaken tomorrow with massive mommy milkers. It could happen. Stranger things had happened.

"That's right, Big Mama, slurp it up," said Mother Moonflow, her words trailing into a low groan. Goose pimples popped to the surface of her titanic breasts. "Keep drinking, Big Mama, I want you to suck me dry. Right on, right on."

Sarah felt gentle but insistent hands on her shoulder, but she ignored them. The hands shook her harder, and this time Sarah reluctantly parted from the teat, her lips making a wet pop as she detached. Sarah's belly felt warm and full, sloshing heavily as she stumbled to her feet. Jesus. How long was she drinking?

"C'mon, Greedy Guts, let someone else have a go," said the weasel, laughing. She led Sarah back toward the circle. Then she lowered her voice and said just to Sarah, "Damn, you *really* went for it."

"Oh shit. Did I fuck up?" Christ, what was wrong with her? Her stomach ached, full of way too much milk. She was in the one place in the world where theoretically it should be impossible for her to look like a freak. But even among these weirdos, she was doing it wrong. She was certain they all must be staring at her, judging the weird stranger who'd spent too long at the tit, but when she looked, no one was paying attention to her. They were too busy lining up to get their own taste.

"Ha ha, naw, you're fine. I did the same thing the first time I drank from Mother Moonflow. Just wait till you start to feel it."

Sarah stared into the center of the ring, where the horse and the wolf had lowered the bird to the floor. "Are they going to deliver a baby high? Is that a good idea?"

"Why not? What could possibly go wrong?"

Sarah wondered what a baby with twenty mothers would look like, what kind of terrible freak monster baby abomination was about to be born into the world. No, that was silly. She knew they were all just on crack; the bird had just fucked a guy and they were all agreeing to this shared delusion to avoid reckoning with that fact. It was perfectly ordinary, perfectly normal.

Just like Andy had said about those weird piles of raccoon bones in the woods. *Perfectly normal.*

Nothing weird is happening. It's all normal.

After the last of the sisters finished drinking from Mother Moonflow, Sarah watched as the wolf and the horse took their positions on either side of the bird.

"When we bring new life into the world, it's just another performance of the cosmic ballet," said Mother Moonflow, her voice booming over the clearing. "If you think about it, life is like a cycle, isn't it? It keeps flowing. And we gotta be true to that. That's what the Green Lady would want. We gotta be true. So even as we welcome a new sister, let's remember the story of the Green Lady. Whoa, dude, here she comes now!"

A second moon wobbled into view from behind the temple, a big round glowing orb hovering twenty feet above the ground.

"The Green Lady lives by the cycles of the moon; she is born when the moon is born; she dies when it dies," droned Mother Moonflow.

The second moon awkwardly navigated through the air over the clearing, moving in fits and starts. Sarah felt like she was losing her mind until it came closer. Then she could see that the second moon was nothing but a big paper lantern, held aloft by a trio of black-clad sisters using long sticks.

"We honor the Green Lady with the pleasures of the flesh! Every day here, when we come together, we give honor to the sacrifice of the Green Lady!"

The black-clad sisters dashed the lantern to the ground, the delicate paper crinkling and crumbling, and the Green Lady herself sprang from the wreckage. It was a trick, Sarah knew, an incredible, theatrical trick. The Green Lady was a massive papier-mâché puppet, her bobbing head and articulated arms manipulated by another trio of black-clad sisters who suddenly burst into view. In college, Sarah had once marched in a protest for university clericals to get a cost of living pay raise, and she remembered watching a bunch of grad students try to maneuver a giant Mr. Peanut puppet holding a sign that said OUR CLERICALS ARE PAID PEANUTS. The Green Lady looked kind of like that now.

The Green Lady hovered over the scene, a monstrous head as big as a Volkswagen slowly twisting back and forth, staring down at them with a painted-on expression. Her body, which Sarah knew must just be a series of wire loops and wooden joints, was hidden beneath the flowing green cascade of the cloth ribbons that made up her hair. Her mushroom cap, carved from Styrofoam, wobbled atop her head. The sisters cheered and hooted.

"Everything's a far-out ride when the Green Lady's there!" crowed Mother Moonflow, one hand snaking between her legs and pressing deep into her snatch. Sarah watched in stupefied fascination as those fingers began to move, like little hummingbirds, in and out, in and out. Sarah could hear deep, throaty moans all around her.

The horse lifted a mason jar of some unidentified oily liquid to the bird's mouth. The bird glugged it studiously and didn't cough once until it was all gone.

Mother Moonflow's breathing came hot and heavy, but she wasn't done with her speech. "But we know the Green Lady isn't alone out there. There's also *him*. The Green Lady's brother, her lover, her rapist, her murderer. The Lord of the Forest. Oh, man, there he is now! What a bum trip, man! Get outta here, man, no one likes *your* style!"

A second puppet careened into view, this time emerging from the tree line, held aloft by yet more puppeteers. The Lord of the Forest was a green giant, with a sparkling jewel at his forehead that even in the darkness Sarah could tell was just a holographic sticker, and antlers made of interlocking cardboard tubes.

The bird groaned and the sisters, or at the least the sisters who didn't already have their masks up and their faces buried between someone's legs, hummed. Sarah could see the hum, rising off the circle of women like steam. Beautiful purple steam. Oh no. The moonflow was hitting. This was way stronger than weed.

"The miracle of childbirth," muttered the horse sarcastically. Sarah was inclined to agree. She did not like to think about babies. The thought of a thing gestating inside her belly, like a gigantic grub, filled her with nausea. She felt guilty about that. Women were supposed to cherish that intimate power to nurture new life, supposed to want to hold that parasite inside them. Even most of the other trans women she knew wanted that. Maybe she was just a big fraud.

She needed to sit down. The circle was already breaking up. Several sisters were sitting on the ground, their heads in their hands. Others were lying down. Quite a few had broken off into smaller groups, where they giggled and pawed at one another and tore at their clothes. *They must be feeling the moonflow too*, thought Sarah.

"It's the eternal cycle, man destroying woman!" called Mother Moonflow, her voice husky, dropping to her knees as she continued to plunge her fingers deep inside herself, all the way to the knuckle, her nipples grazing the grass. "But not anymore!"

The Lord of the Forest fell upon the colossal Green Lady and the two puppets sailed to the ground, collapsing into a heap like the *Hindenburg* going down in flames, but the puppeteers were not finished with their performance. A black-clad sister skittered away from her fellow puppeteers to grab at some mechanism at the crotch of the Lord of the Forest, and then a gigantic papier-mâché cock popped into view like a switchblade flipping open. It was painted pink and red, but Sarah could still see the gray of the newsprint bleeding through. The puppeteers took a running leap, and they rammed the Lord of the Forest into the prone form of the Green Lady; the other group of puppeteers reacted, lifting the Green Lady into the air and shaking her papier-mâché corpse like a terrier shaking a rat.

Sarah had never seen puppets fuck before. But she was so stoned now that she couldn't even trust herself to believe that she was seeing it now.

"Keep him down, man!" howled Mother Moonflow. "Touch yourself; remind yourself that you are woman! He can't stand it! The more you cum, the more you keep him down! Down with the patriarchy! Down with the Lord of the Forest!"

In the center of the circle, the bird was screaming even louder, so loud that she drowned out the few remaining sisters still humming in unison and her screams blended into the huffing moans of women fucking. Sarah couldn't see anything from her vantage point. The bird was lying on the ground, her legs spread, knees pulled in. The horse was kneeling between her legs; Mother Moonflow was hovering over them both, chanting and masturbating. Then all at once, the screaming morphed into a long, drawn-out, wavering grunt and there was a squelching, slopping sound as Athena exploded out in a puddle of red soupy afterbirth. Sarah could smell fresh shit and hear the tinkling, high-pitched wail of a baby.

The weasel beamed. "The baby's here! We got a new little shit in the temple!"

Her joy was infectious. The bad feelings, the fear, it all melted away at once and even Sarah felt a sudden bubbling well of good will in the bosom of her soul. Love was suddenly oozing out of her, so sudden and so intense that she was almost afraid.

The puppets continued to fuck, thrusting harder, deeper, faster.

"The baby's here!" cried Sarah. She couldn't help it. Actually, now that she thought about it, pregnancy was a beautiful thing and childbirth was a miracle. She hugged the weasel close, the joy radiating from her. The entire scene shifted to a beautiful array of dazzling purples and cool refreshing blues. The only thing that Sarah felt now was peace and love and a deep, all-consuming joy. She loved this weasel so much. She had never loved anyone as much as this weasel, this weird little chaser goblin who didn't just tolerate her, but actively wanted her. She didn't even care what deal Skillet had made with the Lord of the Forest—who cared about that, the Lord of the Forest probably wasn't even real. All that mattered was:

"I love you, Skillet," bubbled Sarah. "I want to be with you. I want to stay with you."

"Oh, Sarah, yes! I want you. Oh Gord, I want to be with you so bad!"

They were laughing and crying and putting their hands all over each other. Forget Jade and her self-absorbed bullshit. Forget Madeleine and her stupid penny-pinching payments. Forget the Hell Slut and her thundering jealousy. Forget Andy. Nothing was as important as being here, right now, with Skillet. Not even seeing the goddess again, not even having giant tits. Not even Herman. Sarah lifted the weasel's mask. Skillet's face beneath was green and laced with dark blue veins, sparkling in the moonlight. Her eternal smile was huge, like the Cheshire cat's grin, wider than her face. Sarah was suddenly fascinated by the pores on Skillet's cheeks, the bristles on her scalp. Her eyes looked as big as dinner plates. Every detail of Skillet's face was absolutely riveting.

"The baby's here!" cried Sarah. "Isn't it wonderful? The baby's here!"

Skillet reached up and peeled away Sarah's raccoon face, her fingers brushing Sarah's flushed cheek. Then they were kissing, deeper, harder, tongue sliding over tongue, and Sarah was too stupid, too gone to remember what Skillet had done, how she had made this all happen.

Sarah giggled and the sound rang out, loud and stupid, in the sudden silence of the clearing. No one else was celebrating. At the center of the circle, the baby was still crying. The horse whispered something. Mother Moonflow leaned forward, closer.

"Let me see my baby," said the bird, her voice weak. "Let me see Athena."

What was spreading outward through the circle was a whisper, a vibe, passing from sister to sister as gradually the news permeated through the assembly. Sarah had a sudden thought, a fleeting image half remembered from a dream at Madeleine's house—seeing her own double, herself, unfurl to release a glowing goddess. Was that what had just been birthed into the world? Or was it something else? What had come through Aphrodite's hole? What had just belched forth into existence? A creature with twenty mothers, something that shouldn't be? The sisters were fucking all around her, Sarah stood alone in an ocean of flesh, and she could feel Mother Moonflow's eyes on her from across the clearing, singling her out, resting on her face, seeing her for the first time among all that writhing girl meat and suddenly knowing the truth.

"What's wrong?" whispered Sarah. "What's happening?"

The frogs turned toward her, no emotion visible in their black eyes.

"It's a boy," they said in unison.

The horse passed the baby to Mother Moonflow. It was tiny and wet, red-faced and screaming. Mother Moonflow whispered something to the wolf as the baby, still red-faced, still screaming, passed between hands again. The wolf stared down at the creature in her hands kicking its tiny legs feebly, waving stubby arms without reason. Mother Moonflow said something again, sharper this time, and this time the wolf responded. There was a sudden sickening crunch and the baby stopped crying. The bird tore off her mask, screaming, a piercing howl that filled the night sky, louder and louder, until Sarah was certain her eardrums would burst, until Sarah was certain that there was no way a noise that huge and mournful could come out of a person. There wasn't enough grief in the world to make that noise, but it kept getting louder. There were words in it—"Let me see her! Let me see Athena! Let me see her!"—but Sarah could barely parse them.

I didn't see that, thought Sarah. *That didn't happen. I'm just tripping.*

The wolf wiped her hand across her bare bottom, leaving a ragged red smear on her cheek. Sarah stared. She could feel the world collapsing around her, the ground opening up and dropping her straight into the deepest, darkest pit of hell. The colors were shifting—the beautiful deep purples and mellow blues were disintegrating into sickly yellows and nauseating pukey browns. The trip was going sour.

The Lord of the Forest burst into simulated orgasm, his papier-mâché dick exploding in a shower of red and white crepe paper streamers.

I need to get out of here, thought Sarah. *I need to get out of here right the fuck now.*

But all around the temple, for miles and miles and miles, was nothing but dark, dark forest.

ACT 3: TRANSCENDENCE,

or Liber Secundus

23.

*The Devil's Chapel (*Agaricus basilicus*) is a hypothetical mushroom believed to grow exclusively within the boundaries of the Pamogo Forest. Its appearance and coloration are unknown. It is not known what it tastes like. No one has ever seen a Devil's Chapel.*

—Field Guide to Common Mushrooms of the Pamogo Forest, *T. F. Greengarb (1978)*

The world was moving in slow motion. Mother Moonflow gathered Aphrodite into her arms and pulled her close, burying her face between Mother Moonflow's breasts so that her screams were muffled and Sarah knew she was still crying only by the shaking of her shoulders.

The puppets lay where they fell, like two beached-whale carcasses, abandoned and forgotten in this new crisis. Sisters lay in heaps around the clearing, some crying, some screaming, and a few—apparently too high on moonflow to internalize the new reality—still fucking.

"I'm sorry, Little Mama," Mother Moonflow was saying. "This is just the pits. But it had to be. It had to be."

Aphrodite must have said something, but Sarah couldn't hear. Mother Moonflow shushed her gently.

"No, Little Mama. It wasn't your daughter. It wasn't anything. This is how it must be. There's nothing to see. It wasn't anything."

"I know, Mother Moonflow, I know." Aphrodite pulled away long enough for Sarah to hear those words, punctuated by hiccuping sobs, before she buried her face back into Mother Moonflow's cleavage. The other sisters were scattered around the clearing, consoling one another in small clusters, or shouting and howling and beating the ground with their fists, and the wailing and moaning filled the night air. A woman in a Venetian mask painted with yellow whorls of flame was curled up into a ball several yards away, knees to her chest, face buried in her folded arms.

Mother Moonflow whispered something to Aphrodite, who nodded, and then Mother Moonflow whispered something else to another woman, the cat from earlier. The cat and the cow stepped forward and positioned themselves on either side of Aphrodite, holding her and petting her as she continued to cry. Sarah watched as the wolf wrapped something small in a blanket, stood up, and started to move away from the group. She watched as the wolf passed by the woman in the flame-painted Venetian mask and paused to speak softly under her breath and extend a hand. The Venetian-mask woman shook her head and scooted away. The wolf did not make a second attempt.

She's gonna get rid of the body, thought Sarah dully, but she didn't know what she was supposed to do with that information.

Keep quiet. Don't panic. Breathe. Keep your fucking mouth shut. Act normal. Get Andy and get the fuck out of here, back to Las Brujas or just out in the woods, it doesn't matter where, just be quiet and get out and once you're back in civilization, then *you can…*

What could she do? Tell the cops? The best-case scenario was that they just wouldn't believe her.

Sarah suddenly had the horrifying realization that the wolf was turning toward her. She was going to see the baby.

Don't look, she told herself. *Don't fucking look.*

She looked.

The wolf's massive arms made the baby look even smaller. It was fragile and wet, skin red and tender, the bald head too big for its body now lolling at a sickening angle. Its fingers were tiny, small enough that it would have been able to curl its whole hand around one of Sarah's fingers.

"I need to go," said Sarah.

Skillet looked at her, puzzled, her pupils so big her eyes looked black. "What? Why?"

"I need to go." Sarah blundered her way through the crowd, carefully sidestepping the writhing bodies on the ground and the rubberneckers pushing in to gawk at the dead monster baby. She walked slowly, calmly, not too fast, not too frantic, just normal enough that no one would think to look up and see her. *Just be normal, just walk normal, just stay calm. It's fine. Stay calm and get out. Stay calm and leave.* The crowd was thinning toward the back; if she could just dodge around the corner of the temple, just dodge out of eyeshot, but she could hear murmuring, muttering, chatter slowly building to a crescendo. Something bad was about to happen. No—something worse was about to happen.

Mother Moonflow was coming. For once, she was not wearing that dreamy hippie smile. She was walking right toward her, pointing. "There's one! Get her! Get them both! Don't let these phallic alecs escape!"

In the distance, several masked women climbed onto the

stage, tackling the man in the giant papier-mâché mask and knocking him to the ground. If he resisted, Sarah couldn't see.

"Nonono, stay back!" Sarah tripped over her own feet in a panic. She tipped over and hit the ground with a thud, her glasses falling from her face and cracking against the hard dirt. "Don't come any closer! I'm warning you, Diane Tibbitts!"

Mother Moonflow exploded into a fury. "You would deadname me?! You of all people!" She turned to the crowd. "You see what these phallic alecs bring to us?" Mother Moonflow straightened her back, her spine creaking under the weight of her colossal chest, and started counting off on her fingers. "Violence. Rape. Misogyny. Microaggressions. And this! She did this—with her phallic energy!"

Keep it together, thought Sarah. *You've had bad trips before. What was it that Madeleine said about bad trips? "If you start going bad, just remind yourself, where there's light, there's warmth"?* Sarah stared at a distant flickering torch with an intensity that she didn't think possible, but she did not feel any warmer in the chilly night air; it just made her eyes sting. Her arms broke out in goose bumps and she felt a chill run through her body, even though sweat was still pouring off her in sheets. She knew what she saw. That baby was definitely dead.

"You killed that baby! There was a baby!" Sarah scrambled to find her glasses.

The other sisters were surrounding her now, forming a circle around her. Even Aphrodite, lost somewhere in the crowd, paused in her weeping to watch. Now Sarah couldn't leave. Shit! She should have just gone for the woods. She shouldn't have wasted time. *That's what you get. That's what you fucking get.*

Sarah started to babble, but Mother Moonflow wasn't finished.

"You contaminated the purity of our birthing ceremony with your phallic energy! Your disgusting body, rank with girl sperm! Your filthy mouth on my tit, the sacred font of moonflow! We invited you into our birthing ceremony and you ruined it! It's a real bad scene, man!"

Murmurs of assent rippled through the crowd. Sarah did not think the trip could get worse, but the world tilted and dumped her into an even deeper layer of hell. The violence was coming. Sarah had seen it often enough to recognize it taking shape, and she was stupid for not seeing it from the start, for just sitting here like a lump and letting it boil up around her. In college, there was a frat guy who cornered her at a house party and whose eyes went murderous when he started to suspect she wasn't just a fat, easy lay. There was the blind date who wanted to talk endlessly about the size of her ass and tell her about his bottomless respect for her bravery, only to stomp out of the restaurant in a fury when she wouldn't order dessert. And the one time Madeleine took her clubbing, there was the man who shrieked and pointed and screamed as she emerged from the wrong restroom and chased them both, still shrieking and pointing and screaming, out of the club into the night. But no, apparently she was too stupid to predict the completely obvious tonight.

Sarah felt like she was a kid again getting berated by a very disappointed teacher. Mother Moonflow's breasts flopped against her stomach with every agitated gesture, and she was hunched low enough that her nipples scraped against the ground with every swing. *The friction must be highly sensual*, thought Sarah, because she imagined that she could see the nipples stiffening. *Jesus, what am I doing?* The moonflow made it impossible to think.

She was too terrified to say anything. She was convinced that she had completely forgotten all her vocal training and that the moment she opened her mouth, a man's baritone voice would leap out unbidden. *No, that's crazy thinking. It's the moonflow. Just remember you're having a bad time. Maybe Mother Moonflow will keep talking long enough for the moonflow to wear off. How long does the moonflow last?* Sarah had no concept of time. Stupidly, she hadn't checked her watch when she first drank. Not that it mattered. Her mind was so gone that she was half convinced she would not be able to decipher numbers anyway right now. *Why did I drink so much milk? Fuuuuck. Skillet was right, why the fuck was I such a greedy guts? Where is Skillet?*

Mother Moonflow sneered. "'Where is Skillet?' Looking for your little accomplice, huh?"

Oh. Apparently, she had said that part out loud.

"I know. I know everything. I know what you did. I know you're in league with the Lord of the Forest. I know you orchestrated this all, all to undermine me and to undermine the Green Lady."

Sarah felt like the world was shrinking in rhythmic pulses, gradually constricting around her to choke her like plastic wrap. This was her mother's womb, wrapping her safe and tight and warm. The world was disappearing; soon there would be nothing but womb. She was a helpless baby, asleep, about to be birthed.

"What did he promise you? He came to you in the dark and he whispered into your ear and he poisoned your mind and he poisoned your heart! You're a prophet of the Lord of the Forest!"

The wolf was next to Mother Moonflow now, her narrowed eyes just visible through the holes in her mask. "Wouldn't the prophet of the Lord of the Forest be a man?" she said uncertainly.

"Shut up! Shut the fuck up, all of you!" screamed Mother Moonflow. Her face was red; the vein bisecting her forehead was throbbing. "We're done playing that game! I am done with that bullshit! Open your eyes and look!"

The wolf stared at Sarah for a long moment, and Sarah could feel those eyes washing over her body, taking in her nubbly little breasts, her thick limbs, her shriveled girl dick hidden under the bulge of her gut. It took a moment longer for the light of understanding to appear in the wolf's eyes.

"Oh," said the wolf. "I couldn't tell. I really couldn't."

Mother Moonflow's eyes were hidden behind her glasses, but her mouth was a thin line of rage.

"That's a bum trip, man," she said, the dreamy hippie cadence back. Her voice quavered. "I thought you were cool, but this whole time, turned out you were a total square. Green Lady help me, you're going to pay for what you did to that baby."

The wolf reached for Sarah, and this time, everything went black.

24.

I am certain that I saw it today, lurking by the tree line. It does not have the face of a man.

—Diary of Lazarus Sloane
(California State Parks Archives)

Sunny Delight disappeared sometime during the chaos, and the Hell Slut knew, with miserable certainty, where she must have gone. The Hell Slut was right. Sunny Delight was at the field full of ruined cars, digging under the Studebaker until she found the lockbox. She took the money, all of it, but the Hell Slut, watching from the bushes, wondered if she felt a pang of guilt for it. This was different than taking the money from Mel. That money was hers; she was just taking what he owed her. This? This was stealing. But the Hell Slut couldn't blame her. Sunny Delight didn't know how long it would need to last her. She grabbed the big ungainly key with the little plastic skull key chain and pocketed it.

A twig cracked under the Hell Slut's foot. Sunny Delight gasped out loud and scanned the tree line, obviously afraid that someone had seen her slip away from the temple, someone had followed her here to the car lot, someone was going to end her escape. The raccoons in the trees stared down at her with glowing eyes.

"Not gonna say goodbye?" said the Hell Slut. She had removed her mask. They both had. Now they could talk, face to face.

"It's easier this way." Sunny Delight gulped; it sounded like a toilet plunger in the stillness of the night forest. She didn't need to say more than that. *Are you going to kill me like that baby?* "I can't stay here. It's so messed up. It's all messed up. The Green Lady . . . I can't believe she would want this . . ."

"What the Green Lady wants is what Mother Moonflow says," said the Hell Slut.

"Then Mother Moonflow is wrong! The Green Lady wouldn't want us to kill Athena! He was just a baby!"

"You don't know what you're saying."

"And I know you're mad at that girl for stealing Skillet, but you can't think it's right to kill her!"

"I'm not mad at anyone over Skillet," snapped the Hell Slut. "I don't care about Skillet."

"Yes, you do! I can tell! You love her! The Green Lady told me." Sunny Delight shook her head. "I never should have come here. I never should have got between you two. I never should have ruined things!"

"You don't understand anything."

"I understand enough."

The Hell Slut looked at Sunny Delight and felt a sudden stab of furious jealousy. She was so normal and pretty, she could probably just melt back into society if she wanted to and just live. She wasn't a freak and a killer; she didn't need to live this life. She could go home anytime that she wanted. Not like the Hell Slut. She'd been a fool to think she could keep the love of someone like Sunny Delight. Women like her were relegated to the Skillets of the world. *I never should have got between you two*, she'd said. Like the Hell Slut was destined for a Skillet, like she deserved a Skillet.

"Are you going to stop me?"

"No," said the Hell Slut. "Do whatever you want."

Sunny Delight stood up, shoving the remaining bills into her bra and taking a backward step toward the Sturgeon. The Hell Slut didn't move to stop her, so she climbed in behind the wheel and pulled the door shut.

"She's a good car," said the Hell Slut. "Can't believe she's still running after the hell she went through. She'll get you where you need to go."

"I'm sorry. I can't stay here. Not after that." Sunny Delight paused. "You can come with me. You should come with me."

That was a funny idea. What future was out there for them? They could go live a nice little suburban picket fence existence, maybe even get a nice little whitewashed San Bernardo bungalow—Sunny Delight could be a tradwife, the Hell Slut could be a cop. They could go to Little League games on the weekends, church on Sundays; they could come home and the Hell Slut could beat Sunny Delight for burning the dinner roast. No one would ever think they were anything but a nice, normal couple. But the Hell Slut could see in her eyes that the offer wasn't real. There was that fear there, now that she could see what the Hell Slut was truly capable of. They would never have again what they had before.

She remembered what Mother Moonflow had said the first day they met. *You'll always have a home here with us gals.* That knowledge was more valuable than gold. The Hell Slut couldn't give that up, not in a million years, not for all the Sunny Delights in the world. This was where she belonged. It was the only place she belonged.

The Hell Slut shook her head. "No, you were right. I belong here. I deserve Skillet. You don't want that. Go fuck off. I don't even know why I rescued your dumb ass from that frat guy. You can go back to Mel, for all I care."

Sunny Delight cringed and the Hell Slut regretted her words immediately, but they were already said.

"I'm not going back to Mel. I'm gonna go north."

"There's nothing north."

"Yeah, well. We'll see." Sunny Delight cranked the key and the engine roared to life. "I saw the Green Lady, back when we were in San Bernardo. I felt her presence. And I don't believe that she would want us to do the things that Mother Moonflow says the Green Lady wants. I think Mother Moonflow just says what *she* wants. I think Mother Moonflow just makes us do what she wants. So you're gonna have to figure out who you're loyal to, Mother Moonflow or the Green Lady. I know what I am. Praise the Green Lady."

The Hell Slut watched the car pull out backward and then roll out of the lot and onto the service road. She watched until all she could see were the twin orbs of the Sturgeon's taillights, and then even those disappeared behind the trees. She thought about that promise she'd made to Sunny Delight while they were in San Bernardo, that someday they would travel down to the Bay and together they would kill Mel. It looked like that wasn't going to happen. Mel was going to live. He was going to live and he was going to find some other runaway and get her to turn tricks in the back room of his apartment, and he was going to beat her and rape her and take her money, and he would do it again and again to who knows how many runaways after that.

But maybe Sunny Delight would keep her promise to go north, and then, at the very least, he wouldn't be doing it to her anymore.

He won't be doing it to Sunny Delight anymore, thought the Hell Slut. *At least he won't be doing it to her.*

She watched the darkness left behind in the wake of the retreating Sturgeon for a few minutes more. Then she returned to the thicket.

Virginia Dentata stood in front of the door and crossed her arms as the Hell Slut approached.

"No one talks to the prisoner."

The Hell Slut snorted. Prisoner. How fucking melodramatic could you get? "It's just fucking Skillet. I won't even be a minute."

"I'm sure you got plenty to talk about. You and Skillet are awfully close, aren't you?"

"Go to hell. You think someone else is gonna talk some sense into the little shit? You know it's gotta be me or no one."

Virginia Dentata guffawed. "Fine. Have fun. See if she'll talk to you. She's lucky she still has any teeth at this point." She held up a bandaged forearm to illustrate her point. The bandages were stained red.

The Hell Slut put a hand on her shoulder and muscled her aside. But then pity moved her and she said, just to mollify Virginia Dentata, "Gimme a minute. No one needs to know."

Beyond the door was a small cell, one of many in a temple designed on a whim, and lying on the floor was Skillet, naked, nose bloody, eye swollen shut, trussed up like a holiday ham. There was a low wooden bench opposite Skillet, partially hidden in the shadowy corner, and the Hell Slut lowered her wide ass onto it. It creaked loudly and Skillet stirred under the blood and grime.

"Hey," said the Hell Slut.

"Hey, sister." Skillet grinned and her teeth were all stained red.

"What happened to you?"

"Virginia Dentata, mostly. And Miss Trix. They're real sore about the birthing ceremony getting fucked." Skillet laughed unsteadily.

"Ugh, I'm gonna end those fucking bitches," said the Hell Slut. Then she inhaled through her nose, willing herself back to calm. "Looks like you held your own, though. You really bit the hell out of Virginia Dentata's arm. That shit could get infected."

"Ha ha! Good."

The Hell Slut lit a roach, took a drag, and held it to Skillet's mouth. Skillet sucked in and released the smoke with a dry little gasp.

"Look at us," she wheezed. "Like a couple of noir dykes in that old movie."

"What old movie?"

Skillet laughed dryly. "I dunno. One of them."

"You're in a real fucking jam this time, Skillet. Real fucking hell of a tantrum you're throwing."

"I ain't done nothin'. I'm innocent!"

"Yeah, and those phallic alecs just randomly happened to show up? What's with this fat girl?"

Skillet's eyes darted back and forth. "What do you care? Maybe I just like her, okay?"

"You fuck around all the time, Skillet. You've fucked every sister in the temple. You expect me to think this fat chick means something to you? You two have some deep emotional bond forged in, what, the one day I was gone? Fuck off."

"You abandoned me for the Dank Hole girl! What was I supposed to do?"

"Is that what this is about? Sunny Delight?"

Skillet laughed a loud, shrill, ugly laugh. "Ha! I saw what happened back there. She couldn't even look at you after what you did. You knew that would happen. She doesn't know what you are. She could never know what you are. You've said it before: You do what needs doing. You think the Dank Hole girl could ever understand that?"

The Hell Slut grunted in the darkness.

"I guess not. She's gone now. She was with me when we killed that ranger, so I thought—"

"Yeah, well, killin' a fucking baby's a little different. I know what you thought. You thought you could find someone better than Skillet, huh? You thought she would get you? News flash—ain't no one gets you better than Skillet! Ain't no one *ever* gonna get you better than Skillet! I know what you are. And I'm still here! Untie me."

"I can't. Not this time. I'm sorry, Skillet. Fuck, Skillet, I wish it wasn't like this. Why did you have to do it? Why did you have to go do all this shit?" The Hell Slut's voice cracked just a little.

"You started it. Before that, we were always Skillet and the Hell Slut. Now we're not. Didn't that mean anything to you?"

"You got yourself into a fucking hell of a jam, Skillet. Mother Moonflow's got some real fucked-up shit planned for you."

Fear washed over Skillet's face, possibly for the first time ever. That was funny. Up until this moment, the Hell Slut hadn't been sure that Skillet could experience fear. Everything was a joke to her, a joke or an excuse to cop a feel.

"What's she gonna do?"

"We're about to find out. You just keep your mouth shut. When the time comes, I'll take care of things."

"You got a plan?"

"No. No, I don't got a fucking plan. I barely know what I'm doing. We're probably both gonna get fucking killed, that's what's gonna happen."

Skillet grinned. "We're together again, at least. Heh. We were meant to be together. Remember the first time we killed for the temple?"

"I got such a fuckin' yeast infection from that."

"Ha ha! What a start! And now look at us! Skillet and the Hell Slut, together again. Nice ring to it, don't ya think?"

She put her hand on Skillet's head and scritched her fingers against her scalp. Skillet fluttered her eyelids.

I guess this is what I get, thought the Hell Slut. *I guess this is all I would ever get.*

"It does have a nice ring to it." The Hell Slut pushed herself to her feet and left the room, closing the door behind her with a click.

25.

*The Purple Viscount (*Clitopilus violetus*) has a wide rounded cap of varying violet to purple hues, topped with patchy wart-like scales. It excretes a sticky syrup-like substance when disturbed. It is said to taste of your mother's dying whisper.*

—Field Guide to Common Mushrooms of the Pamogo Forest, *T. F. Greengarb (1978)*

Andy missed most of the ceremony because his mask had extremely poor visibility. He was able to piece together the general story of the Green Lady and the Lord of the Forest by listening to Mother Moonflow's words, muffled as they were by papier-mâché, but he'd lost track of the action by the time that the scuffle began. It didn't help that the lyrics of "Orinoco Flow" tended to overwhelm the dialogue. All he knew was that, all of a sudden, he was being tackled by unseen forces pushing his face to the ground and twisting his arms behind his back.

"This is all just a big misunderstanding."

He tried to protest, but they couldn't hear him through his papier-mâché mask—either that or they didn't care. He was stripped and bound—he could recall dozens of hands tearing at his shirt and ripping off his khakis and boxers, and, worst of all, curious fingers playing with his dick and balls. The sisters cooed and giggled, amused by the novelty of his genitals, and they laughed the entire trek from the clearing to wherever they were taking him. Andy, still wearing his mask, his feet and wrists bound, had little choice but to go along. For the first time since their rescue in the house in the woods, Andy felt fear grip his heart. Sarah kept talking about how this was a cult—only now did he start to see the full implications of what that might mean.

"I'm sure we can talk this out," said Andy, now strapped to a cot in the infirmary and staring up at the painting of the Green Lady across the ceiling. "There's no reason to do any of this."

Doc Clopper stretched a rubber glove over her hand and snapped the cuff, more for the theatricality of it than for any actual medical purpose. She didn't wear a mask or a cap, her gray hair falling over her shoulders, and her only other acquiescence to medical hygiene was a leather apron tied around her waist. After a hard day of doctoring, her tie-dyed T-shirt was spattered with obscure bodily fluids. She held up a comically gigantic syringe—so massive that surely it must be designed only for use on horses or other large quadrupeds, surely not for use on people—and flicked the obviously rusty point to spray a few drops across the room. The syringe was filled with a thick white fluid.

"Listen, pal, I don't like this whole situation any more than you do," she said, peering at the syringe through her glasses. "You think this is how I want to spend my time? Playing nursemaid to some phallic alec who can't keep his phallic energy in his pants? I got fanfic I could be writing."

Andy stared at the tip of the syringe, a fat drop of liquid still clinging to the rusty point. It looked like tetanus waiting to happen. He felt suddenly sweaty and feverish, and fear made his dick shrivel and his testicles retract into tight prickly spheres. He struggled against his bonds, but the leather straps were latched tight and he only succeeded in rattling the cot's metal frame. Doc Clopper waited patiently for the tantrum to pass.

"You feeling better now? Work out your frustrations?"

"This isn't fair! I didn't do anything! I wore the mask just like you asked me to! And I never left that phallic containment-zone stage thing! I'm an ally!"

"This was always gonna happen, right from the start. I dunno why Mother Moonflow thought it was such a hot idea having you phallic alecs attend; I told her from the start that something like this was gonna happen. Now look who has to clean up the mess."

"I didn't even drink any moonflow!"

Doc Clopper rolled her eyes. She placed a metal tray onto the stool next to the cot and began piling evil-looking medical devices upon it. Andy watched, his pulse rising with every new gleaming metal instrument added to the assortment.

"See, that's actually the problem. A smart kid like you, we can't have you all clearheaded for what's to come. For your own sake, you gotta be doped up. It wouldn't be right to put you through it sober. I took a Hippocratic oath, after all."

Apart from the occasional beer after work and a single marijuana joint in college, Andy was a complete naif to the world of psychoactive substances. "I've never done drugs!" he wailed.

Doc Clopper paused, still brandishing the needle. "Never? Well then, you got two choices. You can drink the moonflow, or I can inject it right into you. Keep in mind that with that second option, there is a slight chance that it might cause mushrooms to grow in your bloodstream and kill you, but you'll probably be fine."

Andy looked at the needle again. The idea of drinking moonflow, of losing his mind and his reason and his rationality and becoming so helpless and stupid, like a baby, was utterly repellant. He felt itchy just thinking about it. But that needle...

"I'll drink it."

"You're a good kid. Don't worry about it. Just sit back and enjoy the ride. It's gonna blow your mind."

They put Sarah in one of the raccoon rooms; Miss Trix flushed them out, cursing and shouting, raccoons tumbling from their nests in the rafters. Sarah was still naked—she could vaguely recall, through the moonflow haze, dozens of hands dragging her here after the birthing ceremony, and Virginia Dentata even smashing her glasses and then roughly binding her wrists and ankles with thick twine until she bled and then throwing her here, into a baby crib so small that her legs stuck out through the bars. Without her glasses, it was hard to tell who slapped her around, who smacked her head against the floor, whose hand squeezed at her throat...but she recognized Virginia Dentata's voice hissing obscenities in her ear, and she was not surprised.

"Fucking he-she gonna get what's coming; oh, you're gonna get it now..."

When she was alone, she wallowed in nauseous misery and guilt. She had abandoned Herman. And for what? A chance to see the goddess—who wasn't even real, just a stupid hallucination that, for some bizarre reason, Sarah couldn't get out of her head? What a stupid thing to do.

The walls were painted with happy clowns and smiling cats. *This was gonna be the baby's room*, thought Sarah dumbly, but the painted faces twisted and laughed and leered and she couldn't think straight. In the rare moments when the brain fog lifted and she could remember where she was, she could feel the cords tightly bound around her wrists and ankles. *It's like in a Nancy Drew book*, she thought stupidly, and then the moonflow fog returned and she passed into a world of shadows and illusions.

Someone else was in the room with her, but she had trouble focusing enough to identify her companion at first. Andy was dumped into the crib with her, and they were lying back-to-back, both naked, so that she could feel the sweaty skin of his bony ass rubbing against the sweaty skin of her fat ass. Andy sobbed quietly, his narrow shoulders shaking.

Empty baby bottles littered the floor, and Sarah could see they were stained with white residue. *They're drugging him*, she thought. *He's high too.*

"Andy, is that you?"

"Time has three directions," he babbled in a strained voice. Andy was not holding his moonflow well.

"It's okay, Andy. You're just high. You're fine. Listen to me. I'll talk you through it. How're you holding up?"

"'S cold."

"I know. Me too." He didn't respond, so she continued: "I'm sorry I got us into this mess. I shouldn't have followed that phone glitch. I shouldn't have fucked up their dumb ceremony."

All because she'd wanted to see the goddess again. What a joke. What a stupid idiot she was.

"I'm sorry I got us lost," said Andy. "You were right. This is a cult. I'm so stupid."

He was very stupid, but she felt too miserable with guilt to point that out. "Don't worry about it."

"I want you to know? When I said that stuff about trans women liking *Stalker*? That wasn't me being transphobic."

"Uh-huh."

"And also I wasn't trying to get with Effervescent Bubbles. We really were just talking about interpretation."

"Christ. You don't do drugs, you don't want sex—what do you *do* with all your time? You were right about Skillet, though. We got together."

And what a stupid fucking idea that had been.

"Congratulations?"

"It doesn't matter. Skillet's a chaser. I've met them before, they're just usually guys. She just wanted to fuck cuz I'm fat and I was a rebound. But whatever, who cares now."

Andy paused, like when she had confessed her secret desire for huge breasts. Even in the depths of moonflow delirium, he must have sensed he was outside of his element.

"Are they going to kill us?"

Sarah didn't want to keep talking. She felt like she was explaining to a kid that Santa Claus wasn't real. Luckily, the moonflow made both of their tongues fat and lethargic, and words difficult to remember. So instead they lay there, numb to the world, as reality warped and shifted around them, and waited for their fate.

At some point, Sarah became aware that there was someone else in the room, watching them. She thought it was Jade—but then she remembered she was in an abandoned lumber mill in the middle of the Pamogo Forest and that Jade wasn't here. She was thousands of miles away, probably organizing some new art show right at this moment, and she probably hadn't given a single thought to Sarah in months. Sarah had to concentrate hard to see through the blur of moonflow and recognize her guard—*It's the ginger girl, what's her name, Bubbles? Effervescent Bubbles! That's it.* Sarah tried to talk to her, but Effervescent Bubbles didn't reply. She just sat in the corner and sobbed the whole time. Eventually, someone else came into the room and relieved her. Someone pushed Sarah into a sitting position and shoved a baby bottle of milk under her nose, commanding her to drink. Distantly, a voice in her head told her it was a bad idea. They were keeping her high going. As long as she was high, she couldn't do anything. She would just lie in this room, lazy and stupid, until Mother Moonflow finally decided what to do with them.

Whatever that was, Sarah knew it wasn't going to be good. Otherwise, they wouldn't be tied up.

The hands holding the bottle had black fingernails. It was Pickles.

"Drink up, c'mon," he was saying. "That's a good girl, hmm? Yum-yum, you love your milkies, don't you?"

Sarah looked at him, bleary-eyed, cream dribbling down her double chin. His hair looked like a black waterfall. She could almost see the rivulets of black trickling down the strands of his hair, like flickering LED lights, and she was so mesmerized that she almost forgot to say anything.

"Where's my clothes?" she finally asked. Pickles was blurry without her glasses.

"Lie down and be quiet, please." Pickles lowered her back to the ground. He rolled Andy over onto his back and shoved the bottle into his mouth. Andy's long skinny body looked even longer and skinnier without clothes, and Sarah stared studiously at his sunken hairless chest to avoid looking at his crotch. When she finally looked, she was shocked to see he still had a dick. He had a catheter shoved up there, a long rubber tube leading over to a bedside table, where, she now realized, it emptied into a big glass pitcher. There were several glass pitchers full of bright yellow piss, which Sarah surmised Doc Clopper must be collecting for reasons of her own.

"They're gonna kill us," said Sarah. "Please. You have to untie me. I promise if you do, we'll just leave. We'll never come back."

"Little late for that, don't you think?" Pickles tilted the bottle, and Andy gurgled deep in his throat as he continued to drink obliviously. "You really should *not* have done that. You really have no one but yourself to blame, you know."

Sarah wondered where Pickles had been during the birthing ceremony. She didn't remember seeing him there. Maybe they didn't let him attend. She couldn't remember. This cult made no sense. What was Pickles? The hair, the nails, the way he bowed his head to let Mother Moonflow stroke him like a lap dog... Maybe there was something there, something she could use...

"Look. We're... we're not so different, are we? I mean, are we?" God, it was embarrassing to say; it was such an obvious ploy of desperation, but... she was desperate, after all.

Pickles looked down his nose at her, frowning at her disgusting nudity. "That's cute. You're doing psychology. We are totally different. I'm not some guy who's trying to be a woman. I was never a guy. I'm unbinary."

Sarah laid her head on the floor and groaned. *Oh god. More discourse.*

Pickles pulled the empty bottle from Andy's mouth with a pop and took a seat in the rickety chair that Effervescent Bubbles had vacated. He crossed his legs, placed his hands in his lap, and primly stared at the wall. "But, by all means, keep it up. Did you try this with Effervescent Bubbles? I bet she really responded well."

"We didn't talk. She just cried the whole time she was here."

"Of course she did, poor thing. The whole birthing ceremony debacle...it really hit her hard. Such a sensitive girl. Just really traumatizing for her, you know?"

"What am I even doing here?" moaned Sarah. She felt so woozy.

"Shut up. You're the one who's ruining things. You really thought you could drink the moonflow and get away with it, didn't you? I almost admire the chutzpah. You're really making things difficult for the rest of us, I hope you know that." His voice was rising; he was starting to get agitated. Sarah wasn't sure whether this was a positive development or a negative one.

"That's not fair. Look, Pickles, I get it. Believe me, I get it." Her head felt heavy from the tainted milk, and she had no clue if anything she was saying was having any effect.

"Stop it! I know what you're doing. You think you can manipulate me, but I've worked harder than any of the sisters to get here. I had to! You know why? I had nowhere else to go! They can go live in society! I can't!"

Sarah desperately tried to remember what it was that Madeleine always said that cracked so many eggs. She was violating the prime directive, but frankly, she was willing to risk sending Pickles into a full-blown existential crisis if it helped her get out of here.

"Of course not," she said as kindly as she could muster. "And you've got such nice hair."

"Shut up! Fucking truscum!" Pickles jumped from his chair and kicked Sarah hard in the belly, knocking the wind out of her. She gagged and milk spurted from her mouth and nose. Pickles kicked her again, this time in the crotch, and Sarah bellowed in pain. *God damn it!*

"I can't wait for Mother Moonflow to deal with you! Send you back to the Lord of the Forest, where you belong!"

Sarah felt reality shudder and suddenly she was outside herself, bobbing up to the ceiling, looking down on Pickles kicking her body, which twitched and screamed in response. She rose through the ceiling and up through the building, higher and higher, until she popped through the roof of the temple and up into the night sky, so that she could see the surrounding miles and miles of endless green that was the Pamogo canopy. Was this real? Or was it part of the hallucination?

When she returned to her body, Pickles was inspecting the piss bottles on the nightstand. He nodded in satisfaction.

"Nice and yellow. Doc Clopper will love it."

"Why does Doc Clopper want piss?"

Pickles giggled playfully. "You know how doctors are! They love to play doctor. Or I guess, in her case, I should say they love to play veterinarian!"

He laughed even harder as he crouched down next to Andy, pinched the soft head of Andy's flaccid dick between two fingers, and gently tugged at the hose.

"You know, I saw the Lord of the Forest once."

Sarah blinked at him, still sputtering milk.

Pickles lowered his voice. "Many, many years ago, I went out into the woods alone. I wasn't supposed to, but I was young and foolish and I thought I knew better than Mother Moonflow. I thought I could impress her with my scavenging prowess. Ah, the folly of youth! I was down by one of the old fire watchtowers when I felt eyes on my back and I knew I wasn't alone. I looked up and I saw him."

Inches of rubber tubing unspooled from Andy's urethra as Pickles tugged, hand over hand. Sarah's girl dick flinched in sympathetic pain, but Andy was far too high to even register what was happening. He started to harden under Pickles's grasp, and Pickles chuckled quietly.

"He's not real," said Sarah. "Skillet said it's all not real."

Pickles barked a short laugh. "Skillet's always been a blasphemer. He was tall, ridiculously tall... and thin! Like a scarecrow, arms all dangly and legs too long. And the face! I'll never forget the face..."

"It was not the face of a man," said Sarah.

Pickles drew back, eyes wide. "You've seen him?"

She had seen him. Deep down, she was sure of it. Leviathan's Favored Son must have suppressed it. But somewhere down in the deepest basement of her subconscious, the memory bubbled and boiled.

"No, I've... I've heard. He told me."

Pickles arched a skeptical eyebrow. "That is a highly dubious statement. I don't even think he can form words with a mouth like... like that. I swear to the Green Lady, I've never seen anything like it. I panicked, dropped everything I was carrying, and I ran. I ran back here, to the temple, to the protection of Mother Moonflow and the Green Lady. And I never, ever, *ever* went out there again."

For the first time, Sarah noticed that there were strands of gray hairs mixed in with the black ones.

"How long have you been here, Pickles?"

"I have never gone out there into those woods again." He was trembling, choked by fear, so that he stuttered. "And I never will. I will live out my days and die here in the temple before I ever see that thing again."

"Why are you telling me this?"

"Oh, sweetie." Pickles clucked his tongue sadly. Finally, the end of the tube popped free from Andy's dick hole, and Pickles threw it to the floor. He wiped his hands against his robe as if to psychologically cleanse them of all cock germs. "I just want you to be ready when you meet him."

From Bissau to Palau, in the shade of Avalon
From Fiji to Tiree and the Isles of Ebony

"You're in a real jam, Big Mama."

Sarah awoke to the strains of "Orinoco Flow." The last thing she remembered was Pickles, but apparently he had since vacated the room. Now Mother Moonflow herself sat cross-legged on the floor in front of her. Up close, the markers of her age were more apparent. Her senses heightened by moonflow, Sarah could see the cracks in the façade: the little wrinkles at the sides of the mouth, the snarly gray hairs hidden among the flowing waterfall of black. Her beauty regimen must be even more extreme than Madeleine's to keep age at bay so effectively. Mother Moonflow had her boombox with her.

"I'm glad that we're getting a chance to rap, one-on-one. I feel like we got a lot in common."

"What about Andy here?" Sarah forced her mouth to form words, fighting the numbing effects of moonflow. The world still swam before her eyes, a symphony of outrageous colors.

"Let him sleep—that cat's had a hard day. He ain't used to expanding his mind. Not like us." Mother Moonflow stretched and unfurled, lying down on the floor so that she was facing Sarah through the bars of the crib. She pushed her glasses up to her forehead and fixed Sarah with eyes revealed to be a cold slate gray. Her colossal breasts filled the space between them, her nipples just barely grazing Sarah's chest with every inhale. Sarah struggled to ignore the sensation.

"Like I was saying, we got a lot in common. We're both strong independent women who are also intelligent. We both know what we want. We're both not shy about taking what we want. Listen, Big Mama, I owe you an apology. I shouldn't have said what I said earlier. I got a little heated."

Sarah remained silent.

"I shouldn't have misgendered you. That was real unchill of me. But you gotta understand, Big Mama, I was real mad at the time."

"Of course," said Sarah, nodding as sympathetically as she could. It had worked (momentarily) on that ranger in Las Brujas; maybe she could convince Mother Moonflow she was totally sincere. Maybe her life depended on convincing Mother Moonflow of that. "I forgive you."

"And, anyway, you deadnamed me first."

"Of course," said Sarah. "I shouldn't have done that. I apologize completely. It was my fault. Since that's settled, maybe you could untie me?"

Oh my God in heaven, thought Sarah, *are we having a goddamn therapy session? This is torture.*

"Not just yet. There's just one thing I don't get about you, Big Mama."

"What's that?"

"How'd you kill that baby?"

Sarah sputtered stupidly, milk bubbling from her nose.

"Twenty strong women orgasmed the night of Athena's conception. And tonight we even anointed the dancers with dead dad seed, real potent stuff! I thought your phallic energy was weak, Sarah. You ejaculate girl sperm now. It's probably just a powder or something. There's no way that you sucking on my tit could have caused this to go wrong. And your pal Andy sitting in the bleachers? No way was that enough. We prepared too well. So what happened? I just don't get it. Here, suck on my teat while I talk. We don't want you coming down, do we?"

Mother Moonflow hoisted a breast into Sarah's face, smothering her with soft, warm, pillowy flesh, and a turgid nipple poked her in the eye before it found its mark.

"I don't get why you'd want to be a woman. Women are weak. We live in a whirlwind of our own lusts, unable to withstand the lure of men and their dicks. You know I had to put a padlock on the cellar cuz the sisters kept sneakin' down there? Why would you ever want to be like that? When you're born with the phallic power?"

Mother Moonflow cooed softly and reached her foot between Sarah's legs to gently tickle her girl dick with her toes, but nerves and moonflow kept Sarah from showing even a ghost of a reaction.

Sarah spat out the nipple and gritted her teeth when Mother Moonflow tried to jam it back in.

"But I don't blame you, Sarah. I know none of this was your fault. You're just a sap, same as your pal over there." She nodded toward Andy, who sniffed and smacked his lips in his sleep.

"Are you going to kill us?"

"Naw, I ain't gonna kill you! I need your help. You help me with this one little thing and, heck, I'll forget the whole dead baby fiasco. You help me with this one thing, and you'll both be free to go. We'll take ya back to Las Brujas, and we'll just forget this whole thing ever happened."

It was too much to hope for. Sarah was confident that Mother Moonflow was lying. Even if she didn't blame Sarah for Athena's death, surely she couldn't just let a couple of murder witnesses just traipse out of here? But Sarah could feel the weakest little grasping tendrils of hope clutching at her heart, and it was too seductive to ignore.

"You mean it?"

A smile curled across Mother Moonflow's face. "With the Green Lady as my witness, Big Mama, I wouldn't lie!"

"What's this one thing?"

"I'm gonna take y'all down into the cellar. I'm gonna show you where we grow the King's Breakfast. I know that's what you want. I know that's what you've been after. I saw the way you were jonesin' after moonflow last night. I know you musta had it before, you musta seen something you need to see again, felt something you need to feel again. I bet you saw the Green Lady. She only shows herself to real special gals, I can tell you that. I promise you, Sarah, whatever you saw, what we got down in the cellar is gonna blow it away. That's the real deal. Ain't nothing like the real deal."

"Why are you doing this?"

"Because I know this whole thing wasn't your idea, Big Mama. It was Skillet, wasn't it?"

Sarah's blood ran instantly cold.

"I know everything, Big Mama. Skillet must really think I'm a real idiot, that I wouldn't figure it out. Effervescent Bubbles heard what she said to the Lord of the Forest, and Effervescent Bubbles is a loyal sister, so of course she told me. I know you're here because of Skillet. I know she was working to undermine me. We gotta discipline her, get her back in line."

"Jesus Christ."

"Don't say that name, Big Mama. If you're gonna swear, use her name. Swear by the name of the Green Lady. But we all know how Skillet is, we all know what she is. Don't tell me you got feelings for her? If it makes ya feel better, we ain't gonna do nothing bad—we're just giving her a little slap on the wrist. She'll fuss and she'll fret and make a real big stink about it, but she'll barely feel it, trust me. You just play along. Just say yes, and you can save yourself and save your phallic alec pal over there."

"What are you going to do to Skillet?"

"You don't worry about the whats and the what nots, Big Mama. You let me worry about that. All you gotta do is play along. You want to see the Green Lady again, don't you?"

Sarah tried really hard to think, to parse meaning as she swam through a moonflow haze. She remembered the goddess, remembered those kindly outstretched hands, and thought about grabbing those hands and holding them tight. She felt like she was going to cry, it was so overwhelming. It was so overwhelming she didn't have room for thoughts of Andy or Madeleine or even Herman, and all she had to do was help Mother Moonflow with this one little problem, this one little problem of Skillet—who, Sarah reminded herself, was a little shit who had used her and was also a chaser to boot.

She opened her mouth and she said it.

"Yes."

Sail away, sail away, sail away

26.

*Witch Fingers (*Agaricus strix*) are an uncommon, localized variant of the Mother of Groans, distinguished by tall white crooked stalks terminating in clusters of unusual keratin plates resembling human fingernails. Witch Fingers are the only known fungus to contain bones. They are said to taste of bad decisions rashly made.*

—Field Guide to Common Mushrooms of the Pamogo Forest, *T. F. Greengarb (1978)*

The prophet remained in seclusion. She burned sage and patchouli, filling the sanctuary with thick acrid smoke that scorched her lungs and flushed the little sisters out of their tunnels, and listened to "Orinoco Flow" on loop until the words started to blur into pure noise. The sisters outside the sanctuary whispered and gossiped, passing around flasks of moonflow, waiting for the moment that Mother Moonflow would reach a decision about what was to be done.

The Hell Slut sat on a stump, furiously puffing on a joint, away from the others. But she could hear little snatches of conversation, and every word just made her suck harder on her joint.

"...giving them over to the Lord of the Forest..."

"...Green Lady have mercy..."

"...phallic energy, that's what did it..."

"...it's only fair, after what they did..."

"...is it true? What Skillet did?..."

"Of course it's true," announced Virginia Dentata, her voice loud and belligerent above the fray. "Mother Moonflow will take care of those phallic alecs, just you wait. She'll make sure they pay for what they did to Aphrodite's baby. And Skillet's gonna get what's coming to her."

"You don't know shit," said the Hell Slut.

Virginia Dentata turned slowly, one eyebrow raised. "You got something to say? Maybe you're making deals with the Lord of the Forest too? You're awful tight with Skillet, aren't you?"

"Not anymore," said Miss Trix. "She's got a new beau now. How's your Sunny Delight?" She pursed her lips in a mocking kissy-kissy face, and Virginia Dentata bellowed with laughter.

The vagina door opened, and Pickles emerged in a cloud of incense. Everyone dropped their conversations and turned their attention to him.

"Mother Moonflow invites you all into the sanctuary. You all need to hear what she's about to say."

They crowded inside, jostling for space on the floor, everyone trying to get as close to Mother Moonflow as possible. There had never been so many sisters in the sanctuary together at one time. Sometimes, if she had some important wisdom, Mother Moonflow might summon a sister or maybe two sisters for an audience, but to have all twenty here at once? It was unheard of. They filled the room, sitting in a circle around the central futon, where Mother Moonflow sat cross-legged with the two phallic alecs at her sides, one teat in each mouth. They were still naked, their wrists still bound, their minds numbed. The concentrated heat from many bodies made the room swelter, and the musty scent of body odor overwhelmed the scent of patchouli and drove the raccoons back into their tunnels. A flask passed from hand to hand in the audience, sisters waiting their turn to guzzle deep swigs of moonflow, cream trickling down chins as they drank.

"There's been some real unchill vibes here in the temple lately. And I think we all know why. These two phallic alecs came to us out of the woods, and like good neighbors, we tried to help them. We really did. But look what happened, man! They got their phallic vibes all over everything."

Virginia Dentata, squatting in the front row, glowered in the gloom but did not say anything. Sarah sensed that she was pleased to be vindicated. What a fucking bitch.

"Before I make my verdict, any of you cats got anything else to say? Virginia Dentata? Pickles?"

Pickles hung in the back of the room, nervously gnawing at his fingernails. He looked nauseous but he shook his head.

"I know Aphrodite has some words."

"I do have something to say," said Aphrodite. Her eyes were red and puffy and her voice quavered. She pulled a crumpled slice of paper from her brassiere and smoothed it with her hands before clearing her throat.

Oh great, thought Sarah. *Here we go.*

"This is for the phallic alec that killed Athena," said Aphrodite, reading from a prepared speech. "I was angry at first. I asked myself, why? Why would you take away my Athena? What did she ever do to you? She was just a baby. And then I thought, was it me? Did I do something wrong? What did I do to make you hate me so? But the more I thought about it, it's not anger I feel anymore. Mother Moonflow helped me to realize that this was all part of the Green Lady's plan and that, through Athena's death, we are now stronger. And that's good, it's really good. I'm glad that you killed Athena. I want you to know that, despite everything, I forgive you. I don't have any hate in my heart for you. I just feel sorry for you."

Oh my God, thought Sarah. *Oh my God, I hate this.*

"That's some real wisdom." Mother Moonflow nodded appreciatively. "Now let's talk about the real truth, though. We're all hurting from what these phallic alecs have done, and we all know there's only one thing that we can do. I'm gonna take them down into the cellar."

The crowd exploded into chatter—several women whooped in excitement, but a few others snarled and shook their heads.

Now Virginia Dentata leaped to her feet. "That's it? Mother Moonflow, after all they've done—"

"That's it. These phallic alecs are about to undertake one mega cosmic journey, and afterward, when they really understand, they're free to go."

This revelation prompted laughter from the audience. Sarah didn't like that.

"But first, where's the Hell Slut?"

The Hell Slut came before Mother Moonflow and kneeled awkwardly.

"Big Mama, I ain't gonna lie. This whole thing's been a real setback. I was worried for a bit back there, but I'm glad to know you're still with me. We can't do this without you. You are still with us, right?"

"Yes, Mother Moonflow."

"You're gonna get a chance to show it. Check this."

The door opened again. Miss Trix carried in Skillet and dumped her on the ground, taking special care to ensure that

Skillet missed every pillow on her descent and hit the hard packed-earth floor at full force. Miss Trix flashed a smug grin at the accused before taking her place in the audience. Skillet was nude and black blood crusted her lips. Her breath whistled through her blood-clogged nose.

"Had some time to think about what you did, Little Mama?" asked Mother Moonflow.

Skillet blinked her good eye. She glanced over at the Hell Slut, then at Sarah, realization dawning as she saw Sarah was on the futon sitting next to Mother Moonflow, and giggled hysterically.

"Look," said Skillet, "I'm sorry about the baby. Aphrodite can just make another, if she wants it so bad. Or better yet, tell her to take responsibility for the little shits! God knows someone needs to—"

"You will be quiet. The baby is not the issue, Skillet. We're beyond that. The issue is that you went behind my back and made a deal with the Lord of the Forest to destroy me, to destroy this sisterhood!"

"No!"

"Effervescent Bubbles, please tell the sisters what you told me."

Effervescent Bubbles stepped forward, wringing her hands nervously under the frayed fabric of her poncho. Her eyes darted about the room, but she never looked at Skillet.

"I saw Skillet go into the woods and talk to the Lord of the Forest."

"And what did she say?" coaxed Mother Moonflow.

Effervescent Bubbles squirmed, sweat beading on her brow. "She said... 'I want to see the temple burn to the ground. I give myself to you... Whatever you want, my body, my soul, my pussy, it's yours, I swear it!'"

The room broke out into angry chatter, and above it all, Skillet screeched, "I never said that! I never fucking said that!"

Mother Moonflow held up her hands for quiet. "That's a real grave accusation, Skillet. Most unmellow. We can't have that kinda insubordination in the temple. It ain't good. And since these phallic alecs came from the Lord of the Forest, I think they ought to go back to him. Does anyone object to that?"

The collected women did not object.

"And since you wanted to deal with the Lord of the Forest so much, I think it's time that you meet your benefactor and really understand what deal you made."

Skillet flopped and shrieked. "What the fuck?! What are you talking about?"

"You promised to give the Lord of the Forest anything that he wanted. Anything he desired. Your body, your soul, your pussy. And the Lord of the Forest, he is in all his forms a man. There is only one thing that he desires."

She paused, as if to wait for some objection. Behind her, Pickles was silent, terror writ large across his face. The only sound was Skillet's wheezing.

A lone voice broke the silence. It was the Hell Slut. "Mother Moonflow, you can't do that. You can't do that."

Silence.

"Ain't you still with me, Hell Slut?"

"Yes, Mother Moonflow."

"Then that's the way it's got to be, Big Mama."

The Hell Slut snorted and seethed, but Mother Moonflow continued talking, unbothered.

"Then it's settled! Skillet, you've heard the judgment. Y'all ready to take your medicine?"

There was a knock at the door. The little door, the one painted red. The one painted with a face. Something was back there.

Skillet burst into loud shrill giggles that echoed against the rounded walls of the sanctuary, back and forth, magnifying with every reverberation. Mother Moonflow fell silent and waited for the laughter to die down. Pickles hid his mouth behind his black-painted fingers.

"Skillet," said Mother Moonflow. "You worked to undermine the prophet of the Green Lady. Hell Slut. You've been awful close with Skillet in the past. Too close perhaps. You are still loyal, right? Now is your chance to prove your loyalty."

"I'm loyal to you, Mother Moonflow," said the Hell Slut.

"That's what I like to hear, cats!" Now Mother Moonflow was at the door. Not the main door, but the other one—the small door in the back of the room, the one that came only as high as your waist, the one that was hidden behind piles of dirty pillows, the one that was always locked, the one from which Sarah was certain she had just heard a knock. Now Sarah heard a key turn in a lock, she heard a bolt retract with the grinding of too many years of rust, and she watched, unbelieving, as the door opened.

"Sarah, come with me," said Mother Moonflow. She stood. "It's time you saw what we're all about. Hell Slut, pick up Skillet. Take her and follow me." She turned to Pickles. "Pickles, wake Andy. The rest of you, listen: We've been through a lot, but we gotta look forward. And the best way to heal is sexual healing."

A murmur rippled through the crowd, but this time it was excited, eager.

"You can get started without me. Virginia Dentata, Miss Trix, you two are in charge. Get the atmosphere going. You can use my CDs. The sisters need to heal."

And without another word, she ducked under the doorjamb and disappeared into the dark.

The Hell Slut lifted Skillet over her shoulder and reached into the darkness, fumbling against the wall until her fingers connected with something. She flicked a switch and a bare light bulb shuddered to life, and another one ten feet down the narrow passage back here, and then another one ten feet farther along. Mother Moonflow was already ahead of them, vanishing down the descending corridor.

Sarah could just make out that the passage sloped downward and was pleated with stairs, leading down into the earth.

"You first," said the Hell Slut.

Just play along. Just play along.

Sarah stepped through. Then the Hell Slut, grunting as she squeezed her bulk through the narrow opening. And then lastly came Pickles, leading Andy. Andy swayed unsteadily, blinking in stupefied confusion.

The rest of the sisters remained behind, but the news that they were going to get to have an orgy had already made them forget all that unpleasantness with What Was to Be Done with Skillet. The little square of light, through which Sarah could still glimpse the rest of the sisters, laughing and smiling and pulling off their clothes, grabbing one another in free, joyous embraces, and hear the sounds of Enya music, grew smaller and smaller and farther and farther away, until they started to descend the stairs and then it vanished completely.

27.

More men have abandoned the project, in fear of this bogeyman. The skeleton crew which remains is incapable of completing the work I require. The woods are eating them, I am sure of it.

—Diary of Lazarus Sloane
(California State Parks Archives)

In the dark, there was only the sound of their footsteps, creaking against the stairs, and Skillet's continued laughter.

"Skillet, be quiet," said Pickles.

Skillet kept laughing. She squirmed, but the hands of the Hell Slut gripped her tight.

"Hell Slut, make her be quiet!" hissed Pickles.

"How about you shut up?" said the Hell Slut.

"Ha ha, you got it all wrong," said Skillet. "You got it all wrong."

"Quiet," said Mother Moonflow's voice from farther down the stairs. "You don't understand what's happening at all."

They descended, the sound of Enya's voice becoming fainter and tinnier with every step. Skillet didn't walk. Her feet barely touched the ground. It didn't matter. The Hell Slut carried

Skillet like she weighed nothing, like she was an empty husk. And they went down. And down. And down.

"I didn't really want the Lord of the Forest to destroy the temple," babbled Skillet suddenly. "I was just joking. I don't know why Effervescent Bubbles said that! You can't trust her! She's a total kiss-ass! She's just gonna tell you whatever you want to hear! I never did nothing!"

Out of the darkness, Mother Moonflow's voice intoned, "'I give you my soul, my body, my pussy.' Those were your words, Skillet."

"They were not! I never said that!" Skillet cried, struggling anew so that the Hell Slut's hands clamped tighter to hold her.

Then, more quietly, so that Mother Moonflow couldn't hear, she said, "Hell Slut."

There was no response.

A little louder: "Hell Slut!"

No response.

"Hell Slut, c'mon! C'mon, it's me, Skillet. You know I wouldn't do anything against the temple! You know it. Tell them. Tell them all!"

"You're in a hell of a jam, Skillet."

Skillet was quiet for a moment, and then: "Sarah! Sarah!"

"I'm over here."

"Sarah, remember the good times we had? You know I didn't do it. Tell them!"

Sarah thought about Skillet. She thought about the time together on a dirty mattress in the back of a rusted Volkswagen bus, she thought about Skillet's little hands squeezing and kneading her flesh, and she thought about how the two of them had attempted to break into this very tunnel to get the King's Breakfast, and how they were almost caught and how they had run away laughing and how free and fun and real it was to run away laughing with someone. *Just play along and you'll be okay. It's all an act. It's just some little slap on the wrist thing. They'll do their thing and everything will be fine.*

"Sarah?" Skillet's voice quavered in the dark. Her acting was impeccable. Sarah had not expected Skillet to be capable of such kayfabe.

There was a long pause and then Sarah said, "I'm sorry, Skillet. I'm really sorry."

The stairs eventually terminated in a darkened chamber. They could hear the sound of someone fiddling with another light switch. A bulb flashed twice a good twenty feet down the hall and then died with a drawn out sizzle. The sudden flash disturbed things in the dark, and they scuttled away into the shadows. More raccoons, probably. The tunnels must connect.

"That's a real bummer," said Mother Moonflow. The sound of a match striking. A candle flickered to life.

Now they could see, barely. The flame revealed that the chamber was an unfinished cellar of packed earth and that it wasn't so much a room as the start of a longer tunnel, which continued to slope downward. A cool, dry draft rose up from the depths of the earth to meet them and make the candle flame stutter; the wind carried the musty stench of death. Mother Moonflow, her naked body glowing in the candlelight, moved quickly down the corridor, for she had no fear of what lay ahead. But trepidation seized the rest of the party, and they would have tarried longer but for the risk of being left in the pitch-black darkness.

Sarah stumbled but maintained her balance. She could barely see where she was going, and her moonflow high made the subterranean world around her warp and twist before her eyes. The earthen walls were breathing, pulsing with a barely contained malignancy, and Sarah worried that they might close in on her if she stopped thinking about them for a moment.

"You all right?" said the Hell Slut.

"Fine." Sarah was too high to trust her senses, too high to trust her brain. Sarah remembered seeing the sisters passing around a flask of moonflow back in the sanctuary. She was certain her companions were equally stoned, so who knew what insane thoughts were running through their heads, what monstrous visions appearing before their eyes? Just like at the birthing ceremony, Sarah was certain that the ground could open up beneath her at any moment and tip her into an even deeper layer of hell.

Just play along. Mother Moonflow said to play along. Just play along and it'll be fine. Get through this and you can get out of here.

Andy leaned against the wall, his head lolling. Sarah once again took pains to avoid looking at his crotch and his flopping penis. It felt like looking at your brother naked.

"Andy, you still with us?"

He shook his head.

"It's okay. We're almost through this. I promise you. Come on."

She took his arm over her shoulder and let him lean on her, and they continued downward.

Again, they heard the voice of Mother Moonflow: "They say that the key to building togetherness is self-disclosure. Sarah, you were right. Before I came to the Pamogo, I was known as Diane Tibbitts."

Sarah shivered. She didn't like hearing that name from Mother Moonflow's lips. It felt like something she shouldn't know, forbidden knowledge that could only presage death and misfortune.

The candle flame bobbed down the hallway, and they were obliged to follow.

"The first time that I ever came to the Pamogo, it was an artist's retreat. The younger sisters, they always ask me, 'Oh, an artist's commune? Was that the Summer of Love?'" She laughed. "But I'm not that old, baby! We hung out among the trees, just feeling nature. We spent a weekend here, living in this old abandoned sawmill. I took the King's Breakfast and let the Pig cum in me. That's when I first felt the presence of the Lord of the Forest."

The voice echoed strangely up the corridor, distorted into overlapping whispers by the distance.

"There's something else we got in common, Sarah. You've had the King's Breakfast before?"

"My friend was having a party," said Sarah. Her voice echoed. "And she had the King's Breakfast."

Mother Moonflow spoke again and this time her voice was cracking, too raw with emotion to flow. "I remember the first time that I took the King's Breakfast. It was a real trip, man. I saw the Lord of the Forest and I felt his strength, his power, his cunning—all qualities he possesses in abundance and all qualities that allow him to dominate. I saw his cloak of moss, his antlers of coral fungus, and the face that was not like the face of a man."

Sarah kept quiet. She felt it best not to mention that was not the same thing that she saw when she took the King's Breakfast.

"That sounds . . . difficult."

"You would think, wouldn't ya? But it really opened my eyes. You ever have a revelation like that? It just hits you like a blinding light and you know, you just know, things will never ever be the same. You know that you can't go back, you can only go forward, but it's scary—it's so, so scary. You're stepping into the great unknown and it's gonna cost you everything, everything you've worked for, everything you've ever known or believed or thought was true. But you know it's all a lie now and want to keep living that lie, you desperately do, because the alternative is so terrifying. But you can't. You gotta go forward?"

"Yeah, something like that," said Sarah.

"Now I know the Green Lady is the way, baby. I've been her prophet for all these years; I led all these gals to the truth of the Green Lady. I dedicated my life to her. I shared the Green Lady's revelation with the world, and I knew that women were really responding when my words received dozens—dozens!—of hits on alt.feminism.neopagan.theory. Hell Slut, you remember. You were the first. You and Skillet there."

"I remember."

"But I tell ya, and some of these chicks won't like me saying it, but there ain't nothing like feeling the Lord of the Forest fill you up. It's real mod. I ain't supposed to say it, but ya know how us gals are—who can resist a bad boy? Skillet knows what I'm saying."

Skillet sputtered. "I don't know anything!"

"She's embarrassed now. But just wait, it'll all make sense soon, when ya see the Lord of the Forest for yourself."

Sarah didn't like this situation at all. She didn't like that Mother Moonflow was freely confessing her lifetime of sins. It implied that she did not expect all of them to return to the surface when this was all over. Sarah tried to catch the eyes of her fellow travelers, tried to gauge how they were reacting—but it was too dark.

The tunnel ended in a cul-de-sac. There was, set into the dirt wall, another door, again only waist-high. It was not decorated, but like the door upstairs, it was fastened by a lock and dead bolt. The wooden frame was laced with deep scratches.

Sarah could sense something beyond, slow and rhythmic, like a monstrous heartbeat in the distance. She put her hand to her chest, hoping it might just be her own nervous pulse reverberating in her ears. This couldn't be real. There couldn't actually be something down there.

"You hear that, Big Mama?"

Sarah nodded.

This isn't real. It's all an act. It's the moonflow fucking up my mind. There's nothing through that door.

Mother Moonflow handed her candle off to Pickles and stooped down to unlock the mechanism.

"Before we go in, there's just one last little thing." Mother Moonflow nodded to Pickles, who dug something out of his robe pocket and held it out to the group. Little yellow pills. Leviathan's Favored Son.

"Hey!" said Sarah. "That's ours!"

"Not anymore. It was very kind of you to provide them, though. Makes things so much easier. Each of you, take one."

There was one for Mother Moonflow, one for Skillet, one for the Hell Slut, one for Pickles.

That was it.

Sarah felt the fear rising. No one was offering her a pill. No one was offering Andy a pill.

"Hold on to these for now, cats. You'll know when to take 'em, if things start to get unmellow."

"What about us?" said Sarah, her voice rising with panic. Her heart was beating faster. *Shit, shit, shit. This was all a trick from the beginning, wasn't it?* She was certain, dead certain, that whatever lay beyond that door must be the same thing, of the same sort, as whatever she had encountered in the woods, whatever had been so awful, so terrifying, so bone-chillingly horrible that she had been forced to wipe her memory and wander lost in an unmapped wilderness rather than confront it. And this time, she did not have Leviathan's Favored Son to help her out. She would have to see it, and afterward, she would have to remember it.

Mother Moonflow spoke: "It happens sometimes that you feel the presence of the Lord of the Forest out there in the woods and you just can't take it. It's too much, man. It feels like it's gonna blow your mind like a fuse box, and ya just get so scared ya can't imagine holding that knowledge in your head forevermore. I ain't blamin' ya, it's heavy shit. But we're gonna do some real radical drug therapy tonight. This time, you're gonna look at the Lord of the Forest head-on. Ya ain't gonna blink, ya ain't gonna turn away, and most of all ya ain't gonna scrub your brain afterward. How's that sound for a totally cosmic journey?"

"I don't want that!"

"Hey, Big Mama, don't get so bent outta shape." Mother Moonflow turned and looked her right in the eye. "It ain't so bad. Might take a little getting used to, but, heck, you might even like it after a while. Pickles, you stay here. Guard this door. Let no one else in. Let no one but us out."

Pickles nodded curtly, but his eyes darted about nervously. This entire expedition seemed poorly planned, since the party possessed only a single candle. Sarah wondered how they would see once they passed through this second door. But it turned out to be a moot point, because the room beyond was illuminated quite brightly.

Only down here, in this vast subterranean vault, was there still any evidence that the temple had once been a sawmill; Sarah could see the rusted hulks of old machinery crouching in the corners, circular saw blades casting evil shadows, chains rattling somewhere in the rafters in response to the *slap, slap, slap* of their feet against the spongy floor. Skillet was still laughing. Apparently, this was just getting funnier and funnier.

A nauseating profusion of mushrooms coated the walls, and their white tentacles stretched across the floor of this underground cathedral in thick, spongy mats that squished and shifted under their feet as they continued their trek. The mushrooms filled the chamber in great white piles like snowdrifts—every square inch of ground was buried beneath the lumpy white caps so thickly that there wasn't even a path through the bloom. Wispy white tendrils of free-hanging mycelium dangled from the ceiling like ghostly party streamers. Here and there, exposed rocks jutted out from the walls, protruding beyond the mushroom tangle like crooked teeth. The fungus glowed with a cold, ghostly bioluminescence, so that they could see without the aid of candles.

Sarah did not like this. She especially did not like the sound of Skillet's laughter, so loud and profane in this sacred space that it felt destined to trigger some terrible cataclysm. But it just kept getting louder.

That was when she saw the bodies. They were arranged in rows along the walls, all trapped under a thick cottony quilt of mycelium, so that the little party had to walk down the narrow aisle between the barrows. She glanced at the first body as they passed. It was little more than mummified skin stretched over bones, dressed in the tattered remnants of jeans and a leather vest, a grinning skull visible through the thinned webbing only because it was now too desiccated to provide nourishment to the fruiting bodies anymore. The webbing was thicker around the other bodies, each one cozy in its own fungal cocoon for all eternity, except for the two newest bodies at the end of the line.

Here was Hal Sampson, flabby and soft, still wearing black socks and jockey shorts, head smashed into slurry. Next to him, on a little bier of mushrooms, lay Athena. A bunch of freshly cut daisies lay at the baby's tiny feet.

"A courtesy for Aphrodite," said Mother Moonflow. She reached out and gave a playful tweak to one of Athena's cold little toes with her thumb and index finger. "She carried it for nine months; she's still got some big feelings."

Sarah nodded dumbly.

At the far end of the chamber, Sarah could sense it. No, it couldn't be. It had to be the moonflow. There was no other logical explanation. And yet she'd always known it was down here, but she hadn't really believed. Not really. But there was no denying it now. There was no metaphor to it. There it was, in the flesh. It was asleep, but its dreams were thick and palpable in the musty dungeon, air clogged with spores, thick ropes of blinding white mycelium binding it as it slept until Sarah could see nothing but a solid vegetable mass.

Because here, under the trees and the earth, under the roots of the towering spruce and the mighty fir, under strata of rich black loam and rocky clay, under the carcasses of ancient sequoias and redwoods, and finally under the worms and the slugs and the crawling things that ate them all, the Lord of the Forest slept.

28.

The trees grow so quickly now I feel they will consume the entire world. How is this possible? Navigating these woods is impossible. I cannot leave ever again or I will die out there.

—Diary of Lazarus Sloane
(California State Parks Archives)

Don't be scared, cats. He can't hurt ya."

Mother Moonflow ran her hand along a tumescent vine, thick as a bridge cable, and fingered the joint where it connected to the vegetable whole with sensual calm.

"I planted the first spores down here. I nourished him, I nurtured him. My passions made him grow. You might even say that, in any meaningful sense of the term, I am his mother. He's an impressive specimen, grown so big and vibrant—just look at all these shrooms!"

She gestured expansively to the room, to the mushrooms bursting from the walls and sprouting from the floor, to the mycelium webbing that covered everything. The moonflow made the room spin before Sarah's eyes. It grew suddenly brighter and then dimmer, the cold blue light washing over the world and then receding, almost as if the mushrooms could understand and respond to Mother Moonflow's words with a sinister otherworldly intelligence. The Hell Slut, still clutching Skillet, did not react to the change in luminosity. Neither did Mother Moonflow.

"Hey, but don't worry. He's just a fungus, bound and helpless. All that power? It's all tied up in these little guys." She plucked a mushroom bud from the mass and held it under Sarah's nose. "It's all groovy when we bring the Green Lady into the light and this guy stays down here in the dark. See, I eat 'em and my body—"

"I know. You turn a phallic vibe into a yonic tonic."

"Damn, sis! You're on the ball!"

Tiny bones littered the floor around the throbbing fungal lump—so tiny and fine that they must be the bones of a raccoon. Or possibly a child. Or a baby.

Mother Moonflow kicked aside a scattering of tiny knuckles and ribs; they dispersed among the mushrooms, stirring up a small dust cloud of spores. "She was born of the Pig's seed, right here, in this room. This is where the Pig had me, so this is where I planted the first spores. I hoped that the Pig's lingering power in her would nurture the Lord of the Forest." She shrugged her shoulders. "It was a total bummer, but how else was I supposed to grow more shrooms?"

"Your daughter," breathed Sarah. "Oh my God, it's anthropophagic."

"Damn, listen to that fancy-pants book learnin'! You really are on the ball. Very groovy. We'll stop right here."

The Hell Slut pushed Sarah to her knees, and then Andy.

"I'm freaking out," said Andy. He squeezed his eyes closed, whimpering softly. "I can't take it."

"Hold on, just hold on."

Andy could not hold on. "It's everywhere! It's here! Can't you see it?"

The fungal mound remained still. Andy tipped over onto the ground, shuddering wildly among the mushrooms, destroying whole swaths of fruiting bodies and kicking up yet more clouds of spores. He was still crying.

"You gave him too much," said the Hell Slut.

"You can't have too much moonflow, Big Mama—have some faith! He's just seein' the Lord of the Forest for the first time. It's a lot to take in."

All the while, Sarah waited, heart in mouth, for the arrival of the Lord of the Forest. The fungal mound did not react to their presence, did not react to Skillet's continued laughter or to Andy's weeping, did not react at all. It was as if it were nothing more than ordinary fungus. After a spell, the silence grew embarrassing.

Mother Moonflow rubbed her face. "Let's up the dosage."

From behind, the Hell Slut hooked her fingers into Sarah's nostrils and pulled her head back so that her mouth popped open. She squirmed, but Mother Moonflow was already squeezing more moonflow down her throat. She gagged and sputtered.

"Now, cats, you're really gonna see beyond the veil!"

A wave of heat passed through Sarah's body, and she felt her brain ascend to an altogether new and unprecedented level of consciousness, her mind expanding to touch all the secrets of the universe.

"Check this. Y'all know why only I can turn the King's Breakfast into a yonic tonic? It's cuz I'm not afraid to take the Lord of the Forest's power into my body."

Mother Moonflow waded into the fungal tangle, and Sarah

watched in disbelief as she parted her legs and allowed the Lord of the Forest to enter. She was the prophet of the Green Lady, and this was her duty and her pleasure.

"There is nothing like feeling that incredible strength fill you up," she said with a sigh. "It's great! You're gonna love it!"

Mother Moonflow pumped her hips, up and down, up and down, her eyes closed, her lips wet and slightly parted. They watched as, between Mother Moonflow's legs, the vegetable mass bloomed and cracked open.

Sarah was not prepared for this. Her eyes burned to look away, but she couldn't. She did not have Leviathan's Favored Son. This was a memory that she could not erase, that she could never erase; no matter how long she lived, till her dying day, she would remember this. She felt dizzy and stifled a moan that welled up from her suddenly lurching guts. The world tottered. Her shoulders heaved, and she spewed a torrent of watery vomit across the floor. She coughed and hacked, dribbling thick strands of mucus from her slack lips. Dizziness overtook her, and she had to concentrate to keep from falling face down to the floor.

"Keep watching! Don't look away!" shouted Mother Moonflow, never breaking stride. The fungus was moving, tendrils wiggling. It must be the strange soil acidity. Or maybe it was the moonflow. But the roots around the base of the bulb were definitely moving. Sarah was certain of it. Oh shit. It was real. It was all real.

"Holy shit, the roots—it's alive! It's moving!"

Roots twined around Mother Moonflow's middle, pulling tight, tighter, tighter.

Sarah was mesmerized, her mind suddenly blank. She couldn't think of anything other than this awful sight; the entire world outside of this cellar had totally vanished into a black void, and for her, this was the universe. There was no room in her mind for anything other than this horror.

Mother Moonflow rose to dismount, standing on her tiptoes and wiggling her bottom so that the point of the Lord's root bulb could pop free. It whipped out erect, rising like a spire above the vegetable mass—ribbed, notched, and braided for her pleasure.

Sarah saw something twitch out of the corner of her eye. Tentacles of mycelium slithered along the floor, probing outward from the fungus mass as if activated by Sarah's attention. No one else seemed to notice them.

"That's got him all riled up, baby. Now watch what he does!" Mother Moonflow sauntered up to her and pressed a finger against Sarah's forehead. "Ain't no way to forget that. Now you gonna open right up and take him in, like the phallic alec you are, Big Mama."

Andy rolled around, smacking his face against the floor and babbling incoherently.

Dozens of wire-thin tendrils protruded from the root mass, anchoring it to the floor. Sarah thought that they ought to move, just a bit. The strings quivered and flexed with a sudden malevolent intelligence. She could barely hear Mother Moonflow's words, she was so intrigued by this development. The tendrils seemed agitated, perhaps by Mother Moonflow's pussy, perhaps by Skillet's shrieking or Andy's babble, but most likely, and Sarah knew this fact with absolute certainty all the way down to the cockles of her heart, because Mother Moonflow had offered her a chance to see the Green Lady again and she had said yes.

The tendrils were moving, pulsing. The whole of the mass was cracking open like a spent cocoon, releasing a blast of steaming mist.

More tendrils shot out, grabbing at Sarah's knees, at Andy's feet. She fell, hitting the earth with a solid thud. Then the tendrils were upon the both of them, slithering between their legs and around their arms and up their nostrils and into their sinuses, and Sarah felt herself falling deeper and deeper into moonflow oblivion as she sucked in great lungfuls of spores with every bellowing scream. Reality peeled away, the walls of the basement receding into amniotic darkness, and suddenly she was no more.

Her body lay in this abandoned cellar, covered by festering mushrooms that bloomed and died and bloomed and died in an endless cycle. She lay there for an indeterminable length of time, but not too long, before the raccoons found her—they lapped up her clouded eyes before the jelly had a chance to liquify and pulled the soft flesh from her lips. Her breasts deflated back into her chest. Her guts churned and gurgled, the gases of decomposition filling her intestines until she burst. Maggots ate her from the inside out. Her split body finally folded in on itself, turning to black slime and sloughing off the bone. Time passed. Her face melted, revealing the secret face beneath. The temple crumbled slowly over the course of eons, reclaimed by the forest. Still, Sarah remained dead. Great mats of spongy green moss grew across her ribs. Toadstools sprouted from her empty eye sockets, but no one came to collect them, so eventually they too crumbled to a ruin of dust. Insects filled her empty skull until they too passed from memory.

And all the while, geography changed and shifted beneath her.

One day, a hiker in the Pamogo stumbled across her bones and gave them a fanciful name. They called her the Green Lady, after the moss that billowed in velvety tufts between the slats of her broken ribs and the mushrooms that bloomed eternal from the moist dark cavern of her skull. Even that first explorer could tell there was something sublime about this place. The forest was thicker here, more indulgent, a verdancy bordering on opulence. For some, the Green Lady was just another trail marker, a midpoint between the ravine of Greensleeves and the tree with teeth. But others could, just for a moment, feel the peace of this space, the serenity of the Green Lady, and know that there was much more here. Sometimes they would take that moment with them when they finally left the Pamogo Forest, and maybe they would hold it fast even after that. There were some who might, in time, even be drawn back.

But that lasted for only the briefest flash of an instant, until even those bones crumbled to nothing and all the hikers were gone and with them the memory of the Green Lady, and all that remained was the forest, forever and always, seeping over history and spilling over the world.

But the dissolution of Sarah's body didn't matter, because Sarah wasn't there. She was rising up out of herself in a shower of light, in a brand-new form with a big broad mushroom cap and big perfect golden tits—

`>no no no I can't do this`

`>not now`

`>WAKE&&&&`

Sarah was filled with the incredible, unbelievable, mind-blowing revelation that the Lord of the Forest and the Green Lady were one and the same; they existed simultaneously as one single entity, an entity who could appear in an infinite number of incarnations to an infinite number of people, whom Mother Moonflow saw as a towering figure with peeling coral fungus antlers and whom Sarah saw as a glowing mushroom goddess with big tits but holy shit of course it's so obvious fungi are hermaphroditic of course of course it was going to be this way the whole idea of sexually dimorphic mushroom gods was just silly from the start and—

Sarah struggled to control her racing thoughts, her mind a blur.

`>no no no`

`>not yet`

`>I'm not ready`

>there's one last thing I need to do

>please not yet

>just let me do one last thing

Sarah pulled away, screaming, a sudden pain ripping through her chest like the blade of a knife. She felt the sticky strings of fungal matter pull from her nose, from her mouth, as she moved, and she scrambled to get away. It was too much. Her brain felt like it was on fire.

She tumbled free and staggered across the floor, gasping and wheezing.

"I can't do it! Not yet!" she cried, and she vomited until her throat burned. Bile and moonflow poured out of her.

Sarah and Andy writhed on the floor, screaming and batting at nothing. The Hell Slut watched impassively. She was fairly certain that at some point, once these two had expended all their energy in this manic tantrum, once they were too exhausted to continue fighting the moonflow demons in their heads, Mother Moonflow would ask her to kill them and add them to the rows of bodies down here. The King's Breakfast needed fertilizer. And the Hell Slut was pretty good at killing, after all. And if Mother Moonflow asked her to kill, she would.

Mother Moonflow is the prophet of the Green Lady, she reminded herself. She needed to follow Mother Moonflow. She'd already killed so many, what were two more? She'd already given up Sunny Delight; there was nothing left for her to do except be loyal to Mother Moonflow.

There's still Skillet.

The air was thick with a dense fog of spores, getting denser all the time.

"All that binary thinking's got them trapped, but their minds are finally opening for the truth. We're gonna give 'em a real show now."

"You promised I'd see the Green Lady!" wailed Sarah, still on her hands and knees, still drooling. "Not that!"

"Baby, that ain't up to me. The moonflow's gonna show you what the moonflow's gonna show you. The Green Lady's real picky about revealing herself. Not every woman gets to be her prophet."

"I bet you haven't seen her!" shouted Sarah. She hacked and sputtered, her lungs gummy with phlegm. "I bet you made everything up!"

"I know everything about the Green Lady."

"She's beautiful! A beautiful, glowing presence! With kind hands and huge tits!"

"That's how Sunny Delight described her too," said the Hell Slut. "Except for the tits."

Mother Moonflow looked at her levelly.

The Hell Slut continued: "Sunny Delight said she saw the Green Lady. When we were in San Bernardo."

"Sunny Delight? The tramp? The tramp who cut and ran when things got too real? You think she actually saw the Green Lady? C'mon, you're smarter than that, Big Mama. Don't talk nonsense, let me do my work. Let's finish this little show." Mother Moonflow turned to Skillet. "He's ready for you now."

Skillet shook her head, eyes wide.

"You promised him, Little Mama—your soul, your body, your pussy. Don't pretend you didn't say it. You're brave at a distance, but when you come face-to-face with reality—you don't seem all that brave at all. We gotta put on a show for your phallic alecs. We gotta really blow their minds."

Skillet shook her head again, harder, backing away until she bumped into the Hell Slut.

"He's looking for you, Skillet. He's looking for you to make good on your promise. Usually, you're so eager."

The Hell Slut watched as, behind Mother Moonflow, the fungal mass twitched almost as if in response to the Hell Slut's thoughts. In fact, she was absolutely sure it was twitching in response to her thoughts. She was absolutely positive now that it was not a moonflow hallucination.

"Mother Moonflow, she doesn't want to do it," said the Hell Slut. The root bulb pulsed in animal anticipation, pores leaking white sap.

Mother Moonflow frowned. "Big Mama, you said you were loyal. You said you were with me till the end."

"She doesn't want to."

The Hell Slut hesitated, her attention focused on the throbbing vegetable mass. Sarah was on her hands and knees, vomiting. The Hell Slut almost believed that maybe Sarah could see it moving too.

"She needs to learn before she can rejoin us," said Mother Moonflow calmly, still speaking of Skillet. She grabbed Skillet by the wrist and jerked her forward. Her talons pressed deeply into Skillet's arm, leaving crescent-shaped welts that made her yelp. "It's not a punishment. It's a lesson."

The Hell Slut remembered hearing those words before. *This isn't a punishment, kiddo. It's a lesson.*

The tendrils twitched and throbbed; the mycelium mat beneath their feet seemed to tense and strain.

"Oh, fuck this," said the Hell Slut.

Mother Moonflow did not expect it, and would never have expected it, when the Hell Slut shoved her; she stumbled backward into the knot of tendrils. The yellow pill flew out of her grasp and across the room; the Hell Slut did not watch where it landed. The erect spire whipped back and forth; the bed of tentacles squirmed en masse. Spores rose from the mass in thick clouds.

Skillet scrambled across the floor on her belly like a lizard.

Mother Moonflow twisted free, her long hair flying, and fixed the Hell Slut with furious eyes, flashing over the rims of her shattered glasses. The Hell Slut should have completed the job—she was a professional with pride, after all—but those eyes stopped her. They put the fear in her. How embarrassing! This was an amateur mistake. But she still made it.

"What the fuck are you doing?!" screamed Mother Moonflow. "This is majorly unchill!"

"A lesson?!" cried the Hell Slut, regaining her voice. "You call this a lesson?! This isn't right! The Green Lady wouldn't want this!"

"You don't know anything about the Green Lady!"

The Hell Slut had killed Master Choda and Hal Sampson and Baby Athena and many others on Mother Moonflow's orders, because the Hell Slut was always loyal to Mother Moonflow. But apparently this was where her loyalty ended. Even after everything, she couldn't do *that* to Skillet.

Well. So be it.

The Hell Slut didn't have a good response, so she just said "Fuck you!" again and pushed Mother Moonflow deeper into that nest of writhing tendrils, which were now snaking around the Hell Slut's arms and under her shirt. Behind her, Skillet's hysterical laughter finally gave way to pure shrieks. She went careening, tearing through the webs of mycelium that stretched across the room and nearly pulling corpses from their beds in her haste.

Something was rising from the fungus. Mother Moonflow twisted her head to gaze directly at it, finally cognizant that something was moving that shouldn't be moving.

"Are you seeing this, Big Mama? Are you seeing this?!"

"Fuck, fuck, fuck!" The Hell Slut fumbled with her yellow pill in the pocket of her jacket.

Mother Moonflow gazed upon the rising monstrosity in stunned disbelief. "The Lord of the Forest! He moves! He lives!"

Tendrils whipped out from the bulk of its form, spiraling around Mother Moonflow's neck and chest and belly in great winding coils. Mother Moonflow gagged in surprise, her excitement evaporating. Her hands pried desperately at the coils around her throat, digging her talons between the vines, but their grip was tight and true. Mother Moonflow turned red, then purple, her tongue flopping in her open mouth like a slug, then white, then she slumped over into the writhing nest of fungal tentacles, breaking apart at the impact, an immediate composting process as a living carpet of hungry tendrils engulfed her. She was back to the soil, the nourishing, nourishing soil.

The Hell Slut roared in sudden panic, backing away from the remnants of Mother Moonflow and tripping over her own feet. Tendrils turned their attention to her and stabbed deep into her thighs and gut with murderous intent. She kicked at them, but they came away with blood. The Hell Slut felt something burst inside her and she felt the pain, and she knew this was not like Hal Sampson's bullet hole. She was certain that this time, it was real. Something had punctured her, deep, and she could see the life welling out of her in big black gouts.

Okay. That was fine. She would just put that into a little box in her head to process later. Right now, she had to get free. That was the most important thing. Just concentrate on that. Bellowing, she forced herself to stand. She grabbed the tentacles around her neck and tore them apart. The soft fungus wasn't hard to break, but the tendrils were persistent.

And there were a lot of them. The Hell Slut could feel roots tangling at her shins. With a supreme effort, she pulled away. She tore at the roots, but more kept coming. She could feel herself totter, her body going clammy and cold as her blood drained, spilling across the floor, but she still had enough strength to yank her legs forward, delighting in the brittle sound of roots tearing. She didn't think about that. She put that in a little box in her head to process later. There was only one thing that was important now. She staggered toward the door, toward the sound of Skillet's whimpering, and slumped her way toward salvation. One step, then another, left foot, right foot, ignoring the squelching, squirming sounds of hungry roots behind her, hungry roots dipping into the soil, drilling into the hard-packed dirt that had long since been drained of any nutrients and digging deep, deep, deep until they found the good stuff, hungry roots climbing the walls, putting out runners, mushrooms bursting into flower along the new mycelium veins. Skillet was too busy screaming to appreciate the sight, too busy scratching at the locked door like a dog, but the Hell Slut saw it and she thought it was darkly appropriate.

"We're locked in!" Skillet howled. "The door won't move!"

"Fucking Pickles," mumbled the Hell Slut. "I should have known."

Behind them, the movement of roots became a rumble that filled the chamber and rattled the walls.

"Outta my way," the Hell Slut said, and smashed her fist into the door, again and again, until the rotten wood splintered into sawdust. The Hell Slut pulled back, her bloody knuckles studded with splinters like a cactus. For so long, the Hell Slut had restrained herself, living only by Mother Moonflow's orders. But now she was free to flex the full extent of her power.

The Hell Slut lurched through the ruined doorway and fell in a bloody heap across the floor. It was dark, completely dark. In the far distance, across an endless ocean of shadow, she could see the flickering light bulb that marked the bottom of the stairwell that led back up to the light. It was so very, very far away.

"What's happening? What did you do?" screeched Pickles's voice in the darkness.

"You son of a bitch, if I get my hands on you—"

"Mother Moonflow gave me instructions!" he cried.

"Mother Moonflow is gone!"

Pickles wailed, a sound of utter misery and despair so bereft it almost rivaled the sound Aphrodite had made when her baby was murdered.

"Pickles, gimme a fuckin' hand!" yelled Skillet.

Pickles started to obey, but then he must have seen something in the room behind them, something terrifying and ominous and, worst of all, advancing, because he screamed again and ran off into the darkness, his robe flying behind him.

"Shit!" said Skillet. "Shit! Shit! Shit!"

And something was coming up behind them.

It wasn't just the squishing, squelching of tendrils and roots anymore; the Hell Slut could hear something thumping. One. Two. One. Two. Footsteps. Something with feet was ascending to meet them.

Skillet looked down at the Hell Slut, who was bruised and bloody and battered.

"Ah fuck," said Skillet. "Fuuuuck. C'mon, we gotta go! We gotta go!"

"I'm not going anywhere. I told you I'd take care of things. You go."

A shadow fell across them as something advanced to the landing, standing tall to block the anemic light thrown by the bare light bulbs. The Hell Slut felt an overwhelming urge to turn around and look, to see it clearly in the light, but she resisted.

"Hey," said Skillet, grinning. "It's Skillet and the Hell Slut, right?"

The Hell Slut never saw the thing coming through the door. She was too tired to turn her head to look; even thinking about it required a monumental effort that she just couldn't muster anymore, and besides, her vision was going green around the edges and blurry in the middle. But she heard Skillet bellowing and shrieking and she could imagine, she could just imagine, that right outside of her field of vision, Skillet was launching herself at a god with the fury of a thousand wet cats. That was how Skillet fought, all paws and claws, all teeth and nails, a nasty little ball of rage like a cornered ferret. It was a touching effort, but the Hell Slut was too sleepy to worry when she heard a sudden crack and Skillet's hollering abruptly stopped.

I guess this is what I get, thought the Hell Slut. *I guess this is all I would ever get.*

29.

[unintelligible]

—*Diary of Lazarus Sloane*
(California State Parks Archives)

Sarah saw where Leviathan's Favored Son fell when Mother Moonflow stumbled.

Her head throbbed like it was going to explode. She puked milk and granola until there was nothing left to come out, and then the dry heaves took her until her chest ached and her throat burned.

Andy was still writhing on the floor, grabbing at his face. All around them, slithering tendrils laced themselves into a squirming quilt, and Sarah could barely keep her balance atop the rolling ocean of fungal matter as she wobbled toward him.

"I saw him!" he cried, but Sarah was not interested in whatever hallucination was plaguing him.

"Andy! Can you hear me? Can you understand me?" She grabbed his shoulders and shook him. Andy coughed, his beard wet with saliva, and he stared, wide-eyed, through her for a moment before his eyes focused. "Do you know who I am?"

"Sarah?" He did not sound confident in his answer.

"That's right! Excellent! Do you know where we are?"

"Are we dead? Is this hell?"

Sarah was honestly not sure. "I don't know. Christ, I don't know. Just hold on."

She dropped onto her hands and knees and searched among the tendrils, even as they grabbed at her ankles and wrists. Andy remained on the floor, his knees pulled up to his chest so that he obliviously flashed his dick and taint at Sarah as she worked. The white roots flexed and twitched, and on either side of them, the corpses began to rise from their beds like macabre marionettes dangling from fibrous threads. The older bodies were too brittle and they fell apart immediately, but the fresher carcasses, still held together by dried skin and desiccated tendons, sat up to watch them with mushroom-clogged sockets.

"Oh shit, oh shit..."

She hacked and coughed, struggling to concentrate through a gathering haze of fresh spores. The fruiting bodies were pollinating. Spores spewed from the empty eyes and hanging jaws of the dead men; from their chest cavities, wafting from between their exposed ribs; and from any other parts of their bodies where the creeping fungus had penetrated.

Sarah tore at the tendrils in a blind panic, and the tendrils retaliated by winding tighter, pulling harder, snaking between the fleshy rolls on her sides and between her legs until she bled. She felt the panic rising in her gullet. The walls were washed a hot pink with her falling mood. Her temperature fluctuated wildly, so that one moment she was sweating and the next her teeth chattered.

"Hey, kids," said Andy, addressing a nonexistent class of third graders, his voice dreamy and his eyes unfocused. "Today, we're gonna learn all about Lazarus Sloane and the gold rush! Isn't that exciting?"

"That's real exciting. Tell me more, Andy. Keep talking."

Sarah wallowed among the roots as Andy launched drunkenly into the story of Lazarus Sloane, his adventures in gold mining, the Mexican land grant, the sawmill, mostly everything. Andy didn't mention Sloane's attacks on the Chinese, because that might have raised awkward questions and, as a State Parks interpreter, avoiding awkward questions was always his highest priority, even when he was deep in a moonflow haze.

"That's great, man, keep talking. Stick with me, okay? I'm going to get you out of here."

Andy nodded dumbly. Okay. At least he was better at following her lead when he was in this state. Sarah had to concentrate; the moonflow made the world swim before her eyes. Anything could happen from one moment to the next. A sudden warmth passed over her, concentrating in her chest. "Oh shit."

"What?"

"Andy, I'm really gonna need you to help me here. I'm still hallucinating." She crossed her arms over her chest and when Andy stared at her quizzically, she felt compelled to explain. "Please tell me my tits aren't growing."

Andy stared at her. He was still under the moonflow's influence enough that the power of suggestion was too much and he started to see it too. "Wow," he said. "They are!"

Sarah groaned in annoyance. It was too late, the suggestion was in her head, and Sarah could feel her chest growing hot. "No, they're not! God damn it!"

Concentrate, she thought. *Andy's useless. Don't think about your tits. Think about finding the way out of here.* The building shuddered like a living thing. Sarah very steadfastly refused to think about her breasts, even though her nipples were tingling something awful now.

It's just the moonflow. It's just the moonflow.

There's something in here.

All around, the roots twisted as one—one mind, like a school of fish. Even the corpses took note, skulls suddenly twisting upon bony necks to regard this new interloper.

There's something in here. You felt it before. At the birthing ceremony. In dreams. It's here.

That was when she heard Andy make a noise, a startled gurgle in his throat, and she turned and she saw *it.* It was tall, too tall, neck lolling at a sickening angle so that the crown of its head didn't quite brush the ceiling. In the dim glow of mushrooms, it was a black silhouette, outline hazy. She could see the wispy strands of Spanish moss hanging off it in clumps. It smelled damp. *Please be a hallucination*, she thought desperately, even though she knew with absolute certainty that it was as real as could be.

"He's here, oh Jesus Christ, it's here."

"Who? What is this?" asked Andy. He stared straight at the figure, unable to focus his eyes.

"The Lord of the Forest."

The figure swayed where it stood. Then it started to advance with long, slow strides as if it were moving through water, wading through the growing tangles of mushrooms that sprouted from the seams of the floor.

The Lord of the Forest moved into the light, and Sarah saw the mossy green cloak, the branching antlers of twisted, peeling coral fungus erupting from its skull, the dick that slapped between long, long legs. Its body was white and soft, a solid fungal mass. It didn't have a face, not a real one, just the barest start of one. It looked like the underside of a stingray. The eyes were two long, drooping holes, dark and empty, like if you just poked your thumb into a lump of clay and wiggled it around for a while, and below that was no nose, just a gaping, sucking void of a mouth. But even in the darkness, she could see the rings of teeth looping down its throat.

>"Sarah."

Sarah blinked and looked again. It wasn't actually the Lord of the Forest or any monster at all; it was just Skillet. Of course, the moonflow was messing with her mind, making her see things. The Lord of the Forest was still there, like a transparent silhouette over reality, but if Sarah really concentrated hard, she could see through him and there was Skillet. It was just Skillet. It was okay.

"Skillet? I heard that thing kill you!" Sarah was pretty sure that Skillet's mangled body was right outside this tomb, lying in a heap just beyond the smashed door.

Something was very, very wrong. Sarah felt like the illusion should dissipate; the image of the Lord of the Forest should slowly fade as Skillet came more into focus. But that didn't happen. Both images remained, and the terrible epiphany hit Sarah that what she was looking at was not Skillet and was not the Lord of the Forest, but somehow both simultaneously, an impossible configuration like something you would see in a dream. She understood, with rising panic, that the scene she had witnessed in the cellar was no moonflow hallucination.

Or perhaps, she thought desperately, *I'm still hallucinating.*

>"You got it all wrong, ha ha! Hey, I'm real sorry about losing it before. I got carried away. I was just, you know, really mad. Like, I was so mad and I just thought how I wished that the Lord of the

Forest could destroy this stupid temple and Mother Moonflow and ALL the sisters and even the Hell Slut for abandoning me and going with the Dank Hole girl, and anyway, I just let him in. Turns out it was super easy to do this whole time!"

Skillet's face sparkled in the moonlight, her pupils so huge that her eyes looked entirely black—like one of Mother Moonflow's raccoons.

"Stay back. I'm getting out of here!"

>"Aw, don't be scared, it's still me!"

Skillet tilted her head quizzically.

>"Why are you leaving? Ever since I met you, all you've talked about is leaving."

"I have to leave."

>"C'mon. We could be something. You and me. We had fun, didn't we? You'd give all this up?"

Sarah narrowed her eyes suspiciously. Something was off. Something was very, very different. "Give all *what* up?"

>"Didn't you want to see the Green Lady? You were talkin' about her before."

"No, no, no!" cried Sarah. "Don't fuckin' say that! You're not even real!"

>"It's easy to feel her when you're on this side. I wasn't real religious before, but, man, now I can see why people get that way!"

"She's not here! It's just you... and that thing!"

Skillet giggled hysterically.

>"That thing is me! I'm the Lord of the Forest now! And it fuckin' rules! I'm gonna fuckin' destroy this whole stupid temple! C'mon, do it with me!"

"This is ridiculous. This can't be real."

>"When you saw the goddess and she reached out with her hands, I know you wanted to reach back. It's only scary when you're on that side, I promise. Once you're over here, there's no fear."

"How did you know about that? I never told you about that!" Was this actually Skillet or just a product of her own imagination? If it was just another moonflow hallucination projecting from her own brain, then of course it would know everything Sarah knew.

But what if it wasn't?

What if this was all real?

>WAKE *&&&

>"I know everything now," said Skillet. Her black eyes were like the infinite depths of space. "C'mon. I know you're ready to take her hand now. It's scary when you're alone. But you won't be alone. We had good times, didn't we? I'll be there. I'll be here."

Too many things happened at once.

On the floor, Andy moaned pathetically. Somewhere among the vines, Sarah's fingers brushed against her quarry—the last capsule of Leviathan's Favored Son. She snatched it up.

She was just so tired of all this. She felt that burning sensation in her chest, hotter, tighter, deeper, like she had swallowed just a little tiny spark of the Green Lady and now it was growing, growing, like a weed, like a fungus, traveling through her veins, reaching into her soul, and all she had to do, the only thing she needed to do, the thing that should be so incredibly easy to do, was open up and let her in. That was all that she ever had to do.

"I'm sorry, Andy. I'm just going to keep making stupid decisions until I die."

"Huh?"

She took that opening. She fell upon him and pried open his jaw and pushed the pill into his gullet until he started to gag, but she didn't let up until it went down, and then she massaged it down his throat. He goggled at her in astonishment, coughing and sputtering.

"I'm sorry for this, Andy, but I need you to listen. I need you to get back to Las Brujas, okay? Call Madeleine. Tell her you're gonna adopt Herman."

"What?"

"This is super important! This is literally the only reason I came back. You're the only one who can do it. Madeleine is useless—she'll send him back to the shelter. Don't believe her if she tells you anything else. And Jade... she never liked him to begin with. I literally don't know anyone else."

"Don't act like that," said Andy, coherent for a split second. "We're both getting out of here."

"No. We're not."

She opened up and let the Green Lady in.

Sarah was floating at the ceiling, staring down at herself, at the Green Lady, so she could watch the entire scene unfold. The tendrils enveloped her and split her open. She was torn apart, a gaping maw of big meaty flaps lolling, and the Green Lady burst out in her gelatinous pink sac. The Green Lady pulled her bulk from the ruins that had been Sarah, her flanks swelling, hands scrabbling for purchase against a wooden floor now bathed with blood and slime. The Green Lady gummed at her birthing caul, ripping the slick wet skin and slopping out into the world.

And now they were free. The slime of birth fell away and all that was left was the light, the brilliant blinding light, as Sarah rose to her feet, a brilliant glittering golden light, a being of pure dazzling brilliance who also happened to have big perfect breasts.

The Lord of the Forest tensed and swelled at the sight of her, his member inflating between his legs, barbs popping to life in a circle around his crown. The Green Lady flopped against the floor, screeching and flailing, her back arching into lordosis through pure animal instinct. Andy shrieked and kicked, desperately scooting along the wall.

Sarah felt the tender caresses of stringy roots, no longer threatening, now gentle and soft, winding around her, tighter, tighter, pressing into her butter-soft flesh, tighter, tighter, until a soft little sigh popped from her mouth. The tendrils slipped between her inflating breasts, curling around erect nipples, and slid over the arc of her belly, between her legs, twining around her girl dick and lifting her up out of herself. She felt the world fall away as she rose, higher and higher, through the ceiling.

This is the cosmic journey Mother Moonflow promised, she thought dully. She could feel herself coming apart, her mind blooming into a million fragments like the mushrooms releasing spores, and she could feel herself spreading out and out and out, all through the forest, her toes sinking into the soft loam, her fingers curling into branches, she was in every tree, every root, every dusting of pollen, and every blanket of moss, she was in the alders and the pines and the beechwoods, and she was in the slugs and the worms and the crawling things that ate them all, she could feel the worms winding through her flesh, which was soil, and she could see the great, vast eternity of the Pamogo Forest through eyes that no human had ever used, mushrooms bursting from her sockets, she saw a green map laid out before her, and here and there, among the trees, little glowing lights, like fireflies, roving around and around, and she could simply put her finger on any light and end it with just the merest touch, like squashing a bug, she could end it with a thought, really.

Those were people, she knew, and people weren't welcome in the Pamogo, in the world of the Green Lady and the Lord of the Forest. They were so arrogant to think that the Green Lady was of them, was one of them, that she cared for their adoration. The Green Lady, Sarah knew, was so much older. She had no need for worship; she simply was. She was a beast of the forest, and she would conduct herself as a beast of the forest would conduct itself. She could see the remnants of Mother Moonflow, reduced to particles, returned to the earth, and the ruined body of Sarah, shredded among the mushrooms, and where the Lord of the Forest had found Skillet and the Hell Slut, and she could see Pickles stumbling blindly through the dark of the labyrinth, and upstairs she could see Virginia Dentata and Miss Trix and all the others in their orgy, and she could see Sunny Delight, so very, very far away, piloting a Sturgeon bound for uncharted lands, and she could see, right there, in his pathetic heap, Andy still struggling to parse the miracle swirling all around him as Sarah took him by the shoulders and lifted him up and pushed him out into the woods and placed upon him her grace so that nothing would find him or harm him, and she told him, finally, as her last human words, as kindly as she could, "Go save my little baby Herman, you doofus," and she saw it all. The vines bound her tighter and tighter, probing her in all her places, and Sarah welcomed them as the forest welcomes the mist.

The Green Lady and the Lord of the Forest lived and breathed and walked in the world, and they entwined themselves together, the reunion of worlds, together again, never to be parted, together forever and ever and ever.

Outside, in the sky, the moon was full.

30.

What a fright I look! after so many months of isolation... my body is gaunt, my beard disheveled and my clothes stained with mud. My fingernails have curled into brittle black talons. I smell abominable. I look quite mad. the forest watches.

—Diary of Lazarus Sloane (California State Parks Archives)

Miss Trix and Virginia Dentata could not agree on the best soundtrack for the orgy.

Mother Moonflow had gifted them access to her complete collection of CDs and a five-disc boombox, but Miss Trix, believing that this orgy should heal with an atmosphere of sensual bonding, insisted that they play "Sadeness" by Enigma, and Virginia Dentata, believing that this orgy should get everyone pumped, wanted to play *Jock Jams, Volume 2*. Eventually, they were able to compromise when they realized that an orgy celebrating women coming together should clearly have big AFAB vocals and the best choice was therefore, of course, Kylie Minogue's *Fever*.

Miss Trix sat outside the door, serving as a bouncer. There was, strictly speaking, no need for a bouncer. All the sisters were invited, and since they were deep in the desolation of the Pamogo, the only unwelcome strangers who might try to enter the orgy were now either dead or catatonic. But this playacting gave the whole affair a delightfully risqué aura of exclusivity, and ambience was going to be very important to getting every pussy as wet as possible as quickly as possible.

"Hey, guys, I know we're all bummed about things. Truth is, I'm bummed too. But you know what Mother Moonflow says, right? Good vibes, good vibes."

Miss Trix rolled her eyes at the muffled sounds of Virginia Dentata's MC patter coming from the closed room behind her. Virginia Dentata sucked at it. That was why Mother Moonflow usually ran the orgies.

"Hey, guys, you all feeling good tonight? You ready to feel good? Tonight is all about feeling good. Yeah. Yeah, that's right. We're all having a good time, right? Hey. How about some tunes, huh? Yeah."

The breathy voice of Kylie Minogue invited everyone to come into her world. In retrospect, this was a bad choice, thought Miss Trix. The lyrics were all wrong. Kylie's voice oozed sex, so that Miss Trix squirmed in her seat, but you could clearly hear her addressing her entreaties to "Boy." This was a love song for straights. That was an embarrassing mistake. She should have argued harder for "Sadeness."

But Miss Trix was underestimating the lure of that husky, smoky voice.

Inside the room, Doc Clopper felt moved to touch Aphrodite on the thigh, and Aphrodite, still a depressing sad sack since the loss of her baby, did not withdraw. Soon they were touching each other, on the arm, on the face, and then they were kissing together atop a pile of beaded pillows. And then others were touching and kissing, Marsha Mallow on Zooty Zoot Zoot, Captain Beef Curtains on Charlotte the Harlot, and soon the sound of moaning and gasping nearly overpowered Kylie's darkly seductive techno-pop anthem and the harried "Yeah, we're having fun now, eh? Maybe I'll have some fun now too, eh?" of Virginia Dentata.

There was a chittering, chattering sound. The women were already too deep into their business to notice, but Virginia Dentata turned to look. A raccoon dashed through the crowd, bounded into the center of the room, and bared its teeth at the writhing women. Another raccoon scuttled between Virginia Dentata's legs, brushing her shins with coarse fur. More raccoons were squeezing from holes in the walls, dropping to the floor, and intermingling with the squirming bodies. Great. That was just what they needed. These damn raccoons were everywhere in the temple, but they usually avoided the high-traffic areas. Naturally, they would change that just to fuck up the orgy. As if the sisters didn't have enough issues.

Two sisters, tongues interlocked, rolled over an angry raccoon and immediately howled in surprise. The raccoon squealed.

Other sisters were also starting to notice.

"Hey, hey," said Virginia Dentata loudly. "Don't worry about that, it's just the little sisters. Nothing you haven't seen before. Gimme a sec, we'll get it sorted out quick and then we'll be back to business—"

The little waist-high door with the leering face painted on it flew open and Pickles exploded out, hair flying, robe billowing, a tangle of flailing limbs. The orgy mood now completely ruined, the sisters screamed and yelled. But before Virginia Dentata had the opportunity to demand an explanation for this rude interruption, all hell followed.

Outside, Miss Trix waited. The carcasses of the giant puppets lay in a heap across the clearing, the grotesque caricatures of the Lord and the Lady plugged together in stillborn coitus. A drop of liquid hit Miss Trix on the forehead; she reached up to wipe it away and her hand came away red. She glanced up.

The temple loomed in the dark. No lights flickered in any window. The building glistened in the moonlight in a way that it should not glisten. The walls squirmed with a multitude of pale wet roots, branching and spreading, red with blood, glinting evilly like oil in the moonlight. Spores billowed from the open windows in a fungal blizzard.

There was a great and sudden commotion in the room behind her. It did not sound sexual and it did not sound sensual. It was a panicked roar and then a great pounding against the walls and door, as if a great many hands had forgotten in their fear how to work a doorknob. Kylie's voice shuddered and skipped—suddenly, she was singing "Burning Up," then "Dancefloor," then, quite abruptly, the boombox jolted and flipped to a new CD and belted two lines of Lou Bega's "Mambo No. 5" before dying with a crunch. Miss Trix took a step backward.

She did not move to open the door, but she didn't need to—it quite suddenly opened of its own accord, and a cavalcade of screaming women poured out, tripping and tumbling in their panic. Someone ran into Miss Trix and knocked her to the floor.

It was over in less than a minute. Women were running in circles in a blind panic, screaming and swearing. Some ran into the woods and vanished. Others remained close to the temple, paralyzed by terror. She recognized Pickles in the distance, his open house robe flapping behind him.

"Where's Mother Moonflow? What's happening?"

Miss Trix called out to him, and he paused, only briefly, to look up at her with terrified eyes. The scar across his abdomen looked like a curled black centipede in the gloom of the night. He shook his head, his halo of snarly hair shaking, before lurching into the woods and disappearing. That was not a comforting sign.

Miss Trix peered into the darkened sanctuary, which she had helped to build but which now, in the darkness and stillness of the night, illuminated only by the few remaining torches still flickering around the clearing, was suddenly alien. A stinking red tide, chunky with ground hamburger meat, slopped out and washed over her feet. The inside walls, what little she could see of them, were covered with a fresh latticework of gently pulsing roots.

Then the Lord of the Forest emerged, long, long legs striding. Its maw flopped open, blubbery gummy mouth too floppy to hold shut, lips quivering, whorls of little reptilian peg teeth glistening in the vortex of a gullet. It had no eyes. Its open maw was screaming a scream that was very much not the scream of a raccoon, but a toneless bellow that reverberated through the canopy.

Behind the Lord of the Forest, a plethora of rooty tentacles slithered from the deep void of the open door, gliding over the slick gooey outer walls. Raccoons spilled out of the building in their wake, chattering and screaming.

The Lord of the Forest was very much not interested in people, who constantly chattered in their annoying human languages, spilling words that meant nothing. Even outside, it was offended by the walls that humans built, and it could vaguely sense more humans beyond those walls. A female of the species shouted at it in meaningless human words. It responded in the ancient tongue of the gods, the language that could, with a word, call plants from the dirt and fungus from the rot. The female of the species stared at it, uncomprehending, her human mind too blinkered to even fathom the depths of her ignorance.

Miss Trix opened her mouth to say something, or maybe she was just opening it out of sheer shock, but in any case, it didn't matter, because the Lord of the Forest put long spindly arms like branches forward, curling scabby claws around her shoulders, and scissored her into ribbons. Then it turned to the temple, red ribbons of Miss Trix trailing from between its talons like streamers.

"Hey! Fuck you! Over here!"

Virginia Dentata had uprooted one of the torches still burning after the birthing ceremony. She hopped back and forth, jabbing the searing flame toward the Lord of the Forest while cleverly avoiding its grasp. She must not understand. Her mind was too small; she refused to understand the scope of her situation. The Lord of the Forest was not to be trifled with. It was a god and these humans would do well to remember.

The Lord of the Forest remembered Virginia Dentata, it remembered how she had beat up Skillet and smashed Sarah's glasses, and the Lord of the Forest was ready to end this bitch.

It lashed out with a vine, coiling it around her throat, and pulled her forward so that she dropped her torch. She gawped like a fish, and the Lord of the Forest took the opportunity to snake a vine into her open mouth and down her throat. Her eyes bugged and she retched, drool dribbling from her mouth, as her hands grabbed at the vine in a futile effort to dislodge it. The rough surface lacerated her hands until they were too lubricated with blood to maintain their grip. The Lord of the Forest was unbothered. The vines unspooled into the human, filling her guts and invading her sinuses. More labored gagging and then, quite suddenly, Virginia Dentata's eyeballs exploded in a flash of gore, and white toadstools bloomed instantly from her sockets. The body collapsed to the ground, limp. Tendrils writhed under her skin, more and more, spreading, multiplying, until the fresh body burst into a new mushroom bloom.

A malevolent animal cunning gleamed deep in the empty pits in the face of the Lord of the Forest. It would destroy this building and drive the humans out—as it should be. Already, its roots were hard at work dismantling, destroying; it would tear this abominable structure to the ground, and all that would remain would be the forest. White roots snaked through the temple, prying between boards, pulling apart walls, putting forth mushrooms in such incredible profusion that soon the entire structure would disappear under the multitude of their lumpy white caps.

Nearly two hundred years ago, fleeing his failures on the American River, Lazarus Sloane had made his way to the deserted edges of the great Pamogo Forest and beheld a vast, endless tangle of creepers and lianas, junk hemlocks and gnarled alders, a wet wild woods that was his to tame. His experiments in logging saw little more success than his gold-mining efforts, but he left behind one thing—a massive, derelict timber mill that stood, like a silent sentinel, in the dead center of the forest. Whatever flumes might have been constructed to carry away logs had long since dried up and rotted away, whatever roads might have been paved had long since cracked and warped and returned to dirt, but the mill remained.

Roots wound themselves around the beams and wormed their way between wooden slats. Mushrooms flowered from every pore. The temple stood for a while yet, empty of people yet full of life, because the workmanship was too good to let it dissolve completely. But eventually, it crumbled under the weight of its new gods, and all evidence of its existence was subsumed back into the earth. Such is the way of things.

The Lord of the Forest was in the forest, in the trees and the rocks, in the dark banks of wet ferns, in the rich black loam, in the bones of raccoons and in the raccoons, in the miles and miles of mycelium tendrils underpinning the roots of the redwoods and sequoias, and in the worms and slugs and crawling things that ate them all. The Green Lady was in the forest, in the streams and the caves, in the creeping moss and the hanging vines, in the miles and miles of branches entwined like lovers' arms all across the forest, shielding the deep dark undergrowth. The forest was theirs again, and whatever small influence they'd once had while they were asleep, to turn the feet and twist the necks of foolish humans who wandered into their domain, was now magnified a hundredfold.

Those survivors who still remained, spared for whatever reason, fanned out through the forest, stumbling over roots and slogging through brambles, thighs ripped by thorns and feet bloodied by sharp rocks. There were no paths, and once the spires of the mill disappeared behind the treetops, there was nothing more. The woods were dark and deep. Occasionally, they could hear the shouts of their fellows, muffled by green, but the woods were confusing and the gods of old now held sway.

31.

*The Lady in Black (*Amanita mortis*) is a solitary toadstool with a wide coal-black cap, resembling a wide-brimmed harvest hat, and drooping protruding gills. Its stalk is also black. Consumption of the Lady in Black is invariably immediately fatal and is strongly discouraged. Do not eat the Lady in Black.*

—Field Guide to Common Mushrooms of the Pamogo Forest, *T. F. Greengarb (1978)*

Andy wandered in a daze.

The forest was different now. It was never hospitable, of course, but Andy could sense wary eyes on his back. It reminded him of how Sarah had insisted someone was following them in the minutes before they both lost hours to Leviathan's Favored Son, and it made him wonder if she was right. Were the sisters stalking them even then? Had their rescuers plotted against them from the start? The moonflow glowed in his veins, feeding his paranoia as suddenly everything and everyone seemed so obviously connected. He paused to stare at the fractal patterns unfolding in the green leaves above, losing more hours, until the cold and damp suddenly reminded him that he was naked. He struggled to remember why he was naked, but the last day was a jumble and all he could recall was Sarah pushing him out the temple door.

The forest twisted and turned before his eyes, and he couldn't be sure whether it was real or whether it was the moonflow. He shivered and his teeth chattered; he had no protection against the elements. Every step was agony, the ground rocky and rough under the soft soles of his bare feet, and more than once he sat down among the roots of a cedar or an alder and planned to give up.

But he also remembered that Sarah had entrusted to him a sacred task, the care of a cat, and he pushed forward for that. He kept going.

Eventually, he came across an unfamiliar stream—fresh clean water guttering over smooth stones—and, as thirsty as he was, his instincts told him to wait. He followed the flow of the creek for some time until he came across a body lodged against a fallen tree.

It lay face down in the course of the stream, black house robe and hair weaving in the current. It could not have been dead long; the skin was only starting to take on the mottled gray color of cold blood clotting.

"Hey, bud, you okay?" said Andy. Pickles did not answer, so Andy moved to the next phase of his investigation; he selected a fallen branch from the shore and poked at the body until he was able to turn it over. Something had already eaten away the lips and eyes, and Andy was so startled by the sight that he yelped and dropped the branch. The body fell back into the creek.

He paused for a while, and then he waded into the creek and slowly disentangled the body from its house robe. He plucked at the wet material, carefully, carefully, so that he wouldn't accidently touch that clammy gray skin, and the whole process was especially difficult given that he couldn't bring himself to actually look at what he was doing. He tried to think of Sarah, effortlessly shoving Greensleeves over to get the mushrooms in its eyes, and chided himself for being so squeamish, but these were not comparable situations and he knew it. This body was way fresher, and that made it so much worse. Finally, he pulled it free and the body flipped in the current and started to float away. Andy didn't wait. He lugged the drenched robe to shore and wrung it out as much as he could before he put it on; it was cold and soppy, but it was his only option for clothes. Pickles was not wearing shoes. That was the real disappointment. He really needed shoes.

Andy did not linger after that. The horror of his discovery gave him new energy, and he continued his way downstream, shivering as he pulled the damp robe tightly around him and hoped that his body heat would dry it quickly.

Eventually, he lay in the undergrowth and waited for sleep. In a dream, he wandered a forest of giant toadstools, their flaring caps blotting out a yellow sky, while unseen assailants chased him. He tried to hide, but they always knew where he was. Squatting behind a gigantic mushroom, he saw Sarah and she looked like shit, ferns blossoming from her shoulders, purple tongue lolling. Her feet and haunches were rooted into the soil. Her skin was mottled green and Andy got the impression that, beneath her blanket of moss and lichen and fungus, she was naked as well. Her eyes were gone, her sockets filled with new fungal growth, twisting spires of pink mushrooms. She glowed with an unearthly bioluminescence. He tried to focus on her, tried to see only Sarah or only the Green Lady, but the illusion refused to fade and the glowing silhouette never dissipated completely.

"Am I dead? I think I'm dead."

>"You're dreaming," said Sarah without moving her desiccated lips. "You're supposed to save Herman. That's the whole reason I saved you, you doofus."

"I don't know where I am." His assailants were close; he could sense them fanning out through the woods and closing in, closer, closer. His legs itched to run, but he couldn't end this conversation. "There's no way out of this forest!"

>"Some stalker you are! Here, I'll help you."

She raised her arms to the sky, new roots snapping as she moved, and started to glow brighter and brighter until Andy's eyes watered. He stepped backward, tripping over his own feet, and fell on his butt.

Then he woke up.

The Hell Slut found Andy curled up asleep under a tree, and she couldn't help but feel sorry for him. He looked so pathetic there, wet and shivering, slathered in mud. How could a creature like that expect to survive out here in the unforgiving elements? She considered leaving him here, just moving on without a word, but she felt bad for the helpless creatures of the world, even the ones she killed, and not even her hatred for men could taint the pure pity she felt for this absolute baby. Maybe he reminded her of Skillet or of Sunny Delight, or maybe she just didn't have anything better to do with herself now that she was alone in the world. Or maybe this sad little skinny kid, with his shaggy hair and his scruffy little beard and his slender hands and his lips slightly parted in sleep, just reminded her too much of her first love, the Lady Jesus, and try as she might, she couldn't leave him to die.

Her face was swollen with bruises, and her twice-broken nose was a contused purple. She was covered in blood, her clothes saturated with it, the coppery stink billowing off her in waves. Fresh wounds lacerated the exposed flesh above the neckline of her shredded tank top, and painful electric sparks shot up her left leg with every step, but the deep gut wound that should have ended her? That was fine, disappeared just like Hal Sampson's bullet hole. What were the odds?

The Hell Slut made a mental note to lay off the moonflow. If she kept hallucinating about life-ending injuries, it was probably a good sign that she needed to get clean. Not that she had a choice now.

So she sat down, back against a nearby elm, and smoked a joint as she waited for Andy to wake.

"Sleeping Beauty's up, huh?" she said when Andy finally stirred. "They really fuckin' pumped you full of moonflow, didn't they?"

He flopped around on the ground, shivering in his wet robe, smearing his bare ass with mud. He still wasn't in complete control of his faculties yet.

"That's fucking pathetic. I can't watch this." She tossed him her buckskin jacket. "Put that on. At least it's better than nothing."

The jacket fit her perfectly, but she was much bigger than Andy. On Andy, it came down to his mid-thigh.

The Hell Slut rose to her feet and stretched, spine cracking. "All right, let's get moving. The sooner we get you out of these woods, the better."

"You tried to kill me!" cried Andy, huddling in the oversized jacket.

She looked down at him. "Well, I'm not trying to kill you now.

That was yesterday's doctrine. I'm reformed now. You wanna stay here? Maybe wait for rescue?"

Andy did not.

The Hell Slut knew these woods as well as anyone could. Andy stumbled along behind as she hacked her way through the brush. Occasionally, she would pause to point out a desiccated corpse half-buried among the bracken, still dressed in rags and tatters, a shredded woolen beanie still pulled tight over a bare cranium or a threadbare scarf still wrapped around the exposed vertebrae of a neck.

She did not particularly care for Andy, who was slow and stumbled a lot and kept asking stupid questions the entire way.

"What happened?"

The Hell Slut couldn't answer that question. She wasn't sure why she was still alive. She tried to attribute everything to moonflow paranoia; maybe none of it had really happened, but then again, maybe it had and maybe she was alive because Skillet still felt some sympathy for her, even after everything that had happened. She could even imagine Skillet's stupid little face with that stupid goblin grin. *Really sorry about stabbing you before, ha ha! I just got a little carried away. Ha ha!* That would be just like her. It was a nice thought, at least. She only vaguely recalled one weird final image: the temple teeming with squirming, wormy roots and blossoming with an extravagance of white mushrooms.

The loss of Mother Moonflow was difficult, despite everything. It pained her deeply to lose the woman who'd first said, *You'll always have a home here with us gals*. It really did. She was fairly certain that she had killed Mother Moonflow, although the details of everything that had happened during her trip were sketchy. She suspected that in the days to come, she would not be able to keep this knowledge in a little box in her head.

You'll always have a home here with us gals. Well. Not anymore, it turned out.

"Why do you keep talking? Just be quiet and try to keep up."

It could only be that they, for whatever reason, had the favor of the gods, because the horrors of the forest did not find them; Andy and the Hell Slut slipped into the cool dark woods and vanished. They continued to move through the woods blindly, until finally they found a tree with teeth embedded in its bark. After that, after much hiking, they found a corpse in a canyon wearing the tattered remains of a green raincoat, and after that, surely it was just a trick of the light, surely they were just seeing what they wanted to see, what they hoped to see, but the canopy seemed to be thinning and the trees around them didn't look so unfamiliar. The woods felt less hostile than usual, almost as if some force was guiding them to safety, as if perhaps something inherent and ethereal in the woods was paying them one last little kindness out of the memory of better times.

The Hell Slut spied the first sign of the visitor center through the thinning trees. Andy started to laugh when she pointed it out.

"We're here!" he cried. "We made it!"

He stumbled forward, passing the Hell Slut, who was suddenly stationary. He stopped and looked back at her.

"All right," she said. "This is it for us. I'm gonna leave you here. I'm taking my jacket back, though."

Andy wriggled out of the jacket and handed it back. The Hell Slut took it without a word.

"Where are you gonna go?"

"Maybe I'll go north. I got an old friend up there."

"There's nothing north."

"We'll see. We didn't exactly part on good terms."

"Come inside," said Andy. "You can get a little cleaned up, get something to eat? We could watch *Stalker.*"

"What's that?"

"Nothing. Nothing, just an inside joke. I guess you wouldn't get it. It's a movie."

"Oh. I'd rather not." The Hell Slut turned and tromped off into the woods, and then she was gone.

32.

All Visitors Welcome!

—Sloane Mill State Historic Park informational brochure (circa 1995)

When Andy finally stumbled into the Sloane Mill State Historic Park parking lot, he was filthy, caked in mud, his robe tattered, his body laced with bloody gashes from too many spills over too many logs and too many trees. The Sloane Mill State Historic Park visitor center stood exactly as he had left it, the parking lot empty except for Sarah's abandoned Tercel and a ranger now shoving a ticket under a windshield wiper. The ranger was middle-aged, with a paunch drooping over his gun belt, a salt-and-pepper crew cut, and a mustache. He looked exactly like every other ranger.

The ranger went for his gun when he saw Andy, because that was what rangers did, but then he recognized Andy and didn't shoot. Andy raised one hand to show he wasn't a threat, his other hand carefully clamping his robe together.

"You weren't on-site," said the ranger accusingly. His eyes trailed over the dirty robe. "You're not in uniform."

The ranger had a spare key for the visitor center. He waited patiently while Andy showered and dressed, and then listened to Andy babble about the girl he had taken into the Pamogo, Sarah—no, he didn't know her last name, and she was lost out there now. There was more, but Andy's descriptions made him sound insane, and even Andy couldn't entirely discern reality from moonflow hallucinations. The ranger raised a hand for him to stop, then took out a pencil and notepad and said, "So what you're saying is that during park hours, you left the site?"

"Did you hear anything I said? A girl is lost!"

"I heard you. There's a lot of that going on. You know there was an incident in San Bernardo?"

"What happened in San Bernardo?"

"That's none of your concern. But if you ask me, this was no coincidence. I suspect antifa involvement, maybe BLM. Probably outside agitators from San Francisco. You know how they are in San Francisco. You know the real problem is, Commiefornia is at the forefront of bad laws. Take this whole marijuana decriminalization thing. You know that potheads actually would prefer to be in jail?"

"Sarah is in danger. I think they were planning to hurt her. She might be dead!"

"I'm not done. I was up at the county jail the other day, for training, and one of them told me, 'I'm glad I'm in jail, it's the only way I can get clean.' He totally said that to me! But how are we supposed to get them the jail they need if you can't even search them anymore, huh? Think about it. Then tell me your bleeding-heart politicians are gonna solve that!"

The ranger had a lot of theories, which he expounded on at length, but Andy really just wanted him to leave. The ranger promised that the authorities would get to the bottom of this, that Sarah's killers would be brought to justice, that Andy would be hearing more from them about this.

"Don't worry, I won't tell anyone about you being out of uniform. You're lucky you didn't get yourself arrested. Or worse. Next time, call dispatch and let us know before you go off-site. We need staff on-site during normal business hours."

After he left, Andy never heard from him again.

The moonflow was finally working its way out of his system, leaving him drained and desolate. Andy tried to sleep, but he was interrupted every ten minutes by the call of nature. He spent the night on the toilet, liquid shit pouring out of him. Too much moonflow. On top of everything else, it wreaked havoc with his digestion to the point that by the end, his asshole was raw and screaming, and he was thankful just to finally collapse into bed. He didn't sleep. He lay in bed for hours, staring at the ceiling, listening to nothing.

In the morning, he awoke to see sunlight pouring through the window, and the fact that he woke up indicated that he must have slept at some point.

The days passed in a slow molasses-thick sludge. The sunlight was welcome at first, but the brightness hurt his eyes and made his head throb after the cool gloom of the Pamogo. There were loose ends to tie up too. He talked to Madeleine on the phone. She was upset, screaming; she couldn't understand. Where was Sarah? Andy didn't know. He had no answers. At first, he considered trying to explain, but he remembered only scattered fragments himself. She screamed at him for losing Sarah and called him a bunch of names, which Andy listened to without interruption. They spoke again only once, several weeks later, when Madeleine felt obligated to invite him to a candlelight vigil for Sarah. Andy had not heard anything else from the ranger, which he took to be bad news, and when he called district headquarters about it, they just told him the case was in process. He didn't go to the vigil. Madeleine would be staring at him the whole time, knowing that it was his fault.

Madeleine insisted that she would take Herman, but he knew Madeleine and he knew that Sarah was right when she said that Madeleine was a flake. He drove down to the Bay himself to get the cat. Herman was not happy about it. He yowled the whole trip back to Las Brujas, so distressed that he shit his crate and Andy had to pull off into a Shasta Lake gas station to hose him down.

The rangers, alerted now that Andy had been off-site during working hours, dropped by more frequently, hoping to catch him slacking again. Each time, they left another ticket on the Tercel's windshield, even though Andy always explained to them the situation. Eventually, someone at district headquarters must have said something, because a tow truck came and took it away, and Andy didn't know what happened to it after that.

Things returned to normal fast.

Talking about Lazarus Sloane was a big waste of time, Andy realized. Tourists came, as they always did, sporadically. In the morning, he would wake and open the park—he hoisted the American flag and the California flag, flipped on all the lights in the little museum, dusted the glass display cases, opened the cash registers, and waited for visitors. Visitors came, bored families passing through on their way to Oregon who just needed to use the bathroom but then decided to kill some extra time. They pressed their snotty noses against the displays and left fingerprints all over the glass. They would ask Andy questions about Lazarus Sloane or the Pamogo woods, and then they would nod and stare off into the distance, disinterested, as they ignored his answers. They were just here to waste time; they didn't care.

Headquarters in San Bernardo sent a dictate, informing all parks in the sector that they were to discontinue in-person school tours in favor of digital programs. "We can reach more kids this way," the dictate said. Andy now explained 1860s logging equipment to a computer screen, allowing him to address multiple classrooms at once. Sometimes up to eight classrooms participated in a single call, but usually the teachers canceled at the last minute. The Internet in the visitor center was always buggy, so Andy was rarely able to finish a program without the connection dying. Teachers would then complain to headquarters, and headquarters would then send down a reprimand to Andy.

Everything seemed very sordid and very pointless. The world was a gray blur, compared to the vivid colors he had almost touched.

For the first week in his new home, Herman hid under the bed, mewling pitifully. Andy shoved cans of food under the bed, but Herman refused to eat. Herman was the first cat that Andy had owned in years, so he couldn't remember if that was normal. He would need to eat eventually.

Andy went into Las Brujas and bought a stuffed mouse on a string. He waved it in front of the bed, but Herman didn't react.

Then one night, Herman finally came out, padded into the kitchen, and jumped to the window. He purred so hard that he rattled, a noise Andy had not heard from this cat before. Outside, there was nothing but the parking lot and, beyond that, the darkness of the Pamogo trees.

"What do you see out there, buddy?"

Herman continued to purr. Andy gulped and licked his lips. He didn't want to ask the next question, but he felt compelled.

"Do you see Mama out there?"

Herman settled down, tucked his paws under him, and closed his eyes. He continued to purr well into the night.

Acknowledgments

I would not be where I am today without the uncompromising love and support of my wonderful family: Mom and Dad, my brother Tommy and my sister Muffin, who always believe in me no matter what the hell dumbass thing I am currently doing, and especially my very, very long-suffering wife, who had to read every single early half-baked version of this book. I also want to thank my agents, John Baker and Julie Gourinchas, who saw something in a lowly Internet goblin, who took a chance on this incredibly unsellable book, for their tireless work and awesome dedication in actually selling it; my editors, Angelica Chong and Jenni Hill, whose keen eyes and patient editing did the all-important and thankless work of making this book fit for human consumption; Lisa Marie Pompilio for our gloriously psychedelic cover; and the entire team at Orbit for making this book a reality! While there are too many other friends and well-wishers to mention, I would be remiss not to give a shout-out to Brian Keene, the grumpy horror uncle who first helped me find my footing; my dedicated beta readers, Jennifer Albright, Nicoletta Giuseffi, Eve Harms, Ethan Poschman, Winter Holmes, Cormack Baldwin, Thomas Hale, and B. A. Postma; and the kindness of all Midnight Pals readers and the horror community in general. And a big thanks to Fun Coven, Puppet Pals, Kitty

Sneezes, Volcano Lair, and the Midnight Pals audio Discords! Finally, this book coincides with the arrival of my first niece, Momo—a big congratulations to Matt and Muffin, since they're the ones doing all the hard work raising her! Maybe don't show her this book till she's older, though.

Meet the Author

Bitter Karella

BITTER KARELLA is the writer and horror aficionado behind the thrice Hugo Award–nominated microfiction comedy account @Midnightpals.bsky.social, which asks, What if all your favorite horror writers gathered around the campfire to tell scary stories? His work has appeared in *Seize the Press*, Tenebrous Press's *Your Body Is Not Your Body*, and Ghoulish Books's *Bound in Flesh*. She also dabbles in cartooning and text game design.

if you enjoyed
MOONFLOW
look out for

RED RABBIT GHOST

by

Jen Julian

A cynical young outcast confronts his small town's dark secrets in this atmospheric and haunting debut horror novel from brilliant new voice Jen Julian.

The town of Blacknot is not what it appears, and a place deep in the woods known only as the Night House is calling....

Jesse Calloway didn't plan to return to his repressive backwoods hometown of Blacknot, North Carolina, after only one year away at college, but an anonymous messenger has lured him home. Eighteen years ago, his mother died under unexplained circumstances. Every story he has heard is incomplete. Now the messenger claims to have the answers. But Jesse will have to hunt for them.

Alice Catherine, the daughter of a local pork manufacturer, obsesses over Jesse in turn. To her, he is a key player in unearthing the dark family history she's convinced her father is concealing. Alice knows Jesse must find the answers himself, with the hope that once he does, he'll help her change both their futures.

But Jesse's path to Alice isn't a straight line, and his questions are stirring up issues with locals, including his much older and well-armed ex-boyfriend, Harlan. When an old fling of Jesse's goes missing and Alice's plans start to unravel, it's clear there's more at stake than either of them could imagine. On a collision course littered with psychotropic fungi, time-warping magic, and far too many alligators, Jesse and Alice will need to determine how far they are willing to go for the truth, and whether they can trust each other enough to get there. . . .

1

Jesse keeps his dead mother's things in an old Tarbarrel tin. Pork jerky smell, black pepper and molasses, contained alongside photographs. His mother's senior yearbook picture—her sharp, toothy grin. A Polaroid of her and Aunt Nancy toilet-papering the Confederate Memorial in downtown Blacknot. Nancy was seventeen then, his mother nine, both dressed in bell sleeves and fringe like it was still the 60s, though the Polaroid was taken by Jesse's grandmother in 1982. On the back, an inscription: *Nancy Jane & Constance Louise, getting in trouble.*

Also inside the tin: twelve postcards addressed to Nancy while she was in graduate school, messages in his mother's affected teenage voice—*If you find a man in the Queen City, bring him home so that we might sacrifice him to the swamp gods and ensure the harvest.*

Also: one bracelet of black wooden beads, which he guesses his mother must have worn.

Also: a series of articles from the paper about how they found her, dead, on the banks of the Miskwa River eighteen summers ago, and a small notebook of inscrutable thoughts, facts, and fantasies (Jesse couldn't remember his mother, so he resorted to inventing details), which he wrote when he was a kid. *River highest since 1980—average water temp 71°—she had black hair, pretty face, archy eyebrows—5 foot 1—shoe size 6 1/2, bad at singing—loved* Wizard of Oz, X-Files, *will-o'-the-wisp, animals—spoke French and Spanish—laughed at weird stuff like ghosts—smelled like cinnamon, fixed eggs better than Nancy, came home from work wearing costumes, played chess—*

And so on.

There are many things the tin does not include. According to Nancy, Connie burned a lot of keepsakes and photos in the years leading up to the final breakdown that killed her, including pictures of her and Jesse together. That is his least favorite detail about her, aside from being dead.

Remarkably, he didn't take the tin with him to college. When he packed last August, he decided to leave it right there on the upper shelf of his closet, its time-honored home. Now, after driving back the four hours from Greensboro, he finds that Nancy has used his monthslong absence as an excuse to pack up his bedroom to turn it into an office/meditation studio. All his posters and books and old school projects are stuffed away in boxes, the walls now hung with calming beach photographs, the closet clean of his baggy high school clothes and red Miskwa High sweatshirts.

And the tin, which is not where he left it.

"Where'd you put it?" he asks Nancy, trying not to panic.

His aunt stands in the doorway, looking sheepish. "I mean." She gestures to the boxes. "I put away a lot of shit, hon. It's probably here."

"Probably?"

"I did throw some things out. Your old running shoes were biohazards. What did the tin look like?"

"Like a *tin*," he says. "It looked like a tin. Red. A red tin. It had the Tarbarrel logo on it. It had—all her stuff was in there."

"Her stuff?" Nancy says.

Jesse dives into the boxes. Some are open, some already taped shut. His aunt knows what he's talking about, of course, but in the face of his alarm, she stands calm. Or at least pretends to.

"I'm sure it's here somewhere."

On principle alone, he doesn't like that she's done this, just crunched down and packed away his entire childhood like a whole lot of junk. Trophies for cross-country crammed in with mix CDs, the complete films of Bogart and Bacall. In one box, he finds the many amusing pulp fiction book covers he hunted down in flea markets all over the county, then, digging deeper, a glass hand pipe containing the charred residue of some backwater ditch weed. He bristles at the thought of Nancy finding it. Sure, they used to sing along to Peter Tosh's *Legalize It* on car trips, but that doesn't mean he wants her to have a firsthand view of his indiscretions.

But then, maybe the invasiveness was the point. Maybe her whole meditation studio plan was just an excuse to go through his stuff, to try to understand him one last time, unravel his secrets, account for his high school misery.

"Oh, stop being so *frantic*," she says. "I'll help you."

"Don't!" he says. "Please, don't touch anything else. I'll find it myself."

"But you *know* I wouldn't have thrown that out."

"You just said maybe you did."

She laughs. Her expression is becoming strained.

"But I didn't trash anything *important*, sweetheart. Do you really think I'd just throw out—*that*?"

"Connie's things," he says. "My mother's things."

There's no official moratorium on mentioning his mother's name, though he realizes it's been a long time since it was uttered aloud in this house. Nancy steps back, no longer smiling. Her face flushes with indignation.

After a minute, she says, "You know, you've caught me off guard, Jesse, just being here. You insisted you were staying out in Greensboro for the summer. Since November, that's been your plan, right? Get a job, get an apartment. What happened?"

He can't even tell if she's happy to see him. Sure, when he first got in, she rushed out to the driveway to meet him, and when Dick, his red 1998 hatchback, let out its usual tricky sputter, she laughed and said, "Now, *there's* a sweet sound." All the neighbors must've heard it, too. Must've thought, *Oh, that's Jesse Calloway. Antsy Nancy's boy. He's back from college, finally.* Because he didn't come back for Thanksgiving, Christmas, or Easter. Nancy, who taught film and public speaking at the community college in Kneesville, had all the same breaks he did, so each time she'd drive out to see him, and they'd stay with Minerva, her old roommate from grad school, a silver-haired lesbian. And during every visit, Nancy praised the "culture" of the city (i.e., Greensboro) in comparison to the hick trashfire of Miskwa County, and then she drank too much wine and said she would be happy enough to see Jesse survive his freshman year without alcohol poisoning or gonorrhea, which he guessed was meant to take the pressure off or something. But in all that, there was never any talk of Jesse returning home. Nancy took him at his word.

"The plan," he says to her, "changed."

"It changed," she says. "What changed? You were *adamant* about not coming back here."

He rips up packing tape in snaky strips, one box after another.

"What *changed*?" she asks again.

He finds a plastic bin of photos: Jesse and Nancy at the carnivorous plant garden in Wilmington, another one of him and his grandfather at the Fort Fisher Aquarium, then a few with his former high school friends in their ninth-grade Halloween costumes, grins with retainer wires.

"I wanted to see friends," he says.

"Which friends?" asks Nancy.

"'Which friends?' Why does that matter?"

"Because. Some of your friends have a history of getting you in trouble."

He laughs. "Well, there you go. You got me. I drove four hours to get lit at some redneck barn party. Nothing like the *scene* in metropolitan Blacknot. Endless ragers. Orgies day and night."

Nancy's flush deepens.

"You had a plan," she says firmly. "You changed your mind so fast, that's all I'm saying."

"For all you know, I've been thinking about it for weeks. And anyway, that's got nothing to do with you culling out my shit without asking."

"Oh, Jesse, stop it. Just stop. I didn't—do you seriously think I'd do that on purpose, throw out those things, my *sister's* things...?"

She trails off, her voice breaking. Tears fog up her glasses.

Little fucker, says a voice in Jesse's head. First night home, and you have lied to Nancy and made her cry. Fine work.

"I didn't say you'd do it on purpose," he says, trying to be nicer. "It's fine. It's got to be here somewhere."

"I mean," she says tearfully, "you didn't even take it *with* you. How was I supposed to know?"

In hindsight, yes, maybe the tin would've been safer if he'd brought it with him to college. But he never missed it there. Until a month ago, he was hardly thinking about Connie Calloway at all. Back at school, he was an actual adult, savvy and queer and experienced. He got props for liking David Lynch and owning a discontinued car. It's 2015 and the 90s are cool again. Everything comes back around. Everything reincarnates.

That's what changing your life is like, he assumes: a reincarnation.

Nancy lifts her glasses, squeezes her fingers against her eyes. "I didn't throw it out, I didn't," she keeps saying. "At least, I don't think I did."

And he keeps saying, "It's okay, it's okay, I'm sure you didn't," though really, he just wants to find the damn thing so they can stop talking about it and she can stop crying.

Then, finally, hiding under a pile of Dashiell Hammett novels, there it is. The Tarbarrel mascot—a rosy-cheeked cartoon pig—beams goofily at him from the tin's candy-red lid. He takes a breath.

"It's there?" Nancy asks.

"It's here."

"Good." She leaves the room, swiping at her tears and muttering, "Came all the way back here to fucking worry me."

Sometimes, Nancy takes Jesse's bad decision-making personally, and that is not his fault.

What did she say back in August when she took his shoulders in the campus courtyard? She was crying then, too, their clothes damp with sweat from carrying his stuff upstairs in an elevatorless dorm. She hugged him like he belonged to her, a compact little yin-yang, light and dark. Nancy is honey haired and pink faced, and Jesse inherited his mother's wiry dark curls and brown eyes and sandy-brown skin. But they shared a cringey optimism there, in that courtyard.

"I knew you'd get out of there," she said. "You are going to kick the shit out of this place. You're smart. You bounce back.

You always have." Something like that. He remembers looking around at everyone else squirming in the face of similar talks from parents, grandparents, siblings. Everyone is tough. Everyone is the most genius genius.

"I'm just lucky," he told Nancy.

"You're *not* just lucky," she said. "You'll show them. You're *resilient*."

Then the fearsome Minerva swung back around in her SUV, driving without patience (she and her ex-wife had already seen their two children off to college), and she loaded up Nancy and the empty dolly and the bungee cords, and then, with a kiss and a blink, his aunt disappeared into the shaky summer heat.

Jesse was relieved to see her go. He carried his last box up to his room, a care package Nancy assembled: rolls of quarters, double-ply toilet paper, condoms (*I know you can get these at the health center*, she wrote in a mortifying note, *but still*). He met his roommate, a kid from Cary who introduced himself with a strong handshake, as if they were making a business deal: "Alex Khan. Poli-sci."

"Jesse Calloway," Jesse said. "Undeclared."

"You on Wipixx?"

Wipixx was a social media app Jesse had never heard of, so he didn't understand the question. At the time, he assumed Alex could discern immediately that he was a backwoods clown from a trashfire county.

"I'm sorry, man," he said. "Did you just ask me if I'm *on whippets*?"

Reincarnation indeed.

Jesse reclaims his room. He takes down Nancy's tranquil photos. Goodbye, sand dunes and softly waving seagrass. He tapes up all his pulp book covers in their place. There are at least forty of them, an impressive collection. However, when he steps back to admire them, he's disheartened to see that they don't look as cool or eclectic as he remembers. They look like a mess.

As he rearranges them, trying in vain to make them more aesthetically pleasing, Nancy sticks her head in the doorway.

"Did you even eat dinner?" she asks sharply. "You're like a rail."

He looks at her, startled. "I had something on the road."

"Well, if you get hungry, you know, there's a chess pie in the fridge. That's still your favorite, right?"

Jesse feels suddenly ashamed of himself.

Later, when he goes to the kitchen, he finds the pie in the fridge: a pristine golden disc of butter and sugar. He's not hungry, but he takes the pie out and stands in the kitchen doorway with it, fork in hand.

Nancy is grading finals in the den. The local news plays on mute. The windows are open to the night air of late spring, filling the room with an eggy smell. Nancy notices him standing there, sets aside her papers, and holds out an arm. He comes to sit by her.

"Sorry," he says.

"Same," she says. "I shouldn't have gone through your stuff without asking."

On the news, a young teacher leads a camera crew around his old elementary school. The hallway is lined with scribbly drawings of animals. Jesse experiences a wave of nostalgia. He pokes the chess pie with his fork.

"I know you can't help it," he says, "but you don't need to worry. I won't go anywhere near Pinewood. I promise."

"Hmm," Nancy says. "Thing is, sweetheart, it's Blacknot." She pronounces it the way the old locals do, like Black-*nut*. "If you're here, you're near everything."

Jesse shrugs and looks down at the pie in his lap. He begins to eat it, so sweet it feels like it's burning his tongue.

"You're not going to cut a piece?" says Nancy. "You're just going to eat it like that, like a monster?"

He licks the fork. "Uh-huh."

She digs in herself, and they sit like that for a while, trading the fork back and forth until there's a huge hole in the pie, as if an alien burst out of it. Jesse stares at the hole. Already, his stomach is telling him this was a mistake.

"Of course," Nancy says, "I'm happy you're here. Stay as long as you need."

"Thank you. I know."

"But you should know you won't find a job. Merle hired out your spot at the diner."

"I won't be here long enough to get a job. A couple days, tops."

She reaches out and brushes the hair off his forehead. "This new haircut…I don't know about this haircut. It's a little hipster-y."

He bats her hand away. "No, it isn't."

"What do you think they'll say about you when you're waltzing around downtown Blacknot looking like this?"

"They'll say, 'That kid has his shit together.' I mean, come on, I cleaned off the nail polish. What's the issue?"

She squeezes his cheek. "I just want you to be careful."

"I will, I will. Don't fuss."

He can see in her face that she doubts him; not that he's lying, but that he's making a promise he can't keep. This is often the soul of her doubt, and the soul of his deceit. He believes wholeheartedly any promise he makes to anyone, every time.

He goes to bed early that night. The drive wore him out, he says. By three AM, he's wide awake, listening to Nancy's snores on the other side of the house and staring once again at the collage of book covers on his wall. They're almost disturbing to him now; why is that? He lights a candle. His room is dark and hot. Most of these he didn't even find himself, actually. The best ones—*Alligator-Women from the Swamp Planet*, which features the tagline "They're here . . . and they're *horny*!" and *Attack of the Mutant Mushrooms*, in which the monsters resemble dildos—those were gifts from Harlan. Thrifting is one of few gay activities a closeted man can enjoy in this county.

If Jesse wanted to, he could find other pieces of Harlan all around the room. A pair of jeans, pierced in the crotch by a spring in Harlan's couch. A Union army coat button, which Harlan's uncle found at the battlefield over in Kinston. But only Jesse would know the significance of these things; Nancy wouldn't be able to pick them out.

God help him if she could.

But he's not here for this. He doesn't need this collection. He's not a fucking kid anymore. His aunt's impulse to cull, he feels it, too—though in a different, more volatile way. One by one, he tears the book covers away and takes them down the hall to the bathroom. There, he begins to burn them in the sink. The Alligator-Women curl up and turn black; the Mutant Mushrooms shrivel. The fire flares up unexpectedly and nearly catches the hand towel, and he is forced to open the bathroom window and let the smoke out into the night—

Whoosh. A flood of swamp stench hits him hard in the face. Low tide and hog farm. Confederate jasmine. Stale hot air. The assault seems personal, like this place has been waiting for him. Like it *sees* him. He never wanted to come back here. This stinking, suffocating place.

A rising wave of sugar burns the back of his throat. He leans over the toilet, and it comes up fast. A full-body retching. An exorcism.

That's a bad sign. A terrible idea all around, this trip. But then he returns to his room, drained and shaky, and he sees his phone lit up on the bedside table.

A Wipixx message from Cat:

Welcome home
You want still pictures of your mother?

His heart hammers. This. This is what he's here for.

Yes
Please

Tomorrow come town to bridge 9am
Tell no one